Lucinda Hart lives in Cornwall with her two young daughters. She has an honours degree in Fine Art and Creative Writing, and a Masters in Creative Writing, both from Bath Spa University. She has been writing since early childhood and is now the author of nine novels. Place is very important to Lucinda and her work frequently features her favourite locations.

Oberon Out is the first of her novels to be published by Austin Macauley.

This book is for my family: my daughters Raphael and Aelfrida, my mother Caroline, and my grandfather Alfred. Also for my father Chris and my grandmother Sylvia, who never lived to see it in print. This is for you all with my gratitude and love.

Lucinda Hart

Oberon Out

Austin Macauley Publishers™
London * Cambridge * New York * Sharjah

A CIP catalogue record for this title is available from the British Library.

ISBN 9781528925884 (Paperback)
ISBN 9781528925891 (Hardback)
ISBN 9781528964487 (ePub e-book)

www.austinmacauley.com

First Published (2019)
Austin Macauley Publishers Ltd
25 Canada Square
Canary Wharf
London
E14 5LQ

Maddie's butterfly house is better known as the Magic of Life Butterfly House at Cwm Rheidol, Aberystwyth. This is one of my favourite places and I recommend it without hesitation. If you're lucky, you'll meet Neil there, who knows more about butterflies and moths than any other person I know. Thank you, Neil, for letting me use your place, for letting me hold your Atlas moths, and for telling me about Denmark.

Still in Wales, if you haven't been to the beautiful reservoirs of Elan and Claerwen, you might like to take a look at them online or, better still, visit them.

The Farmers' Market in Bath is on Saturdays in Green Park Station. One of the original farmers' markets, it is lively and vibrant with colour and music.

Thanks also to Mark and Tim for showing me around an NHS Sterile Services Department and for answering my many questions. Behind all the medics, managers, and nurses in all our hospitals are vast unseen armies of people keeping the places going. This book features just one of these armies.

Wotton House and its gardens are based on a real location, sadly no longer open to the public. The gardens would have made a wonderful setting for *A Midsummer Night's Dream*.

Finally, thanks to CL for the title.

Act I

Love in Idleness

"*How now, Spirit.*" Fairy arranges delicate segments of pink and white cake on a long oval platter, and looks up at the man in the doorway.

There are bowls of fruit, jewel-bright and luscious: cherries, strawberries, grapes, and crescents of melon. There are plates of spun-sugar confectionery. There are six Champagne flutes.

"You've done a beautiful job as always, Fairy." RG unwinds the green silk scarf he wears even on these balmy June evenings. "We've had to wait some time for tonight, haven't we?"

"I'm still not sure about him." Fairy strikes a match, dips it to one of the tea lights. "I don't think he's reliable."

"You weren't sure about Peaseblossom either," RG retorts, helping himself to a slice of pink iced cake.

"And I was right," says Fairy, blowing out the match, and standing back to survey the ring of candles gently flickering in the breeze coming through the open casement. "I'm not happy with her doing the Midsummer job. And don't eat all the cake."

"Don't be spiky, Fairy. Peaseblossom has done well. I shall ask her to stay behind tonight. It will suit her well. She won't let us – you – down."

"It's most unwise. Give it to Moth. Look what Peaseblossom did at the christening last month."

"That wasn't her fault. She didn't know the priest was listening. And everything worked out all right with the great-aunt in the end. Now, I need to sort out the money for Moth and Cobweb for the London job. They're a good team."

"Moth and Cobweb are a different class of agent altogether." Fairy pats her silver bun in front of the wall mirror.

"Please try to be agreeable tonight, Fairy. This is a special evening to enjoy the company of all our agents, and to welcome Mustardseed into our family."

He leaves her grumbling in the outer reception and goes through into his private office at the back. The agency occupies the floor above a high street goldsmiths in the centre of Bath. The reception room overlooks New Bond Street. RG sometimes wishes he had taken that room for his office, but then he would not have the fun of irritating Fairy by wandering in, opening the blinds and watching the crowds tramping the pavements below. It was from that very window he first saw Mustardseed some four weeks ago.

It was a Monday lunchtime. Summer rain was falling. Fairy had gone to one of the organic delis under her voluminous umbrella, and RG was standing alone at the front window gazing out through a fine veil of drizzle. The boy was striding down the opposite pavement. He wore jeans and a dark shirt, with a black cap on his head. A siren howled from around the corner in Milsom Street, and an ambulance forced into the queue of cars. Its siren wailed and wailed, strobes spinning, and the boy turned to find the source of the noise. As he turned, RG saw the long tumbling ponytail of russet hair under his cap. The traffic moved on, the ambulance shunted underneath the window, and the boy disappeared into the crowd. RG thought no more of him, until he sorted through the applications for the job vacancy he'd advertised, and saw on one a photograph of the young man with the bronze ponytail. He shortlisted him, interviewed him – with three others – a few days later and, that same evening, rang to offer him the job.

RG counts out fifties and twenties, and slides them into two envelopes for Moth and Cobweb. He checks the time. Nearly seven o'clock. He's asked these two for seven, Peaseblossom for ten past, and Mustardseed for twenty past. As he locks the desk drawer, the bell rings on the street below, and he hears Fairy speaking on the intercom. She's friendly: it must be Moth and Cobweb.

He greets them on the landing, shakes Cobweb's hand, kisses Moth on the cheek. *Fairy is right,* he thinks, as he hands them their money. They are by far the best agents he's ever employed. Moth is a quiet girl, studying for a PhD. Her hair is soft and brown and moth-like, and people don't realise what's beneath that inscrutable exterior.

"Moth, Cobweb, huge congratulations on that assignment. The client called me earlier. He's delighted with your work."

"It was great fun." Cobweb folds his envelope into the inner pocket of his jacket. He's dressed discreetly in black, with dark hair gelled into spikes and his eyes outlined in smoky liner.

RG ushers them into the reception room, and opens a bottle of Champagne with a crack. Bubbles cascade down the flutes in Fairy's hands and Cobweb exclaims over the delicate morsels on the plates. The four of them clink glasses. RG inhales the heady dry breath of the wine. He dreads the day when he may have to call Cobweb in and say he can no longer offer him work. Cobweb's an actor, resting at present but, if his face becomes better known, he won't be able to work for the agency any more. Fortunately, Cobweb is a master of disguise with hats and hair dye and wigs, which make him unrecognisable to most people. For one job he dressed as a woman, but he does that occasionally anyway.

The street bell rings again. Fairy finishes her piece of cake before answering.

"Peaseblossom," she sniffs down the intercom. "Yes, come up."

"Everyone will be here tonight," RG smiles. "Our new Mustardseed is arriving shortly."

He can hear Peaseblossom's feet bouncing up the stairs. She arrives on the landing in a breathless haze of fluffy blonde hair and floral scent.

"Robin," she cries, taking both his hands in hers. "So good to see you again. Is Mustardseed here yet?"

"RG to you," Fairy mutters, as she pours a glass of Champagne for Peaseblossom.

"Those cakes look divine, Fairy." Peaseblossom gulps her drink. "Did you make them yourself? Moth, I just love that shawl. Is it antique?"

Cobweb kisses Peaseblossom's outstretched hand, and she giggles and flushes.

"If you could stay for a few moments at the end, Peaseblossom, I have a job which I think would be perfect for you," RG says quietly.

"He's coming," Fairy announces from the window.

"Thank you, Robin." Peaseblossom dumps her glass on the desk and swipes a chocolate truffle. "Let me look. Which is he, Fairy?"

"The one with red hair," the Fairy says stiffly.

"Oh, isn't he scrummy?"

"You could be his mother."

"Don't be ridiculous. I'm only thirty-three. Moth, what do you think? Quickly! Too late, he's crossed the road. He's at the door."

Fairy buzzes him in. RG pours a glass ready for him. The young man stands a moment in the doorway. He's wearing a patchwork shirt over jeans.

"Mustardseed, dear boy," RG starts, pressing a glass into his hand. "Please meet the other agents: Cobweb, Moth, and Peaseblossom."

"Hi everyone, I'm–"

"Mustardseed," RG interrupts quickly. "No other names here."

"Peaseblossom, come into the office. No, bring your drink, that's fine."

RG holds open the door into the back office. Fairy is starting to gather up the plates and glasses. Moth, Cobweb, and Mustardseed have gone their separate ways. Peaseblossom follows RG and sits in the squashy chair for visitors. RG flicks on his laptop.

"OK, Peaseblossom. I have a very simple job that needs doing this Midsummer's Eve." He looks up at her. "That's the 23rd of June. A week on Saturday."

"Where is it? What do I have to do?"

"It's near Cirencester. You will need to deliver two envelopes to two people. Obviously, you have to deliver the right envelope to the right recipient. We can't have a repeat of the Easter Egg Hunt."

"I'm sorry," Peaseblossom says. "But that wasn't my fault. The Easter Bunny–"

"I know, I know about the Easter Bunny. But you chatted up the wrong person. His wife was rather upset."

"Everything worked out all right in the end, didn't it?"

"That's not the point," RG sighs. "We have to do what the clients ask. It's a job."

"Yes, sorry, Robin. It won't happen again."

"Excellent." RG opens up the file on the laptop. "Now, this assignment is rather delicate. The client's name is Justin Fontaine, and he and his family are old friends of Fairy's. I have to tell you, Fairy isn't sure you are the right agent to do this, but I told her you were perfect, that's it's the kind of environment you will thrive in."

"I won't mess it up. I promise. I thought Fairy was being really sniffy to me tonight."

"Would you like to hear about the job?"

"Yes, yes, of course."

"Mr Fontaine needs two sonnets delivered to two different ladies on the same day."

"Oh, how exciting. Where are the sonnets? Can I read them?"

"They haven't been written yet."

"Am I going to write them?"

"I've been asked to write them," RG says.

"Yes, of course. So, two sonnets for two ladies."

"It's a little more complicated than that. On Midsummer's Eve the client's marrying one of them."

"Who's the other lady?"

"His mistress."

"O-M-G!"

"Quite. So, when I give you the sonnets you must be absolutely sure which is which."

"I will."

"Right, I will ring you when the envelopes are ready for you to collect. And I'll give you directions then." He clicks off the laptop. "Don't let me down on this, Peaseblossom. I will never hear the end of it."

He holds her gaze a moment, wondering if Fairy is right, and if quiet, discreet Moth would be better than plump, bubbly, twice divorced at thirty-three, Peaseblossom. But Peaseblossom will blend effortlessly into a summer society wedding party.

"You can count on me, Robin." Peaseblossom stands – only slightly unsteadily – and reaches for her neon pink handbag.

"Thank you, Peaseblossom. I'll be in touch." He holds open the door. He can't hear Fairy next door; she's probably been eavesdropping.

Peaseblossom goes home and breaks the first rule of the agency as she always does. She Googles the client, and searches for him on Facebook. She can't find Justin Fontaine on Facebook, but she does find out from the net that he's twenty-six years old, the son of a property developer, a graduate of LSE. He's engaged to Clare Greenaway, heiress to the vast shoes and handbags empire. In the past, Peaseblossom has bought shoes and a bag from Greenaway's. She wonders if she should wear a pair of these shoes at the wedding, or whether it will draw unwanted attention on her. Or, more likely, the bride won't even notice. Peaseblossom Googles further, and learns that Justin Fontaine's parents own Wotton House, a manor near Cirencester, well known for its gardens and as a wedding venue. She clicks on the link to the Wotton website, skims through the gallery of photos. Lawns with peacocks, a glassy lake, a yew walk, an Italian garden of crumbling statues, and a celebrity-chef conservatory restaurant. *The food should be yummy,* she thinks.

RG lays aside his italic fountain pen carefully, so it doesn't smudge ink on the two sheets in front of him. He's happy with the sonnets and has inscribed them onto thick watermarked paper. He's spent a little more time over this, as Justin Fontaine is a kind of honorary godson of Fairy's. Fairy is always discreet about her background and her friends, but RG knows enough not to be surprised at her hobnobbing with people like these. Fairy talked to him about this job. She even shed her abrasive manner and acidic comments, so he knows it matters to her, and this is where he doesn't know what to do.

He blots the second sonnet. They're not bad, all things considered. They say what has to be said. Maybe writing poetry is something he could consider as a sideline, for St Valentine's Day maybe. He reads each sonnet one more time, and glances at his watch. Peaseblossom will be here at any moment to collect them, and the directions for the wedding, though he suspects she will already have found out it's taking place at the Fontaines' manor.

He folds each sonnet carefully and slides them inside thick ivory envelopes. This is the hardest part, harder than writing the damn things. He just doesn't know what to do for the best.

Sonnets. A Midsummer wedding in a beautiful garden. Wine and flowers, moths circling the lanterns strung between trees as dusk falls. Peaseblossom can see it all. She can smell the heady roses and honeysuckle, taste the Champagne on her tongue.

But it's not that simple, is it? she suddenly remembers. There are two women, but only one bride.

Peaseblossom is relieved when Robin answers the intercom himself. Fairy would never let that happen if she were in the office. She must have gone home. It's evening now. Probably he asked her to come at this time to make sure they would be alone. Peaseblossom runs up the stairs.

"Good evening, Peaseblossom."

"Are the sonnets ready, Robin?"

"Sit down and I will explain."

She sinks into the soft chair, folds her hands in her lap. On the desk are two pale envelopes.

"These are the sonnets." Robin indicates the envelopes, but doesn't hand them over. "As I said before, you must get this right." He spins the envelopes to face her. "You will see the two ladies have similar initials." The elaborate interlocking initials look very alike. "*CS* and *CG*."

"Clare Greenaway." Peaseblossom points at CG.

"Correct. The other is Claire Sutherland. They have the same Christian name. Are you paying attention?"

"Yes, the same name. Let's hope this guy knows which one he's marrying."

"Peaseblossom."

"I'm sorry, Robin."

He turns over the envelopes. There's a deep red wax seal on each flap. "These remain sealed."

"Of course. I wouldn't open them. Robin, believe me, I wouldn't do that."

He arches his eyebrows. "What happened at the university party?"

"That was a mistake," she mumbles, as her cheeks flame pink.

Why does he always have to bring up these other assignments? It's not easy doing this job. You have to think on your feet a lot, and situations don't always go according to plan.

"Sorry, Robin?"

"I said: the wedding is taking place at his parents' house. It's an evening wedding and a masque. There will be drinks and canapés to start off. Your instructions are to deliver these before the ceremony starts."

At last he slides the two envelopes to her. She touches the hard bumpy seal on one of them.

"Here is a third envelope for you. This contains directions to the house. The gardens are open to the public – but you probably know that anyway – so there is a car park. It also tells you how to deliver these sonnets. Destroy all this before you go and do not take any of it to the wedding. Let me know as soon as the job is done."

"One thing, Robin… Will Fairy be at the wedding?"

"She hasn't decided. If she is there do not speak to her or seek her out or do anything indiscreet."

"Of course not."

"Wear something appropriate. You will need a mask. And don't drink too much, especially if you're driving."

Peaseblossom drops the three envelopes – the two thick off-white ones, and the brown windowless one with her instructions – into her pink bag.

"Is that all, Robin?" she asks.

"That's all, Peaseblossom. Except for me to say Oberon Out."

Peaseblossom clasps her bag to her chest as she walks home. She wants to open the brown envelope – well, really, she wants to open the others more – and see what she has to do, but she can't do it in the middle of Milson Street.

The summer evening is still warm from the day's sun, and the city is alive. Crowds of girls in high heels, a man with his suit jacket hooked over his shoulder, a crusty crouched beneath the cashpoint machine, young lovers holding hands. Peaseblossom sighs. Sonnets. Once she'd had poetry written for her. Luke was no great poet, but she still has his verses in a Quality Street tin under her bed. The power of the words is greater than the sum of their parts; reading them sometimes, in the early hours of the morning, with the soundtrack of traffic, and shouting, and ambulances, she drifts back to that time of her life, when she was young and in love.

She met Luke in the last year of her psychology degree. He was a drama student, with green eyes and shaggy, brown hair. They married in haste, when she was twenty-two, and he was twenty. Not in haste because she was pregnant, or because she'd told him she was when she knew she wasn't, simply because they wanted to, and there was no need for a long engagement, or a fancy, expensive wedding.

Crossing George Street, Peaseblossom smiles ruefully. Her wedding to Luke, at the registry office with two witnesses – friends of hers – was the complete opposite to this Fontaine affair. She quickens her step to get home sooner and read her instructions.

Claire Sutherland wandered down the sunken lane. There was rarely any traffic on this back way. If anything came, like a tractor or an occasional car, she'd hear it, and tuck into the hedge. It was a hot day, August, school holidays. The foxgloves were over in the verges, and most of the poppies. The foliage was starting to look dusty and tired. There were butterflies – a cabbage white, and something darkly speckled she didn't recognise. The sun overhead cast straggly patterns of light and shade on the tarmac before her as she walked. On her right the hedge ended in a straggle of weeds, and there was the wall of Wotton House.

The door was a Gothic arch in the mossy wall, and it was open. Not fully open, just ajar by about eighteen inches. An invitation. It had never, ever, been open before. Claire hesitated, and looked both ways along the lane. No traffic, no walkers, just the sleepy summer air, heavy on her shoulders. She stepped closer to the door and peered in. She couldn't see much: just a tangle of undergrowth and a tree of some kind.

She reached out her hand to the wood. It was faintly warm and rough. The dark paint was peeling off in jagged strips. She stepped forward to the gap. It only took a second. She was in the lane, in the dappled warmth, and then she was in the cool shade of the wall and the tree, and the door was behind her. If she were in a book, it would swing silently shut, and she would be unable to find a catch, or it would be too old and stiff for her fingers, and she would be trapped. Or the door would have disappeared altogether, and she would only see the long, unbroken estate wall, and she would have to somehow scramble up on something and haul herself out that way, bruising her shins and cutting her hands as she fell. Unless she turned her back on the wall, and where the door had been, and walked forwards into the garden, with no thoughts of escape.

Which is what she did.

Tonight Peaseblossom sits cross-legged on her bed, and reads Luke's poems, and fingers the lock of his hair she has kept for ten years. She wonders – as she often does – what has happened to him. The last she heard he was teaching drama. She's found him on Facebook, but his profile is closed, and she is afraid to add him in case he refuses, which he well might. She has these nights, sometimes, when she opens a bottle of white, and reads again the lines of her history, and weeps into her pillow for the love she lost; then, the following day, a little hungover, a little bruised around the eyes, she returns her memories to that closed part of her mind where they sleep safely until she rouses them once more.

It never happens with Graham, her second husband. Well, it wouldn't, would it? It only ever happens with Luke.

The ground underfoot was hard and dry. There were a few fallen leaves, yellow-green and crinkled, dry as paper when Claire scuffed them with her toe. There was no path as such, just a bare strip through the straggly foliage, where tree roots clawed the cracked earth. The air was heavy and still, and hot in her mouth and nose when she inhaled. Perhaps she should go back. She turned, just the once, and the door was still there, still half-open, still revealing a narrow stripe of tarmac. No. Before her, the way turned and, without looking back, she knew the door was hidden, gone.

She ducked under a low branch. The air became cooler and, at the same time she smelt faint sulphur. Only a foot or two from where she stood, the ground fell away into an ornamental lake. The water was low and oily-looking. There were a few leaves, floating, unmoving on the surface. Further out was an island where ducks squatted on the tired grass and, on the long side of the lake was a small, battered building with a turret, and a weathervane on its roof.

Claire started along the edge of the lake. The ground was crumbly, and loose soil slipped into the stagnant water. She walked slowly, carefully avoiding the tree roots jutting up through the thin earth, and she wasn't aware that there was anyone else there until she heard his voice.

"Who are you?"

She straightened, and cracked her head on a branch.

"Hey, watch it."

The boy ran along the narrow ledge towards her. He stopped with only the low branch between them.

"So, who are you?" he asked again.

"I'm sorry, the door was open. I-I just wanted to have a look."

"I didn't ask *how did you get in?* Or *what are you doing here?*"

"Sorry," Claire mumbled again. "Claire. Claire Sutherland."

"Justin Fontaine." He held out his hand under the branch.

She hesitated, then lifted her own to shake.

"What door?" Justin asked.

"The pointy one back there. It goes onto the lane."

"It's always open."

"No, it's never been open before."

"I mean it's never locked. But don't tell anyone else that."

Claire smiled at him. He was about her age, but much taller, with dark hair. His jeans were stained with grass as though he spent a lot of time outdoors.

"You live here, then?" she asked. "At Wotton House?"

"Yeah."

"I've not seen you around. Do you go to school in Cirencester?"

"No, I go away to school," Justin said, and she saw a flicker of something – unhappiness? resentment? loneliness? – in his eyes.

"I–well, I'd better be off then," she said. "Shall I close the door?"

"Don't go," he said. "Come with me."

The night before the assignment Peaseblossom tries on her outfit. She's wearing a shift of pale pink linen – the colour of tiny shells – and a matching jacket. The dress is a bit tight these days, but if she keeps the jacket on, it will be all right. She's added some cream silk roses to a vintage pink hat. She decides against her cream heels, which she bought years ago from Greenaway's, and goes for pink ballet flats instead. She'll be able to move around the garden much more easily in those; she'll be less likely to turn her ankle over going down some crumbling steps or whatever. Imagine falling at Wotton House, and the sonnets tumbling out of her bag.

"It's a boathouse," Justin explained.

"Is there a boat?"

"There is."

Claire gazed at the funny building with its Gothic turret and tiny stained-glass windows. Inside it looked dark and cool. She could just see the shape of a rowing boat moored in the dark oblong of water. The water's surface was fractured with splinters of red and gold sunlight.

"It's beautiful," she said.

"My mother wants to open the gardens to the public," Justin told her.

"How long have you lived here?"

"A couple of years. It was pretty messy when we came, but Mother's had loads of gardeners in. They've planted up the woodland, and tidied up the Italian garden. She's had a massive conservatory built on the back too. She wants to turn it into a restaurant, get into glossy magazines."

"What do you think about that?"

He shrugged. "I'm not here that much, am I? After A-levels, it'll be uni and then a job in the City probably."

He walked on, along the lakeside path. From somewhere ahead, Claire heard faint running water. She ran to catch up.

"A-levels. How old are you?"

"Seventeen," he said. "I'm half-way through them."

"I've just done my GSCEs," she said. "What are you going to do at uni?"

"Economics."

"Oh." Claire couldn't disguise disappointment. She hoped he'd have said art or literature or even horticulture. Not economics.

"It's all been planned for years," he said. "I just have to go with it."

"Of course," she said, but she didn't understand.

She knew exactly what she wanted to study: drama and literature. She was always making up stories in her head. True, many of them were only fractured little scenes, but she loved to experiment with words, and how sentences sounded. Then she imagined them being read aloud, acted on a stage, or in front of a camera. Slipping through the door in the wall, she'd envisaged brambles snaring her arms and a crazy witch-woman, but never a boy, a young man, like Justin, who hadn't bollocked her for sneaking in, but had been friendly and shown her this beautiful lake.

"Do you have any brothers and sisters?"

"No, only me," he said, and kicked gravel on the path. "All the pressure's on me."

Claire had two older brothers. Their council house was cramped and noisy. Justin lived alone with his parents in a huge house – it must be huge – with this wonderful, fairy-tale garden. Their lives were so different. If she hadn't stepped through that pointed door, she would never have seen this garden, and never met him.

At the head of the lake was a waterfall, but many of the mossy boulders were exposed, and only a small jet of water fell down. Justin looked at his watch.

“Look, I have to go now. Come back another day? I could show you the rest of the garden. There’s a lot of it.”

“I’d love to,” Claire smiled. “How do I get in?”

“The way you came today. Like I said, it’s never locked. Give me your number. I think we’re going out tomorrow, but I’ll give you a ring some time after that.” He gestured a sloping path beyond the waterfall. “I’m going that way. Can you find your way out?”

“Can I have your number too?” Claire asked, but he had scrambled up the grassy bank, and she didn’t want to ask louder.

She watched him striding away. He did not look back to wave. The garden was quiet, with just the gentle rush of the waterfall, and birdsong from somewhere. At last she turned away from the cascade and started back along the lakeside path towards the boathouse.

That was lucky, Justin thought, as he ran through the gloomy yew walk. *I like her*. He liked the way she’d seen the open door and walked straight through. He liked her long brown hair and hazel eyes. And he liked her voice. He’d never thought much about voices before, but he liked Claire’s very much. He wanted to hear it again. And he wanted to see her again. He wondered when he could call her without sounding desperate.

The door was still ajar. Claire hesitated before stepping through. She was leaving fairyland. That was daft. She could come back. He had her number. And the gate was always open. As she came out onto the lane she pulled it to behind her. It was heavy and it creaked, and caught on a stone. She tugged until it was flush with the wall. She didn’t want any other girls going through and meeting Justin Fontaine. When the lane curved away up the village she checked over her shoulder: the door was still there, dark in the stone wall. Still there for another day.

The roses in the Italian garden have been left to grow wild, around and over some of the marble statues. The crunch of gravel under Justin’s heels is loud. A gauzy moth brushes his cheek with soft, dry wings. Something moves in the undergrowth. The garden is bleached to coloured greys in the twilight. If he turns, he’ll see the white and silver marquee obscuring the back of Wotton House. It looks wrong, like a spacecraft on the lawn. He crunches past the statues, and under the canopy of the woodland. The bluebells are mostly over; instead he smells the sharpness of damp leaves and soil, after the rain a couple of hours ago. Now the sky is clear of clouds, and the moon speckles the narrow path winding through the grove.

Justin walks on, familiar steps, as the path turns and dips towards the brook that runs through the valley. His steps falter a little, as a ghost flits across the mossy stone bridge. Claire, with her dark hair loose down her back. Across the bridge and up the slope is the hidden dell.

“Fuck, fuck, fuck,” he says aloud, and his voice is as hard and out-of-place as the giant marquee.

This time tomorrow he’ll be married. He can’t change it. It’s happening. The marquee is up, the florists and the photographers are coming, the rings are bought, and – worst of all – his bride has booked the entertainment for the guests.

He walks on, deeper into the valley, before the ghost of Claire can tug him by the arm into the dell. If he goes there, he'll cry.

It was Luke who took the booking. A society wedding in Cirencester, he'd said to Claire and the others in the pub. Some rich bird getting married at the bridegroom's manor on Midsummer's Eve. The perfect job, he'd said over and over again, the perfect job for the Love in Idleness Players. Nothing could be more appropriate. Vicky and Mike were delighted. Simon broke loudly into *I'm Getting Married in the Morning*. Claire didn't say anything. She knew already whose wedding it was.

The Love in Idleness Players were a small touring company in London, set up by Mike and his wife, Vicky, some ten years ago. Over the years, with different actors coming and going, the group became well known for its programmes of Shakespearean highlights performed at parties and ceremonies, and its work with schools and colleges. Mike and Vicky's sixteen-year-old son, Orlando, sometimes took part. He'd already had a couple of TV roles as a teenager. Luke had been with the company for three or four years; so had Simon, the musician. And then there was the newest member: Claire.

"Hey, you're from that way, aren't you?" Mike asked her, as he cracked down his empty beer glass. "D'you know who it is?"

"I know the house," Claire said at last, finished her drink and stood up. Time to get the tube home before it got too late. Or before she betrayed herself.

Claire is back at her parents' house. She has been here for two nights already, as the Love in Idleness players' last booking was at the beginning of the week. The others will be driving down to Wotton in the minibus tomorrow.

She runs her hand down the blue bedroom wall. It's achingly familiar. There's the knobbly bit. There's the felt-tip mark. Her teenage posters are still on the wall, held up by dry fragments of tape: Matisse's *Snail*, Westlife, a couple of Pre-Raphaelites. Her phone on the bedside table lights up with a new text. Justin. '*I can't wait to see you tomorrow.*'

Tomorrow: the day he marries another woman, and Claire can do nothing but watch.

Justin called Claire two days after they met, and asked her if she'd like to meet him in the garden. His parents would be out that afternoon. They'd have the place to themselves. Luckily, she too was alone. Her parents were at work, so was her oldest brother; her second brother had gone out before she woke up, leaving no note, but he wouldn't be that interested in what she was doing, if he came back and found her gone.

It was another hot, dusty day. She chose her favourite summer top, one with tiny pink and blue flowers, and thin pink straps. She brushed her hair and put on lip-gloss.

When she got to the wall of Wotton House, the Gothic door was closed, as she had left it. She pushed it. It was stiff, and jammed; she pushed again, and it gave way, and then she was in the garden once more, the dry earth and curling tree roots beneath her feet.

Justin was waiting at the lakeside. The air was fresher, but Claire could still smell the sulphur from the weeds and silted-up lakebed. Hovering insects whirred above the oily surface; one of the ducks slid into the water with a dull splash.

"Hi," he called, and she waved back.

"I'm so pleased you could come," he said, as she drew level with him. "It's a bit boring here sometimes on my own."

How could it be boring? Claire wondered. She could make up endless stories and adventures in a place like this.

"I mean, it's lovely, and all that," Justin said, as though he had seen her thoughts. "I didn't mean to sound like a brat. I spend a lot of time just wandering round the garden, but it's more fun to do it with a friend."

"Are we friends?" Claire asked.

"I hope so," he said.

He offered her a cigarette; when she shook her head, he pocketed the packet and lighter, and didn't get them out again. They walked along the lakeside to the boathouse. This time he led her in, and she stood on the narrow ledge inside, and moved her hands through the shards of red and gold.

Beyond the cascade, a lawn sloped up towards the back of the house. Claire stopped on the lawn and stared at the Georgian manor, with its deep oblong windows, and the ornamental conservatory.

"That's where the restaurant's going to be?" she asked Justin with a smile.

"That's where the restaurant's going to be." He hesitated, then said, "I don't much like the idea of loads of people tramping about the place. Come on, let me show you the wood."

"You have your own wood?"

"It's not that big. Race you."

He ran off across the lawn. Claire followed, but she was no runner, and he'd disappeared down a flight of stone steps into a sunken walled garden of statues and straggly roses. He jumped out at her from behind a marble bust and she shrieked.

"What are you doing in September?" he asked.

"A-levels," she said. "English, drama, and art. I'm going to be an actress. That's all I've ever wanted to do."

"You'll still be living in Wotton then?"

"Yes."

"That's good. I can see you when I get back for holidays."

The grassy path dipped down into a valley. Tall trees – Claire wasn't sure what kind they were – soared over their heads. Wild flowers grew amongst the grasses; insects buzzed and dived. The way led steeply down and back on itself, and there, in the cleft of land was the jagged green line of a stream. Stone slabs formed a bridge, and Claire stood on them, watching the narrow gush of water shoot below her feet.

"You could put plays on in this garden," she said, straightening up.

"Plays?"

"Outdoor theatre. It would be amazing. *A Midsummer Night's Dream.*"

That was it of course, that was the play. Robin Goodfellow and the Fairy pouncing out from behind these gnarled trunks; Helena chasing Demetrius through the grasses and flowers; Titania and Oberon meeting on this bridge under a silver moon.

They met again, a few days later. This time Justin had a couple of cans of beer and some crisps in a rucksack. Instead of walking along the lake to the waterfall, they sat on a bench by a hidden pool. There were lily pads on the dark water, and a stone fish reared up from the centre of the pool, its mouth gaping wide.

"I get my results next week," Claire said.

"You must tell me," Justin said, flicking open his beer. "As soon as you know."

She shut her eyes, let the sun warm her face. The taste of beer in her mouth, and the stagnant smell of the pond. When Justin went back to school she wouldn't be able to come into the garden. She wouldn't see the leaves turn copper and red; she wouldn't see the toadstools shooting up under bushes and trees. And, worse than that, she wouldn't see Justin.

"What do you know about the people at Wotton House?" Claire asked.

"Not a lot."

Her mother was in the kitchen, preparing a salad for dinner. Claire sat at the table, twiddling her fork in her hand, round and round. She watched the downward flash of her mother's knife, as a tomato fell in slices onto the wooden board.

"I've seen her, the woman, in the post office a couple of times," her mother said, scooping up the tomato, arranging it on a bed of leaves. "I don't think I've seen the man. They've got a boy who's at boarding school. That's what Sheila said."

"I've met him," Claire said, dropping her fork with a clatter.

"Who?"

"Justin. The boy. Justin Fontaine. I've met him. I've been to Wotton House. Well, the garden anyway. It's incredible."

"How did you meet him?" Her mother scraped the pale green tufts off a handful of radishes.

"I met him in the lane," Claire improvised. "He asked me if I wanted to see the garden, and I said yes, and that was that. I've been back. I like him."

"How old is he?"

"Seventeen. He's doing A-levels."

"You're a dark horse," her mother smiled. "I suppose he'll be going back to boarding school this autumn then."

"Yes," Claire muttered. She didn't want to think about that.

'All As and Bs,' Claire texted Justin.

'Clever girl!' he wrote back. '*When are you coming round?'*

It was late afternoon before Claire could escape from her celebrating friends at school. She slipped through the Gothic doorway, through the haze of heat and insects to the lake. Justin was standing on the far shore. He started to run towards her; suddenly she found her own feet running on the crumbly path. She ducked under the branch where she'd banged her head, where they'd first shaken hands. He held out his arms, she ran to him, and he spun her up in the air.

"Clever girl," he said again, and lowered her to the ground.

Claire liked his strong, sun-tanned arms around her. He held her a second, then let her go. She was flustered. She didn't know what to say. She thought for a second – stupid, deluded girl that she was – that he was going to kiss her.

"I've got some chocolate to celebrate," he said. "But it's a bit sticky."

They ate a bar of Dairy Milk by the secret lily pond. Justin asked if she would mind if he smoked, and she said she wouldn't. She didn't want him to, but she didn't want to tell him that. A smudge of cloud covered the sun, and the wind rustled the leaves. In a dark leafy corner Claire saw the glowing red-orange berries of Lords and Ladies. She glanced to the sky, to the cloud. Autumn was coming.

The next time Claire took her watercolours and brushes. She sat on an abandoned log by the boathouse, and Justin lay on a rug beside her. Every so often, as her water muddied, he took her bottle up to the walled garden and filled it from a tap beneath the apricot tree on the golden south wall. Claire painted the boathouse with its coloured panes of glass, turret and weathervane; she painted the island; she painted the fiery Lords and Ladies that now flamed in so many corners.

Later, they walked up through the walled garden, and there was a tall woman with severe dark hair, gesturing to a man in wellingtons with a wheelbarrow. Justin introduced Claire to his mother, Evelyn, who inclined her head coolly. Claire blushed; she had a hole in her jeans, and her muddy knee stuck out.

"I don't think Justin's mentioned you," Evelyn said. "Do you live in Wotton?"

"Yes, all my life," Claire said.

"Whereabouts do you live?"

Claire's cheeks flamed again. "Rowan Close."

Evelyn turned to Justin. "That's the estate, isn't it?"

Justin stared at the gravel.

"That's right," Claire said, and her heart rate was thumping. "The council estate."

"I see. So, Catherine–"

"It's Claire, Mother."

"Claire. Tell me about your family. What do your parents do?"

"Really, Mother, she doesn't need the third degree from you."

"I'm trying to get to know your…friend, Justin."

"Dad's a carpenter," Claire said. "And Mum works at a care home. One of my brothers is also a carpenter."

"What do you think you will do, Claire?"

"I'm going to be an actress."

Justin grabbed Claire's arm and dragged her away, as Evelyn turned back to the gardener, who'd stood there listening to the whole exchange with a grin on his face.

"I'm sorry," Justin said.

Claire shrugged. She didn't come from much, but her parents worked hard, and always had time and love for her and her brothers, which was more than Justin got from Evelyn.

It was the first time Claire had seen anyone except Justin in the garden. Until that moment she could have pretended, with her storyteller's mind, that it really was a magic kingdom, and they were the only two people who knew the way in. Day by day the garden was changing, the light growing cold, the seasons turning, time relentlessly sweeping on.

"I asked Mother if you could come in when I'm away," Justin told her. "If you want to paint, or just have a wander. She said you could."

They were on the sofa in Claire's house, watching TV. Claire hadn't invited him; he'd just turned up one afternoon, and her mother had answered his knock, and called Claire down from her room. She felt odd and disconnected, sitting cross-legged on the sofa in the living room, with a familiar cushion at her back, watching the moving images on the screen, but not taking them in, whilst next-door in the kitchen her mother was talking to her brother until he thumped off upstairs to his bedroom. This wasn't the world she knew with Justin.

"It wouldn't be the same without you to talk to," Claire said, and she was afraid of encountering his mother among the trees.

"I know," he said. "I'm sorry. I just thought you might like to."

“Thank you,” she said, but she doubted if he really had asked his mother. Claire didn’t think Evelyn would welcome her into Wotton House garden. She wasn’t the type of visitor Evelyn was after; she wasn’t the type of friend she’d want for Justin.

It was Justin’s last day before he returned back to school. He walked with Claire back along the lakeside. The water was higher now after some rainy days. The leaves were damp as they brushed Claire’s face. The end of summer had come, and Justin was leaving with it.

“Stay in touch,” he said to her at the gate, the pointed Gothic gate she’d sneaked through all those weeks ago.

“Of course,” she said.

It was evening, and the light was failing under a streak of mauve cloud. Claire shivered, and shoved her sketchpad into her rucksack.

“Well, I’ll see you, old bean,” said Justin.

He didn’t close the door after her; instead he stood there in the archway, and when she turned he waved, and then, at last, she saw the dark door closing, separating her from him. He was inside, and she was outside.

The next weekend Claire stood before the Gothic door again. She wondered if Evelyn had locked it from the inside, but no; when she pushed it, it groaned over the stones and tree roots.

She walked alone by the lake, she sat for a moment on the bench by the lily pond; she hesitated at the mouth of the grotto, where rainwater dripped from above, splashing onto the stones at her feet. She was uneasy, kept looking over her shoulder. No one was there, just the faint rustles and sighs of leaves and water and birds. She saw a few toadstools, red and orange, amongst the mulch and debris on the ground. There were slugs too, and snails, in the damp, dark corners. The wind was chill, and it ruffled the oily surface of the lake and the cobwebs between the leaves. Claire found she was running back to the wall and the door. Without Justin and the summer sun, the garden was hostile. She would not come back alone.

Why am I thinking of that day? Claire wonders.

It’s a hot summer night, and she casts off the duvet, but she can still recall the cool dampness of that autumn morning; she can still smell the decay on the air. Of all the times she has known the garden, why does she find herself thinking of that day?

Because she feels the same unease, the same fear, the same knowledge that nothing stays the same.

“I’m so sorry,” Justin had said to her, when she told him about the booking Luke had taken. “Clare had no idea it was you. I mean, she doesn’t know anything about you. She just thought it would be wonderful to have Shakespeare in the garden at Midsummer.”

“Does she like Shakespeare?” Claire asked.

“I don’t think so.” Justin evaded her eyes. “Not like you. She’s not like you in any way. But at least I will have you there. I will be able to see you. I might be able to get away.”

“Justin, it’s your wedding day,” Claire said sharply. “You won’t be able to get away at all.”

"I'm not ever going to leave you," he said.

That was two months ago. Claire reaches for the quilt again. Shakespeare in Wotton garden was her idea, long, long ago, before he'd ever met this bloody Greenaway heiress. Shakespeare at Wotton belonged to a summer's day when she'd stood on the mossy bridge, seen Oberon and Titania and their company flitting amongst the silver tree trunks.

When Justin came home to Wotton after his A-levels, the gardens had been open to the public for three months. The conservatory and its kitchen had been blocked off from the rest of the house. There were wrought iron chairs and tables, noisy on the stone flags, and a long bar where cakes and light lunches were served. He hated it, he told Claire. He hated the intruders in the garden. He hated the crunching of their feet on the gravelled walkways, the wrappers he sometimes found on the surface of the lake, or shoved into the crevices of the grotto.

If he got the grades he needed – and he was pretty sure he would – he would be going to LSE in the autumn.

"You won't come back here then," Claire said.

They had hacked a way through the undergrowth in the woods, away from the signposted trail. To the left the brook ran under the stone bridge. It was a midsummer evening. The last of the bluebells were hazy beneath the trees. There was bright campion, and the scent of wild garlic. A few moths rose from the foliage as they walked.

"Of course, I will," he said. "It's only three years."

"And then you'll be working in London," Claire said. "You'll never have time to come back here."

She was applying for literature and drama at university for a year's time. She did want to go to London, but she'd never been there alone, and wouldn't have any idea how to manage. Justin wouldn't have time for her. He'd have his own friends, his own life. There would be no place for her in London with him, so she was hoping to get to Bristol. Her grandparents lived there; she could stay with them in the week, and come home to Wotton at the weekends. It was easier. Safer.

"I'll always come back," he said. "It's my home. And you're here."

"I'm here?" Claire echoed.

Justin stopped and turned to her. The ground had dropped. They stood in a secret dell. Claire could no longer hear the sigh of the stream over stones. She looked up, and the tall trees kaleidoscoped up to the mauve-grey sky.

"Claire," Justin said, and reached out to her. "You're here. I'll always come back here because of you."

She moved towards him, and then his arms were around her, one hand under the flimsy top she wore, and she cried out at the touch of his skin on hers.

Claire starts awake. Through the gap in the curtains the sky is light: a mother-of-pearl luminescence. She can hear birds in the trees at the foot of the garden. It's Midsummer's Eve, and today her lover is marrying someone else. A fragment of her dream returns. She was in the dell again. No, not that memory, not today.

"I've never done this before," Claire blurted out at last, as Justin pulled her down gently onto the grasses and flowers. "Have you?"

He hesitated, and she knew his answer, and felt hot pain in her eyes and throat.

"Only once," he said at last. "I was drunk. It didn't matter. You matter."

The soft tickle of grass and leaves beneath her, the sky darkening to amethyst between the treetops, the thick smell of garlic, the rustles of a creature in the undergrowth. Afterwards he lay his head on her chest, and she stroked his hair.

"Was that all right?" he asked, lifting his head.

His face was flushed still, and his eyes anxious.

"It was lovely," Claire said.

Was it? She didn't know. When she walked up to the garden that evening, she never thought this was the day it would happen. She was changed now. Would she look different in a mirror? Would other people read her face and know what had happened on the scented bed of earth and leaves and flowers?

Justin's room overlooks the back lawn. When he yanks the curtains back, the marquee is still there, that alien spacecraft of silver and white. He can't see the Italian garden beyond it; all he can see are the tall leafy treetops of the bluebell wood where he walked last night. He has kept the window open all night, and now he hears the unearthly shriek of one of the peacocks.

It's still early. Luckily, Clare and her family are staying in an expensive hotel in Cirencester, and not here at Wotton. Justin needs this one last morning with his memories.

The only person he's talked to is Aunt Effie. She's not really an aunt; she just sort of came into his life during his teens. It's someone from Aunt Effie's weird agency who will be coming today to deliver two sonnets to Claire and Clare.

"This is not right, Justin," Aunt Effie told him sharply on the phone, when he first approached her about this. "Think very carefully about what you're saying."

"I have thought," he said wearily. "There's nothing else I can do. There's no way out."

"There's always a way out, if you look for it," Aunt Effie sniffed.

"Not for me. I have to do this. You know why."

"You can always change your mind," she said. "About anything."

"You can always change your mind," Justin says aloud, standing at his bedroom window, watching the fabric of the marquee shiver in the dawn breeze.

Until when? At what point will he pass the moment when he cannot halt what he has started? Aunt Effie has sent him a photograph of the woman – the agent – known as Peaseblossom, who will be coming to the wedding party today. She – like everyone else – will be masked. Will he know who she is?

Peaseblossom cannot settle. She is always jittery before a job. This one is even more stressful because Fairy will be there. Robin said she hadn't decided whether or not to go to the wedding, but Peaseblossom knows she will be there, and she'll be watching like a hawk for the slightest error or indiscretion, so she can go back to Robin and say Moth should have done it instead. Peaseblossom doesn't think this sounds like an assignment for Moth. Moth is too standoffish and inscrutable. She wouldn't be able to mingle socially with strangers at this kind of wedding. She wouldn't even dress properly. She'd go in some hippie thing with tie-dye and mismatched beads. Peaseblossom secretly likes Moth's image, but it wouldn't do for this. Not at all.

She reads through her instructions one last time. She can't take them with her. Someone might see them. Once, on a job at the Birmingham Holiday Inn, she left the client's details in the Ladies. And if anyone's going to find her instructions today, it'll be Fairy. Obviously.

Right. CS and CG. She's got it. Damn Robin. He shouldn't have made the initials look so alike.

Claire doesn't know how to spend the morning. The others are driving down from London in the minibus and will get to Wotton about lunchtime. Orlando is coming with his parents as he is acting at the wedding; Simon's eight-year-old, Alfie, is also coming. It's his first time travelling with the players. He's going to be an elf, in a green hat, looking cute.

Claire watches her mother watching her with a worried face. She is waiting for Claire to say something. She knows very little. She doesn't know that Claire and Justin, after years apart, have been lovers for the last couple of months. She thinks only that Claire and the Love in Idleness players are providing the entertainment for her old boyfriend's wedding. She doesn't know that Claire is walking along secret paths and through leafy groves in her mind. She doesn't know how Claire is dreading seeing Justin today with his bride, how afraid she is.

Peaseblossom only gets lost once finding Wotton House. There are signs for the open gardens but, when she reaches the private drive, there is a notice saying the garden is closed today. She follows a Jag down the leafy drive. In her rear-view mirror a sports car appears with the roof down. Peaseblossom's small Getz is going to look a poor relation here.

The lane opens out into a vast gravelled car park. Yes, most of the cars are expensive: sports cars, 4x4s, BMWs, Mercs and so on. In the far corner there's a minibus with writing on the side. Peaseblossom shunts forwards to read what it says. *Love in Idleness Players: Touring Theatre Company* and an interlocking pair of masks. It must belong to the actors who are doing the entertainment. Justin Fontaine's mistress is one of them. Somehow, she has to find out which one she is and give her the sonnet, and somehow, she has to approach the bride and get her away from all her gushing attendants. Peaseblossom is grateful it is a masked party. She knows neither bride nor groom, and will have to bullshit if anyone asks her. Bullshitting will be easier behind a mask of pink and silver.

She parks opposite the minibus at the edge of the car park. Behind her are gently sloping fields, open country. She moves her driving mirror and checks her hair. Her mask is on the passenger seat under her hat. She slides it on, and tweaks her hair once more. Then she jams on her hat. She's never worn a mask before, and she feels both protected and vulnerable. People are climbing out of cars wearing a variety of masks: some beautiful like hers, other comedy ones from joke shops. She watches them for a moment. It's actually very unsettling. She doesn't want to get out of the car now.

At last, she opens the glove compartment and takes out the two sealed envelopes. What has Justin Fontaine said to his two women on this day? Is he having second thoughts about the wedding? Is it a guilty conscience and, if so, about which woman? Clare Greenaway is certainly rich, but does he love her?

What's love got to do with it? Peaseblossom sighs as she gets out of the car and locks the door. She's only been in love once, and now that is just a memory.

She crunches across the car park after the other guests. The soles of her ballet pumps are very thin, and the gravel is hard and painful. She clasps her bag – brown suede from Greenaway's – tightly to her side. Inside are the two envelopes.

She passes a shuttered ticket booth and follows the path. Through the shrubbery she can see the white façade of Wotton House. The path opens into a large courtyard in front of the house. There are flowers around the door and the lower windows. At the side of the house is a strip of grass. The people in front are going that way. Peaseblossom straightens her mask and walks on.

The grass is softer under her feet. There's a huge marquee on the lawn, with silver pennants lifting in the breeze. It hides her view of most of the gardens, but she can see a single tall, sturdy tree at the far end of the lawn. To the left is a grassy bank, scattered with daisies and buttercups, unlike the formal lawn, which is green striped and bare of any flowers. On top of the bank are trees, including a monkey puzzle and, amongst these, a peacock struts with his tail folded in a turquoise train.

She stands still a moment, unnerved by the company. The faces around her are elegant, hostile, ridiculous. There are narrow glittering bands worn across eyes, like her own mask; Cameron and Blair and Thatcher; Frankenstein's monster, Dracula and Edgar Allan Poe; Disney characters and an Egyptian death mask. It's all a bit creepy.

A drink. That's what she needs. Just the one for courage. Then she must find out where the players are and which one is Claire Sutherland.

Obviously, it was never going to last. Claire and Justin came from such different worlds, and were embarking on such different lives: him in the City, and her as an actress. That first summer, before Justin left for university, they met whenever they could in the gardens. They sat on benches and on rugs in secret corners, and talked and ate chocolate; later, when the gardens closed, and the crowds had gone, they'd wander hand-in-hand up to the dell on the far slope of the bluebell wood. Justin came to her house some days. He was never snobby about her living in Rowan Close, and sat happily at the cramped dinner table, or squashed with Claire on her narrow bed. He never invited her inside Wotton House, and she never asked to go in. The furthest she went was into the conservatory restaurant, where she once drank a cup of Earl Grey and ate lemon cake, while Justin scowled at the noise of visitors scraping their chairs and shouting.

She kept Justin secret. She didn't tell her friends about him. She kept herself to herself in the holidays, so it wasn't that difficult. She would always prefer to read, or write, or go for solitary walks, than hang out with the girls in coffee bars or at the cinema. He wasn't like them; they wouldn't understand. Sometimes she didn't understand either: what would a boy like him see in a girl like her?

She cried when he left for university. He promised he'd come back for a long weekend in the autumn, and he did, but it was wet and cold, and the days were short, and they could no longer throw down a blanket in the bluebell wood. The ground was sodden and mulchy with rotten leaves and mould and toadstools. Instead they drove out in Justin's car and he came to her house but, to Claire, Justin was so completely part of Wotton gardens it felt unhinged, unreal, not to be there with him.

She wondered if he would invite her up to London for a few days, but he didn't. Once, at Christmas, she asked him if he was seeing anyone else in London. *Of course not*, he said, but he evaded her eyes, and that night she cried until she thought she would vomit. She remembered what he'd said that first time in the dell, that he had only done it once before when he was drunk, and she realised that too was probably not true.

A year later, Claire went to university in Bristol. That Christmas, Justin told her he wasn't coming home to Wotton; he was spending Christmas with friends in France. He might come for a few days at New Year, but he couldn't be sure. A couple of days after New Year, Claire saw his car parked in the village with a red-haired girl in the passenger seat. She ran home before Justin could come out of whichever shop he'd gone into.

Different worlds; different lives.

Claire knew the redhead came from the same world as Justin. Not only would she have been inside Wotton House, she'd probably be staying there too.

Different worlds; different lives.

The Love in Idleness Players have been given the old potting shed in the walled garden as their tiring house. For the first time in her life Claire went into Wotton House along the formal drive. She met up with the others at the village pub, and got into the minibus next to Alfie, the over-excited elf. Some masked relation of the bride met them and walked them down to the potting shed. *I know the way*, Claire wanted to shout. *That's where the apricot tree is*.

The potting shed has an arched Gothic window like the red and gold windows of the boathouse. There's the apricot tree, and there's the tap where Justin filled her bottle with clean water many summers ago. Of course, the potting shed is no longer simply a potting shed: the floor has been cleaned and levelled out, the walls whitewashed, and there is now a quirky display of old gardening tools, and some shards of pottery that were dug up by the lake at Wotton.

Claire wonders if Evelyn will recognise her when she's performing, and whether she will remember the conversation they had in this walled garden, when she told Evelyn she was going to be an actress. *Well, I bloody did it,* Claire thinks. *I came from a council house, but now I'm an actress*. She wonders if she will see Evelyn. Everyone but the players is masked, but Claire's sure she'd recognise that arrogant posture anywhere.

Peaseblossom gulps her wine quickly. She hasn't seen anyone who looks like they might be a member of a troupe of players. Everyone is wearing expensive gowns and summer suits, with strange heads nodding on their shoulders. It's going to be much harder finding people when she can't see their faces. There's the bride, Clare Greenaway, in a flowing pink gown, with roses fastened in her pale blonde hair. She's wearing a Pierrot-style mask: white with a single black tear on her cheekbone.

Peaseblossom wanders into the marquee. There are bowls of pink roses and white lilies, and the smell is overwhelming.

"I hear Clare's invited some travelling players," she says to the Wicked Witch of the West at the drinks table. "Do you know when they're going to start?"

"Oh soon, I would think. Or everyone will be too pissed to take in the culture," the woman says, helping herself to a plate of canapés.

"It's so romantic," says another guest, a short, dumpy woman, with a leopard-skin mask. "*A Midsummer Night's Dream* on Midsummer's Night."

"Jeez, they're not doing the whole bloody thing, are they?" Gollum in a suit looks at his watch. "They'd better get cracking."

"Don't be silly, Edwin," the Witch interrupts. "It's only a few scenes from the play to get us in the mood."

"The mood for what?"

"I think it's beautiful," the leopard woman says. "Clare's amazing, so creative. Fancy having actors at your wedding."

"There's Justin." Gollum snatches a sliver of smoked salmon and gestures to the mouth of the marquee.

"Are you sure… Oh yes, I think you're right."

Peaseblossom looks too. In the doorway is a tall, slight man, with a leafy green head. He's bending down to talk to a hunched woman with very thin legs. He has his arm around her shoulders. Even with an owl instead of a head, Peaseblossom knows who it is: Fairy.

Justin feels a right idiot in the Green Man mask Clare got for him. She said he had to wear it, as it was his garden, his woodland, where they were getting married. *In fact,* he thinks, *the whole masque thing is ridiculous and pretentious, like the marquee and the piles of flowers inside it.* He wants nothing more than to rip off the stupid mask and run away down one of the secret pathways.

"She's here," Aunt Effie says.

They're standing in the mouth of the marquee. He's aware of someone disguised as Gollum, striding towards him, while shoving food in his face. It might well be that bore Edwin, who's married to a friend of Clare's.

"The one in pink," Aunt Effie gestures.

Just inside the marquee is a young woman in a slightly too-tight pink two-piece, with a flowery hat, and a brown handbag she's clutching most defensively to her side.

"Do you want to change your mind?" Aunt Effie asks.

"Justin." Edwin claps him on the shoulder. "The condemned man and all that. Too late to back out now."

"Justin?" Aunt Effie interrupts sharply.

He hesitates, ignoring Edwin, looking at the plump woman in pink, knowing what's concealed in her bag.

"No," he mutters. "No."

Aunt Effie shakes her head and moves away.

"OK, everyone, ready?" Mike asks.

Claire feels sick. In the damp warmth of the old potting shed she shivers. She's wearing a simple long cream dress; Vicky is wearing the same in a soft green. They'll add coronets and capes and so on as they change characters. Orlando is playing Puck; he has a woven crown of twigs and leaves on his head. Alfie insisted on wearing his elf suit in the minibus. It's a bit crumpled now, but he looks sweet with his pointed green hat and copper hair.

"Go on then, Si," Mike says. "Give them a bit of music."

"And don't mention the Scottish play," Alfie yells, as his father picks up his lute.

"Alfie," Simon and Vicky say together.

Claire doesn't think Macbeth – there, she's said it in her mind – can bring her any more bad luck than the day already holds.

"Claire." Luke starts towards the door.

She scoops up her skirt and follows him. Outside it is bright, and she screws up her eyes.

"You realise," Orlando is saying to his parents, as she leaves. "We're the only people here who aren't masked."

I realise, Claire thinks.

Masks affect behaviour. Peaseblossom knows this. She's studied psychology. Somehow, the guy with the lute has drawn the milling wedding guests like iron filings, and they're following him past the silver and white marquee towards the giant, thick tree at the far end of the lawn. Beyond its sturdy trunk, Peaseblossom can see some blowsy roses and marble busts and statues. It's the sunken Italian garden; she has seen it on the internet. She walks with the crowd, one hand on her bag. The entertainment has begun. Soon after the players have finished, the wedding ceremony will start. She has to fulfil her task before then. She glances around. She can't see Justin Fontaine in his Green Man mask anywhere. Clare Greenaway and her hangers-on are on the left. The peacock has fanned open his train, and the feathers shimmer with iridescence. *They're bad luck,* Peaseblossom thinks, and looks away. That owl head, the dreary grey dress, the thin legs. Fairy's watching her.

Claire hardly saw Justin after New Year. Later that year she and her friend Sadie moved into a small flat in Bristol, and she didn't come home at weekends as much. Once her mother said she'd seen Justin in the village. Claire didn't ask if he was alone. She didn't want to know; she didn't care; it didn't matter. And in everyday life it didn't. She met other men; she dated fellow students; she had a sporadic affair with one of the lecturers. She didn't fall in love, but that was because she would not allow herself to. She told Sadie about Justin, about the garden, the lake, and the secret dell in the bluebell wood. She also told her about the redhead in his car. Sadie said Justin was a waste of space. Claire nodded and agreed, but the smell of bluebells always made her cry.

When she did go home to Wotton she didn't walk down the lane past the estate wall with the Gothic door. If she had to go that way in the car with her parents, she would stare at her entwined fingers in her lap. Only sometimes did she look up and see the door. It was still there, but it looked like it had been re-painted, as it was now a uniform, shiny black. It was never ajar, always firmly closed. Like the door to her memories.

It's all the wrong way round, Claire thinks. She and Luke are standing behind the vast cedar tree above the Italian garden. The people coming towards her are all masked. She sees that Greenaway woman as Pierrot, there's Simon Cowell, Freddie Mercury, JFK, someone in a Ned Kelly helmet. At university she'd gone out with a Fine Art student for a while. He said he wanted to make a piece of art which reconstructed a life class, where the model was fully clothed, but the artists behind the easels were naked. *That's what this is like,* she thinks.

"*Now, fair Hippolyta.*" Luke, as Theseus, takes her hand and gently pulls her away from the tree.

As Claire opens her mouth she sees the Green Man on the edge of the crowd.

Peaseblossom stumbles forwards and snatches at her mask. Under the tree, holding the hand of a girl in a long cream gown, who may even be Claire Sutherland, is Luke. Her Luke. Her hand fumbles on the mask and she tears it away, and the elastic snaps against her cheek. He looks older – he must be thirty-one now – but his hair is the same chestnut brown.

Luke, she wants to cry aloud, as he leads the girl by the hand down the steps into the Italian garden, down to the frothy pink and white roses and the ethereal statues.

The lutenist picks up his instrument again and weaves through the crowd, drawing them back up the lawn towards the yew walk. Peaseblossom holds her broken mask in her hand, and pushes the other way. Luke and the girl have disappeared from the Italian garden. Peaseblossom runs down the steps, nearly turns her ankle over in her hurry. Her heart rate is soaring. She stops in the middle of the sunken garden, but he's gone. Completely vanished. There's a gate at the far end that looks like it leads into woodland, and another on the right that's not properly fastened. That's the way he must have gone. Peaseblossom crunches across the gravel. Her feet hurt through her thin soles. When she reaches the gate, she puts her hand on the clasp. *He touched this a moment ago,* she thinks. She's about to open the gate, when she hears steps behind her. She spins around and cries aloud. It's only Fairy in that sinister owl mask. Peaseblossom reaches guiltily for her bag.

"Peaseblossom."

"I haven't found the right moment yet," Peaseblossom says. "I'm just working out the best way to do it discreetly."

"Never mind that." Fairy stops walking, looks back over her shoulder.

There is no one else around. They are alone in the Italian garden.

"What have I done?" Peaseblossom asks, and wishes she didn't sound so desperate. She wants to go back to the others now, to see the next part of the play, to see Luke again. Without her mask, he will see her. She has to find a chance to talk to him today.

"Those sonnets. Give them to me. I want to tell you something."

"I won't mess it up, Fairy. I know it's important to you. Robin said so."

"The sonnets."

Peaseblossom slides her hand into her bag, and pulls them out. Two envelopes: CS and CG. The two sets of initials look very alike and it takes her a second to tell them apart.

"You must swap these," Fairy says.

"What, open them? I can't do that. I promised Robin."

Fairy takes the envelopes from her. "Look at these initials, Peaseblossom. They are very alike, aren't they?"

"Yes, but I know which is which."

"You must give them the other way round. This one here–" She indicates the envelope addressed to CS. "This one must go to the bride. The other one goes to the actress. That's the woman we've just seen."

The one with Luke. The one who held his hand and walked with him through these roses.

"But my instructions were to–"

"I know Justin. I've known him for many years. He'll thank me in the end for this."

"What's in the sonnets?" Peaseblossom asks.

"Never you mind. Just make sure you hand them out the wrong way round. I can't imagine that's too difficult, Peaseblossom. You usually manage to get things wrong on your assignments."

"Robin's pleased with what I've done," Peaseblossom cries.

Fairy sniffs. "I was hoping he would have listened to me, when I talked to him about this job."

"You mean get Moth to do it instead of me?"

"I meant that he would have swapped the sonnets himself, but he assured me he couldn't do it."

“Perhaps we should open them first and check.” Peaseblossom holds out her hands for the envelopes. She must get out of this sunken garden, and back to the players.

“Absolutely not,” Fairy says. “There is no need. He was adamant that he could not do it. I didn’t ask him again.”

At last she holds out the two envelopes. Peaseblossom takes them, glances down at the interlocking, swirling initials. Fairy turns away and walks unsteadily across the gravel to the steps. Peaseblossom puts the sonnets away safely and follows Fairy back to the stone steps, the giant cedar and the lawn beyond.

Claire sighed and turned into the lane. She never walked this way, not even now, so many years afterwards. Now it was time to put the ghosts to rest. She had come back to Wotton for her father’s sixtieth birthday. It was the end of February, still cold and blustery. The hedgerows were wintery, with half-dead bony brown foliage. Claire shoved her hands into the pockets of her parka. She would walk to the Gothic door and then along the lane a little, along the estate wall where, only a few feet away, was the lake and the island, the ducks and the boathouse.

The door was ajar, just as it had been that long-ago summer, the start of everything. Claire stopped walking, and gazed at it. This was no trick of memory and eye; it really was open. A car came along the lane towards the village, and Claire tucked into the hedgerow. Once it passed her, she ran across the lane to the door.

There was mud scuffed up at the bottom, smearing a brown film over the paintwork. There was a single long scratch running down one of the panels. Through the gap, Claire could see the hard, bare earth and the skeletal trees and shrubs. If she just took a step and then another she could cross that threshold and, within a moment, she would be standing on the edge of the lake. It would be deep and brown with the winter rain, painted in a palette of sienna and ochre under a white sky.

She had never been back inside the gardens. Once or twice she had looked at the website, seen the photographs of the statues in the Italian garden, the strange little boathouse, the soaring trees above the drifts of bluebells. Now the door was open, the magic door, the way in. It was open and inviting her to step inside. Still she hesitated.

Suddenly, she was aware of someone behind her in the lane. She swung around.

“Claire,” said Justin.

Her hands fluttered and she shoved them back into her pockets.

“Justin.”

“Jesus. Claire. It’s so good to see you again. What are you doing here? I mean, I didn’t think you still lived at home. Come here, old bean. Give me a hug.”

Claire stood rigid; Justin had to reach out to her. They hugged awkwardly hampered by thick coats. Justin took her face in his hands.

“It really is so good to see you again. What are you up to?”

“I’m back for my Dad’s birthday. It was his sixtieth yesterday.” Claire was gabbling, feeling childlike and foolish.

“Are you still in Bristol?”

“No, I’ve been in London the last few years,” Claire said. “My friend and I moved up after uni. She knew London and helped me settle in. She’s gone to America now. I live on my own.”

“London? You’ve been in London all this time, and you never told me?”

Claire looked beyond Justin to the knobbly brown hedgerow. “I didn’t think you’d be interested anymore,” she said at last.

"I'm sorry," he said. "I treated you very badly. You didn't deserve it. I don't know what happened. I was living up there and it's another world and you were going to Bristol and–"

"It doesn't matter," Claire said.

A tractor came snorting along the lane, its red paintwork splattered with mud and grime. They stood aside in the half-open doorway as it lumbered past, leaving thick muddy tracks on the tarmac.

"So, what are you doing now?" he asked.

"I'm part of a travelling theatre group called Love in Idleness. We tour a lot of the time, take plays to schools and places without theatres. That's the bread and butter. The jam is special bookings for house parties and weddings."

"That's fantastic. You made it as an actress. That's wonderful. I'm so pleased."

Claire looked at him. He looked tired and under stress, but he did also look genuinely happy for her. It was so confusing.

"Sorry, I've only been talking about me." She stopped, embarrassed. "What about you? Are you living here?"

"No, I'm leaving this afternoon," he said. "Back to London."

"I'm going back later too," Claire said.

"Are you driving? Or getting the train?"

"Train."

"Let me give you a lift. It's no trouble."

"No, no, I'm fine. Really. Thank you, but the train's all booked."

"I'd love to give you a lift. I'd love to talk to you again. Please." Justin smiled at her. "I'll pick you up. You tell me when."

This is a bad idea, Claire thought. *I shouldn't do it.*

She knew he would come. She never thought for a moment that he'd stand her up. He drove into Rowan Close in a black Alfa Romeo and parked outside her parents' house. Claire hugged her parents and shouldered her tatty rucksack. Justin opened the boot and put it inside, held the passenger door for her.

"You never told me what you were doing," Claire said, as they drove through the village.

"I work for Greenaway's," Justin said. "You know, the shoe people."

"Oh, yes. Right. What as?"

"In the finance department."

"I didn't imagine you were a buyer for stilettos. What's it like?"

"It's OK."

"You don't sound very convincing."

"Oh Claire, I don't know."

"If you're not happy, you should look for something else. Everyone wants help with money these days."

"It's not that simple. I should have said before. I'm getting married."

"Married," she said. One word. It shouldn't hurt so much. "Who are you marrying?"

"Clare Greenaway," Justin muttered, and swore at the car in front.

"Oh, I get it. When's the great day?"

"In June. Look, let's not talk about all that. I want to hear about you and your theatre company."

"Why don't you want to talk about your own wedding?" Claire needled.

"Because I don't," Justin said.

Fairy wanders into the marquee. Peaseblossom didn't like to overtake her, but now she can run to where the guests are gathering for the next scene. Her leather bag thumps her hip as she runs. Her phone is in the bag. She should phone Robin and tell him what Fairy said. She should open the sonnets and see what they say. She must follow her instructions to the letter. She should do as Fairy says. She must find Luke.

The crowd is milling where the yew walk opens out onto the lawn. Peaseblossom is at the back and can't see. She squeezes between a fat man disguised as Michael Jackson and the dark fingers of the yews.

It's two other actors, a man and a woman. Peaseblossom can't remember much of *A Midsummer Night's Dream*, not that she would dare tell Robin that.

"*Therefore hear me, Hermia*," the man says.

That's right: Hermia and Lysander. She really should brush up her Shakespeare. Robin's often coming out with quotes and references which Cobweb always knows and understands.

Peaseblossom sees a sudden movement through the gnarled yew branches. It's a boy, eight or nine, dressed in green with a pointed hat and red hair. He slides through a gap between the trees and grins at Peaseblossom.

"I'm an elf," he says.

"So, I can see," she says. "Are you in the play?"

"Not really," the elf says. "That's my dad. The one with the lute. And that's Mike and Vicky. Then there's Claire and Luke. And Orlando. He is in the play. He's sixteen. I'm eight."

Peaseblossom looks over to where the actors are. The woman in cream – Claire – has joined the other two. She must be Helena. Peaseblossom stands on tiptoe, but she can't see Luke anywhere. She can't really listen to what the actors are saying. Neither is she listening to the elf.

"I said: who are you?"

"Oh." Peaseblossom is flustered. "I'm a…friend of Clare's."

"How do you know Claire?" the elf asks. "And where's your mask? Everyone else is wearing a mask. Why aren't you wearing one?"

"It broke," Peaseblossom says.

"That's silly," the elf says. "Now you look different to everyone else. How do you know Claire?"

"Not that Claire. Clare. The bride."

"The bride? Claire's not the bride."

Peaseblossom sighs, but this persistent elf might be useful. "The bride is called Clare as well," she says.

"I'm called Alfie," the elf tells her.

"Alfie the Elfie?"

"There isn't really an elf in this play, you know. Orlando, he's Puck. He's like a bigger elf. I'm an extra elf."

"So, what do you do?"

"Anything useful," he says.

"Anything?"

Justin pressed his card into Claire's hand when he left her.

"Please call me," he said. "I can't believe you've been in London and I didn't know."

Like the reverse of that first day when they met in Wotton gardens, when he took her number, but did not give her his. This time he folded her fingers around the shiny oblong of card. She glanced down at it: the Greenaway's typeface she had seen in so many high streets, then his name and numbers and email in Times New Roman.

"OK," she said. "I will."

He looked at her a moment, and she knew he was waiting for her to offer her own number, but she didn't.

That night, in bed in her garret in Highgate, lying beneath the sloping ceiling, her head raced with everything that had happened. When she'd woken up that morning – just a bit hungover from her father's birthday meal – she was in her old room. It was all familiar and all strange. Like the lane past Wotton gardens.

Claire hadn't planned to walk that way, until her feet found themselves approaching the estate wall, and she knew the time had come. She could so easily have not been there, and she would never have met Justin, never spoken to him, or travelled to London with him.

It must have happened for a reason, she thought, and reached out to her bedside table: bright pink alarm clock, torch, a pile of books, and a small lozenge of amethyst. And one shiny business card. Claire picked it up and stared at the letters in the half-light.

The next day she called Justin.

"You never told me your name."

Peaseblossom jumps at the tug on her sleeve. It's the elf again. Alfie.

"I told you mine," he says. "If I tell you my name, you have to tell me yours. It's rude not to."

"Oh," Peaseblossom says.

She's never any good at this. She always intends to have a false name ready before each assignment, but somehow she always forgets.

"So, what is it?"

"Penelope," Peaseblossom invents.

The crowd has moved on to the bank on the far side of the lawn, behind the wedding cake marquee. Luke is lying down on the grass, with his arm across his eyes. Peaseblossom elbows through the crowd to the far side, where Claire Sutherland steps out from behind the monkey-puzzle tree. Luke sits up, rubs hair from his face.

"*O Helen, goddess, nymph, perfect, divine!*" He stumbles to his feet, reaches out to Claire, and his mouth freezes for a second, looking beyond.

"Luke's forgotten the lines," Alfie says.

"*To what, my love, shall I compare thine eyne*?" Luke gazes at Peaseblossom, then, at last, turns back to Claire.

"I thought he'd forgotten it, Penelope."

"You still here?"

"I'm still here," Alfie says. "What's wrong with Luke, do you think? He was looking at you. He probably wonders where your mask is."

Peaseblossom glances around. She can't see that owl mask anywhere. Not that that means Fairy isn't watching her from somewhere. She opens the clasp on her bag, slides her hand in, finds the two thick envelopes.

"Alfie." She bends down to the elf's ear. "I need someone to do something for me today. An elf would be the ideal person to do it. Would you like to help?"

He wrinkles his freckled nose. "How much?" he asks.

"How much?" Peaseblossom echoes. "I thought you said you'd do anything useful."

"I would," he says. "But elves have to be paid."

The crowd drifts off around them, following the lute player, Alfie's father, down the lawn. Peaseblossom looks for Luke, but he's gone once more. She has to find him before the players leave. She has to deliver the bloody sonnets, and she's running out of time. She takes a note out of her purse and waves it under Alfie's nose.

"When the job's done," she says.

"What do I have to do?"

She hesitates for a moment. Should she be doing this? But if she doesn't, she may miss her chance to see Luke.

"Pay attention," she says, and shows Alfie the two envelopes. "I've been asked to give these to Claire and Clare. That's your friend, Claire, the actress, and Clare, the bride."

"Did you write those?" Alfie points at the interlaced letters of CS. "It's really messy. I can hardly read it. Let's see the other one."

"No, I didn't," Peaseblossom says.

"What's in them?"

"I don't know. And they mustn't be opened. Claire and Clare will know if they've been opened, and then I won't pay you."

Alfie rolls his eyes. "I won't open them."

"Good. OK."

"Claire's called Claire Sutherland," Alfie says, looking at the envelopes. "That must be hers. It looks a bit more like CS than the other one."

"The other one's CG. That's Clare Greenaway, the bride."

"What do I say to them?"

"Just say you have a special delivery for them."

"They might ask who from."

"It's a secret. They'll know when they open them."

"Will they give me a tip?"

"Alfie! I thought you were a helpful elf."

"Even helpful elves have to be paid."

Peaseblossom ignores this. "Do you know who the bride is?"

"Is she wearing a wedding dress?"

"No, not yet. She's got a kind of clown mask on."

"OK, cool. Can I watch Orlando first? He's doing a Puck bit in a moment. His mum and dad are Titania and Oberon. Next time I might have a proper part."

"You must do it before the wedding starts."

"I thought this was a wedding."

"This is the party before the wedding. So you must do it at the end of the play, before the bride goes off to change into her wedding dress. And, Alfie, if you speak to Luke…" She trails off. She doesn't know what to say. She can't give her real name now. "Tell him an old friend is here today who'd love to see him."

"Who's the old friend?"

"Me."

"You're not that old. You're older than me obviously. And older than Orlando. And older than Claire too, I think. I must go. I want to watch Orlando. I'll find you when it's done, and you can pay me."

Alfie shoves the sonnets into the pocket of his tunic and starts to run down the lawn towards the cedar tree.

Peaseblossom exhales. That's the sonnets taken care of. Now she can concentrate on finding Luke.

Shit! She never told Alfie to swap them. *Oh Jesus.*

"Alfie, Alfie!"

Peaseblossom runs after him. One of her ballet shoes comes off; she scoops it up in her hand, and runs across the grass. Alfie's small green form is vanishing into the masked crowd, as he elbows his way to the front.

Peaseblossom is breathless, when she reaches the spectators. She's right at the back. She jumps up to see over the shoulders in front of her. She cannot see the elf anywhere.

"Excuse me," she mutters, and pushes between a woman in an elaborate black glittering mask, and a man wearing Frank Zappa's face. Frank Zappa swears as Peaseblossom treads on his foot, even though she has no shoe.

In front of the giant cedar tree Titania is reclining on the ground with a circle of flowers in her hair. Oberon stoops over her, squeezing the juice of love-in-idleness into her eyes.

"*...think no more of this night's accidents*," he says.

There's a young fellow there with them, wearing a coronet of leaves on his head. Puck. Orlando. Suddenly Peaseblossom sees a movement behind the giant lined tree trunk. A bright green tunic, the glint of red hair. She ducks and runs across the front of the spectators. She can feel Puck's dark eyes watching her scuttling, bent over, shoe in hand, holding her hat on.

"Alfie, Alfie," she hisses, drawing him behind the trunk.

"Sssh," he says, peering around the tree. "Titania's waking up."

"Those envelopes I gave you."

"I've got them safe."

"I forgot to tell you you've got to give them the wrong way round."

"The wrong way round? What, upside down? The writing's so bad, I don't think they'd notice anyway. Why didn't you type them? Can't you use a computer?"

"I didn't bloody write them. Now, listen. No, show me them again."

Alfie sighs and takes the envelopes out of his pocket. They're a bit crumpled. Peaseblossom crouches down beside him.

"This one that says CS. That must go to Clare Greenaway. And the one that says CG must go to Claire. Your Claire."

"Are you sure? That seems a bit silly. Claire's called Claire Sutherland. That's CS."

"I know, I know. The person who wrote them made a mistake, and then it was too late to fix it. Like you said, the writing's bad, so the ladies probably won't notice."

"What about Luke?"

"Luke?" Peaseblossom flushes.

"Do I still have to tell him you want to see him?"

"Yes. Yes please."

"You're sure about this? These letters? They go the wrong way round?"

"Yes. Like I just said."

"Have you had something put in your eyes too?" Alfie asks.

And Justin met her that same night. They went for a drink, then back to Claire's tiny flat. She made coffee, and offered him whisky, which she rarely drank, but that night she poured two generous measures into tumblers, and they sat together on the floor, on her threadbare black and white rug. And Claire brought the bottle of Talisker down onto the floor with them, and topped up the glasses, sloshing some onto her fingers, and Justin took her hand and sucked the whisky off her skin.

Justin has not been watching the acting. Not even when it's Claire. He almost can't focus on her. He's seen her eyes swing to his Green Man mask, but he can't read her thoughts, sees only Hippolyta's haughtiness, Helena's hurt. He wishes that, like in *Four Weddings and a Funeral*, someone will leap forward from the crowd, rip off a mask, and yell that he cannot marry Clare Greenaway because he doesn't love her, because he loves someone else. Sometimes he's caught sight of that owl mask, and he knows Aunt Effie is watching him. She's also watching that woman in pink, and so is he.

At any time he could have gone over to her, told her he knew she was from the agency and that he no longer wanted the sonnets delivered. Seeing Claire drifting around his garden – their garden – in that filmy, cream gown, with her hair tumbling down her back, he felt sick with the knowledge of what was going to happen. He could stop it. He had that choice, that power.

Then he saw the agency woman running, bent double and clutching a shoe, across the front row of the spectators to grab a small elf from behind the cedar tree. What the fuck was going on? Claire had told him that Simon, who's a single father, would be bringing his son as an extra elf, but why the hell was the agent chasing him so desperately across the garden?

Alfie trots down the steps behind the cedar tree. He is in a sunken garden. There are roses there, and pink and white petals have scattered on the gravel beneath his feet. There are statues too. Some only have heads. One has no arms. If he had a marker pen, it would be fun to draw a moustache onto one of those cold white faces. He checks behind him. Everyone's moving back up the lawn, past the marquee, following his dad's lute. Alfie chuckles. He thinks the wedding guests are probably getting a bit knackered with all this marching up and down the lawn to see bits of the play. They'd probably rather be in the marquee with the food and wine.

There's a bench amongst the roses. Alfie sits down cross-legged like an elf. He takes out the two envelopes Penelope gave him. They're a bit scruffy now. He tries to smooth them down. So she wants him to give the wrong envelope to the wrong person? That can't be right. If these are so important, she wouldn't have put them in the wrong envelopes to start with. He considers the two sets of initials. It really would have been easier if Penelope had typed them. Or whoever it was who did it. Whatever she said, he thinks Penelope did write the envelopes, but she's embarrassed to admit she muddled up the contents. What are the contents? Alfie holds one up and turns it this way and that, but the envelope is made of thick paper. It feels like there is only one folded sheet inside. He checks the other one. Again, one folded sheet but he can't see anything. They are both sealed with a red blob of wax. Alfie's never seen a letter sealed with wax before, except in films. He rubs his finger over its rough surface. Claire wouldn't be cross with him if he opened her envelope, would she? Then, at least, he could see what one of the envelopes contained. But it would have to be the one with the bride's initials, wouldn't it? Supposing when Claire gets hers she realises she has been given someone else's letter? Then she would have to find the bride and swap letters. *Why is Penelope writing to them both?* Alfie wonders. He's almost certain it is Penelope. She couldn't properly tell him who they were from, so it must be her.

He's just about to break open the wax on the envelope marked CG, when there's a shriek from behind him. He jumps, stifling a shriek himself. The peacock is slowly revolving. Its tail has opened into a giant fan of blue and green eyes. They're unlucky, Alfie remembers. Everyone knows that. Guiltily, he shoves both letters back into his pocket.

They went to the Tate Modern, to the museums, to Highgate Cemetery. One evening they went to Swan Lake because Claire loved ballet. Some nights Justin took her to hotels; sometimes he came back to her tiny flat. He never took her to his Chelsea apartment; she never asked to see it. She knew he didn't live with Clare Greenaway, but her things would be there, her presence would be there. She wouldn't want to see that flat, just as she had never wanted to see inside Wotton House. She was still the girl from Rowan Close.

"Why are you doing it, Justin?" Claire asked.

They were cuddled together under the duvet on her narrow single bed. Claire wanted to sit up, reach out for some water, but she was too content to move.

"Doing what?" Justin asked, but he stiffened, and Claire felt the tension in his muscles. He knew what she was talking about.

She hesitated. This was difficult to say.

"Why are you marrying her?" She still could not say her name when she was talking about the woman Justin was going to spend his life with. It was obscene on her lips.

Justin sighed, shut his eyes, pulled Claire close.

"I have to," he said.

Claire felt cold and slithery inside. "Is she pregnant?"

"No. God, no. Not that."

"It's just that…you don't seem that fond of her when you speak about her."

"I'm not." His eyes were still closed.

"So…what…why? If you don't love her?"

"I don't love her." He opened his eyes, looked at Claire. "I never have. But I have to marry her. She comes with considerable benefits."

"The money?" Claire was horrified. Justin already had money: family money and a fat salary. He couldn't be that shallow, could he? To marry someone he didn't love because she was an heiress.

"Things are very difficult," he said. "My father's lost almost everything. The last few years he's had an impossible gambling problem. He's run up huge debts. My mother took an overdose at Christmas. We nearly lost her. If I marry Clare, it will really help things at home."

"There must be another way," Claire said. She remembered the spiky snobby Evelyn in the walled garden, tried to feel compassion, but couldn't.

"There isn't another way to get several million. If I don't do this, my parents will lose Wotton, my mother might kill herself. I can't have that. I have to marry Clare. She's OK, you know. It's just not real love."

"Have you ever felt real love?" Claire asked.

"I have," he said. "I do now."

What will Claire do when she receives her sonnet? Justin gulps the wine he's picked up from the marquee. Someone's talking to him, but he's not listening. He feels somewhat light-headed, but he hasn't drunk that much. He shouldn't be making wedding vows in this state. He glances over to where his mother is standing. She too has a drink in her hand. She's thinner than ever and, beneath that mask, he knows her face is gaunt and lined, the face of a much older woman. She will exhale with relief once the vows and the rings are exchanged.

"I'm not ever going to leave you," he had said to Claire. "You and me. We're something special. Whatever happens I will find a way to see you."

He knew Claire was finding it hard. He'd had other affairs while he was with Clare Greenaway and been unfaithful to girlfriends before. He knew which girls were cool with being the other woman. Claire wasn't one of those. She was uncomfortable and sad. And he was guilty. He should never have put her in this position. He should never have treated her so badly years before. None of the women he'd taken for lovers had ever understood him in the gentle, unassuming way that Claire had so many summers ago at Wotton. If he could change things, he would. But the wedding date was set for Midsummer's Eve, the players booked, the guest list drawn up. It was unstoppable.

"A play at a wedding," Claire had said sadly. "In a wooded garden on Midsummer's Eve." And then she had turned away to hide her tears, but he had already seen them.

And now, any time soon, Claire will be handed an envelope. She'll look at it, and not recognise the writing, but she will probably wonder if it's from him. Then she'll open it, and draw out the paper within and, in fourteen lines, her world will fall in pieces, because the sonnet Justin asked Robin Goodfellow to write to her is one telling her that he will always treasure their time together, and their shared memories, but that he cannot take her into his future.

And while Claire – his lovely, gentle Claire – is reading that, somewhere else in the garden Clare will also be opening an envelope, and her sonnet will tell her how Justin is looking forward to spending his life with her, her alone, and that no one else holds his heart. *Jesus fucking Christ,* Justin thinks, nodding inanely to the couple talking at him. I should have sent them the other way round. If only I had done that. He looks round wildly. He can't see Aunt Effie or the agent. The guests are trudging back down the lawn for the final scene of the play. He knows it's the final scene because Claire told him how they were ending it. The lute player is leading everyone past the giant cedar, through the pink and white Italian garden to the first trees of the bluebell wood.

A clown mask. That's what Penelope said. There's someone on the far side of the crowd with a clown mask, but surely that's a bloke. Alfie sidles through the throng. The play is nearly over. It's Orlando's final speech coming up. Then it'll be the wedding bit proper. He's got to deliver these before the wedding. Claire's is easy, but the clown one is harder.

"Excuse me, is that Clare's mask you're wearing?" Alfie asks the man. "If she's swapped masks I need to know. I need to find Clare urgently."

"Clare's busy at the moment," the clown says. "I'm sure you can find her after the wedding."

"No, I need her now," Alfie says, but the man and his companions have moved on, ignoring him, past the big tree and into the sunken rose garden where he almost opened one of the envelopes.

The sunken garden is filling up with wedding guests. Alfie, on the edge of the lawn, is higher up, but he can only see the backs of their heads. His dad lowers his lute.

"*If we shadows have offended,*" Orlando calls down. He's astride a branch of the tall tree at the furthest end of the rose garden. "*Think but this, and all is mended.*" He leaps from the branch to the ground, and some of the wedding guests gasp and one woman cries out.

Alfie thinks quickly. He must find the bride first. She will be going back to the big house after Orlando has finished to get ready for the wedding. If he waits at the top of the lawn, he'll see her. He must. Claire can have hers later. He trots back up towards the house, stopping off in the marquee to help himself to some nibbles. Really, this job of Penelope's is making him worry an awful lot. It just can't be right to give someone a letter meant for someone else. He likes Claire. What would she tell him to do? Give the right letter to the right person. That's what Claire would say. Alfie knows Claire and trusts her a lot more than he does Penelope. He'll do what Claire would say. The right letter for the right person.

The players are standing in a line, bowing to the guests in the Italian garden. Peaseblossom can see Luke's eyes searching the masked crowd. He's looking for her. *I'm here, I'm here*, she wants to shout. It has been so long since she saw him. So long since he saw her. What will he make of her? She pulls in her abs. At least the jacket hides the tightness of her shift. She's wearing both shoes again but, even though it is a warm and dry evening, one foot feels cold and a little damp from the grass on her tights.

It was all her fault with Luke. She drove him away.

"I want a baby," she said to Luke.

They'd been married a year. Luke was just finishing his drama degree. She was working in a bookshop, because she hadn't walked straight into a psychologist's position, as she had naively imagined she would. She didn't mind the bookshop, but the money was awful, and sometimes she felt so trapped. She was only young, but already she found herself peering into prams and buggies, sometimes fingering baby clothes if she was alone in Tesco, imagining what it would feel like to feed tiny arms and legs into those pastel suits.

"What?" Luke said, but she knew he had heard. His eyes were wary and he fiddled with the fork he had laid down on his empty plate.

"A baby," she said again, and reached out to clasp his hand across the table. "I really want a baby. You want a family, too, don't you?"

"Well, yes, one day," he said at last. "But not now. Not yet."

"Why not yet?" she asked. "I really want to do it now. When I'm young. When we're both young. I don't want to be one of those old mothers at the school."

"Jesus, you're hardly old."

"It might take some time. We should start trying now."

Luke untangled his hand from hers. She stiffened. This wasn't going right. Luke should have leaped up from his chair, sent it crashing to the lino and scooped her in his arms, telling her how much he wanted to make a baby with her. She had taken a couple of candles into their tiny bedroom, laid out her sexy red lace babydoll. If she'd been taking oral contraceptives, she would have ditched them, but they all seemed to make her nauseous, so they'd always used Durex, and there was nothing she could do about that. She had considered chucking them out too, but if Luke had responded as he should have, as she was certain he would have, he wouldn't have used them again anyway.

"It's too soon," he said. "We've got loads of time. I'm not ready for this. We haven't any money."

"Babies don't need money. They need love." Peaseblossom wished she hadn't had so much wine. She could feel tears starting and, once she started, especially after drinking, she couldn't stop.

Luke laughed. "I think you'll find they need a bit more than that," he said. "Cots and clothes and nappies and prams and so on. None of that's cheap."

"We could get it second-hand. They don't need much, Luke. They need love, and we'd give it that, wouldn't we?"

"Not now," Luke said. "Really. Neither of us have got our jobs sorted out. I want to act. You don't want to stay in that place forever. Let's get ourselves sorted out, then talk again in two or three years."

"Two or three years? I want this now. I want to be a mother. I want someone to love."

"You've got me," Luke said. "You said you loved me."

"You know what I mean."

"I didn't say *no*. I said *not now*." He pushed back his chair, picked up their two plates, carried them to the sink. "I'll wash up, then I'm going to bed. I'm really tired."

"It's only nine o'clock. We never go to bed this early."

"You don't have to." Luke squirted washing up liquid into the bowl, came back to the table for the glasses. "You stay up if you like. I'm tired."

"You weren't tired half an hour ago," she said, and stumbled into the bedroom.

Their flat was so small she could hear the sounds of Luke washing up – the spray of the tap, the clink as he stacked plates and saucepans on the drying rack – and, no doubt, he could hear her sobs too. Her red babydoll lay on the pale bed covers like a splash of blood. Blood: the symbol of womanhood, motherhood. She snatched it up and shoved it into the bedside drawer, tugged out a T-shirt instead. She couldn't walk out of the bedroom carrying the candles back to the living room, so she threw them into the bottom of the wardrobe, tumbling on top of her boots and trainers. Her mouth tasted foul: red wine and garlic. She wanted to clean her teeth, cleanse her mouth with Listerine, but she couldn't move from the bed.

Of course Justin had considered breaking up with Clare and calling off the wedding. Finding Claire again at that Gothic garden door had been as wonderful as finding her that first time by the lake. She was tied to him, to his younger self, to the garden that he loved. She came from a world apart from his but, when they were together, it didn't matter. He made excuses to Clare to be with her; he knew he was on thin ice; he knew how easily he could be caught out. *Would that not be for the best?* he often wondered. Then the wedding would be cancelled and Claire would never have to see him make his vows to another woman. And then he thought of his parents, and what his mother had done on Boxing Day the previous year and he knew if he jilted Clare, he might lose his mother. He would just have to find ways to see Claire as well when he was in London. It wasn't going to be easy, working for Greenaway's, but he would bloody well find a way.

They lived in a bubble for those few months. He did not introduce her to anyone he knew. Once, as they were going into a restaurant in Soho, he took her arm and tugged her out straight away, as he had seen a couple who were friends with the Greenaways.

"We'll have to go somewhere else," he said. "I'm sorry. That could have been awkward."

And she didn't introduce him to any of her friends either. He knew she mainly hung out with the others in her acting troupe: Mike and Vicky and their teenage son, Luke and Simon. There was one night, at her flat, when her phone went, and it was Luke, and he was obviously asking her to meet him and the others to discuss something, and she said she was feeling ill.

"If you need to go, go," Justin said when she hung up.

"No," she said.

Peaseblossom sits on the bench in the Italian garden. The air is scented with roses. Wedding guests drift back towards the marquee and the house. It's almost time for the ceremony. She can't see Clare Greenaway anywhere, and wonders for a second if Alfie has delivered the first of the sonnets. Luke and Claire and the others are at the centre of a group, accepting compliments on the performance. Luke's eyes stray from the faces in front of him. Justin Fontaine joins them, his Green Man mask hanging loosely from his fingers. Surely, he would love a few moments with his mistress before he commits himself to someone else. Peaseblossom gets up, straightens her hat, which somehow has managed to stay on, and crunches through the gravel to the iron gate. As she walks, Luke peels away from Claire and Justin.

"Luke," she says.

"I never thought I would see you again," he says. "And there you were, and I thought it couldn't be you, but it is."

He opens his arms and Peaseblossom falls into him. He kisses her cheeks, and at last her pink flowered hat works loose from its pin and slides down her back to the ground, but she hardly feels it fall.

"You look lovely," Luke says. "All pink and white and rosy."

"You look…grassy," Peaseblossom says at last, almost unable to speak.

Luke's cheesecloth smock is stained green with grass, and there's even a streak of blood on one of the sleeves from a hidden graze.

"It's so lovely to see you," Luke says.

Peaseblossom thought she could wear Luke down over the next few weeks. She gave up meat and told Luke it was to make her healthier and purer for conception. She gave up alcohol. She even bought a glossy hardback book called *Conception to Birth*, and left it out on the sofa.

She wheedled, she reasoned, she shouted, she cried. But Luke would not budge. He didn't want a baby yet. He wanted to establish his career as an actor. He wanted more financial security, a bigger home, more stability. The rows became bitter. He yelled at her one night that he should never have married her so young, and now she was wanting to turn him into a father, and he'd never even had time for a life of his own.

In truth, Peaseblossom didn't know why she was so desperate to have a baby, but soon the idea preoccupied her all the time. Tears burst in her eyes when she saw a furry bald head carried against a father's cheek or bobbing along in a Tesco trolley.

"What are you doing here?" Luke asks. "I mean, are you friends with the bride?"

"Er, no, not really."

Justin Fontaine turns around. Without the mask, Peaseblossom sees a haunted young man, with floppy dark hair. He looks at her, with a question in his eyes. For a second she thinks he is going to speak to her, say something about the sonnets, but no, of course not. Claire is there. Claire looks sad and tense.

"You go," Peaseblossom hears her say to Justin.

Justin stalks through the Italian garden, with his mask under his arm. Claire stands very still, watching him. He doesn't even acknowledge Luke and the woman he's talking to. Claire walks slowly towards them and picks up the woman's hat.

"Your hat," she says and, for once, the effort of speaking is like wading through treacle.

Luke and the woman are facing each other, holding hands left and right. Claire feels awkward standing there grasping the hat. She drops it onto the bench and follows Justin up the lawn. By the time she reaches the cedar tree she's crying.

"Almost time for the nuptials," Luke says.

"I don't want to see that," Peaseblossom says. "I'm not a friend of anyone here. I don't need to be at the wedding. I want to talk to you."

They are alone in the sunken garden now. The heat of the day is fading, as the sky turns a milky amethyst. The scent of roses is overwhelming.

"Will you walk with me?" Luke asks, and offers his arm.

Peaseblossom slides her arm through his, turns once to see Fairy perched like a malevolent owl on the edge of the lawn, lets him lead her though the iron gate and into the wood beyond.

Alfie hasn't seen anyone in a clown mask who might be the bride. He's panicking now. It'll soon be the wedding, and his dad and the players will be returning to London. And he's got to tell Luke an old friend wants to see him. And he's still got to find Penelope, so he can be paid. He leaves the revellers on the lawn and runs back down the tunnel of yew trees to the potting shed.

"Claire, Claire!"

"What is it, Alfie?"

Claire's crumpled on the floor with her back against the whitewashed wall. *She looks sad,* Alfie thinks. Maybe he can cheer her up with his delivery.

"Come out here a moment," he says.

"Oh, Alfie, must I?"

"Yes," he says. "I need to speak to you."

"Can't you… Oh OK." She stands and follows him outside. "Are you all right?"

Alfie hesitates. He needs to check one more time.

"If someone told you to do something and it's wrong, like obviously wrong, would you do it? Or would you do what's right?"

"What are you on about? Has something happened? Where's your dad?"

"In the tent drinking beer. I need to know. Would you do what was right?"

"Can you be more exact?"

"You'd do the right thing, wouldn't you?"

"I suppose so."

Alfie looks at her. He's never seen her look quite like this before, as though there isn't any point in anything anymore. He's unsettled.

"Don't worry about it. I was only thinking about something," he says. "I've been asked to give you this letter." He pulls an envelope from his pocket. Yes, CS. Those are Claire's initials. It's the right thing to do.

"Who's it from?" she asks.

"Penelope."

Claire looks puzzled. "Who's Penelope?"

"The pink lady." Alfie holds out the envelope. This is his last chance to reclaim it, to do what Penelope said.

Claire takes it from him. She doesn't even look at the front.

"I'll read it later, Alfie," she says. "I don't feel well at the moment." He follows her into the potting shed. She drops the envelope into her bag, unscrews a bottle of water and drinks. Alfie hovers. He could still do it, reach into her bag and swap it. No, he's done the right thing.

"What does the bride look like?" Alfie asks.

Claire stiffens with the bottle to her mouth.

"Tell me everything," Luke says.

"Everything? That's a big ask."

Above their heads the trees – birch and beech, Peaseblossom thinks – soar into the evening sky. There are clicks and whirrs from the undergrowth, and the scent of wild garlic. The last of the bluebells are bruised and mauve amongst the grasses. There's no one else around. They can't see the house or the marquee; they can't hear the inane chatter of the wedding guests. This could be a real wood, a real forest, where lovers and fairies meet in secret groves.

Luke pulls a wry face. "Have you had your babies yet?"

"No," Peaseblossom says.

"I'm sorry," Luke says, and squeezes her arm.

Peaseblossom blinks. Sometimes she thinks she will never be a mother. The pain of seeing other babies – friends' babies or those she passes on the streets and in shops – has dulled over time because she has applied her own anaesthetic, but it's an anaesthetic that wears off too soon. She glances at Luke, wonders as she has wondered so many, many times what their child would look like. Fair like her, brown-haired like Luke? Blue eyes or green?

"I'm back in Bath again," Peaseblossom tells him. "After…after everything…"

"I'm sorry," Luke interrupts. "I'm so sorry. I never meant for things to get so horrible and out of hand. I was so unkind to you. I don't know why. I loved you so much, but I couldn't do what you wanted."

"Neither could anyone else, obviously," Peaseblossom says.

The track curves round and drops into the valley. There's a tree close to the path, with a lined, twisted bark, streaked with green and gold lichen. Peaseblossom stares at the colours, and they jump as her eyes fill up.

"I've been divorced twice now," she says.

"Twice? Oh no. What happened? Who did you marry?"

"His name was Graham. He was a bastard. We parted after only a few weeks."

"You poor old thing."

"I wouldn't stay with a man who treated me like that, who hit me because I cooked the wrong thing for dinner."

"Jesus, no. Did you report him?"

"Of course not. I told A & E I'd walked into a door. Like everyone else does. Next time I had to ring my dad, so he could drive me to another A & E. After that I didn't bother. Then I left."

"How are your parents? I always liked them a lot."

"They're fine, yes. They always liked you too."

This was true. Peaseblossom remembers too well her mother berating her for bringing up babies so soon with Luke. And she was right. What had bringing up the subject done for her? Nothing. She lost Luke, who she loved so desperately. She married a bastard. She had unsatisfactory affairs with men: several were married, one was ACDC, one was an alcoholic, another a fantasist.

"Nothing," Peaseblossom says quietly.

"What?"

She shrugs. "Nothing."

"No, please tell me."

"That was what I said. Nothing. I have nothing to show for all the time since we were together. No man, no children, no proper job. I'm never going to be a psychologist, you know."

"It never suited you."

"Actually, I think a lot of it's bollocks anyway."

She turns to him, and his eyes, which are the colour of lichen, crinkle at the edges, and he laughs, and so does she.

They walk on, and the path is damp. There must be a hole in her shoe because she can feel her tights are wet. Not just cold, but wet. Stone slabs make a bridge over a green-black stream.

"If only we could have done the play here," Luke muses.

"Look at you. You made it as an actor then."

"Well, kind of. We do a lot of work with schools, community groups and so on in London. I've had a few other parts. I was in Bath last summer with *What the Butler Saw*."

"At the Theatre Royal?"

"Yes, did you go?"

"I would if I'd have known."

They cross the stream, and the path winds down further, following the water.

"Why are you here?" Luke asks suddenly. "You said you didn't want to see the wedding. I don't understand."

"It's complicated," Peaseblossom says.

"Where's Clare? Has anyone seen Clare?" Alfie asks.

Some of the guests have removed their masks now, and he can see their faces. Many are flushed from too much wine.

He's taken the remaining envelope out of his pocket. It's the one for the bride, the one that Penelope wanted him to give to his friend Claire.

No one answers him, then suddenly someone taps him on the shoulder. He turns around. The person who tapped him is still wearing a mask. An owl mask. He can just see a pair of bright owl eyes through the slits. She has very thin legs, like a bird; he wonders if she has claws inside her shoes.

"Why do you want Clare?" she asks, and he realises, even with her mask, that her eyes are on the letter in his hand.

He glances down at it. He's holding it so only the wax blob is visible.

"I've been asked to give her something before the wedding starts. It's very important."

The owl lady watches him a moment. He senses she wants to say something, that she wants to snatch the envelope and tear it with raptor claws.

"Who asked you to give it to her?" she asks eventually.

"Penelope. The lady in pink. She said it's very important, and I can't find Clare, and she's going to get married in a minute."

"She went in to get changed a while ago," the owl lady says. "Look, she's in the conservatory in her wedding dress. Go now, quickly."

Alfie looks beyond the marquee to the long glass conservatory. Yes, there's a bride. She's wearing a long white or cream dress that trails on the floor behind her. She's got flowers in her hair. There are women fussing round her. Two are wearing long, pale pink dresses. They must be bridesmaids. One's adjusting the flowers on Clare's head.

Alfie sprints up to the conservatory and opens one of the wide glass doors.

"Clare," he shouts.

The bride looks up. Yes, he's got her at last.

"I have a special delivery for you," he announces.

"Who are you?" one of the bridesmaids asks.

"Alfie," he says, and thrusts out the letter. "Clare, this is for you. It's from–" He's not supposed to say who it's from. It's a surprise. Oh no, he told Claire it was from Penelope, because she didn't know who Penelope was.

"From who?" Clare smiles down at him as she takes it from him. He can smell her perfume, see beads glinting on her dress.

"It's a secret," Alfie says. "I'm not allowed to say, but you have to have it before you get married. Which is obviously quite soon."

"What is it? Who's it from?" The women close ranks.

Clare glances at the front, at the initials CG. Alfie crosses his fingers behind his back.

"It's a love letter from Justin," one says.

"Oh, don't be daft," Clare laughs.

"Look, it is, it's a poem. It's–"

Alfie watches Clare's eyes on the text.

"What?" she says. "What?" she says louder, shoves it into the hands of an older woman. "Mum, Mum, what is this? What's he playing at?"

"Clare, darling–"

"No, no, this can't–"

"Let me look."

"Where is he, the bastard?"

"It's not real, is it? It's a joke."

"Not much of a joke."

"He doesn't want to marry me," Clare cries. "He doesn't want me. How could he do this? How could he do this? On my wedding day? In front of everyone."

"He can't do that," her mother shouts.

"It must be a prank," a bridesmaid suggests nervously. "It's not even his writing. Anyway, he couldn't have written that."

"That's even worse," Clare howls. "He's got someone else to write it and he's given it to some boy to give me."

Alfie doesn't ask for a tip. He runs out of the conservatory with tears in his eyes. He got it wrong. Penelope was right. He should have listened to her. Now the bride is distraught, and the wedding about to be cancelled, and it's all because of him. He runs down the lawn, through the milling wedding guests, into the sunken rose garden where he sat earlier. He flings open the gate, doesn't bother to shut it, lets it clang to by itself. He only stops running when he reaches the safety of the trees.

Claire's on the point of telling Mike and Vicky. She's never mentioned Justin to them. All she's ever said is that yes, she grew up in the village and she knows the house. Now, she doesn't think she can cope with the journey back to London in the minibus, with Orlando crowing because he's got some girl's number, as he usually manages to do wherever he goes, and Alfie babbling, and Vicky going on about the bride's dress, because she has insisted they stay long enough to get a glimpse of what Clare Greenaway is wearing.

"Alfie! Alfie!"

Simon comes running into the potting shed.

"He's not here," Mike says, hauling up his rucksack, and setting it on his shoulders.

"What? Jesus. I can't find him anywhere."

"He was here a short while ago," Claire says. "When I came back on my own. Probably fifteen, twenty minutes."

"Can you come and help me look for him?"

"Of course," Claire says.

"We'll come too." Vicky pushes Mike to the door. "Perhaps he's with Orlando?"

"Orlando's chatting up some girl in the beer tent," Simon throws over his shoulder as he runs up the narrow path to the yew walk.

"He might be with Luke," Claire suggests, running after him. She's still wearing her cream gown, and she has to lift it to run.

"Haven't seen Luke either, but I reckon he can look after himself."

The lake, Claire thinks. Could Alfie have gone off exploring and fallen into the lake? *Oh Christ, no.* Where else could he be? The boathouse? The grotto? The woods? Memories slam into her like bullets as her mind races round the garden.

"We'll go down here." Mike gestures down the path towards the lake.

"OK," Claire says. "That's to the lake and the grotto."

"There's a lake?" Simon interrupts.

"Down there," Claire gestures where Mike and Vicky have gone. "I'll do the wood. Simon, you stay round here in case he comes back. Find Orlando or Luke, ask them if they've seen him."

Claire scoops up her dress and runs down the lawn to the cedar tree. It seems familiar. Of course, she and Justin raced down here so many moons ago. There seems to be some sort of disturbance by the marquee, but she doesn't bother to listen. She doesn't even look for Justin. She has to find Alfie.

Alfie can't face his dad. He can't face Claire, who will also have received something horrible. He can't face Penelope and ask for payment. Why was Penelope sending nasty letters on a wedding day anyway?

He scuffs down the path through the woodland. The trees are very tall, and their leaves make a soothing noise. There's another noise too, the sound of running water. Alfie scrambles off the path to the left. Yes, there's a stream, narrow and shallow, bubbling over mossy boulders. Perhaps he could just lose himself in the woods and never have to see anyone again. That makes him cry because he wants to see his dad and Claire and Orlando and his friends, but how can he face anyone after what he's done? He was only trying to do the right thing.

The path crosses the stream and he squats down and trails his fingers in the water. It's very cold. He straightens. He can hear voices from the undergrowth up the opposite slope. He trots through the grasses and flowers. The ground slopes away into a hidden dip. Alfie gasps and feels his face go hot. It's Luke and Penelope, on the ground, and Penelope has discarded her jacket, and her skirt is all bunched up round her middle, and Luke's got his face down there. Penelope howls and Luke raises his head and kisses her. She turns her head, and Alfie forgets to duck in time.

"Alfie," Penelope squeaks, and shoves Luke off her, and fumbles with her dress.

"Alfie," Luke says.

Alfie stumbles backwards and trips over a fallen log. He cries out as his head hits the ground, which is pretty hard and couldn't have been very comfortable for Luke and Penelope.

"Alfie, Elfie." Penelope lifts his shoulders from the ground. "Oh Alfie, don't cry." She sits down on the log and wipes his eyes with her fingers. "Are you hurt? Is your head hurting?"

"How do you know Alfie?" Luke asks. His shirt, like Penelope's dress, is stained with grass. He's holding her jacket over his arm.

"I did it wrong," Alfie chokes. "I'm so sorry, Penelope."

"Penelope?" Luke asks.

"Did it wrong?" she asks.

"I thought it couldn't be right, what you said, about giving the letters the wrong way round. I did it the right way round, but I think I got it all wrong, because Clare was so upset, and I don't think she's getting married after all."

It's cool and quiet under the trees. All Claire can hear is the scuffle of her shoes on the steep path. The gate into the woods was swinging loose but that could have been anyone. She can't see anyone ahead of her. If she follows the path, she'll come to the lake where Mike and Vicky will be searching for Alfie.

"Alfie!" Claire calls.

"He's here."

She recognises Luke's voice. Alfie must have gone off with Luke. She runs on, down the slope and there, coming over the stone bridge are Luke and Alfie, and the blonde woman who was holding hands with Luke earlier. Her dress and jacket have grass stains smeared all over them. Alfie hangs his head.

"Alfie, sweetheart. Your dad's going spare. He couldn't find you."

"He was with us," the woman interrupts.

Claire glances at her and at Luke, at their rumpled clothing, and high colour, and doesn't believe a word of it.

"Let's get you back to your dad," says Luke.

Peaseblossom has Alfie by the hand. As they come up the steps onto the lawn, Fairy, now without her mask, steps out from behind the cedar tree. Peaseblossom feels Alfie stiffen beside him.

"Who's she, Penelope?"

"Why's he calling you Penelope?" Luke asks.

"Not now, Luke."

If Alfie didn't do what Fairy said, no doubt she's in for a right bollocking.

"A word, please," Fairy says to Peaseblossom.

Luke looks confused, as he leads Alfie up the lawn to where the guests are milling and shouting. Claire Sutherland drifts off to the left, away from the crowds, towards the yew walk.

"Congratulations, Peaseblossom."

"Fairy, I'm so sorry. I thought Alfie would be a good delivery boy, more believable than me." She smiles as Alfie throws his arms around his father's middle.

"I said *congratulations*," Fairy says. "You did what I said. Thank you. It's rather awkward at the moment, as you can see, but Justin will thank me in the end. He really could never marry that woman. Not now he's found Claire again."

Peaseblossom is dazed. She's lost her hat – no, it's on the bench in the Italian garden where Claire Sutherland dumped it – and she's lost her tights somewhere in the woods, and her bare legs are scratched. She's found Luke after all these years, and he still loves her. He told her that. He told her he'd never met anyone he could love like he has always loved her. Alfie didn't follow Fairy's instructions, but somehow Fairy is pleased, and thinks he did.

"What's happening?" Peaseblossom asks, gesturing up the lawn. "Why isn't he marrying her?"

"Because he doesn't love her."

"I don't understand. What was in those envelopes?"

Fairy follows her gaze to the commotion outside the marquee. Clare Greenaway, with her wedding gown trailing behind her on the lawn, raises her hand and cracks Justin Fontaine across the face. There are gasps and shrieks. Clare stumbles back towards the house, her pink bridesmaids trailing with her. One puts her arm around Clare; Clare knocks it aside. Justin holds a hand to his cheek, as people surge up to him.

"He asked RG to write two sonnets," Fairy tells Peaseblossom. "In effect he was dumping his mistress and telling the bride how much he loved her. I've known Justin for years. I know it's the actress he really loves. I couldn't stand by and let him ruin his life by marrying the wrong person. That's why I asked you to swap them."

"I told Alfie to swap them," Peaseblossom says. "But he says he didn't. He says he agonised about it for ages but, in the end, he thought it couldn't be right."

"He must have got muddled," Fairy says. "The bride definitely got the sonnet I wanted her to get."

Claire bumps into Vicky outside the potting shed.

"Have you found him?" Vicky cries.

"He was with Luke," Claire says.

"That was lucky. Mike's still down at the lake. I'll phone him. Then let's go and see what the bride's wearing."

"I think there's some kind of hold-up," Claire says. "I don't know what, but there seems to be a lot of confusion and noise."

She follows Vicky into the potting shed. Vicky jabs her phone.

"No bloody signal. I'd better go up by the house."

"I'll see you in a bit."

"You look done in," Vicky says, walking backwards across the walled garden, waving her phone for a signal. "We'll just see the dress, then we'll get off. Sure you want to come back with us?"

"I'm sure."

Claire can't face this night at her parents' house, just down the lane from Wotton House. She needs to be on her own. She's just got to get through the journey.

"Mike, it's me. Yes, he's fine," Vicky says. "Come on back."

Claire picks up her bag and water bottle, runs her eyes around the inside of the potting shed. She won't come to Wotton again. Justin said he would find a way to see her once he's married. He might; he might not. But she won't ever come to Wotton again. Not now that woman will be here, stamping on her memories.

She reaches down to zip up her bag and touches the corner of an envelope. The envelope Alfie gave her. Who did he say it was from? She can't remember. It's sealed with red wax. She frowns, dumps her bag on the floor, and takes the envelope out into the evening sunlight of the walled garden. Vicky has gone. She's alone. She breaks the seal and draws out the paper.

"I should phone Robin," Peaseblossom says, and takes her phone out of her bag.

"You can tell him from me that you and your little helper have done an excellent job," Fairy says.

Fairy's never been this nice to her before.

"I don't understand how they ended up that way round," Peaseblossom muses aloud, as she finds the number in her contacts. "Alfie swears he didn't swap them over."

"I wonder…no, he refused."

"What?"

"Remember, I told you. I asked RG to swap them at the office, but he refused. I think he must have done."

"So, if Alfie had done as you'd said, Justin would have got married?"

"Yes, it looks that way."

"He's coming over." Peaseblossom drops her phone into her bag. She'll ring in a moment.

Justin Fontaine strides down the lawn, shaking off a dark, bony woman.

"That's Evelyn, his mother," Fairy says quietly.

"Just leave me alone," Justin shouts to his mother. "I'll talk to you later. Right now, I want a word with Aunt Effie."

"Aunt Effie?" asks Peaseblossom.

"That's me," Fairy grimaces.

Justin's cheek is bright from Clare's hand. He looks like he's about to cry. Peaseblossom wants to give him a hug, but it's Fairy he stumbles towards. She puts her thin arms around him.

"It's for the best, Justin," she says. "You know that."

He nods, leaning down on Fairy's shoulder.

"How did it happen like that?" he asks. "They were meant to go the other way round."

Fairy disentangles herself from him.

"I think Mr Goodfellow must have had a helping hand in this," she says, giving Peaseblossom a look. "Sometimes, things don't go quite according to plan, but the outcome is happier. Isn't that right, Peaseblossom?"

Peaseblossom nods. She wonders where Luke is, if Alfie is OK. She must find Alfie and tell him he did the right thing in the end.

"You're from the agency," Justin says.

"Yes," says Peaseblossom.

"Thank you," he says stiffly. "And thank you to your delivery boy."

"Have you seen Claire?" Fairy asks. "Your Claire?"

"No," he says. "She will have it by now, won't she?"

"I think so," Peaseblossom agrees.

"I'm going into the woods," Justin says. "I can't go back there." He gestures towards the marquee and the house. "Not yet." He gives Fairy a quick kiss, and squeezes Peaseblossom's arm, then he runs down the steps into the Italian rose garden.

"Claire, you won't believe what's happened to me today," Luke says, as Claire comes out of the yew walk.

"What's going on?" she asks.

"It was like something in a film," Luke says.

"What's going on?" Claire asks again.

There are discarded masks on the lawn. People are leaving the garden. Everyone's talking loudly.

Poor, poor Clare.
How could he do that to her on her wedding day?
Is he seeing someone else?
Disgusting.
He should have done the decent thing weeks ago if he didn't want to marry her.
She'll never get over it.

"Luke!"

"The wedding's off," he says at last. "I believe the bridegroom sent the bride a letter or something telling her he couldn't marry her."

"He did what?"

"Yeah, I know. Poor girl. Lucky escape, I reckon."

Claire can't see Justin anywhere. She can see his father, with his arm around Evelyn's shoulders. Evelyn is sobbing.

"Tell the others I'm not coming back to London tonight," she says.

"You're not?"

"No, I'm staying on another night at home."

She daren't run down the lawn. Not with Evelyn there. She lifts up her long cream skirt and turns back down the yew walk. She must find Justin. She doesn't know what to say to him. She has no words, but she must find him. She cuts through the walled garden and down to the lakeside path. Below her the lake is still and glassy, the trees reflected on its surface. She wants to call out for Justin, but she can't fracture the peace down here. She startles a duck resting on the stubby grass by the boathouse. When she reaches the corner of the lake, she still hasn't found Justin. There's the branch where they shook hands, beyond the shrubbery is the arched door in the wall.

Claire's breathless and slows her step. The path winds away from the lake and into the lower trees of the bluebell wood. The hem of her gown is muddy. She's hot and dishevelled. She doesn't care. Under the trees she can smell garlic and foliage. She can hear the hum of insects amongst the flowers. Small moths flutter up from the grasses as her skirt brushes them.

He's standing on the stone bridge, looking down the valley. Claire stops. She doesn't call out. She simply stands there a moment watching him, as he watches her. Then she picks up her gown and runs the last few yards up the path to the bridge.

"I must phone Robin," Peaseblossom says once more, as she and Fairy start walking back towards the house.

Luke's coming towards her with Alfie.

"Alfie Elfie," Peaseblossom cries.

"I'm so sorry, Penelope."

"What's going on?" Luke asks. "Why does he call you Penelope? What's he done wrong?"

"I'll explain later," she says. "Alfie Elfie, come here."

The little elf steps towards her.

"I know this sounds weird," she says. "And I didn't know this either, but the wedding was meant to be called off. So everything happened as it should have because you made the right decision, and it was me who was wrong. So, don't you worry." She hands him the five she'd shown him earlier.

"But she was so upset." Alfie takes the note diffidently.

"Your friend Claire would have been even more upset," Peaseblossom says.

"Why would she be more upset?"

"I'm completely lost," Luke says.

"Luke, are you and Penelope getting married?" Alfie asks.

Luke laughs; Peaseblossom flushes.

"We've already been married," Peaseblossom says, but when she looks at Luke over Alfie's head, he smiles at her, and she wonders if maybe, just maybe, she might not ruin things this time, if she takes it gently.

Alfie points at a moth that's swooping over to the grassy bank. He takes Luke's hand, and tugs him over to find it. *Luke would make a lovely father,* Peaseblossom thinks, and hits green on her phone before she starts crying.

"Agent Peaseblossom."

"It's done, Robin."

"Thank you, Peaseblossom."

"Robin, did you tamper with the sonnets?" she asks.

"*Thou speak'st aright*," Robin chuckles.

Peaseblossom gives Fairy the thumbs up. Fairy shakes her head and walks away up the lawn.

"So the client isn't getting married now?" Robin asks.

"It would appear not." Peaseblossom's heart rate settles. Robin swapped the sonnets after all. He and Fairy both intended the wedding to be cancelled. She and Alfie did everything right.

"*The king's a beggar now the play is done, all is well ended if this suit be won.*"

"What?" Peaseblossom asks.

"*All's Well That Ends Well*," Robin says.

"Oh, yes, it seems to," she agrees.

Robin sighs. "The play, Peaseblossom. The play."

Act II
Where the Wild Thyme Blows

"What's he said to you about this job then?" Fairy asks, peering over her glasses at her computer screen.

"Nothing much," Moth says. "Just that I'll be going out of town."

"Hmm. He's taken all the calls for this one. Very secretive. I don't know what it's about, but he's spent most of the morning looking at pictures of caterpillars."

"Caterpillars?"

RG appears in the doorway to Fairy's office.

"Moth, my dear. Thank you for coming. Shall we talk?"

Moth follows him to his room and sits down. RG clicks the door to, and slides behind the desk.

"Are you enjoying the summer?" he asks.

"It's getting a bit hot for me," Moth says.

"Sounds like you could do with a trip to the seaside."

"Are you sending me to the seaside?"

RG turns his laptop around to face Moth.

"The Atlas Moth," he says. "Have you ever seen one?"

On the screen is a photograph of the great silk moth. Its tawny wings are patterned with black and white, veined like stained glass.

"In a butterfly house once."

"Excellent. Did you know the adults never feed?"

"They only live for a couple of weeks, I think," Moth says, then, "You're not sending me to Asia, are you?"

"Ah no, Moth. And I don't think you need a passport to get to Wales these days."

"I'm going to Wales? To the seaside?"

"Your first port of call." RG clicks on his laptop again. "Wonderful creatures, those silk moths."

"What have silk moths got to do with it?"

"You're going to find out," RG smiles. "You're going to a butterfly house."

"A butterfly house in Wales? That sounds great."

"I knew you'd like it," he says. "Let me explain. I don't know how long the assignment will take. To start with you need to go to Aberystwyth. I take it you know where that is?"

"Yes," Moth says.

"The butterfly house is outside the town. You'll go there to meet the client, who will tell you more about what she needs. I don't know the full story, but I know that she wants you to find someone for her. Someone she's not seen for twenty years."

"Is the missing person in Wales too?"

"If we knew where he was, he wouldn't be missing, would he? No, not in Wales, but probably not far away. Don't worry about that for now. Take a few days to get ready and then let me know when you'll be leaving. I will sort out accommodation and so on. I'll keep in touch with you on this one. You might need support with the logistics."

"Will I have some time to enjoy the seaside?"

"I'm sure you will, Moth. You must bring me back a stick of rock. It's a long time since I've had rock. How is your car these days?"

"It should be all right. I had new tyres recently."

"I'll email you the details and directions for the butterfly house," RG says. "The client's name is Madeleine Pryce, known as Maddie. She's the owner." He stops a moment. "I think, in the circumstances, you will need another name. Moth in a butterfly house? That wouldn't do. Let's call you Mo. I'll tell her you are called Mo."

"And she's looking for someone from her past?"

"I'll leave her to talk to you about that." RG folds down the laptop. "Right, I've just sent you the link. Let me know when you can leave and, for now, I'll say Oberon Out."

Maddie's apprehensive. Tomorrow, this agent called Mo is arriving at the butterfly house to talk to her, and the whole sad, sorry tale will come out. Maddie wonders if she should ever have contacted the Robin Goodfellow Agency, whether she should have tried to do it on her own or, more sensibly, just forgotten about the whole thing. Forgotten about him. No. She will never be able to do that. She never has been able to. Not for twenty years,

It was a few weeks ago, when everything changed, and tectonic plates moved beneath her feet. Vanessa had just left with her friends for three months' summer travelling in Europe. For the first time in her life Maddie was truly on her own in the house, with only the dogs for company. It was a strange feeling, sometimes it made her light headed.

She drove into Aberystwyth. It was just an ordinary Monday in June. She had no premonition of what was to happen. She parked in the retail park and ran across the road into Chalybeate Street. It was warm, not hot. There would be a blue breeze on the seafront. She went into Mecca, the tea emporium, chatted with the proprietor who she'd known since he first opened the shop, bought red-wrapped packets of scented tea, and stepped out onto the pavement again.

"Maddie? Maddie Vaughan?"

The man in front of her removed his sunglasses. Dark hair cut short, an earring, the swirl of a tattoo on his neck above his collar.

"Dave?" she asked, as a memory surge of nausea jolted through her.

"I knew it was you."

"I've been Maddie Pryce a long time now," she said.

"Of course. Are you still up in the hills? Still sheep farming?"

"Still in the hills, not sheep farming any more. We gave that up before my husband… Are you here for a visit?"

"Yes, visiting the family for a few days."

"Where are you living now?"

"Worcester. I'm the manager of a haulage firm. Where the hell does the time go? So, do you see any of the others? Not seen you on Facebook."

"I'm not on," Maddie said. "I don't really see anyone. I think most have moved away."

"Katie's in Cardiff with the BBC," Dave said. "Don't you talk to her? And what about Sian? She's had four kids. She's only in Tywyn."

Dave's cousin, Katie. His ex-girlfriend, Sian. They were all at school together so many years ago.

"I don't have much time. I keep myself to myself."

"You always did, didn't you?"

Dave scuffs his shoe along the pavement edge, fiddles with his shades. Maddie wonders if she can escape. It's too much, coming out of nowhere like that. Dave, Katie, Sian. The names of long ago.

"Actually, Maddie, I thought of you a few weeks ago," Dave said.

Don't, Maddie wanted to shout. *I don't want to know. Whatever it is, I don't want to know.*

"I was in a pub in Ludlow," Dave said. "And I saw someone from the bad old days. One of our teachers."

"Dave–" Maddie felt hot prickles over her skin. No, it couldn't be. There were lots of teachers.

"You'll remember him," Dave said. "Will Richards."

Moth leaves her motel in Aberystwyth. It's a hot day in early July, but it's raining, and the green fields are blurred with mist. She opens the window for fresh air as she heads inland. Further into the heartlands are the giant folds of the Cambrian Mountains.

Driving west the previous evening, with the setting sun blazing her eyes, Moth had pulled over into a lay-by and climbed out of the car on stiff legs. There was no other traffic, only the faint cries of sheep from the pastures below, and the white splash of a waterfall tumbling down a deep cleft in the mountain, a course as old as time itself. Moth felt very small and alone in the green-gold wilderness and was suddenly relieved to hear a distant engine. She turned and saw a van coming, tiny and white, following the serpentine road around the curves of the landscape.

She'd seen the sign for the butterfly house the previous night as she drove on towards the coast. Now she sees it once more through the drizzle, and turns right down an overgrown lane. The hedges brush the car with foxgloves and poppies. The sky is grey and heavy with summer rain. Droplets from the leaves scatter onto Moth's arm through the open window. The colours of the landscape are fresh and watery. The lane curves through a flat-floored valley where sheep graze on the rising hillsides. On the right is a tumbling stream – no, a river – cascading over mossy boulders in a froth of white. The road follows the bank of this river, seeming to get nowhere, then suddenly she is there. On the left a gravel car park and a low-lying building and, behind it, the glass roof of the butterfly house.

'Cambrian Butterflies,' says the huge signboard. There's a picture of a blue and black butterfly. Moth parks under a dripping tree, turns off the engine and gets out. The car park is muddy with puddles of rainwater. RG told her to take wellies to Wales because it always rains. She hasn't actually got any wellies; instead she's wearing her Caterpillar boots. *Which are kind of suitable,* she thinks with a smile, as she locks the car.

She crunches across the wet gravel to the entrance. Inside there is a café to the right with a glass cabinet of cakes, and photographs of butterflies on the walls. A few tables are taken. Moth smells steam and cake and coffee. On the other side is a gift shop. A couple of people are looking at the display of bright mugs. There are two women behind the desk. On the far wall is a densely beaded curtain to the glasshouse. Moth hovers in the doorway. She has been told to come to the shop.

"I'm looking for Mrs Pryce," she says.

The two women look up. One, who is tall and dark, slides out from behind the counter.

"Hello. You must be Mo," she says, offering Moth her hand. "I'm Maddie. Would you like to look at the butterfly house before it gets busy?"

"Yes please," says Moth.

Perhaps Maddie will talk while they are in the glasshouse, or maybe she wants to get to know Moth first.

"You might want to take off your hoodie," Maddie says. "It's pretty warm in there. I'll put it behind the counter."

Moth peels it off. The shop assistant is wrapping mugs in coloured tissue for the customers.

"This way then."

Maddie parts the curtain; behind it are folds of black plastic. Moth shoulders through these, and the heat smacks her in the face. There are twisting gravel paths between tropical bushes. Creepers and vines hang down from above, tapping Moth on the head. There are giant blooms – purple and pink and orange – and butterflies everywhere: spiralling in the air, fluttering at the flowers, resting on leaves. Moth recognises the narrow red and black wings of the Postman, and the clumsy Owls feeding on trays of ripe banana segments. She inhales the heat, the scents, the colours.

"It's wonderful," she says. "I haven't been to a butterfly house since I was a kid."

"Thank you," Maddie says.

Moth watches Maddie snap off a long tendril of vine. She's tall and thin with dark hair on her shoulders. She looks angular and gawky: if she were a butterfly, her wings would be ragged and awkward.

It's early, and there are only a few people in the glasshouse at this time. Rain drums gently on the roof overhead. Moth feels sweat on her back already, and her hair sticks to her neck. She remembers the picture on RG's laptop.

"Have you got Atlas moths?" she asks.

"They'll be by the pool." Maddie squeezes past some children.

Moth pauses to look at a red and black swallowtail clinging to a leaf at her head height. It has a scarlet body and head. Its wings are shiny and unblemished. Moth thinks maybe it has recently hatched. As they entered the glasshouse she saw netted cabinets: they must be the hatcheries where caterpillars live and where pupae hang. She catches up with Maddie at the pool. A gentle cascade of water runs down the rockface on the back wall and falls into a stony pond. Goldfish flicker in the green water. Maddie points. Three Atlas moths are resting on the damp rocks.

"They don't fly much, do they?" Moth says.

"The females usually stay close to where they hatch. They use pheromones to attract a male."

"I love them," Moth says. "They make me sad though. It's terrible that something so beautiful only lives a couple of weeks."

"But, Mo, this is only a small part of their lives," Maddie says. "They've had other existences as caterpillars and pupae. It's only us who value the imagos the most."

"I suppose," Moth agrees, watching the huge moths, unmoving beside the cascade.

"I think the transition from caterpillar to moth or butterfly is the most amazing thing in the world," Maddie says. "Look, there's a Blue Morpho."

"He's on your signboard," Moth says, as the blue and black butterfly swoops away.

"They're the most popular. The Atlas moths are a close second."

"Do you have any other moths?"

"There should be a couple of moon moths somewhere. Hard to find them being green. I've got Death's Head caterpillars. They're only tiny at the moment, about a centimetre. See that guy there?" Maddie points to a young man in jeans, crouching down in front of another netted cabinet in the far corner. "That's Gary. He's my entomologist. I'd introduce you, but it's a bit awkward. He might wonder why you're here."

Gary straightens with a newly hatched Owl on his hand. He glances over to where they stand, and waves. Maddie waves back.

"Have a look around. I'm just going to speak to him a moment."

Left alone, Moth walks down a gravel pathway. There is another feeding station with banana rings and segments of orange. The Owls are there, drunk on sugar. Moth doesn't know many tropical species, but she recognises the distinctive glasswings from Maddie's website. There are flame-coloured longwings she has never seen before, and one that is lime green, but it flies off before she can look closer. There are many swallowtails – black, yellow, green – and the extraordinary scarlet-bodied ones. Another Blue Morpho. She gazes up at the ceiling, and peers behind the leaves and shrubbery, but she can't see the moon moths anywhere. She's hot now and sweating. She knows her face will be shiny, and her jeans and T-shirt are sticking to her skin. Maddie is still talking to Gary. He opens one of the hatcheries; Maddie squats down to look in, straightens, asks him something, gesturing with her hands. Moth laughs as one of the bright orange butterflies lands on her bare arm. She'd love to feel an Atlas settle on her, but there's little chance of one swooping down from the cool, dark, peaceful waterfall.

"How did you do this?" Moth asks as Maddie comes up to her. "What gave you the idea? Have you always loved butterflies and moths?"

"Always," Maddie says. "I used to keep caterpillars in plastic boxes when I was little. I had butterfly posters on my bedroom walls. I was hoping to study entomology at university but…I got married and Vanessa was born, and my husband was still farming at that time."

"How long have you had this place?"

"Seven years. Owain – my husband – rented out the grazing land when he became ill. He died last year, and it's just me and Vanessa, except she's gone off travelling with her friends. They're somewhere in Italy."

A large party of people comes through the black folds and into the glasshouse.

"Shall we go out for a bit?" Maddie suggests. "You can come back later."

"I'd love to."

"But we should talk about why you're here."

"If you're ready." Moth slides through the curtains into the coolness of the gift shop. She shivers in the sudden change of temperature.

Maddie hands her back her hoodie and puts on her own jacket. Outside, the rain has stopped. The hillsides and trees glow with washed green.

"We'll walk up to my house. It's just up the lane. I'll show you the dam and the reservoir on the way."

She leads Moth out of the car park, which is now much busier, and onto the road. Through the foliage Moth sees the stone wall of a dam with water falling down to a riotous waterfall below.

"The reservoir is behind the dam. It's only small." Maddie hesitates. "Not like the ones at Elan. Have you seen them?"

"I've not been there, but I've seen them on the telly. *Countryfile*, I think it was."

"They're part of my story."

"Is that your house?" Moth points to a whitewashed house on high ground overlooking the inky reservoir. There's a 4x4 parked outside.

"Yes. It was the farm."

"Let's go in and you can tell me what I can do to help. I believe you need me to find someone for you."

"That's right. I've not seen him for twenty years. Twenty years."

Maddie opens the front door. Two black and white collies come out to greet her. She bends down to fondle them.

"I'll make some tea," she says. "And, yes, we must talk. I'm sorry I've been evasive. It's just now you're here it's happening, and it's been so long, and I can't talk to Vanessa because she's away but it's really important to her as well."

"Who are you looking for?"

"His name's Will Richards. If it weren't for him, I'd never have had the butterfly house." She smiles sadly. "If it weren't for him, I'd never have married Owain either."

"Who is Will Richards?"

"He was my biology teacher at school."

This close to the ground Maddie could almost imagine what a caterpillar's eye view might be like: the blades of grass, the leaves, the grains of soil, the other tiny creatures. Sheltered under the hedge of the school field, the caterpillar moved quickly over loose pebbles and earth. Maddie heard voices. A group of kids coming towards her, shouting. Sian, Katie, Dave, a few others.

"What you doing in the hedge?" Sian shouted.

"What you looking at?"

"Nothing." Maddie scrambled to her feet.

There was a grass stain on her shirt and soil on her bare legs. It was September, the second day back at school. She was fifteen.

"Can't be nothing. You wouldn't be down here on your own for nothing." Dave dropped to his knees, started crawling under the hedge.

Maddie glanced down. The caterpillar was only inches away from his hand.

"Down there." She gestured in the opposite direction.

"What?" he said, and deftly she bent down and scooped the caterpillar into her hand.

"Urgh, yuck," Katie squealed. "That's gross. What the hell is it?"

In Maddie's palm, the caterpillar curled into itself in fright. It was dry and slightly rough to the touch. She cupped her other hand over it.

"Elephant Hawk moth," she said defiantly.

"You don't know that."

"Yes, I do."

"Show us then." Dave was on his feet.

Another figure was coming nearer. Mr Richards, the new biology teacher. Tall and rangy with sandy-red hair and wire glasses. Maddie exhaled in relief. She started walking towards him, the caterpillar safe in her hands.

"Come on, you lot," Mr Richards called. "Lunchtime's over."

Maddie stopped a few yards from him and looked back to the gang by the hedge. She hoped they hadn't hurt or frightened any other caterpillars down there. Katie and Sian were now sitting on the grass, with their skirts hitched up.

"Come on!" Mr Richards called again, and reluctantly they stood, tugging their skirts down over their hips. Then he looked at Maddie.

"What's your name?" he smiled.

"Maddie. Maddie Vaughan."

"What are you hiding, Maddie?"

"It's a caterpillar, sir."

She opened her hands. The caterpillar had uncurled and was standing still on her palm. It was grey-brown, like an elephant's trunk, with startled eye patterns on its head.

"He's a beauty. Do you know what he is?"

"Elephant Hawk," she said again. "All the hawks have a hook on their back ends."

"That's right," he said. "Do you like caterpillars?"

"I love them. And butterflies and moths. I want to work with insects. That's what I'd really like to do."

She glanced around the field. The others had gone; she couldn't even hear their voices. There was just her and Mr Richards and the caterpillar.

"You need to put him back. It's time for registration. Where did you find him?"

"In the hedge. I was just watching him, but the others came and they might have hurt him."

"Let's put him back. Show me where he was."

"I've never seen an Elephant Hawk moth," she told him, as they walked together towards the hedge. "I saw a Privet Hawk about a year ago. He was huge."

She crouched down and let the caterpillar slide off her hands.

"Do you know a lot about caterpillars, sir?"

"Yes, they're one of my interests." He stopped as though he had been about to say more and thought better of it.

Together they watched the caterpillar scuttle into the darkness under the hedge. Maddie felt the treacherous sting of tears in her eyes. The following summer it would be a neon bright moth with pink and green wings. If it survived the winter.

"Let's go, Maddie," said Mr Richards. "The bell went some minutes ago."

Reluctantly she walked back across the field with him.

"I'm in your biology group last thing," she said, suddenly brightening.

"We won't be doing insects unfortunately," he said.

"What are we doing?"

"We'll go through the year's syllabus this afternoon."

They reached the school building.

"I'll see you later then," Maddie said. "It's history now."

"I'll see you later, Maddie," he said.

"That was the first time I spoke to him," Maddie says. "The day of the Elephant Hawk caterpillar."

"Hadn't he taught you before?" Moth asks.

"No. Our previous biology teacher had left. He started that September. I sat there in the biology lab that afternoon, wondering how the caterpillar was getting on. I must have been in my own little world because at one point he said, *Maddie, are you writing this down?* But not in a nasty way."

Moth smiles. She's trying to work out the narrative here. Maddie wants to find her old biology teacher. If it weren't for him, she would never have had the butterfly house and never married her husband. Was Maddie's husband something to do with Will Richards? Moth isn't sure. Now she's started, Maddie just wants to talk; all Moth can do is let her, and see how the story develops.

Maddie was in goal again. That's where you ended up if you were tall and no good at sports. Then you'd concede lots of goals and everyone else could blame you for it. The spindly netball post swayed a little in the breeze. Down at the further end of the court there was a scuffle. A whistle. Girls' voices, indignant. Sian, the opposing shooter stood on the white line as far as she was allowed. Maddie loitered by the post and wondered if anyone would notice if she simply left the game. There was an autumnal chill in the air, though it was still only September, and Maddie felt gooseflesh on her legs and bare arms. She wore neon Bermuda shorts under her netball skirt, but they held no warmth. A Small Tortoiseshell wheeled across the court, bright orange against the tarmac. Maddie wondered again about the caterpillar she'd found the previous week.

The match moved down the court towards her. She sighed. Sian shoved against her, waving for the ball, yelling at her teammates. The ball bounced off the rusty metal ring. Maddie pretended to move for it, missed. Up it went again, and this time it fell through the hoop. Sian whooped. Maddie retrieved the ball and chucked it down the court. Back in the school, people were doing interesting, useful things like biology and chemistry, languages and art, and here she was in a smelly red bib getting berated by Katie for allowing the goal in. The butterfly came fluttering back.

At last, the final whistle. Maddie struggled to get the horrible bib over her head. She wondered if they were ever washed. She felt smelly, though she'd hardly done any running about. She might just have time for a quick wash when she got home before she went with her father to see Owain.

Owain Pryce was a sheep farmer in the hills by Ponterwyd. He lived alone and had never married though he was in his forties. Maddie's father had recently taken over his accounts and the two had become friends. During the summer holidays he'd taken Maddie with him to the farm a couple of times. She played with the dogs, and Owain promised her a puppy one day if her parents would allow it, but Maddie knew they wouldn't.

One hot day, while her father and Owain were working on the books, she went out into the sunny valley, and listened to the bleating of sheep, the tumble of water, and the hum of insects. She explored the marshy riverbank, finding butterflies, caterpillars, and dragonflies. She paddled through the water to a mossy boulder where she stood, her bare toes curling for a grip, and felt the cold breath of the river on her skin. The sun was high, flashing off the water below her; when she turned her face to the hard blue sky she almost slipped into the current with dizziness. She slithered off the rock and splashed back to the bank, weeds slapping at her ankles. She dried her feet on the grass, slipped on her pumps and started walking slowly back towards the farm, past the weir and then up to the dam to gaze into the peppermint-green water. The surface broke as a fish moved. Dragonflies skimmed the surface. One of Owain's dogs came trotting down the lane and together they made their way back to the farm.

"This is Owain, the man you married?" Moth asks.

"Yes," says Maddie. "Though I'd never have believed it then. I just loved coming up here to the reservoir, the river. I loved the countryside. And Owain was lovely, really kind. He talked to me. I was an only child, more used to adult company, I suppose, and he told me about the hills and the farm and we got on really well and became friends. Sometimes he'd come out to meet me by the river, and I'd show him things I'd found, plants and insects and so on. I envied him so much living up here on his own."

"Was Owain enthusiastic about the butterfly house?"

"Not at first," Maddie says. "But he'd known me a long time and he knew how much I wanted to do it. Vanessa wanted it too, and he could never say no to her."

Moth's eyes stray to a framed photograph on the dresser behind Maddie.

"Yes, that's them." Maddie twists around and takes the picture. "Owain and Vanessa. It was taken a few years ago but I prefer it. He looked so ill towards the end." She passes the photo to Moth.

Moth sees a man with unruly grey hair, long on his shoulders, with his arm around a teenage girl. She has russet hair and freckles. She's wearing a sun top and a complicated pink and mauve beaded necklace.

"It was cancer," Maddie supplies, twisting her hands as Moth looks at the image. "Bowel cancer."

"I'm very sorry." Moth hands the picture back, and knows the words are inadequate.

"Vanessa was nineteen in May," Maddie says. "She's going to uni this autumn to do botany. She's travelling with friends at the moment. I worry all the time."

"You must," Moth says. "Easier these days with email but even so…"

"She's all I have now."

"You must have been very young when Vanessa was born," Moth ventures.

"Seventeen," Maddie says.

Moth drinks her tea. What brought a young girl and a sheep farmer together? Was it a whirlwind romance, or did love grow slowly over time? She wonders what Maddie's parents made of the marriage: Owain must have been about thirty years older.

"I'm sorry, I'm messing this up. I should be telling you what I need your help with. God, it's hard. Sometimes it's really hard. You are the first person I've spoken to about this. No wonder it's all coming out wrong. I don't know how to say some of it."

"You want help finding your old teacher, yes? Can you tell me why?"

"Will Richards," Maddie says. "My biology teacher and–"

"Was he a friend of Owain's?"

"God, no, they never met."

"You said if it weren't for this Will Richards you wouldn't have married Owain or opened the butterfly house."

"That's right." Maddie's smile is crooked. "I don't really know when it all started. I just know that my last autumn at school I realised I was in love."

"With Owain?" Moth asks, suddenly realising too late how wrong she is.

"No. With Will Richards."

Rain streaked down the minibus windows. Through the murk Maddie gazed at the fold of green hill to the left, and the peaty stream that bubbled beside the road. Wet sheep grazed on the grass; several times Mr Richards had to brake suddenly because one had strayed onto the road.

It was a rainy September day, just after Maddie's sixteenth birthday, and the geography class was visiting the great reservoirs at Elan. The day before, the geography teacher had told them that Mr Powell from history and Mr Richards from biology would be joining them, each driving one of the buses and chaperoning a third of the class. *Please, please let me be in his group*, Maddie urged silently as the names were read out. She wasn't in the first group with the geography teacher; she wasn't in the second with Mr Powell. That meant – surely – she was with Mr Richards. Her name was read out. She would travel in his bus, look at the dams and the countryside with him. She pretended she'd dropped something under the desk, and leaned down, fiddling with her sock, to hide the flush of happiness she knew was on her face.

The weather forecast was for rain on the high ground. If the weather was too bad, the trip might be postponed to another day, and Mr Richards might not be able to come. Maddie felt sick when she woke to a squally shower, but no one suggested cancelling. It always rained in Wales, especially in the mountains.

They'd left the other two minibuses in the main car park at Caban Coch dam. Mr Richards was taking his group to Claerwen first; then they'd return to the Elan reservoirs, and another minibus would shudder across the spindly bridge that marked the submerged dam of Garreg Ddu, and through the dwindling forest to the bleak uplands of Claerwen.

Water had been gushing over Caban Coch when they passed it. Maddie had seen the lakes many times as a child, seen white water pouring over every dam, seen the mud and silt and broken branches below the water line in times of drought. She thought the reservoir by Owain's house was like Elan in miniature: the dark water, the stone dam, the riotous steam, and the marshy banks where she searched for insects and snails, flowers and toadstools.

The hills opened out and there suddenly was the black face of the Claerwen dam, weeping a slimy film of water. Mr Richards swung the bus into the gravel car park.

"I hope everyone's got a hood or a hat," he said, turning around to the passengers. "We're going to get wet. Leave your picnics in the bus, and we'll head up to the top of the dam."

Pools had formed in the uneven car park. A few sheep pecked in the wiry grasses. Some of the kids ran across the lane to the lavatories. Maddie stood, just watching the stream. It was russet and fast flowing after the rains. She felt the heavy power of the black water behind the dam. She couldn't imagine the pressure, or how the dam held, or what it must feel like to live in the little farm beneath it. A sheepdog raced in one of the bumpy fields. She was glad Owain's house was above the water level of his reservoir. If the Claerwen dam cracked, an icy tsunami would roar down the valley engulfing everything before it, drowning sheep, uprooting trees, splitting dwellings.

"What are you thinking?"

She turned sharply at his voice.

He was wearing a green wax jacket and faded jeans. He took off his wire glasses and wiped rain from the lenses.

"Just thinking about all that water," she said. "I wouldn't want to live in the farm." She gestured to the farmhouse, squat against the lower hillside. "Think what the lake could do."

Mr Richards replaced his glasses and tugged on his hood. "I think everyone's ready now," he said. "We'd better go."

She crossed the lane with him to join the others milling outside the lavatories.

"OK, guys, the only way is up." He pointed to the track winding up the hillside. "Wait at the top for me."

Some of the boys raced up ahead. Sian and two other girls giggled and followed them. To the left the monstrous dam loomed over the path. The sound of the falling water was louder. White noise.

"I have to bring up the rear," Mr Richards said to Maddie. "You go on."

"No," she said. "I'll walk with you."

He didn't say anything. Where the path narrowed he gestured for her to go first. He had a long stride. He did not get out of breath. Maddie's legs ached as the road fell away below her. The boys were at the top, shouting and scuffling. She stopped and bent down to examine the colours of a snail's shell.

"I wish I could be small enough to hide in the grasses," she said, straightening up. "I'd love to know what the world looks like from down there. I would love to know what a caterpillar thinks when he bumps into a mouse or whatever. I want to know what goes on inside a chrysalis. Is it a caterpillar or a butterfly? What does it think and feel?"

"I studied entomology," Mr Richards said.

"You did?" She stopped and he almost cannoned into her.

"Yes. I worked abroad for a few years. Then I took up teaching."

"Why?" Maddie asked. Why the hell did he give up a career like that to teach biology in a secondary school?

"I got married," he said. "It wasn't a suitable lifestyle for a married man."

"Oh. Of course."

Maddie glanced at his left hand. He wore a plain wedding ring. She had seen it many times, as he gestured with his hands at the blackboard or pointed at something she'd written in her folder.

He shoved his hand into his pocket as though he'd felt her gaze on in. Sian had told her the rumours about his wife. Mrs Richards was unbalanced. Some people said she was nuts.

"Come on, sir!" someone yelled from the top of the path. "What you two talking about?"

Someone else wolf-whistled and there was laughter. Maddie flushed and scrambled up the final slope of wet grass.

They stood on a small tarmacked car park cut out of the rocky hillside. There were a couple of cars, and a few people milled in bright anoraks. A stream gushed down the rockface, through bright ferns and lichen, and pooled on the ground, splashing water crystals in the air. Maddie pushed back her hood and let the rain sting her face. Mr Richards led the group towards the road across the dam. He was saying something about its construction, how it was built after the war to extend the reservoirs at Elan to provide more drinking water for Birmingham, something about the drainage direction and gravity. The Claerwen dam was the biggest and tallest of the dams at Elan; its reservoir held more water than any of the others. It was officially opened in 1952.

"How old were you then, sir?" one of the boys asked.

Maddie didn't catch Mr Richards' laughing reply. How old was he now? Forty something. Younger or older than Owain? It was hard to tell. Owain was stocky and dark; Mr Richards was tall and spare with fading auburn hair.

Maddie leaned over the parapet and looked down the steep curved face of the dam. White water fell from under the road and down the stones to the river below. From here she could see the farmhouse, and the black and white dog still running in the field. She could see the grassy, stony trail they had climbed up the hillside. The falling water was mesmerising; it looked both light as air and heavy as mercury as it slid down the dam.

"Maddie."

Mr Richards. She ran across the road to where the others were, peering over the opposite balustrade into the black waters of Claerwen. Raindrops pock-marked the surface, which rippled roughly in the wind. The hills on either side of the reservoir were bleak and bare of trees, blurred into nothingness by the mist. Maddie felt the cold, the intense cold, seeping up from the deep, dark water, and understood in an instant that she would remember this day forever, because this was the day she knew had fallen in love with Mr Richards.

He was standing on the higher walkway above the dam road, saying something about the opening of the reservoir. She wasn't listening to his words, content just to hear his voice. Was this the day she had fallen in love with him or was it a couple of weeks earlier when she held out her cupped hands to show him the Elephant Hawk caterpillar with its grumpy grey face, and she knew she'd found an ally?

"You can go as far as the end of the dam," Mr Richards said.

Not Mr Richards, Maddie corrected. Will Richards. Will. He had a name. He wasn't just a teacher any more. He was the man she loved.

The others ran on, along the curve of the dam. Will took off his glasses again and rubbed at them.

"I'd hoped we could bring our picnics up here," he said to Maddie. "But we'll have to eat in the bus."

She climbed the steps to where he stood. The others had gone, shouting, squabbling, laughing. Maddie watched the bright blurs of their anoraks in the austere grey landscape. She moved a little closer to Will. It was just the two of them, standing above the deep heart of Claerwen. The power of the lake seemed to tug at her with its own force field; she could imagine how easy it would be to fall into that inky water, to feel it dragging her down, the cold closing over her. She shook her head, afraid at her thoughts, and gazed along the shoreline.

"Can you go up there?" She gestured to a rough track that wound along the edge of the lake.

"Yes," he said. "It goes to the head of the reservoir. You can't drive along it, not in an ordinary car." He stopped and smiled at her. "Or in a school minibus."

"Have you been there?"

"Several times."

"What's it like?"

"Lonely. Wild. Remote. Sometimes frightening."

"Sounds exciting," Maddie said.

He didn't answer and she felt his eyes on her profile. She blushed, glad of the cool drizzle on her face.

"Why do you go there?"

"To get away, to be on my own, to be part of the landscape. There are insects, birds, plants up there. There are sundews growing in the moss."

"I want to go," Maddie said.

"Not today you can't."

I want to go with you, she added silently. *I want you to show me the sundews*.

Will hollered at the others. "Come on, let's go back and have lunch." He jumped down to the road.

The rest of the class straggled back towards him. The boys mobbed around Will asking him things. Maddie held back.

"What were you talking to him about?" Sian demanded.

"Who?"

"Him. Sir. You were talking to him."

"Oh, just stuff."

"You fancy him." Sian jabbed her in the arm.

"I do not."

"Yes, you do."

"Let me show you what he looks like. Looked like." Maddie jumps up. "Help yourself to tea. Just running upstairs."

At the bottom of her wardrobe is a shoebox. She lays it on the bed. Until Owain died this was in the attic where Vanessa would never find it and where Owain did not have to feel its presence. Maddie glances at the illustration of the shoe on the box. Fifth year school shoes. Shoes worn that year. Worn on those occasions. Some of them. Since she brought the box down from the attic after her conversation with Dave in town, she's only looked in it once, made a cursory glance inside. Now she finds a tightness in her throat as she drops her hand inside, and the delight and despair of that summer twenty years ago floods her mind. A photograph and a dried stem of wild thyme, crumbled to dust.

She jams on the lid and runs down the stairs. She can hear Mo talking softly to the dogs downstairs.

"Here he is." Maddie opens the box again and takes out the picture. *Claerwen, August 1992* in her rounded handwriting on the back. That day.

"I'll need a photo," Mo says. "Perhaps you could scan it. I'm not taking your only copy."

"Yes, yes, of course," Maddie says, and the tightness in her throat has now become a constriction, because this is happening too fast, too hard.

Mo studies the photograph and Maddie remembers taking it. She remembers him tugging his shirt across his chest, the heat of the sun, and the cooling breeze over the lake. After that nothing was the same.

Mo smiles up at her and hands her back the picture.

"Did you take it?" is all she asks.

"Yes." Maddie puts it away and taps the box lid down firmly. "It was at Claerwen. Not the day of the school trip, obviously. Later. After I left school." She waits for Mo to say something about Will, about his appearance, about his even being on a lonely hillside with a sixteen-year-old girl, but she doesn't.

Maddie and Sian stood at Maddie's locker. Maddie had to get her chemistry folders out. She locked up slowly, wanting to loiter in the science block in case Will appeared. On the days when she didn't have biology all she could hope for was a glimpse of him in the corridors, on the field at lunchtime, or around the science department. She and Sian trailed into the chemistry lab.

"Is that everyone?"

He was there in the chemistry class, at the board.

"Mr Jenkins has gone to a funeral today," Will said, as Maddie pulled out her wooden stool, sat down, ran a hand through her hair to give it a bit of bounce. "You'll have to be patient with me, as it's a while since I've done any chemistry." He tugged down the roller blackboard and wiped away an old diagram. "Today we're doing reversible reactions."

"I bet you're pleased," Sian whispered to Maddie.

"What?" Maddie busied herself with her folder, her pen, her textbook.

"That we're having him today." Sian nodded to the board where Will was writing up the first equation on the formation of ammonia.

Maddie didn't have to answer; Sian squeaked as something hit her in the back.

"Hey, who was that?"

Maddie also turned around.

At the next bench Dave was sniggering with his cronies. Sian threw the eraser back at Dave. More laughter from the boys.

"OK, you lot, pack it in," said Will. "Page 90. Dave, where's your text book?"

"Left it at home, sir."

"I know where Mr Jenkins keeps them," said Sian. "I'll get you one."

"Thank you, Sian," Will said.

Maddie watched Sian bending into the cupboard to retrieve the book, and how she postured around the boys' table.

"What's with you and Dave?" she asked when Sian came back.

"Wouldn't you like to know?" Sian countered, turning again to pout at the boys.

Not really, Maddie thought, copying the formulae. When she glanced up, Will was watching her and she met his gaze. Sian would have blushed and fidgeted and bent her head to her work. Maddie just smiled and Will looked away first.

Five minutes to go. Will wandered around the room, answering a few questions. The boys had given up the pretence of working. Sian slid off her stool and shimmied over to them once more. Left alone, Maddie watched Will correcting something for one of the other girls. He straightened up, saw her on her own and came over to her.

"Everything OK, Maddie?" he asked.

"Everything OK," she repeated.

"Do you understand what we've been doing?"

"I understand."

"But not all reactions are reversible," he said.

It was the last Friday before October half term. The sky was pewter, and rain squalls blew in from the west. At lunchtime Maddie went to the library on her own. Sian was probably fussing around Dave. Maddie had seen her doodling Dave's initials on the inside of her biology folder.

There weren't many people in the library. She didn't really want to borrow anything over half term; she would just rather be there than in one of the stuffy classrooms, or out on the windy, muddy field.

She closed the door quietly behind her, A few kids glanced up. She padded towards the stacks, headed for the natural history section. Suddenly she heard Will's voice on the other side of the bookshelf. Quietly she parted the books. He was there, just feet away, talking to Mr Powell from history. She'd looked at most of the insect books before, but she slid out the best volume on butterflies and moths. It did not have many withdrawals stamped on the front page. Still standing, she flicked through the coloured plates, hardly breathing, trying to hear what the two men were saying.

"Very difficult," Will said. "She won't want to do anything with me, but I'm not spending the whole half term in the house."

"Weather's not going to be good," Mr Powell said. "Best day's Monday, they said, getting worse throughout the week."

"I thought I'd head up to Clywedog on Monday," said Will. "I haven't been there since I came back to Aber."

"Clywedog in the rain. Had enough of all that on the Elan trip."

Through the gaps above the books Maddie saw Will and Mr Powell moving away. Quickly she turned her back to the room, tugged her hair over her shoulder, and hunched into the book. She let a few moments pass before she turned around again. They'd gone. Just the same bored-looking kids and the Special Needs teacher sorting out some papers in the far corner. Maddie shoved the book back on the shelf.

Clywedog. It was another reservoir, another huge dam. Her parents were taking Monday and Tuesday off work to spend some time with her. Could she get them to take her to Clywedog on Monday? Her geography project on Elan had to be in after half term. Could she make up some excuse about wanting to go to Clywedog to compare Elan with another reservoir, a more modern one, with a different dam? She left the library, her heart rate skipping.

It was remarkably easy. Maddie's parents were surprised at her request to go to Clywedog, but said, of course, they could go if she needed it for her work. Maddie felt guilty and tried to think of things she needed to find out and do there. She hadn't been there since she was quite little. There was an old lead mine; she remembered a picnic one sunny summer when her father sat on what must have been a spring near the mine ruins and stood up with soaking trousers. There was a narrow plank bridge called the miners' bridge that spanned the tumbling river as it flowed away from the dam.

"Haven't you left it a bit late?" her father asked. "If the project has to be in next week?"

"I only just realised what a good idea it would be," she said. "Visiting another dam. A much newer one," she added, to make him think she knew something about Clywedog.

Her parents said they could have an early lunch and then drive over. Maddie didn't know what time Will would go there. Why exactly was he going there anyway? Just to be by himself in the landscape? Maddie worried that an early lunch might not be that early, and they'd be late leaving and would miss him there.

They left shortly after noon. Maddie's father drove, Maddie sat in the front with him, and her mother snoozed in the back with a picnic bag for afternoon tea. Maddie wore a patterned scarf and carried her notebook and camera. She had a spare film in her coat pocket. She didn't really know what she could do when she got there. She hoped her parents wouldn't ask her too much about the project.

The rain came as they drove out of Llanidloes. Her father put on the wipers and they squeaked across the glass. Then there, suddenly, was the dam, a great buttress spanning the valley.

There was only one car at the viewpoint. It was not Will's dusty black estate car she'd seen him getting into at school. It was only early yet. They couldn't have missed him. Had he changed his mind? Was he coming another day? She got out of the car. The wind tugged at her scarf and hair; rain splattered her face. Below was the giant arc of the dam. There was no water pouring over it. Built in the sixties, it was heavier and uglier than those at Elan with their arched bridges and the Baroque towers that housed the valves for drawing off the water. The dams at Elan were either straight across the valley or gently curved. Clywedog was convex to the water; it looked like it was being pushed forwards, that it would surely burst.

Maddie removed the lens cap and snapped a few views of the dam and the reservoir behind it. The autumn colours of the opposite hillside were faded in the thin afternoon light. She took out her pad and sketched the dam, copied down a few facts from the visitor information notice. Her hair was everywhere. She was freezing. If he appeared now, she would look a tangled mess, but she didn't think he would care. She pocketed her pad, and pointed the camera at the ruined lead mine far below at the foot of the dam. There were a few people wandering around the ruins. She'd know his stride anywhere. He was not there.

Her father opened the driver's door and came to stand beside her.

"We can go down to the bottom as well," he said. "Are you getting what you need?"

"Yes," she said, flicking through her notebook to show him her scribbles and drawings.

"It's bloody bitter up here," he said, and got back in the car.

Maddie glanced around. Still just the one other car. He wasn't up here. *Please let him be down below,* she thought, opening the passenger door.

As her father pulled into the lower car park she saw Will's car. She had got the right day and he was here.

"We'll come over to the mine with you," her father said.

They crossed the narrow bridge. The river foamed beneath them. The sky was dark, threatening more rain. Maddie's hands were numb. She took the rest of her film, random shots of the grey stone mine buildings – grim as lead itself – and of the dam, rising up between the hills. She wandered through the ruins, tried to write down a few words. Raindrops scattered on her page.

“We’re going back to the car,” her mother called.

“OK.” Maddie walked on up the grassy rise.

There was only one family amongst the ruins: parents and two small kids. She thought she might cry. He was here, somewhere, but she couldn’t find him. Her parents had gone back to the car, no doubt for a hot drink and a biscuit. They wouldn’t wait forever for her. She stopped walking, just stood there, watching the kids running and yelling. One fell over, started bawling. She didn’t wear a watch; she didn’t know how long she’d been there, how long she could wait. Soon, her father would come to find her, then they’d be driving out of the car park, leaving Will’s car behind, and he’d never know she’d been there.

The family was moving towards the bridge, the father carrying the howling youngster. Maddie took a hesitant step after them. She stopped, turned. A lone figure was coming swiftly down the hillside. Wax coat, jeans. She whipped open her book, starting sketching the dam from beneath. The rain blurred her pen lines and stung her cold fingers.

“Hello,” she said as he drew level.

“Maddie. What are you doing?”

“Geography project,” she said, hoping he would be hazy on what was required of the project. “The Elan one. I want to do well, so I thought I’d look at this dam too. I’d like to take geography for A-level.”

“I hope you’ll take biology as well,” he said, wiping his glasses carefully, the way he had on the top of the Claerwen dam.

Maddie swallowed. “I will,” she said, shoving her book into her pocket. “Will you be teaching it?”

“Yes,” he said. Then, “How did you get here? Who are you with?”

“My parents,” she said, disloyally wishing they could be spirited back to Aberystwyth and she could go back with him in the muddy old estate car. “They’re back at the car, warming up.”

“Don’t you need warming up too?”

“I think I probably do,” she said, and he took her frozen hands and held them between his own frozen hands.

“Better?” he asked.

“Much better,” she said.

“What did you say to your mum and dad?” Moth asks. “Did they see you with him?”

Maddie smiles. “Yes, we walked back to the car park together. It was raining again, and so cold. I asked him why he was there, and he said he just loved the mountains and the lakes, and needed time by himself. I judged what Sian said about his wife was right. I’d heard him in the library saying things were difficult. I felt strange. Sad that he was unhappy at home, but it meant maybe there was a chance for me.”

“You introduced him to your parents?”

“I felt guilty,” Maddie says. “But they didn’t suspect anything. They didn’t think I would be so devious. I still feel guilty to this day.”

“What happened then?” Moth asks.

“Do you think I was dreadful?” Maddie asks suddenly.

“Not dreadful,” Moth says. She knows she has to handle this carefully. “I can’t imagine falling in love with any of my teachers, but perhaps I was unlucky at my school.”

Maddie laughs. “I wouldn’t have chosen any of the others either.”

“What was it like at school, after you saw him that day at the dam?”

“Painful,” Maddie says. “I knew something had happened, a boundary had been crossed, but I was only sixteen and I didn’t know what to do. I knew it was dangerous, but I didn’t care. I couldn’t tell anyone. No one at all. Sian used to make comments but then she got all wrapped up in Dave and pretty much forgot it because I didn’t rise to it. In biology and chemistry Dave and his friend moved over to sit with us so that took the pressure off me a bit. I’d sit there remembering the feel of his hands around mine.”

“Did he ever speak about it?”

“No, but he was thinking about it, as I was. Every day I would wonder if it would be the day when he said something, but he didn’t. Sometimes in class he would draw up a stool and go through something with me, and I just wanted to reach out for his hands again.”

Maddie didn’t know what to do. She returned to school after half term, expecting Will to say something about that wet afternoon at Clywedog, but he didn’t. She handed in her geography project, with a few references to the dam and surrounding countryside. She shared a workbench with Sian and the two boys in biology. When Will marked her work he never added a personal comment – well, he wouldn’t, would he? She gazed at his spiky red scribbles in the margin, and wondered what he’d been thinking when he wrote them, whether he’d done it at home, and whether his difficult wife was in the room with him.

One Saturday afternoon in town, she and her mother were in an antiques and junk shop at the top of Great Darkgate Street. While her mother picked up blue and white patterned plates, and examined an enamelled box, Maddie sifted through a box of prints. She was bored, frustrated with life. She never seemed able to speak to Will alone; this both irritated her and relieved her because she didn’t know what to say, how to pick up again from Clywedog. There were gloomy etchings, pen and ink drawings of churches, an eastern design of peacocks and blossom. She reached right to the back and pulled out a drawing of three hawk moths: the Death’s Head, the Privet, and the Oleander. She went hot. Only a couple of weeks until the school broke up for Christmas. She could give this to Will. The drawings were dark brown, with the palest washes of colour: pink, gold, green. She couldn’t buy it with her mother there. She would not be able to explain its subsequent disappearance. Quickly she shoved it right to the back of the box.

Her mother bought a blue and white plate. The assistant wrapped it in bulky layers of newspaper. Together they left the shop and started down the road.

“I need to go to the bank,” her mother said.

“OK, I just want to go and look for something,” Maddie said.

“What d’you need?”

“Secret,” said Maddie. “It’s nearly Christmas. You can’t come with me.”

As soon as her mother went into the bank, Maddie ran back up the street to the antique shop. The print was small enough to go in her rucksack, as long as she was careful not to bend it.

The last day of term. They could wear their own clothes. Maddie wore a shirt and jeans. That’s what Will would like. Sian had a glittery pink top and a short skirt. Katie had a tinsel halo on her head. At lunchtime a gang of boys helped the caretaker prepare the hall for the afternoon disco.

The moth print was in Maddie's locker. It had been there for some days, wrapped in silver, but she wanted to give it to Will on the last day. She was desolate. She wouldn't see him at all over Christmas. He'd be at home with his crazy wife, or out alone in the windswept mountains, but this time she would not be able to follow him.

She loitered in the disco. Through the flashing coloured lights she saw Sian and Dave. Dave was waving something over Sian's head. Mistletoe. The thump of the bass drove Maddie's heart rate up. The girl next to her said something but she couldn't hear the words. The curtains had been drawn at the long windows to darken the hall. Mr Powell was squeezing through the crush of bodies. His face was green, then pink, as the lights changed. Maddie peeled away from the wall.

"Have you seen Mr Richards?" she asked him.

"What?" he said, bending down to her.

"Mr Richards. Do you know where he is?"

"Over there a few minutes ago." Mr Powell pointed towards the other end of the hall, then shoved through the door, letting in a slice of light from the corridor.

Maddie turned to where he'd gestured. She could just see Will against the far wall. He was watching the DJ. He hadn't seen her. Her foot scuffed something on the floor. A spring of mistletoe. Just a few berries and a couple of leaves. She couldn't see Sian and Dave anywhere. Maybe it wasn't theirs. Quickly she bent down, picked it up, and shoved it in her shirt pocket. Someone buffeted her as she stood up. Still he wasn't looking her way. She squeezed past the dancers until he was only a few feet away. He turned to her and smiled.

"Can I have a word?" she asked.

The music was so loud surely no one could overhear her.

"I need to give you something," she said. "It's in my locker. By the biology room."

Will glanced around, looked at his watch.

"Yes, you left your coat in the lab," he said. "I put it away for you. I'll see you there in five minutes."

Maddie spun around and shoved back through the mob. She knew he was watching her. She flung open the hall door. The noise subsided as it swung to, but the bass still thudded in her bloodstream. The corridor was empty. She ran down it, down the steps, through the doors. The disco noise faded further and further. Some kids were hanging about down the left-hand passage. She turned right to the science department and the locker area. It was deserted. She opened her locker and brought out the print. Still no one was around. She crossed to the biology lab. The lights were off. The sky outside was dull and metallic. She shut the door and did not turn on the lights. Her footsteps were loud on the tiles. She walked through the lab to the further door, which led into the science storeroom and then on into the chemistry lab. Empty. She returned to Will's room and sat on the desk at the front, facing the blackboard with his blurred chalk marks on it. She swung her legs and waited. Anyone looking through the glass door panel would think the room was empty.

The door opened with a click. Will came in and shut the door.

"Maddie," he said.

He walked over to her, stood in front of the blackboard, in front of her. Only feet from her.

"For you." She handed him the slim parcel. "Happy Christmas. It's perfect for you."

"You shouldn't have," he said.

"You'll like it. Open it."

He unfastened the tape and peeled back the silver paper. Maddie watched him.

"That's really lovely," he said. "Thank you very much. You're right. It's perfect for me."

"Yes," she said.

The mistletoe was in her shirt pocket. She waited.

"I feel awkward now," he said, placing the print on the desk. "You've given me a beautiful gift and I don't have anything for you."

"You'll have to improvise," Maddie said. Still watching him she pulled the mistletoe from her pocket. "Give me a kiss."

"Maddie," he said again.

She let the mistletoe fall to the floor as he bent his head to hers. He kissed her very gently on the mouth. She slid her arms around him, and this time he was not gentle. He tugged her off the desk, so she was standing with him. She opened her mouth to him. His hands were inside her shirt, running up her back.

"Maddie, Jesus, fuck," he said, letting go of her, raking his hair. "I–"

"Don't say you're sorry," she said.

"I can't. I'm not." He grabbed her hand. "Is this what you want?"

"Yes," she said, breathless. "Don't you?"

"You know it is."

"Come with me. There's no one here." She pulled him through the further door into the storeroom.

He glanced around the shelves of chemicals, the microscopes, the test tubes and petri dishes.

"I told you. No one," she whispered, her back against the door.

He pulled kisses from her mouth. He twisted her hair in his fist. He tugged open her shirt and her bra and ran his hand over her breast. She bit her lip. It was like a huge balloon inflating somewhere inside her. When he took her nipple in his mouth she cried out.

"Not here," he said, holding her shirt across her. "Too dangerous."

"Where?" she asked. "When?"

"I don't know."

"I can't bear it, Will," she said.

"We'll find a way," he said. "Can I ring you at home?"

"Not at the weekend." Maddie clumsily fastened her shirt. "And it's nearly Christmas."

"I can't before Christmas."

"I have to see you," she cried. "I have to see you before we come back to school."

"When are you parents working?"

"They go back the Monday after Christmas," she said. "That's ages."

"I know, chicken, but I can't see you before then."

She didn't ask why. "Ring me then at home," she said. "After nine."

"I will. I promise."

"I can't wait."

"Nor me. Come here."

He kissed her again, hard and demanding. She was hot and melting inside.

"Now, go," he said.

Maddie ran back into the biology lab. The door was still closed. She opened it carefully. A couple of boys were coming out of the Gents, but they didn't see her. They shambled away past the lockers. She followed them back towards the hall. The music grew louder and louder. She turned twice to see if Will was behind her, but there was no one. She wanted the darkness and the crowds of the disco, where no one could see the guilt and ecstasy she knew was in her eyes. The boys went ahead of her into the hall. Suddenly she remembered the mistletoe on the floor in Will's lab. She should have picked it up, should have kept it. She reached for the hall door before it swung shut. Through the portal, she saw the flashing lights, the moving shapes of the disco dancers. She slipped inside into the hot, coloured darkness. Her body ached with a longing she'd never felt before. She wanted him again, now. She caught her breath at the memory of his mouth, his hands.

"I can feel it now," Maddie says. She glances at Mo. "In just a few minutes I'd gone from despair to…I knew he wanted me, but I'd not been able to say anything. I didn't know how, and he knew it couldn't come from him. We were both waiting for me to do something, and that was to give him the picture. I wonder if he still has it?"

"It was very risky, wasn't it?" Mo says. "To kiss you in the school like that?"

"God, yes, of course. But, you know, it was just crazy." She can remember the feel of the wooden door, hard behind her back, the sour smell of chemicals, the chill of the unheated room on her bare skin, and the heat inside her, consuming her.

"If I find Will," Mo says, "will he be pleased to hear from you?"

"I don't know," Maddie says. "He must be in his sixties now." She smiles sadly. "So much time gone. I loved my husband. It's not that I've just waited for him to die, so I can find Will again. I know it looks like that, but it's not."

"Nothing is what it looks like," Mo says.

"No," Maddie says. "It's not. I loved Owain and I was devastated to lose him, but Will's always been my first love, do you know what I mean?"

"I understand."

"I think you do," Maddie says. She stands. "I must let the dogs out and I'll make us a sandwich. Come on, girls." The dogs scamper after her to the back door.

Moth stands, stretches, and walks to the front window. The rain has passed and the sky is clear and pale. She can just see the car park at the butterfly house. It is full now with cars. Some kids are running on the grass above the dam. The surface of the reservoir is dark and glassy. She will make time on her trip west to see the great lakes at Elan, and maybe the Clywedog. She wants to stand where Maddie stood with Will. She wants to capture the folly, the despair, the love, of that summer twenty years ago. How long were they lovers? How did it end? Maddie said if it weren't for Will, she would never have married Owain. She was only very young when she got married. She says she loved Owain. *How did she transfer her affections that quickly? Nothing is what it seems,* Moth thinks ruefully.

"Did he meet you that Christmas holiday?" she asks, returning to the kitchen, where Maddie is assembling a loaf, cheeses, and salad on the workbench.

"I can't tell you what it was like, that wait." Maddie holds aloft a bottle of white, pours two glasses. "I was so afraid he'd change his mind, that the days would pass, and he'd think he couldn't do it. Back then, no one had mobiles or email. People couldn't trace you. I couldn't ring him. All I could do was tell him to ring me on a day my parents were supposed to be at work. If one of them had stayed at home, there was no way I could warn him. I was terrified something like that would happen, and he'd ring and I'd have to hang up on him or, worse, one of my parents would take the call."

"But they did go to work?"

"They did."

"So what happened?"

He didn't speak at first.

"Is that you?" Maddie asked.

"It's me," he said quietly. "How long have you got?"

"Most of the day."

"Can you get to the school by ten?"

She glanced at the clock. In fifty minutes she could see him, be with him. The last few days had been terrible. She'd enjoyed Christmas with her parents and Boxing Day with her grandparents in Aberaeron, but the waiting, the fear, the longing, was always there. Her heart had skipped and soared, and sometimes she couldn't catch her breath. At night, she curled into a ball with her face in the pillow.

She hung up. She didn't know where he'd called her from, or where his crazy wife was. He'd spoken quietly so maybe he was at home. She didn't care. He was meeting her in under an hour. She hadn't asked him where they were going, how long he'd got.

It was cold out, bitterly cold, that no-time between Christmas and New Year. She pulled on her hood, even though it was not raining. She could not let herself be recognised or delayed. She got to the school at five to ten. It looked barren and windswept with no one around. She tugged her hood on further, facing away from the road, and waited for his scruffy dark estate car. Glancing sideways, she saw him pull into the kerb. He reached over to open the passenger door, and she scrambled in.

"Hi," she said, suddenly shy.

"Hi," he said. "We need to get out of town."

She fiddled with her seat belt. He hadn't touched her. He wouldn't, not until they'd left Aberystwyth behind.

"Where are we going?" she asked.

"North," he said. "Over the river."

"Will, these last few days…since school broke up…"

"I know," he said.

She hadn't seen him again on the last afternoon of term. Not since he'd sent her from the chemical store with his touch still hot on her skin. He'd not come back to the disco, and she'd been accosted by Sian and Dave and Katie wanting to know where she'd been, and one of Dave's awful friends threatened her with mistletoe, and the thought of any other person touching her made her feel faint, and she'd escaped to the cloakroom and stared at her reflection in the grimy glass as though she had been branded with Will's kisses.

"Maddie, it's not that I don't want to kiss you," he said. "But I want to get away from here first. What we did the other day was–"

"Wonderful," she said.

"It was," he agreed ruefully. "But so dangerous."

"Yes," she smiled at him. "That made it more wonderful."

"What am I going to do with you?" he laughed and, at last, took her hand, as the narrow road fell away beneath the car, and the flat grey beach at Borth spread northwards to the soft dunes of Ynyslas and, beyond those, the glassy Dyfi estuary.

"You'll think of something," she said as they hurtled down to the coast.

"How's the revision going?" he asked. "For the mocks?"

"It's OK," she said. "I'm supposed to be revising today."

It felt both natural and odd to be talking about school, about exams, with him, as they trundled up the long straight road through Borth. Some houses had sandbags lying around the doors. The sea wall looked grey and grim and cold.

"Where were you working before?" she asked. She remembered the day in the library when he told Mr Powell he hadn't been to Clywedog since he'd come back to Aberystwyth.

"Liverpool," he said. "My wife's from up there. She didn't want to move to Aber."

"What does she do?"

"Do?"

"Do for a job?"

"She doesn't work," Will said flatly.

Maddie didn't answer. They left behind the last of Borth's pastel-painted houses. The pale grasses of the golf links blurred into a sunken marshy plain.

"The Rosy Marsh Moth lives there," Will said, gesturing to the spiky grasses and stagnant pools. "It's about the only place in the UK where you can find it. They thought it was extinct. There's load of great stuff here. Orchids, adders, spiders, birds."

"Can we come and look at them one day?"

"I don't know," he said at last. "It might be too close to home."

"We'll just have to look for those sundews at Claerwen then," she said.

"We can do that," he said, then, "I've been so looking forward to today. I was afraid you'd have changed your mind."

"Never."

Now he was there beside her, with his scruffy jeans and sandy hair, long for a teacher, and his left hand on her knee, and she wondered suddenly what would have happened before the day was out. She knew about the mechanics of sex, of course, and she'd laughed with Sian and the girls about it, but until that heady moment in the biology lab no one had ever touched her like that, or kissed her. She felt a hot flare inside at the memory; she wished he'd just stop driving and take her in his arms once more and kiss her again and again.

"Are we going to Aberdyfi?" she asked.

"I thought so," he said. "I don't think anyone knows me there. Does anyone know you?"

"No one," she said, though her parents did have friends there, but surely, she couldn't be so unlucky as to see them. She would have to keep her hood on. "What will we do there?"

"We could walk on the beach," he said.

"It's freezing."

"I can keep you warm," he said. "I've done that before."

"Were you pleased to see me at Clywedog?"

"I'm always pleased to see you," he said. "Since we first met and you had the caterpillar."

"Will, please can we stop?" Maddie asked. "Before we get to Machynlleth?"

Already she could see the spindly railway bridge spanning the river Dyfi. They were almost at Machynlleth. Once they crossed the river they had to go all along its northern bank until they reached Aberdyfi. Maddie couldn't wait that long.

"OK," Will said.

He indicated left and pulled onto a patch of rough ground under the trees. A white van roared past. He turned off the ignition, unclicked his seat belt.

"I can't wait till we get there," Maddie said.

"We can't do much here, chicken," he said.

"Just kiss me," she said.

"You must think we were awful."

"First love isn't awful," Moth says. "There's everything to make it exciting, and everything to make it doomed. That makes it romantic."

Maddie finishes her wine. "It was doomed," she says. "But it was magical. He was so much older than me, he was my teacher, he was married…but he was gorgeous and clever and kind and fun, and we had things in common, things we could talk about. Nature, moths, butterflies, plants. I was only just sixteen."

"What if you hadn't been sixteen?"

They crossed the Dyfi over the stone road bridge. The river swirled beneath the arches, brown and swollen. The road wound on, through the trees, towards the mouth of the estuary and the coloured houses on Aberdyfi's sea front.

Maddie huddled down in the car seat, his touch still stinging on her skin. He'd laughed when he found she wasn't wearing a bra, but he'd only kissed her for a few moments at the roadside. She knew he wanted more. So did she. She was frightened. No, she couldn't be frightened, not with Will.

He parked in the car park on the sea front. The wind roared in off the sea. Across the estuary were the dunes at Ynyslas, the jumble of houses of Borth and the land rising to the clifftop monument.

They ran down the steps to the sand. The smell of salt and mud. Maddie stood at the water's edge, her eyes burning with the cold. Will, behind her, wrapped his arms around her and rested his chin on her head.

"Thank you for coming," he said.

"I wanted this so much," she said. "After Clywedog…I thought you liked me."

"I did," he said. "I do."

"Did you think about me?"

"Did I think about you? All the time. But I couldn't let anyone know that at school."

"They won't." Maddie said. "No one will know anything."

"They mustn't ever know."

"I won't tell anyone," she said, then, "Will, are we going to…?"

He nuzzled her neck and bit her cold ear.

"Do you want to?"

"Yes." She kept her eyes on Borth.

"Is it, I mean, have you…?"

"No."

"Maddie." He turned her around so she was facing him. "I really, really want to, but it doesn't have to be today. Are you sure?"

"I'm really, really sure," she said.

They went up the sandy steps to the car park. He asked if she wanted to buy anything to eat, and she said no. He unlocked the car and she got in, slamming the door on the icy wind.

"We'll go up the Happy Valley," he said, starting the ignition. "We can find somewhere quiet. No one'll go up there today."

It only took a few moments to reach the lane winding inland. The hillsides were bleak and wintery. Maddie wished it were summer and that Will could make love to her amongst wild flowers and butterflies.

They did not pass any vehicles; when the road spilt Will chose a narrow rutted lane.

"It doesn't go anywhere," he explained. "We'll be safe here."

"OK," she said. "I haven't, I mean, I'm not…" She flushed, feeling awkward and young and unable to say what she thought was required of her.

"It's all right, chicken," Will said. "I have. Just in case you wanted to."

"I do want to," she said.

"I won't hurt you," he said.

"I know you won't."

Maddie's pushed away her plate and is crying.

"I'm sorry," she says, at last looking at Moth and raking her hair. "I haven't talked about any of this before. It was so beautiful."

"We all need to cry sometimes," Moth says.

"You don't look like someone who'd cry. You look very competent and contained."

Moth smiles, shrugs.

"It wasn't great," Maddie says at last. "It was so cold. I was scared someone would come along. I didn't really know what I was doing, but he was lovely. Afterwards he just held me and kissed me and I felt so special. I felt beautiful, desired. I suppose I felt loved." She fiddles with her empty wine glass. "I miss him," she says at last. "I've always missed him. We were together for nearly a year. I was crazy about him."

"Did you see him again that Christmas holiday?"

"No. My parents had time off after New Year and then we were back at school. That night when they came home I thought they'd know, but they didn't say anything. I thought I must look different, be different. I was so excited about going back to school because he'd be there, but so uncertain because I didn't know when I'd be able to see him again, and I had to see him again. I felt I couldn't live, I couldn't breathe, without him."

"And he didn't call you or anything?"

"He couldn't. It was terrible not hearing from him. All I could do was look forward to school."

First day back at school. Maddie and Sian were at the lockers before morning registration.

"Sian, I need you to help me," Maddie said.

"Help you with what?"

Maddie closed her locker. She'd prepared it all. It was just a question of speaking the lines without giving herself away as a liar.

"I might sometimes need you to cover for me with my parents," she said. "Over Christmas I met someone. I'm sort of seeing him. He's at the university. You know what my parents are like."

"The university? How old is he?"

"Twenty," Maddie said. "So you can see, they wouldn't like it."

"How did you meet him? What's his name? What's he doing at the uni?"

"His name's Stephen. He's doing art."

"How did you meet him?" Sian demanded again. "Come on, we'd better go. It's nearly time."

"He knows some people I know. We met over Christmas."

"Didn't he go home for Christmas? Where's he from? Have you got a photo?"

"He's from Birmingham. He only went back for a few days."

The corridor was full of kids shambling to registration. Over their heads Maddie saw Will. The first time since he dropped her off outside the school a week ago.

"Morning, sir," said Sian.

"Morning Sian, Maddie," Will said. "Did you have a good holiday?"

I thought you liked me.

I did. I do.

I really, really want to.

I'm really, really sure.

"Yes," Maddie said, and found she could meet his eye, without blushing, without stammering, as he met hers, and she knew then they could do this.

"I'll see you later," Will said and strode past them.

"So, have you got a photo of him?" Sian demanded, shoving Maddie through the double doors.

"Photo of who?"

"Stephen, stupid."

"Oh. No. No, I haven't."

"What d'you want me to do? Say you're with me and that?"

"Maybe sometimes. Not every time. Would you do that? Please?"

"Has he got any single friends?"

"I thought you liked Dave," Maddie said, opening the door to the registration room.

"Hmm, but an older man would be much better. You obviously think so. Have you done it yet?"

Maddie hesitated.

"You have, haven't you?"

"Only once," she said at last.

Biology. Sian had left at lunchtime for a dental appointment. It was just Maddie and the two boys at the workbench. Will was working his way round the room signing off homework. He sat in Sian's place beside Maddie and reached out for Dave's folder. Maddie watched his hand, the way it held the pen. She balled her fist to stop herself placing her hand over his. He wrote something in the margin of Dave's page and handed the folder back. Dave's friend shoved his folder across the wooden table. Will asked him something about his work. Maddie closed her eyes, just listened to his voice.

"Maddie," he said at last. "What have you got for me?"

"Dave!" One of the boys on the next table yelled for Dave. Dave and his friend shambled over to see what was going on.

Will scribbled his initials in Maddie's folder.

"Half four this afternoon," he said so quietly she thought she'd imagined it. "I have an hour."

"Where?" she breathed.

"End of your road." He stood up. "That's fine, Maddie. Boys, come and sit down. We've got another fifteen minutes."

Someone on the boys' table had brought up a question about action potentials. Will went through it on the board. Maddie couldn't take in the words. She sat, doodling circles on the back of her folder, wondering whether Will was really thinking about neurons, or whether he was thinking what she was thinking. When the bell went she left the lab without looking back. She collected her coat from her locker and took it with her to geography. She didn't want to be delayed. She was glad Sian wasn't there to dawdle with on the way home. She needed to run back and wash and change and be at the end of the road at half four. He'd said an hour. Her parents would be home by five thirty. During geography, Maddie drafted the note she could leave them. *Gone to Sian's to see her after the dentist.* No, her mother might ring Sian's mother. *Gone to Sian's to do some biology. Home by 6.* That would have to do. She thought she might have to bring some clothes to school and keep them in her locker. If she was going to meet Will after school, she wasn't going to do it in uniform.

She ran home with the note in her pocket. The house was empty. She put the note in the kitchen where her parents would see it. Quickly she washed and changed her clothes. As she was about to leave, she hid her biology books under the bed. She tugged her hood on again, although it was not raining.

When she saw his car approaching she looked both ways. No one was looking; none of the neighbours were about.

"I've missed you," she said when she got in.

"You only saw me this afternoon."

"You know what I mean."

"Yes," Will said. "I do."

"What were you thinking about when you were doing the action potential stuff on the board?"

"Nothing to do with ion channels," he said.

"I left a note," Maddie said. "I said I'd be at Sian's."

"Sian doesn't suspect anything?"

"No, I told her I'd met a guy from the university, and that my parents wouldn't approve because he was twenty."

Will laughed.

"How would you have spoken to me if the boys hadn't moved?" Maddie asked.

"I don't know. I'd have thought of something."

"I was going crazy wanting to see you."

"I know, chicken. Same here. If I ever arrange to meet you and I'm not there, it's not that I don't want to see you, it's because something's come up and I can't get there, OK?"

"Sure," she said uncertainly, then, "Where are we going today?"

"We'll go up to Ponterwyd."

"How do you know these places?" Maddie asked.

"I know the countryside really well," he said. "I saw some of these places and thought *wouldn't it be wonderful to fuck a beautiful girl there*?"

"Am I beautiful?" Maddie asked.

"You're very beautiful," he said.

He dropped her at the end of her road. She ached for him to kiss her goodbye, but he quickly took her hand and said *see you soon.* The lights were on in her house. Her parents were back. It was just after five thirty. As Maddie put her key in the lock her stomach contracted. She was empty-handed. She had no biology homework in her arms. She opened the door as quietly as possible, called out a cheerful hello and ran upstairs before either of her parents could accost her. In her room she kicked off her shoes and threw herself down on the bed. She lifted her top and ran a hand over her breasts where she could feel bruises starting to bloom. She'd only been away from him for moments; already she missed him.

The biology mock exam was in the gym. It smelt of feet and rubber. Maddie arranged her pens on the single desk. Sian turned around to give her the thumbs up. In the front row Dave had dropped something on the floor and was feeling with his hand to find it. The deputy head handed out the papers, face down on the desks. Maddie dampened a flare of panic. Probably Will was teaching another class or something. That's why he wasn't there. She was good at biology. She knew she would finish with plenty of time, and had been looking forward to sitting there for the last half hour, just watching him as he paced along the rows of desks. Instead all she'd have to watch was the grumpy deputy head.

"Mr Richards, biology," said Maddie's father.

"In the corner." Maddie gestured to where Will was talking to Dave and his mother.

It was parents' night. They'd just spoken to Mr Powell from history. Maddie's teachers were all pleased with her work. She was predicted to get As and Bs for everything. Will was the last on their appointment card.

Dave and his mother stood up. Maddie had been watching Will all evening, as she trailed round with her parents. She'd caught him watching her once or twice. It was getting harder to meet. February was brutally cold, and there had been snow on the mountains. Maddie's parents weren't keen on her being out on her own after dark. She still said she was going to Sian's to work in the evenings, and some nights she really did go there, but Sian questioned her too much about her imaginary boyfriend, and Maddie was no longer sure Sian believed her that the romance was still going on. Maddie's parents hadn't said much about her suddenly going to Sian's after school. They suggested she should invite Sian over instead sometimes; Maddie said she liked going to Sian's because Sian had a dog, but she did ask her around once or twice just to cover herself.

As she and her parents sat down opposite Will in the school hall she remembered the biology class last Friday. They hadn't met for over a week. Towards the end of the class Maddie said she was just going to ask Mr Richards something. She took her folder to the front, writing *when?* on a blank sheet of paper.

"Sorry, I'm a bit stuck," she said. "Can you just explain this?" She held the folder between them, gestured vaguely, didn't look at him.

"Of course. It's like this." He picked up his pen, wrote *Saturday 2 railway station* whilst talking about the nervous system. Then very quickly and quietly he tore the page from the folder and pocketed it.

Luckily, her parents were decorating the living room that weekend, and she was able to go into town, with the excuse of meeting Sian, Dave, and Katie. She didn't know how Will had managed to get a couple of hours on a Saturday afternoon. She didn't ask.

"Maddie's one of my star pupils," Will said to her parents.

"You're hoping to do biology for A-levels, aren't you?" her mother said. "With chemistry and geography."

"Yes, that's right," Maddie said, suddenly resentful.

Here, sitting between her parents, she was a child again. She wasn't a child when Will screwed her in the back of his car in a country lane, when she took him in her mouth in a deserted car park.

"I wanted to stand up, upturn the table, yell that at them." Maddie smiles. "Well, OK, of course I didn't really, but it was so frustrating. I thought Will would see me as a child again, and I'd proved to him I wasn't. That parents' night I was even pissed off with him as well. It's hard to explain but I felt he'd been disloyal somehow, talking about me as a schoolgirl."

"But what else could he have done?" Moth asked.

"I know. But at the time…it was all so painful. I wanted this man so much. A quick fuck in his car just wasn't enough anymore. I fantasised about his wife dying. If he hadn't been married…"

"If he hadn't been married, would he have shacked up with you?"

"Yes, I think so," Maddie said. "Not till after I'd done my A-levels I suppose, but yes, I think he would have. I did mean a lot to him."

"Did he ever say anything about his wife?"

"Very little. She was called Catrina. She was in her thirties. I realise now she suffered from terrible depression, but then she was just crazy. She'd had her womb out very young, endometriosis or something, and so she couldn't have children, and that was part of it, I imagine. And that she and Will were simply so ill matched. Anyway, it was difficult. I knew my alibi was wearing thin. I kept saying I was at Sian's, but surely sooner or later my parents would say something to Sian's parents. I was lucky in a way because they didn't really like Sian's parents. I wanted so much more than he could give me. It was so cold and dark it was almost impossible to get away. And then, that spring something amazing happened. Just for one day."

Will seems different, Maddie thought. *Almost hyperactive, frenetic.* She couldn't tell if it was good or bad. When it was time to pack up at the end of the lesson, she scooped up her keys in her palm and, as she stood up to leave, dropped them quietly on her stool.

Outside, by the lockers, Sian was fooling around with Dave, chasing him, trying to wrest something off him.

"I'll see you in geography," Maddie said vaguely and doubled back to biology.

The door was closed. It was afternoon break. She went in. Will was standing at the window looking out. He turned as he heard her shoes on the floor. He opened his fist where her keys glinted.

"I have some news for you," he said.

He was smiling but still her heart thudded.

"Good news," he went on.

He snatched a textbook off the windowsill, opened it at random, in case anyone should come in. It fell open on the illustration of male genitalia and they both laughed.

"Dave's bent the spine," he said.

"What's the news?" Maddie asked.

"I shouldn't be saying this… I'm saying this as your lover not your teacher," he said quietly. "Can you skive off on Friday?"

"To be with you? Aren't you working?"

"Catrina's going to Liverpool for a few days. Her mother's birthday. She's going on Thursday afternoon on the train. The do is on Sunday. I will have to go up for that. I'll travel on the Saturday, then we'll come back on the Sunday night."

"You're taking Friday off?"

"If you can."

"I can."

"I'll say I'm ill. I'll meet you at the station about half nine."

"I want to kiss you," Maddie said.

"No way," he said. "You can in four days."

Maddie felt her eyes brimming with tears. A day with Will. She hadn't had that since the first time in Aberdyfi. And he was going to lie to the school to be with her. He must want her; he must want her as much as she wanted him.

"Your keys, I believe?" He dangled the key ring.

Maddie took it and, for a second, their hands touched.

"I don't know how we managed it for so long," Maddie tells Moth. "We made arrangements to meet when we passed on the corridors, sometimes in the classroom. We never kept anything in writing. If we ever wrote anything, we'd destroy it. There was so much to lose, but it was so exciting. I became distant from the other kids. I was living a life they couldn't even guess at. They'd never have thought it of me, Mo. I'd have been the last person they'd have expected to have an affair with a teacher."

"If it happened now, you'd be using texts and Facebook. And you'd have got found out."

"It was more exciting the way we did it. Texts make everything so easy. We had to really work to be together. Twice he didn't turn up, and once my mother wouldn't let me go out. I was furious. I slammed into my room, imagining him waiting for me. Even though he'd had to stand me up twice, I never wanted to do that. I was distraught at not seeing him, then I realised I had to get a grip or she'd be suspicious and start asking questions. But we had so few times together and I was getting very angsty. And then his wife went to Liverpool."

Maddie loitered in the neighbouring streets until she knew her parents would have left for work. Then she went back to the house. It was quiet and odd at this time of day. There was a lingering smell of toast, and her father had left his dirty mug on the table. Quickly she ran upstairs to change. She'd never bunked off school before. Her class did not have biology that day so, with luck, no one would realise that Will was not there either.

"What did you tell the school?" she asked him as they left the station car park.

"I said I'd thrown up," Will said.

"And we've really got all day?"

"Until you have to get back."

"Where are we going?"

"Somewhere different," he said.

"Somewhere different?"

"My house," he said.

Maddie knew where he lived, of course, but she had never walked there, never stood outside his house.

He parked on the drive and dug out his keys.

"Put your hood on just in case," he said.

As soon as he had closed and locked the front door he grabbed her, kissed her, shoved her coat from her shoulders.

"My beautiful girl," he said between kisses.

"Am I your girl?" she asked.

"I don't have any others," he said. "Come upstairs."

The door to the front bedroom was closed. He took her into the back room.

"This is my room," he said. "Only mine."

She stood in the doorway. There was a double bed and several shelves of books. She glanced at the volumes: insects, birds, wild plants, Steinbeck, Kerouac, Tolkien, some contemporary crime. His spare glasses were on the bedside cabinet, and his jeans and shirts were thrown across a chair. It looked like it truly was his room, where he slept and read and dreamed, and not something he'd crafted for her benefit.

They'd never had sex in a bed before. Maddie loved the space and the warmth and the softness of the pillows under her.

"I want it to be like this always," she said, as she lay with her head on his chest.

She felt him tense.

"I'm sorry I can't give you more," he said.

But you can, you could, she wanted to cry. *You could leave her.*

Instead she said, "What's going to happen, Will?"

"What do you mean?"

"I mean this, you and me." She stopped, feeling her way through the words. "I want to be with you."

"You are with me. I'll try to make it easier."

"Do you want to be with me?" she asked.

"Very much."

She closed her eyes, let her mind drift, breathing in the smell of his skin, the sex, the bedclothes. Even if he left his wife, she could never tell her parents, not while she was still at school, in his class. She sighed. Over two more years until her A-levels were done. Perhaps she shouldn't take biology next year, but she wasn't sure she could bear to not be with him at school. And her parents would want to know why. She felt a treacherous tear and she coughed it back before it slid onto his skin. It was a beautiful, special day. The future could not be solved in an instant.

Will went downstairs and came back with a bottle of white wine, fruit, cheeses, a crusty baguette.

"What's funny?" he asked as she grinned at him.

"I was just thinking about them at school," she said. "And us here."

"Close your eyes," he said, and fed her grapes and strawberries, and slid her down the bed where the bread crumbs prickled her skin as he drove himself into her once more.

"It wasn't just sex that day," Maddie says to Moth, then smiles.

"You had time to talk to him," Moth suggests.

Maddie's telling her far more than she expected. She sees the conversation is a huge relief and release for Maddie, who has kept all this locked in her heart for so long.

"Yes, and I wanted assurances for the future, and I soon realised they weren't coming. I knew nothing could change until I'd left school, but I wanted to know he was thinking of how we could be together then. After that day at his house I wanted more and more of him. What we did in the country was wild and exciting, but I also wanted some comfort and security."

"Did he say anything about the future?"

"Not really. Just that he would try to work things out, whatever that meant. I couldn't understand why he stayed with her. I still can't. And she must have been mad. She was married to a gorgeous, sexy, lovely man and she didn't want him."

"It happens all the time."

"We sat in bed and ate chocolate and looked at books. He had a beautiful book of tropical butterflies. We talked about the Birdwings. Do you know them?"

"I've heard of them. Do you have any here?"

"No. They're huge, bright-coloured things: green and yellow, with black…like stained glass. The biggest butterflies in the world. I'm sure you've seen pictures of them."

"Is one orange and black and very poisonous?"

"No, you're thinking of the Giant African Swallowtail."

"It must have been hard to leave him that day, especially as you knew his wife wasn't around."

"It was the worst of both," Maddie tells her. "I had to go by four when I wanted to stay all night. And I knew he'd soon be driving up to see his wife. A chance like this wouldn't come again. You have no idea how hard it was to walk away."

"I'll walk home," Maddie said.

She wanted some time between Will and her parents, and she didn't think she could bear to just jump out of the car at the end of the road without cuddles and kisses.

"I can give you a lift, chicken," he said.

"You're ill, confined to your bed."

"Perhaps we should go back to bed." He played with a length of her hair. "It's been fabulous."

She nodded. She ought to say something like *enjoy your mother-in-law's birthday*. But no, why should she? He knew how she felt.

"I'll see you on Monday," she said.

He kissed her long and hard, and he tasted of chocolate and wine. When he let her go, he tugged up her hood.

"Goodbye then."

"Goodbye," she said, and stopped at the door. "Drive safely. I couldn't bear anything to happen to you."

"I'll be careful, I promise."

Her hood blew off as she walked down the drive. She let the wind tug her hair. It had rained and the pavements had a slimy film of water. One of the street lamps had come on, pale and eerie. She walked slowly. Her muscles ached and she was raw and stinging inside. She could pretend she'd gone to school, or she could tell her parents she felt ill when she got there, and she'd gone home.

She let herself into the house and filled a glass of water at the kitchen tap. She'd fallen so badly from her high she was shaky. Will was there at home on his own and she couldn't be there with him because of her parents, and the next day he'd be driving to his wife and her family.

She trailed upstairs with her glass of water. In her bedroom she cried and cried, choking and clawing the pillow. In the hall below the clock struck five. Slowly she sat up. Her parents would be home soon. She had to get a grip. She ran a bath. It would buy her time; she could bathe her face and breathe the scented steam. As she sponged herself she felt disloyal, washing Will from her. She wondered what he was doing now. Was he lying on the bed, amongst the tangled sheets, fanning through the butterfly book? Had he opened another bottle of wine? Was he thinking about her, and did he miss her?

She heard her parents come in, call for her. She shouted back. When she came out of the bathroom in her furry robe her mother was coming up the stairs with clean laundry in her arms.

"How was today?" she asked, leading the way into Maddie's room and dropping clothes on the rumpled bed.

"I wasn't well," Maddie gabbled at last. "I got to school but I felt bad, so I came home."

"What was the matter? You should have called me at work."

"I didn't want to worry you. I just felt sick, queasy, dizzy, you know."

"Are you all right now?"
"A bit better, yes."
"You'll be able to manage dinner?"
"I think so."
Maddie's mother took the rest of the washing away. Maddie waited until she heard footsteps going downstairs once more, then stumbled into jeans and a jumper. She ran her fingers through her wet hair and studied her reflection. Could she pass as ill? She'd have to. It was too late now.
She trotted down and into the kitchen. Her mother was at the sink preparing vegetables.
"What have you eaten?"
"Eaten?"
Grapes, strawberries, chocolate. Wine.
"You've not eaten a thing, have you? There's no washing up." Her mother gestured to the small pile of breakfast crockery.
Maddie almost cried aloud. It was obvious she hadn't been in the house. There wasn't even a dirty cup or chocolate wrapper.
"I had some water upstairs," she said quickly. "I didn't feel like anything else, but I'll have a cup of tea now."
"Are you sure you're all right?" her mother demanded, and turned to her father. "She came home ill and didn't call me. Now she hasn't eaten."
"I'm fine." Maddie dropped a tea bag into a mug. She realised she was starving. "I might have a couple of biscuits."
"Someone was asking after you today," her father said, swiping a biscuit from the packet.
"Me?" Maddie asked warily.
"Owain Pryce. He rang me at work. He said he hadn't seen you for ages and asked how you were. I said you were working hard for your exams. He said if you had any time over Easter, you could go up for the lambing if you wanted to."

Easter holidays and the countdown to the end of school. Maddie smiled ruefully to herself. A year ago, she'd never have believed she would prefer school time to holidays. She just wanted the Easter break to go as quickly as possible. Will had been evasive about when or how they could meet.
"Are you going away?" she'd asked him.
"No, no," he said. "It's just I don't know what I'll be doing. You know. It's only a couple of weeks. I'll be thinking about you even if I'm not with you."
"We can find a way. Surely we can find a way?"
"I don't know."
"You are going away, aren't you? You're going away with her."
Will looked wretched. "I'm not sure," he said at last. "Catrina wants to get away for a few days. Nothing's booked, and it won't be for the whole holiday. It's just I can't tell you right now what's happening."
"No problem," Maddie lied, and she knew he didn't believe her. "I mean, why should it be a problem? It's me you want to be with." She stopped. She sounded petulant.
"The time will go really quickly," he said. "I thought you said you were going to see your dad's friend on that farm? Help out with the lambing?"
"I will," Maddie said.
"Well, that'll be great. Really interesting."

"Yes," she said.

That was the day school broke up. Finally, she got him to agree to phone her at home if he could, when her parents were at work. She gave him the dates they were taking off. If their plans changed and one of them answered, he was to do a wrong number.

A couple of days into the holiday Maddie walked into town. She didn't want to meet Sian and the others; she didn't want to do anything. She'd waited at home all morning in case Will rang; by early afternoon she suspected he wasn't going to. In fact, she suspected he wasn't going to ring her at all during the holidays.

She wandered through town. She saw some boys from her history group and had a few words with them. They'd never been that friendly before. She saw they suddenly looked at her with new eyes, and she knew she'd changed. Will had changed her. They asked her if she wanted to hang out with them that evening. She said no, and felt their gazes on her back as she walked away.

She came to the bottom of Great Darkgate Street and was just about to cross when she glanced over at the opposite pavement. Only yards from her stood Will with a woman. His wife. Catrina. Maddie stepped back from the kerb. They crossed to where she stood. Will was talking to his wife. She was haggard and skinny with short hennaed hair. Suddenly Will looked up and saw Maddie, shrinking against the shop front. He didn't smile, he didn't acknowledge her, he didn't say *Catrina, meet Maddie, one of my biology pupils. My star pupil.* He just walked on with his wife towards the Prom. Maddie waited on the corner, watching them, as the boys had watched her.

"I ached for that man, Mo," Maddie says. *I still do*, she thinks to herself. "I still do," she says aloud.

She looks up at Mo, who is the only person she's ever talked to like this. Mo is just watching her with even brown eyes. *Tomorrow she'll have gone,* Maddie thinks. *Gone to find Will, but I'll feel I've lost a friend.*

"I came up here," she tells Mo. "I came up for the lambing. Owain was really busy and didn't have a great deal of time to talk to me, but I found I enjoyed just being here, out of town. I knew there was no chance Will would turn up or phone or anything and, in some ways, it was a relief. I knew he was going away with her, that ratty, skinny baggage I'd seen. At least this way I was in the countryside, learning about sheep and so on, playing with the dogs, messing about in the river as I'd done before. I caught the bus to the main road and walked down the lane to the farm. Sometimes my dad picked me up in the evenings. I think Owain knew even then I was escaping from something or someone, but he never asked. I remember one evening waiting for my dad, we were just standing by the river talking. He was smoking. He offered me a cigarette and I said no. He said how grown up I'd become. It was like the boys at school. They were all seeing me in a different light suddenly, as a woman, not a girl, and that was because of Will. It's little things, isn't it? When you've known that kind of passion, it marks you out. I don't know how my parents never noticed it."

The last Friday of the holidays. Maddie didn't go to the farm. She had schoolwork to do that she hadn't started. She stayed in bed until her parents left, then went down and ate cereal, and tried to stir herself to get her maths out. It was a warm day, a sunny day, a day to herald the coming of summer. She'd imagined that, during the summer holidays, when she and Will were both off school, they'd be able to meet up lots; suddenly, after Easter, she felt a squeeze of uncertainty.

She shoved the cereal bowl to one side and opened her textbook on the trigonometry chapter. She rummaged in her rucksack for her pens. She was uneasy. In three days' time she'd be back at school, back in biology. She hadn't heard from Will at all. The last time she'd seen him was with his wife in town.

The phone startled her. She dropped her pencil and it rolled onto the floor. She padded into the hall.

"Hello," she said.

"It's me. How have you been? I've missed you, chicken."

It was so good to hear his voice. She wanted to say something bitchy about his wife, about his silence, but then again, she also just wanted to talk to him, to be with him. He asked about the lambing and what she'd done in the holidays. She said she'd done stuff with friends, but she hadn't really, and she hadn't even needed Sian as an alibi, but she didn't want him to think she'd spent the whole holiday crying over his absence. He never mentioned what happened in Great Darkgate Street and she knew he never would.

"I can't wait to see you next week," he said. Then, "I have to go." He hung up without saying goodbye.

"I love you," Maddie said to the buzzing receiver in her hand.

Maddie's table was rickety. She wondered if the people who set up for exams had to measure the distance between tables. Will placed the exam paper face down on her desk. She thought about the previous evening, when she was supposedly at Sian's revising biology. Will had taken her up out of the town but he had no time, and they'd only been able to kiss and cuddle; then he drove her back to the railway station and she was left alone and unfulfilled.

Biology was important. She could not think about him like that, not until she'd finished.

"OK, everyone," Will said. "We'll finish at 12:03. Good luck to you all."

He wrote 12:03 on the blackboard which had been brought into the hall for the exams. Maddie turned over her paper.

Maddie watched Will leave the school hall. The lights were down and the shadows flared with green, pink, and yellow from the disco lights. It was the leavers' Prom: exams were over and so was school. She wore a straight cream cotton dress with capped sleeves. She hadn't danced with any of the boys; she'd hung around on the edge of the crowd, watching Will as he watched her in the half-light.

Sian and Dave were dancing in the middle of the floor. Maddie glanced around quickly. No one was watching. They were dancing or eating or snogging, and no one would notice her slipping through the throng to the door and the balmy June evening beyond.

The sky was a milky lilac. Maddie could hear the thump of the disco in the building behind her. She lifted her long skirt and ran to the field. She stopped at the edge of the grass, looked behind her. No one. She stepped onto the field. From where she stood she couldn't see Will. They would not have long before they were missed. She ran to the thicket and slithered down the bank behind, where Will caught her in his arms and swung her round.

"You look beautiful," he said.

"You look different," she said. "I've never seen you in a suit."

"You probably won't again. No one saw you leaving?"

"No, no one."

"We can't be long but I couldn't not kiss you tonight."

"Can't we leave now, go somewhere? It's a beautiful night."

He hesitated. "Aren't your parents picking you up?"

"Oh. Yes. Shit. What about here?"

"You'll mess up your lovely dress, and then everyone will know."

"I don't care."

"I do." Will tensed. "What was that?" he whispered.

Maddie heard it too. Voices coming closer. She ducked her head to see through the foliage. A flash of bright pink. Sian's Prom dress.

"Shit," she breathed. "Sian, Dave and the others."

"Fuck," he muttered.

Maddie slipped her arms around him under his jacket. If anyone found them there together, down the bank, hiding behind the bushes, there was no escape, there were no lies that would be believed. Will kissed her silently on the top of her head and held her to him.

Scuffling and giggling.

"Dave, stop that immediately." That was Sian.

"Aren't you coming in the bushes?" Dave jeered.

Maddie closed her eyes against Will's shirt. They should never have done this. It was far too dangerous. There was no way out from behind the bushes, and Sian and the others were only a few feet away.

"I am not," Sian squealed.

"Thought you had some fags, Dave?" one of the boys asked.

"Ah, yeah, somewhere. Here, catch."

Maddie turned her head. Through a chink in the leaves she saw Katie putting something – a jacket? – on the grass and sitting down. Cigarette smoke on the air.

"What the hell is Jenkins wearing?" Dave said, and the others laughed. "He smelt of moth balls." He threw himself down on the grass and pulled Sian on top of him. "What you doing next Friday night?"

"I don't know," she said. "Are you taking me out?"

"Rhys Merricks is having a party in the barn. Do you want to come?"

"Maybe," Sian said.

"Ah, come on, Sian, it'll be great. He said you're all invited."

"I'll come," Katie said. "He always fancied me."

"No, he didn't."

"He did. He wanted to take me to his Prom last year, but I was too young. So there."

"No way. He'd never have taken you. He preferred Maddie."

"Where is Maddie?" Sian wondered, as though she'd only just realised Maddie wasn't there.

Will stroked Maddie's hair. *I didn't like Rhys Merricks* she wanted to say.

"I haven't seen her for ages." One of the other boys. "She must be inside."

"Sian, ask her to come next weekend," Dave said.

"She won't be interested in Rhys," Sian said. "She's got a boyfriend at the university. He's called Stephen."

"You met him, Sian?" asked Katie.

"Well, no, but she asks me to cover for her. You know what her parents are like."

Maddie felt her cheeks flame. She felt disloyal to her parents and to Will and to herself, and she was terrified that, at any moment, she would find she could no longer stand in silence, hardly breathing.

"Don't believe you," Dave said.

"Nor me," said his friend.

"I asked her to show me his photo, but she never did," Sian said thoughtfully. "But if she hasn't got a boyfriend, why does she want me to cover for her?"

"I just meant he wasn't at the uni," said Dave's friend.

"So who is he then?"

"You mean you don't know? Were you asleep in biology, then? You sat next to her, for fuck's sake."

"Someone in biology? Dave, stop that, you'll tear this dress."

"It's Mr Richards. Didn't you see the way they went on? How he looked at her and how she looked at him? They were always sneaking about and saying things. Do you know what they were saying?"

"What were they saying?" Katie asked.

"Exactly. They never let anyone hear them. I tell you, that's why she needs you to lie for her, Sian."

"Oh, don't be so stupid. Maddie would never do that. I know she likes him, but she wouldn't be that daft. Neither would he. I'm going in. It's cold."

"He's got a point," said Dave. "Well, bugger me. Maddie and Richards."

"Don't you dare go spreading that rumour, Dave."

"All right then, where is she? Where is Maddie? I bet we'll go back in there and he'll have disappeared too."

They got up, the girls brushing grass from their dresses.

"It's not true," Sian kept saying. "She wouldn't do that. I mean, Maddie? She just wouldn't."

Dave chucked the empty cigarette packet into the bushes. Maddie watched them walk away. Dave had his arm around Sian. Katie was tugging on her jacket.

"We can't both go back inside," Will said.

"Let's leave. You can drop me home early."

"No," he said. "Not today. Not after that. You go in. Say you felt sick or something."

"What about you?"

"I'll go now."

"I don't like that cretin Merricks."

"What cretin?" Will asked distractedly.

"The one having the party. He was the year above us. Before you came–"

"Chicken, I don't give a shit about some guy and his party. I just want to get us out of these bushes before anyone else comes. Now go back to the hall."

"When will I see you?"

"I'll call you at home."

"Give me a kiss."

He kissed her but she knew his eyes were on some point above her head. He let her go and climbed up the bank. She scrambled up after him. She trod on the hem of her dress. She realised she was cold from standing still so long, and from the fear of being discovered in Will's arms. She ran back to the school. The sky had darkened to twilight. The disco noise swelled as she opened the door. Her bare arms fizzed with the sudden warmth. She took a glass of juice from the drinks table. Someone prodded her in the back.

"Where've you been?" It was Dave.

"Sorry, I felt a bit queasy."

"Ah. Right," he said, then, "Don't suppose you've seen Richards, have you?"

"Richards?"

"*Mr* Richards."

"He's here somewhere," Maddie said.

Maddie shivers, recalling the cool wind on her arms, the smell of cigarette smoke through the leaves, and the thick taste of fear in her mouth. She sees again the sky darkening to dusk. Shadow time. Moth time. Now over twenty years ago, but she can remember it all.

"Until then," she says, "I hadn't really considered the possibility of other people finding out. I was shocked that they'd seen how we were in biology. I didn't think anyone would have known. We were so discreet. At least, I thought we were."

"Kids can be pretty sharp," Mo says.

"And I was in my own world. I thought I was untouchable…that night in the bushes I felt real fear. If they'd found us down there, they'd never have believed it if we'd denied it. I suddenly realised as I stood there with him that someone might work things out and then I had to ask myself: if that happened what would Will do?"

Maddie stands at the front window, gazing down at the butterfly house and the stream. If it weren't for Will, she would never have all this. She's told Mo that, and it's true. She loves her butterflies and her home. She loves the valley and the river. She loves Vanessa and she loved Owain, but she thinks of Will every day.

"I think about him every day," she says, and her voice is raw, and she can feel the sting of tears again.

"Where did Owain fit in?" Mo asks at last. "You'd been to see him at Easter."

"He was my friend." Maddie turns around. "He was kind to me. Sometimes I had to escape out of my life and I'd come and see him. He didn't ask me awkward questions. If I went down to the river and sat on the bank and cried, he didn't embarrass me. He didn't tell my parents. I knew I could trust him with anything if I had to."

"Did Will make you cry a lot?"

"Not Will, not until…it was the whole thing. I wanted to share my life with him and he was married. When school broke up, we met up and went off in the car: the Happy Valley again, into the hills. But never enough, only odd days. I knew the hourglass had been upended. It was upended the night of the Prom, and the sand could only flow one way."

No, Moth thinks. It was upended long before then. It was upended the day Maddie and Will first kissed in the biology room. She watches Maddie come back to the table and sit down, worrying away at a scrap of tissue in her hands. Moth tries to see beyond Maddie to the young girl she was once, bursting with a passion she could not control.

It's a job, an assignment, to find Will Richards and bring him back to Maddie, but already it's gone far beyond that. Moth knows the words and emotions spilling out of Maddie have never been spoken, never been shared, before. It's like Moth is the first person to uncover a mosaic, but when she brushes away the earth and dust, she finds it is broken and damaged, wounded by time.

A hot Sunday in August. Maddie's parents were in the garden. She hesitated by the phone again. It was Will's birthday. She hadn't seen him at all the previous week. She wanted to ring him, but she didn't dare. Her parents could come in at any moment; Catrina could answer the phone. Worse still, there might be no answer and she would know they were out somewhere, doing something, just the two of them, spending his birthday together.

The next day Will phoned her at home and told her he would collect her from the end of her road on Tuesday morning at ten.

"We'll have a field trip," he said. "I'll get a picnic on the way."

"What sort of field trip?" she asked.

"It's a surprise."

He was late. She waited at the end of the road. It was another hot blue day, and she couldn't wear a hood. She hopped from one foot to the other. Had something happened? Had Catrina stopped him coming out? Had she overheard him on the phone? Maddie knew he sometimes used a phone box near his house and sometimes he called her from home. *I take the phone up to my room*, he'd said, and Maddie imagined him lying on that bed, with her voice in his ear, and smiled and cried for a day that had gone and would never come back.

Nearly quarter past ten. Was he trying to call her at home? Maddie took a few steps back towards her house, stopped, looked back. His car was coming, and she exhaled in relief.

"I'm sorry, chicken," Will said. "I was late leaving home and I had to go shopping." He gestured to a couple of bags on the back seat.

"It's been so long," Maddie said, and took his hand from the gear stick.

"I know, I'm sorry."

She didn't ask if he'd had a good birthday. She didn't want to know what he did with his wife, what present she'd given him. Instead she just said, "I have your present here. I'll give it to you when we get there. Where are we going?"

"Back to Claerwen," he said.

Back to Claerwen. Almost a year later, and she was going to Claerwen with him. Not in a school bus this time with Sian and Dave and that lot, just her and him in his car, with a bottle of wine on the back seat and his birthday gift on her knees.

"Will there be sundews?"

"There might be," he said, then, "but we won't have time to go all the way to the head of the lake. I would love to take you there but we can't do it today."

Maddie didn't answer. She didn't know if he was referring to her or to himself but, between them, they would never have enough time to find the sundews. *We should go there for a few days*, she wanted to say, *find somewhere to stay*, but she knew he would tell her he would not be able to, and she couldn't see how she could do it either. She cast aside the thought before it dragged her down and tears stung in her eyes. They might not make it all round the long, jagged reservoir, but it was a hot and sunny day, and they'd left town behind them, and no one could chase them now.

"Red kites," she said, watching a few wheeling dark shapes over the mountainside.

"The source of the Severn is up there," Will said. "And the Wye."

"Have you found them?"

"Yes. I went years ago."

"On your own?"

"With some friends from university. It was really wet and muddy."

He's done so much, Maddie thought. *He's lived a whole life before he met me. This time last year, we didn't know the other even existed.*

The road to Elan was busy with holiday traffic. There was no water gushing over Caban Coch. The sun brightened the dark water of the lake. At Garreg Dhu the road split, and they crossed the arched bridge over the submerged dam.

"It's a different feel once you cross the bridge, isn't it?" Will asked. "Elan's great, but Claerwen…it's something else isn't it?"

"It's where–" Maddie started and stopped. *Where I fell in love with you,* she thought.

"Where what?"

"Nothing," she said, and he glanced at her quickly, then back to the road, where the sheep jumped out from behind wire fences, and the Claerwen River cascaded over mossy stones.

He went straight up the steep road to the top of the dam. There were several other cars parked under the craggy cliff. People were walking along the dam, leaning over, as Maddie had once leaned, to look down the rugged stone face or into the sparkling water. He turned off the engine and kissed her, and she handed him his birthday present. She noticed how he carefully kept the red paper and silver ribbon, balling it all together to throw away later. She'd got him a new book on British moths with beautiful colour photographs. She wanted to write something inside it, but she knew she could not.

"I know you know them all anyway," she said, "but the pictures are so lovely."

"Thank you," he said.

He put the book on the back seat and shoved the shopping into his rucksack. He handed her a rug to carry, and a couple of tatty volumes on wild flowers. It was so different from the last time they'd been here. Then the mist and rain wreathed the lake and the mountains. Today the sky was hard and bright, and the water glinted. The hillsides were green and gold. A red kite swooped over Maddie's head only a few feet above her; she could see its russet body and the white bands beneath its wings.

"Come on," Will said, and took her hand.

The water was low in the reservoir, revealing gritty screes on the banks. Foxgloves grew along the high-water mark, pushing through the pebbles and dried weed.

"We're not going up here?" Maddie gestured to the dirt track and the foxgloves.

"It'll be quieter on the other side," Will said. "There's no road."

They walked across the giant dam. Maddie ran up the steps to the high parapet and gazed down into the indigo water, as she had done last time. Looking across the reservoir, she could follow the faint line of the track, hugging the ins and outs of the flooded valley.

On the far side of the dam was a five-barred gate, padlocked and rusty, and a stile precariously hanging over the water. Will chucked the rucksack across and swung himself over the gate. Maddie handed him the rug and the books and climbed up. The spindly gate trembled as she jumped down beside him, and the padlock jangled.

They were right on the edge of the lake here. Below the surface – a foot down, or maybe ten, Maddie couldn't tell – was a flat, amber coloured rock. She could feel the cold rising off the water. A fritillary of some kind fluttered and swooped away from the straggly foxgloves.

"It's so quiet," Maddie said.

She thought, if she listened hard enough, she would hear the water: not the tiny splashes of fish, or ripples breaking against the back of the dam, but the essence of it, its breathing, its existence.

Will started along the track. After a few yards it narrowed and all but disappeared. Maddie followed him as he climbed the shoulder of land. Sheep raised their heads and regarded them with topaz eyes. As they climbed, the lake dropped away, and Maddie could see its broken shape, the exposed gravel, and the bright flowers. Even the dam seemed far away and small. A Harrier jet roared out of nowhere, slicing the sky with its dark blade. The sound growled away into the hills like remembered thunder.

"How about here?" Will said, and she threw the rug down and flattened it onto the bumpy grass. He tumbled her to the ground and held her down. "No one will hear you scream," he said into her hair and kissed her all over her face.

Later, they lay on the rug, sticky with fruit and chocolate and wine and sex.

"Where are the sundews, then?" she asked, turning to him.

"A long way up there." He pointed towards the distant tip of the lake.

Somewhere in those distant gold hills were the sundews, tiny red damp mouths lifted to the sky. Maddie sat up and reached for her camera.

"I want a picture of you."

"No," he said.

"Go on, just one to remember today by."

As she said it, the words sounded ominous, shadows across the day.

"I hate photos," he said, fiddling with his shirt to cover the bright flare of sunburn on his chest. As he looked up Maddie clicked the shutter.

"Oh, Maddie, I said no," he said.

"Thank you," she said, and kissed him.

He lay down on the rug with his arm over his face. Maddie drank the last of the wine from the bottle. It was red, bitter, and made her thirsty. She watched the light shifting on the lake. A red kite soared high overhead. Sheep called across the hillsides.

She looked down at Will. He seemed to be sleeping. She wanted to move his arm, so she could see him, and because it looked so uncomfortable, but she didn't want to wake him. Waking him meant packing up the rug and the empty bottle, and stumbling back down the hill to the reservoir and the five-barred gate, the dam and the car, and she didn't want that. Not yet.

She knelt up to photograph the lake, and the faraway hills where the sundews grew, then lay down beside him, careful not to wake him. She didn't care if she fell asleep too. She didn't care if they slept until evening. She closed her eyes, but she didn't sleep; she listened to the sounds of the hills and of Will's breathing. She tugged absently at a clump of leaves, brought her hand to her nose to smell the sharp scent on her skin. Thyme. She picked a strand and twiddled it between her fingers.

Will started awake. Maddie reached out to him but he sat up stiffly, ignoring her.

"Jesus, look at the fucking time," he said, twisting his watch on his wrist. "You shouldn't have let me sleep."

"What's wrong with sleeping?" Maddie asked.

Will grabbed the remains of the picnic and stuffed it in his rucksack. He tossed her shoes at her.

"Come on, we need to get going."

"It's only half four," she said.

"Your parents will be home soon."

"It doesn't matter. I'll say I was with Sian."

"It's an hour's drive. Come on." He grabbed the rug and thrust it at her.

She stumbled to her feet and gathered it up. Will was already striding down the hillside. Maddie shivered. A film of cloud had streaked over the sun, dappling the water and grass with shadows. She ran to catch up with him, the rug trailing in her arms and catching around her feet.

The water lapped at the gravel. A bee whirred around the foxgloves. Maddie could hear a car engine from somewhere, and voices of people on the dam. Everyday life was crowding closer. Will threw the rucksack over the gate and vaulted over. He didn't wait to make sure she got over all right. She paused a moment, straddling the gate, gazing into the dark water to the amber coloured rock beneath the surface.

"There's no rush," she said, as they reached the road over the dam.

"Your parents," he said shortly. "They mustn't know about today."

"They won't," Maddie said, then fell silent, trying to match his long stride.

She kept her head down, did not look up at the other people loitering on the dam. A dog barked from somewhere – the farm below maybe? – and another Harrier jet shot across the sky, growling away behind the hills. Will opened the boot and threw the rucksack in.

"I'd like a drink." Maddie said.

He handed her a water bottle. "Keep it with you," he said, getting in behind the wheel.

Suddenly he reached round, grabbed the moth book and the birthday wrapping paper, and flung open the door again. Maddie twisted round and watched him throwing them into the boot as well.

He roared down the narrow road. Maddie gazed out at the grass, the sheep, the twisted trees, through a film of tears. Their perfect day was spoilt, ruined, and she didn't know why. The road wound on through the woodland and then over the bridge at Garreg Ddu.

He hesitated at the junction. "We'll go this way," he said, wrenching the wheel to the left. "It's quicker."

The road ran along the edge of Garreg Ddu reservoir. Will came up hard behind another car travelling slowly through the bends.

"Move it, move it," he muttered.

The road rose again to the Pen y Garreg dam with its green-topped tower in the centre. The car ahead lurched unsteadily into the viewing area and Will roared on. Maddie didn't know what to say. Now she just wanted to get home, even though she would have the problem of her parents when she got there.

They reached the final dam, the gracious curve of Craig Goch. The reservoir blurred into muddy marshland as the road twisted away. Will took the mountain pass for Devil's Bridge and Aberystwyth.

Maddie shifted her feet. She'd pulled her socks on too fast and one had twisted and was uncomfortable. She was thirsty but her bladder was swollen. Her eyes felt gritty. She fiddled with the twig of wild thyme, letting the scent stain her fingers.

The way was steep and narrow and Will drove recklessly, forcing past cars coming the other way. He hung on the back of a car ahead until finally it turned off at Cwmystwyth.

"For Christ's sake," she said at last. "What the hell's the matter with you?"

"We're late," he said. "We're very late. We should have left no later than half three."

"It doesn't matter," Maddie said again.

"Will you stop saying that? It may not matter to you, but it does to me."

"It's nothing to do with me, is it? It's you. You're the one who wants to rush back. I thought this was our special day."

"You shouldn't have let me sleep."

"You never said anything about time. You never said you had to leave by half three. What's so urgent anyway?"

"Nothing."

"Something's urgent," she said, and knew she shouldn't force it, but he'd been so lovely until he woke up as the sun was sliding down the sky.

"All right, you want to know. I have to get back because I'm going out tonight."

"Going out?" she said.

"Yes, with Catrina. We're meeting friends for dinner in Machynlleth."

"Tonight?"

"Yes, tonight. Late birthday and all that, and we have to be there by half seven, and I have to get washed and changed and I'm really, really late and I am going to be in such shit."

"It's not my fault!" Maddie cried. "You didn't tell me you had to get back. You said it was going to be a special day for us."

"Yes, well, it could have been, if we'd left in time."

How could it be? Maddie thought. How could it be a special day if he was rushing home to go out with his wife? It was never really her day, Maddie's day. She pocketed the thyme. The sun made her eyes ache. Or maybe she was about to cry.

"I'll have to drop you somewhere." he said. "I can't go right into town now. I'm sorry."

"Where?" she asked.

Will indicated and swung into the kerb. "Here," he said. "Sorry, you'll have to walk from here."

She unclicked her seat belt, turned to him to speak.

"Maddie, please, just get out," he said, his eyes on the driving mirror. "I have to go."

She opened the door and got out. Her jeans were sticky. The twisted sock hurt under her foot. She threw the water bottle onto the passenger seat and slammed the door. She hoped he might reach over and open it again, or wind down his window and call to her, but he swerved out into the traffic, without a wave. She stood there, watching his car shoot away from her. She could smell the thyme on her fingers. She started walking towards home. She couldn't even be bothered to rehearse what she would say to her parents.

She put the key in the lock and opened the front door as quietly as possible. The TV was on. She could smell cooking: something with tomatoes and garlic.

"Where have you been?" her mother demanded.

"With Sian. Sorry I'm late." She started towards the stairs.

"Why didn't you leave us a note? Look at you, what's happened? Have you fallen out with Sian?"

"I'm fine."

"You're not fine at all. I thought you were going to eat with them?"

"Eat with them?"

"With Sian and Dave. That is where you've been, isn't it? I called Sian's mother. She said they were getting the train to Borth this afternoon, and going to get fish and chips… I thought you were with them…you haven't been to Borth, have you?"

"I need to go upstairs. I need a bath."

"Maddie, where have you been?"

"Nowhere," she yelled stamping upstairs. "Nowhere, nothing, nothing matters."

Wednesday morning. Maddie's parents went to work. For a few moments she thought her mother wasn't going to leave her.

"I'll ring you at lunch time, Maddie." Her mother stood in the bedroom doorway. Maddie was huddled under the quilt, but she felt hot and sweaty. Her eyes were stinging from crying most of the night.

"You don't have to."

"I will. Please be in, Maddie."

"I'll be here."

Of course, she would. She wasn't going to be with Will. He would rather go out with his wife than call her. When her mother rang at lunchtime she answered the phone, said she was fine, that she'd eaten a sandwich. She hadn't; the thought of food made her nauseous.

On Thursday lunchtime, the phone went again. Maddie's mother hadn't said anything about ringing, but Maddie guessed it would be her, checking up again.

"Chicken, it's me," Will said.

"Will," she said and she crumpled down on the floor because she felt queasy suddenly.

"Can you talk?"

"Yes," she said.

"I'm really sorry. I was a bastard the other day. It wasn't your fault. I was under such pressure to get back. I should have taken you out another day. I just wanted to see you so much."

"It doesn't matter," she lied, and it felt as though the stress and pain of the last day and a half was pouring, flooding, out of her, staining the carpet, leaving her lighter, buoyant.

"Can you get away for an hour? I could pick you up at two."

"Yes," she said.

He collected her from the end of her road. He didn't kiss her but he took her hand and squeezed it, and she gripped his fingers until he let go to change gear. He drove out of town, through Clarach to Borth, the way he had the first time they'd escaped together. The main street of Borth was crowded with tourists. Bright buckets and fishing nets hung outside the shops; there were ice-cream signs and menu boards on the narrow pavement.

"Did you enjoy the meal?" Maddie asked at last.

"No," he said. "I was so late and Catrina was going crazy and I would have much preferred to be with you."

Maddie didn't answer.

"It's true," he said taking the bumpy lane through the dunes to Ynyslas. "I know you might not believe it, but it's true. I didn't want to go, but I had to. I was thinking about you the whole time."

The road led directly onto the sands. Cars were parked in a crescent in front of the dunes. Across the wide estuary was the pastel-painted terrace of houses on Aberdyfi's seafront: pink, lemon, blue, green, lavender. Somewhere on the opposite shore she had stood on a freezing winter day and looked over to these pale dunes and, beyond them, to the jumble of Borth, rising to its knobbly knoll, and Will bit her ear and said he wanted to make love to her.

He turned off the engine, twisted around to her and took her hands.

"I am sorry, Maddie. I really am."

"OK," she said.

"It was such a wonderful day until then. I ruined it."

Maddie smiled but she knew it was a wobbly smile.

Will looked out of the windscreen to where some kids were running with a kite on the sand flats.

"We do need to be careful," he said. "You know what I mean. The Prom. You're doing A-level biology. So's Dave."

"I can deal with Dave. He's an idiot."

"Not such an idiot."

"He might not get the grade," Maddie said. "We'll see tomorrow when the results come out. Will you be there?"

"No," Will said. "You'll do well. We must be careful. We mustn't talk at school. Not when anyone else can hear."

"All right," she said.

"Would you like to go out next week? How about Wednesday?"

"Definitely."

"We could go up to Nant y Moch."

"I'd love to," she said.

"OK. Wednesday then. I'll pick you up about ten thirty from your road. If there's any problem or change of plan, I'll call you. If you can't make it, I'll understand. I won't ring you unless there is a problem."

A problem. Catrina.

"I'll make it," Maddie said.

It was Thursday. Almost a week until she would see him again. He kissed her, slid his hand inside her shirt and her body responded with a jump; unfulfilled, it became a deep ache.

"I should stop," he said, drawing away. "It's too public here."

Maddie fumbled to do up her shirt, cursing the tourists, the dog-walkers, the kids with their kite.

"It will be quiet at Nant y Moch," he said, and fired the engine. "I'll take you back."

They drove back through Borth, along the cluttered main street, then up the cliff road to Clarach. The sun glinted on the sea, and the horizon was hazy. In a few moments they were back in town again.

"Drop me at the station," Maddie said. "I can walk home."

"Good luck for tomorrow," Will said. "I know you'll do fantastically well."

He kissed her again and she opened the door and scrambled out. She straightened her shirt and saw she'd buttoned it up wrongly. A woman with hefty carrier bags was looking at her strangely, almost angrily. Maddie met her eyes, wanted to stick out her tongue or give her the finger. The woman looked away and Maddie went past her, smiling to herself and gradually the ache inside her subsided.

"He wasn't there that Friday when we got our exam results," Maddie explains to Mo. "I wanted to see him, of course I did, and part of me hoped he'd surprise me and be there, but he wasn't. It was for the best really. My mother came too and all the other kids were there. I did well. I was very pleased with my results. So were my parents. I think they started to forgive me for what they saw as my awful behaviour earlier in the week."

Maddie woke the following Tuesday at half seven. She could smell toast. Her father was talking downstairs, her mother replied quietly, her father again saying *go on, go back to bed.* Then footsteps on the stairs. Maddie was alert. Her mother was ill. She was going back to bed. If she was still ill on Wednesday, would Maddie be able to get away to go to Nant y Moch?

A few moments later her father banged on her half-closed bedroom door.

"Maddie."

"I'm awake."

He opened the door and hovered in the doorway, already looking hot in his work clothes.

"Your mum's got a migraine," he said. "I've told her to take the day off and go back to bed. You can keep an eye on her, can't you? I'll ring up at lunchtime to see how she is."

When he'd gone, Maddie curled on her side and stared at the wall. She was starting to dislike herself. She should be concerned that her mother was ill, but all she could think about was how she could get away to see Will the next day. She was deceiving her parents, lying to them every day. She wished she could tell them about Will, that everything could be open. She smiled crookedly. What would they find the worst thing? That Will was her teacher, his age, that he was married? She rolled onto her back. It was useless. She could never tell them and, because she could never tell them, she would have to continue as she'd started, and make sure they never knew.

She slept awhile and woke a couple of hours later, hot under the duvet. She went out onto the landing. Her mother's door was shut. She had a shower and went down to get a drink. The post had been. She collected the mail – nothing for her, there never was – and dumped it on the table. *This time tomorrow I will be with him,* she thought. About twelve her mother came down in her nightshirt and made some more tea.

"Are you better?" Maddie asked.

"A bit, yes," her mother said. "I'll go up and have a wash, then we can have some lunch."

Maddie rummaged in the fridge for salad and cheese while her mother went upstairs. She heard the whoosh of the shower, her mother's feet padding across the landing.

The phone rang in the hall. It could be Will, changing the time he could pick her up. Maddie shot out of the kitchen; her mother came down the stairs. They almost collided at the phone. Her mother picked it up and gave their number.

"Yes? No, I'm sorry. Goodbye."

She clicked the phone off. "Were you expecting a call?"

"Uh, no," Maddie said. "Well, only Dad. He said he'd ring you."

"That was a man. He said it was a wrong number."

"It must have been then."

"Maddie, is there something you want to tell me?"

"No," Maddie said, and went back into the kitchen.

The phone rang again. Her mother still had the receiver in her hand; she answered.

"Yes, a bit better, thanks. Going to have lunch with Maddie now."

Maddie poured herself some juice. Will had phoned. He'd phoned for a reason. Now he wouldn't phone again. Anything might have happened. He might be ill. She didn't know what to do. She chucked some salad into a bowl and cut some cheese. Her mother was still talking. *Her migraine can't be that bad,* Maddie thought sourly, taking her plate to the table.

"Are you going to work this afternoon?" she asked when her mother came in.

"Do you want to get rid of me?"

"No, I just thought if you were better…"

"Sorry if my headache has inconvenienced you."

"It hasn't," Maddie said. "I was only asking."

"What's going on?" her mother asked. "Are you…I mean, do you have a boyfriend?"

"Boyfriend? No thanks." Maddie ate tomato and looked out of the window.

"It's just you were so upset last week, that day when you were late, and I think you were expecting a call today."

"Last week was…" Maddie shrugged. "Just me being silly."

"You can talk to me," her mother said.

I wish I could: Maddie almost said it aloud. She wanted to throw herself into her mother's arms and cry and cry. The pain of her love for Will was too much, too heavy. If she could only tell someone, if she could just hear them say *everything will be all right*, it might ease a little. If she knew she wasn't alone.

"There's nothing to say," Maddie said. "Really."

The next day she waited at the end of the road as she'd arranged with Will. It was cooler and there had been an early shower. The sky was a pale grey. Somehow it all felt ominous. He didn't come. She checked the time. He was ten minutes late. Fifteen. Twenty. After she'd stood there for half an hour she knew he wasn't coming. That was why he'd tried to call her. If she didn't matter to him, he would just not have turned up. She must matter. He had wanted to explain to her. He probably wanted to suggest another day. She started back towards her house, looking over her shoulder just in case. Nothing.

Something was wrong. Maddie dug out the scrap of paper from her bedside drawer with Will's address and phone number on it. She unfolded it, took it to the phone. She dialled the first few numbers then hung up. She couldn't do this. Yes, she could. If he couldn't talk, he could pretend she was a wrong number. This time she dialled the whole number. It rang out. A woman answered. A woman with a Liverpool accent.

"Could I speak to Mr Richards please?" Maddie said. "It's Maddie. I'm from school."

"From school?" Cartrina repeated.

"Er, yes, one of his A-level students."

"It's not term time. Can't it wait?"

"No, I need to speak to him."

I should never have done this, Maddie thought, as she heard Catrina calling for Will. She wondered if he were upstairs in his den, and if he were thinking of her and wishing he were at Nant y Moch with her.

"Yes, hello," he said abruptly.

"It's Maddie," she said quietly.

"Yes, Catrina said. Why do you want to speak to me?"

"Is everything all right? When you didn't come I was–"

"I can't talk about this right now," he interrupted her, coldly, angrily. "I'll see you at school and we can talk about it, OK? Bye now."

The line went dead.

Maddie would have done anything – anything except never see Will again – to lose those few moments. It was the worst, stupidest thing she could ever have done. She knew when he tried to call her that he couldn't meet her; she should have known the reason he couldn't meet her was Catrina.

He didn't call her again at home that holiday. Once when her parents were out, she picked up the phone and wondered crazily about ringing him again at home. She was so desperate to hear his voice, know that he wasn't still angry with her, because he hadn't been acting for the sake of his wife, Maddie knew that. He was furious that she'd phoned his house. Now she dreaded going back to school.

On the first morning of term, she was given her timetable. The first lesson was biology with Will. She felt sick. She walked to the lab with Dave. The door was open. They followed the rest of the class in. It was a small group now. Maddie and Dave sat together. Maddie felt even more sick. Where was Will? At last he came in. He looked thinner and stressed. Maddie ached to put her arms around him.

"Sorry I'm late," he said. "OK, we'll go through the A-level syllabus."

"He's in a right snot today," Dave muttered to Maddie a few moments later. "Can't you give him one before the next lesson?"

"Shut the fuck up," she hissed at him.

"Maddie, Dave, if you want to talk, go to the common room."

Maddie gasped. Will had never spoken to her like that before. Even Dave looked startled. She felt a hard lump in her throat.

"Jesus," Dave said.

Maddie watched the second hand miserably circling the clock, nibbling away the minutes. At the end of the lesson she packed up her stuff slowly. Dave dashed out of the room to meet his pals for a cigarette. Maddie waited until everyone else had left. Will was cleaning the blackboard; his lovely spiky writing dissolved into puffs of chalk dust. He turned. They were alone. Maddie glanced at the door, walked over to him.

"Will."

"What the hell were you playing at?" he said quietly. "Don't you ever do that again."

"I'm sorry," she said and her voice was thin. "I'm really sorry."

"I'll pick you up at the station after school," he said. "Go straight there." He didn't smile. He didn't even look at her.

"Will, what's–"

He strode away from her to the door. She stood alone in the room.

Maddie felt sick all day. She couldn't eat at lunchtime. She couldn't concentrate in geography or chemistry. By the time she arrived at the station she was shaky with fear and sickness. He arrived immediately. She opened the door.

"Where are we going?" she asked, and hoped her voice didn't shake.

Will kept both hands on the wheel. When he changed gear, she slid her hand over his; he shook free of her and grasped the wheel again. She stared out of the window.

"I said I'm sorry," she said at last.

"We have to talk about this," he said.

"No," she whispered. "I won't ring you again. I'm sorry."

He took the coast road for Clarach and Borth again. Maddie didn't dare break the silence. As they left Borth behind and passed the golf links on the seaward side Will sighed heavily.

"I can't do this anymore, chicken."

"Do what?" she said, but she knew, she'd known since the terrible day when she called him at home.

"I can't see you any more. I'm really sorry. "

"I'll be really careful. No one will ever know."

He braked abruptly on the sands at Ynyslas. Across the estuary was Aberdyfi, mocking her, reminding her of a beautiful day, long gone.

"They already know," he said. "Your friends know. My wife knows."

"You wife knows?" Maddie cried. "How?"

"Because you fucking rang her up, that's why."

"She can't know because of that."

"It only confirmed what she already knew. I must have been stupid thinking I could do this. Someone saw us at the railway station when I dropped you off. Someone saw us kissing."

"Who?" Maddie felt a slimy sensation in her stomach.

"Our neighbour. Catrina found the wrapping paper in the car boot, you know, from the moth book."

A discarded chrysalis.

"She knew I was always going off apparently on my own. Sometimes I called you from the house and she was downstairs. Oh fuck, it's all such a fucking mess. I should never have started this."

"You wanted to," Maddie choked.

"Yes," he said. "I did, but I don't now. I just can't."

"I love you," she said.

"Maddie, don't."

"I don't care about your wife. I'm not asking you to leave her. I just want to be with you. Will, please."

"I'm sorry," he said. "It was wonderful, lovely. You've no idea."

"Then it can be again."

"I'm married. I'm your teacher. I'm too old for you. It's all crazy. Great fun, but crazy, and it has to end now." He fired the ignition.

"Do you want a break for a couple of weeks?" Maddie asked.

"I don't want a break," Will shouted, as they bumped back up the track through the dunes. "I want this to end. It has to end. I have to repair the damage with Catrina. She's not well. I haven't treated her kindly. I have to give her my time now. I know it'll be hard at school. It'll be hard for both of us, but we'll just have to cope with it. It's only two years."

Two years. Two years of being near him and wanting him and loving him.

"You're a lovely girl," he said. "One day you'll meet–"

"Just shut the fuck up," she spat.

Maddie's crying again. She stumbles up from the table and tears off more sheets of kitchen paper.

"I had to go home that evening to my parents and pretend everything was OK," she tells Mo. "It was one of the hardest things I've ever had to do, but their fussing would have been worse. I didn't know what to do. I couldn't bear two years of being at school with him and not having him. Then I thought he would miss me and want me back, then I thought he wouldn't. I didn't sleep that night. I looked terrible in the morning. I thought I was going to throw up."

"Did you see him at school the next day?"

"Only at a distance on the corridor. We didn't have biology until the last period. After lunch was a free period. I walked out and got the bus to Owain's. To here. I hardly knew what I was doing, where I was going. I just had to get away. I couldn't face him in class."

"Owain must have known something was wrong."

"He did. When I arrived, he stopped what he was doing and brought me in – into this room, this kitchen – and made me tea and gave me a shot of whisky and asked me what was the matter. He said he wouldn't tell my parents, but he could see I was distraught, and I could tell him."

"Did you?"

"I had to tell someone. I just had to. I think it would have killed me if I hadn't. I told him I'd been in love with Will for a year and that we'd been together since Christmas. I told him Will was my teacher and married. I told him Catrina had found out and what Will had said to me at Ynyslas."

"What did he say?"

"He asked what Will thought of me, and that was hard. I thought he loved me, but if he loved me, surely he would never have left me?" She smiles at Mo. "I know now it's always more complicated than that."

"It is," Mo says quietly.

"I told him my parents must never know and he agreed."

"What did he think?"

"He was sorry for me. He was kind. He didn't give me advice. It was enough just to tell him, just to share it with another human being. I knew he was fond of me, and I knew he wouldn't judge me. He didn't, but he said I would have to face Will sooner or later at school, and that I mustn't miss any more biology. So the next day I went to biology. Will was in a foul mood again. I tried to be nice and friendly, hoping he would realise how much he would miss me, but he didn't respond. I didn't wait for him at the end; I left with Dave. Dave asked if we'd had a tiff, and I started crying, and he seemed really shocked, like something that had once been a bit of a joke was something serious, and he said *I'm sorry Maddie, I was only joking, I didn't know you liked him that much*, and I said I didn't, I was just being silly. So Dave started going on about Rhys Merricks, the guy who had the party, and how he liked me, and I just didn't have the energy to tell him to shut up. I didn't want anyone else. If I couldn't have Will, I'd just die a lonely old spinster. I didn't want anyone else to touch me."

Mr Jenkins stood in front of the board in the biology lab. Behind him were the dusty remains of Will's scribbles. Maddie slid onto her stool, put her bag on the workbench and hugged it to her. Something was wrong.

"Mr Richards can't come in today," Mr Jenkins said. "So you've got me. I know that means a lot of you have me twice today. I'm sorry about that. Mr Richards says you're doing homeostasis, is that right?"

A few grunts of assent.

"What's the matter with him?" Dave asked Maddie.

She shrugged, dragged her books and pens out.

"Is Mr Richards ill, sir?" Dave asked.

Maddie looked up. Was he ill? Was he distraught at how he had treated her? Had he found another girl, younger, perhaps from the year below, and told her to skive off for a day and… She choked aloud. No, not that. He wouldn't. He loved her.

"No, he's not ill," Mr Jenkins said, turning and wiping down the board.

That evening Maddie lay on her bed. Downstairs her parents were talking. The TV was on: probably the news. Something was wrong with Will. It was something to do with her, she knew it. He couldn't stand the thought of seeing her, he hated himself for how he had behaved, he loved her and wanted her back and couldn't bear to be near her in case she refused him. As if she would.

Her mother called up to her to come and eat. She swung her legs to the floor and the room tilted. She felt sick. Her pulse was skipping. She just knew something awful was happening.

She went downstairs and sat at the table. Her mother gave her a plate of chicken and potatoes and salad. The meat glistened and looked greasy. Chicken. *I can't do this anymore, chicken*. She didn't think she could eat it. The potatoes were hard in her throat. Her parents asked her what she wanted to do for her birthday. Did she want to go out for a meal? Did she want to do something with Sian and Dave? Did she want to invite anyone else? her mother asked pointedly.

"I don't want to do anything," Maddie said.

Her mother tried to press her on what was making her so unhappy.

"It's nothing." Maddie dropped her knife and fork onto the congealed heap of potatoes.

"Did you hear the local news?" her father asked her mother, as he helped himself to more chicken.

"Hardly. I was getting the dinner."

"Some woman tried to kill herself this morning. She walked into the sea."

"What, here in Aber?"

"Yes," he said.

"What on earth makes someone want to do that?"

"She must have been very depressed," he suggested. "Or unbalanced."

"Who was it?" Maddie asked suddenly.

"They didn't say," her father said. "They wouldn't give details like that."

"This morning? It happened this morning?"

"Yes, very early. They said her husband didn't know she'd left the house. Someone saw her and got her out."

If only they hadn't. It was Catrina. Maddie knew something was very wrong. Will wasn't at school. Mr Jenkins said he wasn't ill, but wouldn't answer any questions about why he wasn't there, and a crazy woman walked into the sea. *If only she'd kept on walking,* Maddie thought. If only she'd walked and walked until the water picked her up and flooded her throat and lungs. If only she were dead.

"Yes, it was Catrina," Maddie says. "Things like that don't stay a secret. By the next day people were talking about it. We had a history teacher look after us in biology. Mr Powell. He came to Elan with us that first day." She stops talking, watches Mo, waiting for judgement in her eyes, but there is none. "I wanted her dead," Maddie says. "She wanted to die, and I wanted her to die, but someone saved her."

"Did Will come back to school?"

"I never saw him again. They got a supply teacher in. A woman. They said Will's wife was unwell, but we all knew. The supply teacher was supposed to be covering for him until half term. Half term! It was so far away. I had the most miserable birthday ever. I thought maybe he would find a way to call me, to say happy birthday, but there was nothing. I don't know if he even remembered." Maddie shrugs. "I kept thinking about how twelve months ago I was falling in love with him, that it was that half term when we met at Clywedog and he first held my hands. The last day before half term I asked the supply teacher if Will was coming back and she said no, a new teacher would be starting after the holiday. Later I went looking for Mr Jenkins, the chemistry teacher. I asked him what was happening. He didn't want to talk to me but in the end he said Will and his wife had gone back to Liverpool. She wasn't well and they were going back to be near her family."

"And he never got in touch to tell you this?"

"Never. And something else was happening too." She looks at Mo, expecting Mo to have realised.

"What?" Mo asks.

"I realised I was pregnant," Maddie says.

Half term. Maddie stood on the Prom, and the wind tore her hair. The sea was grey and angry. She couldn't see the horizon line: it blurred into thick clotted clouds.

Claerwen. That was when it must have happened. The last time Will made love to her, the last time he ever would, he'd given her a child. A sudden squall hit her in the face, making her cheeks sting.

She wondered what Catrina was thinking as she stepped into the sea, further and further, the salty water dragging at her clothes. She wondered whether that was what she should do. She could never tell her parents about the baby. They would make her kill it. She could never kill her child. Will's child. It was all she had left of him. She could never tell them about Will. Never. She was trapped. All she had was the ice-cold steely sea.

Or Claerwen? Perhaps she should go to Claerwen one last time. She could hitch there. Walk up to the dam one last time, mount the steps to the upper parapet, lean over and gaze into the black water, and let go. She remembers leaning over, thinking how easy it would be to simply drop over the edge: the splash, the burning cold, then nothing.

She started walking north along the Prom. The sounds of the town – the traffic, voices, a car alarm somewhere – were muffled. All she could hear was the fear in her head.

A man in a wax jacket peeled himself away from the railings. For a second, she thought of Will in his scruffy Barbour and faded jeans, but this man was short and dark. This man was looking at her strangely. Owain.

"Maddie, how are – what on earth's the matter?"

In two strides he was beside her with his arm around her, and she turned her face to his chest and sobbed, choking on wax, sheep, and the salt of the wind.

"What has he done?" Owain asked at last.

He took her arm and led her to one of the benches on the Prom. She stumbled down onto it, huddled up against Owain, stared out to sea, and told him how Catrina had been the woman who'd walked into the sea, how Will had left without even saying goodbye, how his child was growing inside her, and how she wanted this baby more than anything else, but that her parents would never allow it.

"I don't know what to do," she said. "They'll never let me keep it."

"They want what they think is best for you," Owain said. "They want you to stay at school and go to university. You can't do that with a little one."

"I don't care. I can do all that later. I can't do this later. This baby is all I have of him."

"Can't you get in touch with him?"

"No," she said. "What's the point? It was like he hated me at the end."

"I doubt that, Maddie," Owain said.

"He would hardly look at me. He won't be interested. He'll probably tell me to get rid of it too. I can't do that. It's not right, and I love it. I love it already."

"When is it due?" Owain asked.

"May, I think. So I have to tell them soon. I can't hide this. They mustn't ever know about Will. They can't. You said they can't."

"Have you seen a doctor? Are you sure about this?"

"I'm sure."

"But you haven't seen a doctor?"

"No."

"You need to see a doctor," Owain said. "You'll need scans and so on. I don't know much about it, but you'll need to be looked after."

"I can't tell them. You know what they're like."

Owain didn't speak. Maddie turned and looked at him. He was staring out to sea.

"When I saw you, I was thinking of killing myself," Maddie said.

"No," he said abruptly. He grabbed her arms. "Don't even say that. That's never the answer."

"But they'll make me kill my baby," she cried.

"What if the baby's father was there to support you?"

"He's not. He's married. He's gone."

"All right. Suppose he wasn't married, suppose he was here, suppose he married you. They couldn't do anything then, could they?"

"You're being cruel." Maddie jumped up. "He's not, he won't."

"Maddie." Owain grabbed her and tugged her back. He was strong; she let herself fall to the hard bench again. "I'm sorry. I was thinking aloud. What I meant was, well, what if, as far as your parents were concerned, and anyone else, what if the baby's father married you? I'm asking you to marry me."

"You? You're not the father. What are you on about? I can't marry you."

"Listen. You tell them it's my baby. Marry me. Then you can have the baby, and no one will know it's not mine. No one except you and me."

"You don't want to marry me."

"Actually," he said. "I would. We're good friends, aren't we?"

"Yes," she said dully.

"And I agree with you about your parents. If you marry me, you just have the baby. No problem."

"But it wouldn't be yours. You wouldn't like it."

"Of course, I would. It's a baby. It's not its fault."

"It's not mine either."

"I mean it's not the baby's fault that you can't be with its father, but maybe I would do as a reserve." He took her hand. "I know you don't love me. I know you still love this Will. I know this isn't what you'd have chosen, but it might just help you out, and farmers are meant to have wives, you know."

She smiled. A wave broke on the shingle. She turned to look at Owain.

"But people will find out."

"They won't if we don't tell them. Your parents know you come to visit me. So. That's when it happened. I'm happy to stand by you and say that."

"But why? Why would you do that for me?"

"Because I'm very fond of you, and I can't have you getting ill with worry when you need to take care of yourself, and maybe I'd like a family now."

"Why aren't you married?" Maddie asked.

Owain shrugged. "I thought I was going to be once, but…"

"She hurt you."

"Yes. So I do know what it's like."

"What about the baby? Would we tell it? Him, her?"

"No. We must get all this straight now. No one else knows. Not your parents, not your friends, not my family, and not the baby. No one will know except you and me."

"And they didn't," Maddie says. "They never knew. No one."

Moth wonders how she did not realise hours ago that Vanessa was Will's daughter.

Maddie finds the photographs – the one of Will at Claerwen taken before the sun went in and his love turned cold, the one of Vanessa and Owain. Moth takes them from her and holds them together.

"They're very alike," she says. "Will and Vanessa."

"When she was little she asked me why she had red hair when both Owain and I were dark. I told her it was a recessive gene. That it sometimes pops up."

"Your parents believed you?"

"Yes. They weren't happy. They weren't happy at all. I left school. My father thought Owain had betrayed him. I felt terrible. He was helping me out, he was doing what he could to let me have my child, and my parents were angry with him. We got married in the New Year. I cried a lot."

Moth smiles, puts down the photos.

"Two strange Christmases. One year I was waiting for Will to ring me, the next I was getting ready to be married."

"You didn't have any more children?"

"No, only Vanessa. I would have liked more but it wasn't to be. You know why I called her that?"

"Red Admirals," Moth says.

"Her full name is Vanessa Claerwen," Maddie says.

Moth wants to ask what Owain thought of the middle name, and if he knew why Maddie had chosen it, but she can't. Some things she just can't ask.

"So we had to take her to Claerwen quite a lot," Maddie says. "The first time it was unbearable. As time went by it blunted. The pain was always there, but I was expecting it, it couldn't knock me off my feet any more. We'd walk across the dam, and I'd look into the water, and feel the coldness coming up and it would numb me. I've never been over that gate on the other side. I've never seen the sundews. Maybe I never will. Maybe they're not really there." She reaches into the shoebox and pulls out the stiff twig of thyme. "I picked this that day. I remember the smell on my hands as he drove home to go out with Catrina."

"Why do you want to find him now?" Moth asks.

"Vanessa should know her father."

"But what about Owain? She thinks he was her father. It would destroy nearly twenty years of her life. And if you tell her, you'll have to tell your parents, and Owain's family, friends…"

"Owain's parents are dead. His sister is in a care home on the Lleyn. She has dementia; she thinks Owain is still alive and she doesn't know who I am. As for my parents… I have to do this for Vanessa."

"You don't," Moth says. "I don't think you've thought it through, what it would do to her."

"Owain wanted me to. The day he died he said something. Vanessa had gone out of the room. She couldn't bear it any more. I was there. He said *tell Vanessa... I love her.* That was the last thing he said. I don't think he just meant I should tell Vanessa he loved her. She knew that. He wanted me to tell her about Will and that Owain loved her anyway. That was what he meant."

Moth sighs. "Nothing will be the same again."

"I know, I don't care. I have to see him. I have to know he's all right. I have to tell him about Vanessa and…everything."

"It's not just for Vanessa, is it? It's for you."

"I don't know." Maddie looks away. "Yes, it's for me. Please, Mo. Mr Goodfellow said you could find him. I can't do it myself. It's been too long. I've looked for him on

Facebook, and for Catrina. They're not there. I don't know what to do. Earlier this summer I was in town and I bumped into Dave from school and he said he'd seen him in Ludlow."

"Yes, Mr Goodfellow is making enquiries there," Moth says.

"I thought maybe I should just drive to Ludlow and look for him, but that's ridiculous and I wouldn't know what to say to him."

"Even taking Vanessa out of it, I'm afraid you're setting yourself up for a huge disappointment. Supposing he's still married?"

"That doesn't matter. I don't care. I have to see him. I have to tell him. I want him to come here and see the butterfly house, see what I've done with my life. I want to tell him about Owain and Vanessa. I want him to know I didn't just give up when he went. Will you find him for me?"

"I will," Moth says. "I can't put him in the car and drive him back here, but I will do my best to find him and tell him whatever you want me to tell him."

"Thank you," Maddie whispers. She stands. "The butterfly house is closed now. Would you like to have another look before we lock up?"

"I'd love to."

Moth follows Maddie out of the farmhouse and down the lane. She's been here a day. She feels heavy with the weight of loss and pain Maddie carries.

The car park is almost empty. In the shop the assistant is straightening items on the shelves.

There's no one else in the butterfly house, except Gary. Moth has forgotten to take off her hoodie, and she prickles with sweat. Gary gestures to the red and black swallowtail, still spread on a hanging leaf.

"He's not fed all day. I'm going to get some glucose."

"They have to feed as soon as they hatch or they'll die," Maddie says distractedly. A glasswing hovers around her head.

Moth takes off her hoodie, rolls it up under her arm. Gary has swished through the black curtains and the beads to find glucose solution.

"I want him to see this place," Maddie says quietly. "I want him to see I have filled my life with butterflies and moths and caterpillars."

"I know," Moth says. Unbidden comes the image in her head of Will making love to Maddie in the butterfly house, in a rainbow cloud of swallowtails, Postmen, Morphos and Atlas moths.

"Call me," Maddie says. "As soon as you have anything. Please."

"I will. I promise." Mo unlocks her Citroen, chucks her bag and hoodie onto the passenger seat.

"It's his birthday on the sixteenth of August. Wouldn't it be a wonderful present for him, to know he's got a daughter?"

"Certainly different," Mo says.

"Call me any time of day or night. You've got my mobile, haven't you?"

"I have. I'll speak to you soon." Mo starts the ignition, puts the car in gear.

"Will you come back?" Maddie asks suddenly. "Back here, I mean? To the butterfly house?"

Mo smiles. "I will," she says, "I'll bring someone with me next time. Someone who'd like it very much."

"That would be lovely," Maddie says, and wonders who Mo will bring. A boyfriend probably. She has told Mo everything in her heart, but she knows nothing about Mo.

The little car bumps down the lane. Maddie waves until it disappears around the bend.

Alone at last she realises she has a burning headache. She needs a drink of water. She needs a lie down. She stumbles back up to the house. It feels too far to walk; she thinks she may faint. She stops by the little dam, listens a moment to the river rushing over the mossy boulders below.

Owain was like a dam. A solid, strong dam like Claerwen. He held back waters that were deep and frightening. But when he died, it was as though the Claerwen had split apart with a giant chasm, and the dark wild flood surged through: unstoppable, relentless, consuming.

Moth checks her mirror; there's no one behind her. She pulls into the side of the lane, by a five-barred gate. Foxgloves brush the side of the car. She turns on her mobile phone and waits to see if the signal bars flare. In the mountains there might be no signal. Through the open window she can hear the calls of the sheep, and a drowsy humming from a bee inside a foxglove cup. The phone cheeps. A text from RG. '*Ring me when you can*,' he says. '*Good news*.'

Good news. That means he's found a lead in Ludlow. *Is it really good news?* Moth wonders. Shouldn't Maddie just leave the past where it is and concentrate on her butterfly house, her daughter? Will's daughter as well.

The signal bar wavers and dies. Moth will call RG later. She moves off again, up the winding lane. At the main road she turns west for Aberystwyth.

Maddie lets herself into the house. She runs water into a glass, gathers up the shoebox, the photograph of Will, the bony twig of thyme, and carries them upstairs to her bedroom. Mo has gone to find Will. She's going to tell him that Maddie owns a butterfly house and would like to see him. She is not going to tell him he's a father. Maddie kicks off her shoes and lies down on the duvet.

Will lives in Ludlow. It's not that far away, not far at all. She and he are separated by the giant Cambrian Mountains, the cold, dark lakes at Elan. Has he ever come back to Wales? Why has he left Liverpool? Is he still married to Catrina and, if he's not, who shares his life now? He might even have children of his own. Not with Catrina, because she couldn't but, if he'd left her, he could have met someone else. But if he left Catrina, why didn't he try to find Maddie? Perhaps he did. Perhaps he found her married to Owain, living on a sheep farm. The same thoughts, the same questions that have tangled in her mind for twenty years, until they tighten into knots so intricate she wants to tear her head apart. If Will had come back for her, would she have left Owain? He allowed her to keep her child; he was kind. Her loyalty to him would have kept her faithful to him, wouldn't it? Over time her pain calcified into anger. Years passed. Will could at least have tracked her down to apologise for his behaviour that autumn, but there was nothing but silence. Did he ever think of her? Did he miss her? She must meet him again because he should know he has a daughter. And for the other reason too, the one she finds hardest to explain, hardest to admit to, hardest to ignore.

Moth trundles through Machynlleth, past the clock tower, following the road for Aberdyfi. It's further than she thought, but she wants to see the wide, shining estuary Maddie described, the candy-coloured houses on the seafront, the beach where she stood with Will one freezing winter day. Leaving Machynlleth, Moth crosses the Dyfi over an arched stone bridge. The road to Aberdyfi follows the bank of the estuary. Moth can see the spindly railway bridge spanning the saltings. She reckons the countryside hasn't changed much in twenty years: what she sees is what Maddie and Will saw as they escaped over the river that day.

When she gets to Aberdyfi she parks in the seafront car park. Although it's evening, it is July, and there are still a lot of cars. She goes through the gate and down the steps to the beach. Some children are fishing with neon nets in the murky channel. Across the water are pale sand dunes, turned gold by the westerly sun. *Ynyslas,* Moth thinks and, further down the coast, the jumble of houses at Borth.

She takes out her phone and rings RG.

"Agent Moth, my dear," he says.

"I'm sorry I couldn't ring earlier," she says. "I was with the client. It was a long story."

"And where are you now?"

"At the seaside." Moth smiles, remembers their first conversation about this assignment. "Just standing on the beach, thinking about what she told me today."

"I have news on the whereabouts of Will Richards," RG says.

"Is he in Ludlow?" Moth asks.

"That's not where you will meet him."

"Oh."

The wind has blown a straggle of Moth's hair into her mouth. She tugs it out. It tastes of the sea. She turns her back on the estuary, looks at the long terrace of tall, thin houses, coloured like sweeties.

"He's camouflaged himself in woodland."

"I don't understand."

"Think about your own name. Moth."

"Moth," she repeats. "Is that a clue?"

"He was an entomologist."

"Yes," she says.

"I love it when things work out so beautifully. In two days' time you will meet him. My instinct paid off."

"It's something to do with moths," she says at last. "Or butterflies. Does he have a butterfly house too?" That would be too strange.

"He does nature talks at the Wyre Forest," RG says. "The next one's on British moths. On Saturday afternoon."

When RG hangs up Moth quickly calculates time in her head. She could leave Aberystwyth first thing in the morning, go back to Bath, and drive up to the Wyre Forest the following day, but it's a hell of a lot of driving. She would rather take her time, and visit Claerwen on her way east. She dials another number on her phone. There's a voice she wants to hear very much.

It's been a wet summer, and white water is pouring over Caban Coch dam. The mountains soar up green and mauve, and the sun on the water hurts Moth's eyes. She leans over the balustrade to where the water cascades down the stone wall of the dam, and to the channel beneath, stained blue and rust with algae.

She crosses the road to the parking area hewn out of the mountainside. The gravel is churned up with sheep shit. There are a couple of sheep investigating scraggy grass at the bottom of a spindly tree.

Moth drives along the lakeside road. Below her, through the trees and summer foliage, is a narrow footpath and the blue-silver water of Caban Coch reservoir. The road turns to the right as the reservoir bends, and there is the viaduct stretching across the neck of water to the opposite wooded flank. Moth brakes.

On the other side, the trees crowd to the road, overhanging the narrow arm of the reservoir. Moth feels a fluttering in her breast. She is almost there, almost at Claerwen. She thinks of Maddie in the school bus bumping along this same road, the first stirrings of love inside her, but no perception of the heartbreak to come; she thinks of her, beside Will in his battered car, uneasy and sad that he had no time to take her to the sundews, but happy he was there beside her; she thinks of her with Owain and little Vanessa, choking down her pain like phlegm.

The trees thin out, and there is a wide stream – the Claerwen? – tumbling riotously over boulders. Sheep raise their heads as Moth drives by. Some are half-crouched under the wire fences; some stray into the road. Maddie told Moth to look for a steep narrow road on the right, leading up the mountainside to the top of the dam.

There are a few stunted trees, bent double from the wind, rugged boulders stained with moss and lichen, and still more sheep. Moth drives slowly, and the valley opens up beneath her. Suddenly there it is: the dam. Water seeps over the edge, under the arches of the road viaduct. It's not cascading like it was at Caban Coch, just sliding down the great grey-black wall in a silent sheet. Moth parks in the parking bay. Grasses and ferns hang down, and a spring splashes out of a rock cleft, splattering the tarmac. She gets out, slams the door, crosses the road.

There's the path, zigzagging up from the lower car park. That's where Maddie and Will climbed with the geography group. She walks to the road across the dam. On the near side is a gate, closed, and, beyond it, a gravel track, just wide enough for a vehicle, winding around the edge of the lake. *The way to the sundews,* she thinks. At the shoreline is a narrow scree of gravel where leggy foxgloves grow. Moth starts walking across the dam road. She ignores the other people standing around, pointing, taking photos with their mobile phones. She goes up the steps to the higher level, rests her hands on the stone ledge, speckled gold with lichen. She's standing over the very middle of the lake. Today, the water hardly moves, just a gentle sigh of exhalation as a fish jumps or the wind ruffles the surface. It's thick, black, inky water. She cannot guess at its depth.

She walks on. Something is soaring high overhead. She looks up. It's a red kite, and another, gliding high over the water. At the far side of the dam there's another gate, padlocked, and, beside it, almost sliding into the water, a wooden stile. A little rotten-looking, a little unsteady. Moth looks into the shallows and there, somewhere below the surface, is a lozenge-shaped rock, amber in colour. Moth feels a sudden ache in her eyes. She looks over the gate where the grassy track blurs into the hillside, and wonders where on that rounded flank of land, Maddie and Will threw down their blanket and made love, and created a life. She wonders how Maddie ever came back to this place of silent, stark beauty, where it all began, and where it all ended full circle.

Moth puts her boot on the gate, about to swing herself over, then stops. It's not her place to go there, not her memories to trample on.

Maddie shoves her trolley around Morrison's. Not so very far from here, Will once pulled in to the kerbside and chucked her out to walk home alone after their day out at Claerwen. And it's only a little further on to his house. Maddie's only been there once since Will left. She'd just passed her driving test; Owain had bought her a red Nissan Micra. She'd strapped Vanessa into her baby seat and driven to Will's road. Slowly she drove along until she saw his house. The front door was the same – white – and there were net curtains at the windows. There was a silver car on the drive. Maddie stopped, and gazed at the house for a few moments, glad that Will's room was at the back and that she could not see that window from the road. Vanessa started crying, and Maddie quickly found space for a three-point turn and drove home to the farm.

Now she dithers in the fruit aisle, selects a couple of mangoes and some bananas. She feels almost shaky being out in town on her own. Only this time yesterday she was crying into the remains of her lunch while Mo watched her with calm brown eyes. Maddie feels adrift now Mo has gone. On her way to Morrison's she drove into the motel car park, but Mo's Citroen had gone.

Maddie knows Mo is going to meet Will. Last night she phoned with the news that Mr Goodfellow had found out where Will was going to be on Saturday. Maddie asked her where it was but Mo would not say, only that she would be there too. She promised to call Maddie as soon as she had any news.

Maddie moves the trolley on towards cheese. She thinks she knows where Mo is today: Claerwen.

When Vanessa went to school Maddie was lucky. Because she was so young when she had Vanessa, the other mothers were girls several years older than she was. She remembered some of them, from being in higher years at school – some by name, some by face – and one or two even remembered her. She had years to prepare herself for Vanessa's move to secondary school. Sometimes she saw some of her old teachers around town; she knew some would teach Vanessa. She only went to the secondary school when she had to, for parents' nights and such. Every time she stepped into the hall, she remembered the coloured darkness of the Christmas disco, the sudden quietness of the corridor beyond. On the field the thicket of bushes, where she hid with Will's arms around her, grew and spread its branches. She never once went to the science department. Mr Jenkins had long retired by the time Vanessa went to the school and had been replaced by a sharp-voiced woman; a pimply young man taught biology. There was no whisper of Will at that school – except for his daughter.

Moth has chosen a seat at the back of the room in the visitors' centre. There's a good crowd for a Saturday afternoon in July. Many of them know Will; she thinks they may be from a moth club. The windows are darkened, but open, and she can hear the noises of the forest car park outside: voices, car engines, dogs, once a mobile phone. She turns back to the man at the front.

Will Richards is in his early sixties now. He is tall and lean, as he always was. His sandy auburn hair has faded to a gold-white, and is thin on the top. He wears wire glasses, faded black jeans and a T-shirt. He looks like a monochrome version of the man photographed at Claerwen with bright hair and sunburn, and the green, gold and blue landscape behind him. She can hear the Welsh coast in his voice.

He's talking about British moths, in particular the hawks. Later in the summer he will lead a moth hunt in the forest. He changes the slide. It's a close up of an Elephant Hawk caterpillar, grey and segmented like an elephant's trunk, with the surprised eye motifs on its head. Moth ignores the slide, watches the man. Does he remember bending over one of these twenty years ago, held in the palm of the girl who became his lover? Someone at the front asks a question about the caterpillar. He answers, gesturing at the picture. The slide moves on to the neon pink adult moth. Someone else is saying something about having seen several of them. Moth flexes her legs. Away from Maddie and her world of butterflies, lakes, stolen kisses, and lost love, Moth assesses Will

Richards. He is not a tragic golden hero surrounded with sparkling moths and butterflies; he left Maddie without so much as an explanation; he never once enquired after her; he didn't even care.

She tries to listen to what he's saying. He's knowledgeable and he loves moths, she can tell this. At the end of the talk she doesn't ask any questions. Will rolls up the blinds and the sunlight shafts into the room. The screen is still on, now a faded image on the wall. People get up, reach for bags and water bottles. Some stop to talk to Will as they leave. Moth waits, pretends to be studying some nature posters on the wall. Will is packing up, turning off the computer. It's just the two of them now. She wants to run out, go back to her car and drive home, leaving Vanessa with her memories of Owain. Instead she crosses the room to Will.

"That was very interesting," she says.

He smiles, and his eyes crinkle behind the glasses. *A nerdy Clint Eastwood,* Moth thinks. He's still attractive.

"Will you be joining us on the moth hunt?" he asks.

"I don't think I'll be in the area. I was just passing through on my way back from Aberystwyth." She watches him carefully, but he doesn't give away anything. "You're from Wales," she says. "Have you heard of the butterfly house at Ponterwyd? Cambrian Butterflies? I was there the other day."

"I've not been to Wales for years," he says, and she thinks he is now uncomfortable.

She notices he does not say he has not heard of the butterfly house. Surely he has? There aren't many and it must be one of the nearest to him. Why hasn't he even investigated it? She glances to his left hand. There is no wedding ring; no pale band of skin to mark the ghost of one recently removed.

"I wonder if we could talk for a few moments?" Moth asks at last. "I'm not playing games with you; I've been asked to find you. I need to speak to you."

"To find me? I don't understand."

"You're Will Richards, formerly of Aberystwyth?"

"Yes, but like I said I haven't been back there for years. Almost twenty years. Not that I haven't wanted to, but it just wasn't possible." He shuffles his papers, prepares to leave.

"My name's Mo." Moth holds out her hand. "Please. Could we go outside and have a talk?"

"Who has sent you?" Will pockets his flash drive and mobile phone. He looks at her warily.

Moth holds open the door. He doesn't speak as they leave the visitor centre. The afternoon sunlight is hard and bright through the canopy. There's an empty picnic table.

"Let's sit here," she suggests.

"Who has sent you?" he asks again, as he perches on the bench.

"You said it wasn't possible to go back to Wales. Why was that?"

Will takes off his glasses, and cleans them on the hem of his T shirt. "Things didn't work out for me there." He replaces his glasses, looks away from Moth. The wind rustles the leaves on the giant trees. Some kids and a dog are playing a few yards away. Will watches them, does not look at Moth. "I wanted to go back. I wanted to…repair things…but I couldn't. I couldn't go back to Aber in case I saw…her there. She must hate me."

"She doesn't."

Will snaps his head around.

"Maddie sent me to find you." Moth hands him Maddie's business card with its Blue Morpho motif.

"What?" He stares at the card. "Maddie Pryce. Is this Maddie Vaughan? Cambrian Butterflies. She owns this butterfly house? How do you know her? What do you know?"

"I don't know her well," Moth says. "She hired me to find you. I was with her the day before yesterday. She was telling me about that last year at school, your affair, how you left without saying goodbye." Moth checks herself. She's angry. She must not be angry with him.

"Maddie Pryce?" Will says. "Who has she married? Is she happy?"

"She married a family friend, Owain Pryce. A sheep farmer in Ponterwyd."

"Owain Pryce? But he was so old..." Will trails off. "Are they happy? Have they got a family?"

"Owain died last year," Moth tells him. "Yes, they were happy. They gave up sheep some years ago and opened the butterfly house. It's doing very well. I'm surprised you haven't been there."

"I'd heard of it. I just couldn't go back there. And, maybe, I wondered if..." He shakes his head. "My little Maddie running a butterfly house... Did they have children?" he asks again.

"Maddie's got a daughter. Vanessa."

"Vanessa. What else?"

"Maddie wants to see you."

Just hearing her name – Maddie – on someone else's lips after all these years unsettles him. Sometimes, in the early days, after he'd fled Wales, he'd whisper her name when he was alone, and wonder what she was doing, and who she was with. Whether she was thinking of him. He knew he should call her, write to her, do something, but there were no words to excuse how he had treated her. When he left, he left everything behind him. It was the only way. In time, he believed he would stop whispering her name, stop wondering, stop caring.

"Vanessa," Will says at last. "How old is she?"

"In her teens," Mo says evasively.

"She must have married Pryce very young then."

"She did."

"Was he good to her?"

"Very good." Mo's voice has gone hard. Will looks up at her. She's watching him. "He loved her and Vanessa. If it weren't for Owain, she'd never have had the butterfly house."

Will swallows a sudden flare of anger. What this woman has said is true. He could never have helped Maddie open a butterfly house. He could never have turned their shared love into a business, a future. He could never have offered her anything.

"You don't like me," he says. "You don't know me, but you don't like me."

"I don't know Maddie either, but I don't like what happened to her," Mo says. "I don't like how you behaved. I don't like knowing you left her...you left her all alone with no word from you. She didn't deserve that."

"I know."

"You left her all alone. You treated her badly. She told me about Claerwen."

"About Claerwen?"

"How you promised her a day out looking for sundews, and how when it came to it you didn't have time to do that, and then how you blamed her because you fell asleep and all you could think about was rushing home to your wife, and turfing Maddie out on a street corner."

"It wasn't like that," Will interrupts.

"What was it like then?"

He puts his head in his hands. He can feel the warmth of the sun and the coolness of the breeze. He can hear the voices of picnickers and the rumble of a lorry on the main road, just beyond the trees. He lets all this wash over him until he can hear in his mind the distant calls of sheep, the sudden piercing roar of a Harrier jet; he can smell cold water, wine, and a young girl's soft hair.

"I got it wrong," he says. "I should never have gone to Claerwen with Maddie the day I was going out with my wife. It was stupid and insensitive, but I wanted to see her. I thought I would be back in time, and Maddie would never know, and we'd have had a lovely day. It was all getting too much to handle, and Maddie – well, she was sixteen. She didn't understand what it was like to have the responsibilities of a marriage. That was when it all fell apart. I don't think I'll ever go to Claerwen again."

"I was there yesterday," Mo says.

"What was it like?" he asks quickly.

"It was beautiful. I don't think it's changed much in twenty years from what Maddie was saying."

"We went there on a school trip," Will says.

It was soon after he started the job. He had to drive one of the buses. He doesn't remember much about it, but he does remember talking to Maddie, telling her about the sundews. She said she wanted to explore the lonely fringes of the lake and suddenly, overwhelmingly, he wanted to take her there.

"I don't know how it happened," he says. "She wasn't the first girl I'd noticed. Yes, look like that, why don't you? But it happens. Ask any teacher. Even ask female teachers. You spend your days with young girls, young men, on the verge of adulthood. They're fired up with life and expectancy. It's intoxicating. So she wasn't the first girl I noticed, but she was the first one I ever entered into anything with."

"Entered into anything with?"

"I loved her."

It's the first time he's ever said it aloud. He never thought his mouth would ever form those words, that any other person would hear them, and now he's said them to a stranger with unflinching eyes sitting opposite him across a wooden picnic table.

"I loved her," he says again. "But it got out of control. Because I loved her, I suppose. If I didn't I would have let it go, stopped it, whatever, but I couldn't. I had to see her. I had to take risks. I thought no one noticed but they did. My wife. Even some of the kids at school. I don't know how I could have been so naïve. I wanted to be, I guess. It was madness, a wonderful madness, and I never wanted it to end."

"Neither did she."

Will ignores the barbed comment. "That summer, Claerwen…Catrina was already suspicious. My neighbour saw me with Maddie and told her. I was appallingly late after Claerwen, and I didn't just dump her on a street corner and think no more about it. I went home, Catrina was furious. We had to race to Machynlleth and then she was hardly speaking to me. The meal was awful. God alone knows what the other people thought. I kept thinking about Maddie. I felt a bastard, but there was nothing else I could do. I knew the shit I would be in, and I was. Sometimes I wonder if only I had picked another day to take her to Claerwen, whether things would have been different. That was when it all unravelled."

"You can't keep things like that secret for ever. From the very beginning it was a time bomb."

"You're right, of course. Hindsight and all that. As I said, I'd never done anything like it before. Neither had she. We didn't know the rules." He stops suddenly. "What happened at the end? Did she know what Catrina did? Did she know why I left?"

"She heard someone had walked into the sea and she worked it out straight away."

Will sighs. "I should never have gone like that. I didn't know what I was doing. My wife tried to kill herself. She'd done stupid things before, but not like that. I didn't know this side of her when I met her. If I had, I wouldn't have married her. She said we had to leave, go to Liverpool, near her family. She knew I'd been seeing someone; she didn't know who. I think she knew it was someone from the sixth form, thanks to my neighbour. I never told her who it was. So, we went. I didn't have a choice."

Mo looks at him.

"OK, I had a choice, and possibly I made the wrong one. But Maddie, oh Maddie, she didn't understand. She didn't understand the way we'd have been viewed, she didn't understand the implications for my job…did her parents ever find out about me?"

"She says not."

"Just as well. It must have been so terrible for her in those early days when I went."

"Oh, it was. You've no idea."

"I can imagine. You seem to think I was having a ball. I was stuck in a horrible city I hated, with a woman who was losing her mind, her ghastly family on my case all the time, the recriminations, trying to get the house sold in Aber… I worked as a supply teacher for the first year, then luckily I got a post."

"Are you still married to Catrina?" Mo asks coolly.

"No."

"Is she…?" Mo looks away. *At last you are uncomfortable,* Will thinks.

"Yes, she's alive. She tried to do herself in a couple more times, then ten years ago she left me for a man she met at a therapy group. We're not in touch."

"You could have called Maddie then."

"And what good would that have done? She was already married to Pryce."

Will swallows the angry ball in his throat. He's jealous of Owain Pryce. Owain Pryce married Maddie. Owain Pryce has been making love to her for nearly twenty years, he's given her a daughter and a home. He's watched her grow older; he's given her her dream with the butterfly house. Will hasn't done any of these things. He looks away. He doesn't want this woman to see him falter.

"It might have helped her to come to terms with things."

"I don't think so. I thought about it, but I knew she would have made a new life. There was no point my contacting her and, from what you've told me, I was right."

But he's dead now, Will thinks. *Pryce is dead and Maddie wants to see me.*

"She did go to university?" he asks.

Mo hesitates. "No," she says at last.

"What a waste. What a fucking waste. She was such a clever girl."

"I don't think her life's been a waste. Not at all. She's achieved a lot."

Will swings his long legs over the wooden bench, wanting to walk away with Maddie's card in his pocket. He doesn't want to talk to this woman, Mo, any more, but she's his only link to Maddie. He must let her acid words fall off him, scorch the ground instead.

"You said Catrina left you ten years ago?"

"Yes, that's right."

"So what's your situation? I am sure Maddie will want to know before you go to see her. If you choose to see her."

If I choose to see her, Will thinks. *Do I have a choice?*

"I live alone," he says guardedly. "Yes, there have been a few women since then, but I never re-married, nor lived with anyone."

"Do you want to ask me anything?" Mo asks.

Everything and nothing, Will thinks.

"I don't think so," he says instead and, at last, stands.

"I was employed to find you and tell you where Maddie is. I've done that. The rest is up to you, but please, please, don't do anything that will only hurt her again."

"I never meant to hurt her," Will says. "By the time I realised what she meant to me it was too late for her not to be hurt."

"It's not too late now." Mo stands, climbs over the picnic bench.

Will watches her walk through the dappled light to a small hatchback. She doesn't look back. She unlocks the door and gets in. The door closes. He waits for her to drive away and out of his life, but she doesn't. He can just see her behind the wheel. It looks like she's on the phone. Who would she be speaking to? Maddie? Could Maddie's voice be only that distance away? He looks again at the card in his hand. He'd never quite dared to make the connection between Maddie and Cambrian Butterflies in his mind. He simply knew, from when he'd first heard of the butterfly house, that he would never be able to go there. Butterflies and Aberystwyth were a potent, delicious toxin he could not sample.

Still Mo doesn't drive away. Is she waiting for him to get up and go? Does she want to see which is his vehicle? Is she going to take down the registration plate? Follow him home? It's unnerving being watched from behind a windscreen. For want of something to do, he takes out his own mobile, turns it on. He taps Maddie's number into it. Now it will only take a couple of clicks to find her again.

He doesn't know what he'll say to her. No words are adequate after twenty years, after her pain and his lies. What will she look like? Will she still wear her hair, long and dark, down her back? He last saw her as an emerging imago; what will life have done to her wings?

At last he stands, pockets the phone and card. He walks the short distance to his Golf and gets in. In his mirror, he can see Mo's car is still parked under the trees. He swaps his specs for the sunglasses in his glove compartment and fires the ignition. A loud flare of discordant jazz on the radio. He silences it, and swings out of the parking space. As he passes in front of Mo's bonnet, he glances swiftly at her. She's still on the phone. She doesn't acknowledge him. He drives on, without a wave or a hoot, and joins the traffic on the main road.

Moth hangs up from Maddie. She tries to imagine her in the farm kitchen on the far side of those giant mountains and deep, dark lakes. *I'll see you soon*, Moth has just told her. *I'll be coming back with someone very special I want you to meet*. Now it's time to speak to that someone and tell him she'll soon be home.

The phone rings out. At last a woman's voice.

"Hello, Mum," Moth says. "It's me. How's he been?"

"He's right here," her mother says.

Moth smiles. She can hear him squeaking.

"Cosmo, it's Mummy. I'm coming home."

Act III

Green Figs and Mulberries

"Do you like jam, Mustardseed?" RG holds out a plate of jam tarts.

Mustardseed picks up a raspberry one. "Uh, yes, I like jam."

"Good, good. Which is your favourite? I think I prefer apricot." RG selects the apricot tart and places it delicately on his side plate.

"I like raspberry," Mustardseed mumbles through the pastry. "I like the little seeds."

"Oh yes, the seeds." RG chuckles and bites into his tart.

Across the desk Mustardseed drinks from his cup of Earl Grey. Next door Fairy is on the telephone. RG can't hear what she's saying, just the rise and fall of her voice. Sometimes, when he is in there with her, she keeps the headset jammed on even if she's not on the phone, just so she doesn't have to talk to him.

"What about pickles, chutneys, marmalade?" RG asks.

"Yes, I like those too. Sometimes. Some of them."

"Dressings, marinades, mustard?"

"Is this about a job?"

"A job has come up, yes. More tea?" RG hovers the china teapot over Mustardseed's cup.

"To do with jam and pickles?"

"In a way, yes. I am just ascertaining that you would be the right agent for this job."

"I've done all right, haven't I? With the other jobs?"

"You've done splendid work," RG says. "I'm delighted with you. I think this new job will be perfect for you. Yes."

"So what is it? When is it?"

"It's a local job. In Bath. Three days' work." RG taps on his laptop. "Thursday the 18th until Saturday 20th. But you will need to meet the client before then to receive instructions."

"The client is instructing me? Not you?"

"Yes. The client is Ms Gemma Thompson. You will need to meet her on Thursday, Friday or Saturday of the week before."

"And what am I doing?" Mustardseed eyes the plate of tarts. RG swiftly hands it to him; he takes the blackcurrant.

"An excellent choice. Ms Thompson has to go away for a week and needs someone reliable to take care of her business for her."

"Oh." The blackcurrant tart collapses as Mustardseed bites into it, and crumbs speckle onto the desk.

"Not very cloak and dagger, this time, I'm afraid. But it is three full days' work, plus your first meeting with the client. You will need the agency's van as you will be transporting things."

"What things?"

"Consumables." RG hands over a card with a telephone number on it. "This is the client's number. Call her and arrange to meet her. You can pick up the keys to the van nearer the time. Happy?"

"I think so. I mean, yes."

RG calls aloud, "Fairy, could I have a dustpan and brush in here please?"

Mustardseed glances down at the crumbs on the floor and desk.

"No questions? Excellent. Then I'll say Oberon Out."

Gemma Thompson noses her car into Green Park Station. It's not yet eight o'clock. She sees him at once, leaning against one of the supporting pillars, hands in pockets, a cap on his head. Gemma parks in an empty space, kills the engine, and watches him a moment. She knows this is him, the young man who phoned her a few days before, who goes by the name of Mustardseed.

"Mustardseed?" she'd echoed. "Is that what I have to call you?"

"That's my name," he said, and then, more gently, "I can't tell you my real name. It's against the rules. You could call me Mr Seed, I suppose."

Gemma floundered. "Why Mustardseed?"

"It's from *A Midsummer Night's Dream*," he explained.

"Yes, of course," she said.

A Midsummer Night's Dream. They'd done that at school. Or rather, they'd watched the film, and then been taken outside into the sunshine to re-enact parts of the play. She remembers she was supposed to be chasing Alex Davidson through a wood, but he wasn't interested, and her friends giggled because she really, really liked Alex Davidson, and she went red and forgot her lines, even the bit about being as ugly as a bear, which is all she can remember of it now.

Gemma opens the car door. It's a Thursday, and the market is quieter than on Saturdays when the parking bays are all taken with huge vans from the farms, bearing earthy vegetables, slabs of crimson meat, bread, cakes, and cheeses. It's chilly, as it always is in the converted station building, and she pulls on her mittens.

The young man turns at the sound of her boots on the ground. He peels himself from the pillar, strides the few yards towards her, offers his hand.

"Gemma? How do you do? I'm Mustardseed."

"Hello." Gemma takes his hand in her mittened one. She feels shy all of a sudden, as though it's a ridiculous idea to employ a stranger to run her market stall. "You're early," she says, and knows how stupid this sounds, but she has to say something.

"You said eight," he smiles at her. "If you say eight, I will be here at ten to. Can I help you unload anything?"

"Thank you," she says. "You won't have to set up tables and take them down at night. I use one of the booths." She gestures to the row of stalls with striped awnings. "There's just one thing," she says, opening the car boot. "I'll have to introduce you to everyone. They can't call you Mustardseed."

"OK… They can call me Robert."

"Is that your name?"

"No. It's my brother's name."

"Will you remember to answer to Robert?"

"I will," he says. "Are you going to call me Robert?"

"No," Gemma smiles. "I'm going to call you Mustardseed."

Mustardseed walks home to his attic garret in Park Street. He knows he has to make some big decisions about his future, but right now he can't bear the thought of leaving Bath. Not in the autumn, with the high blue skies, and the falling russet leaves in Victoria Park which match his unruly hair. When he applied for the job at the agency on a whim, he never thought he would stand a chance. RG has given him several jobs now. He's done them well and the clients have been satisfied. And now this one. It's a strange one. He's simply working in Green Park Station running a stall selling Gemma's home made jams and chutneys. She's given him a jar of raspberry jam to take home today.

He likes Gemma. She's not pretty really, not like the girls he would usually go for. She's neither tall nor short, neither fat nor thin, with pale brown hair on her shoulders. He thinks her eyes are a greeny-brown. He's sorry he won't be working with her on the stall.

"I do three days a week here," she had explained to him. "I make the stuff on the other days. People like the market in the autumn, especially on Saturdays with the farmers. All those beautiful vegetables. I love the autumn."

"Me too," he said.

He wanted to ask her why she was going away, why she had to approach the agency to run the stall, why she didn't have a friend or relative who could do it. He wanted to ask her all kinds of things, but he couldn't, so instead he offered to run up to Sainsbury's at the far end of the market and get some treats for them both.

"Did Mr Goodfellow tell you why I'm going away?" she asked breaking a triangle off a Toblerone.

"Oh no. He just said you were going away and you needed cover for the stall."

"If you turn up for your pitch regularly you keep it," she explained. "If you don't turn up and someone else approaches the manager with a similar stall he could give it to them." She indicated the CD stall. "He's always fighting off the competition. Everyone thinks they can peddle a few CDs, sell off a vinyl collection. And now there are two other people wanting to sell preserves and herbs. So my stall has to be here every week."

Mustardseed served two women. One of them spoke to Gemma, asked after her grandmother.

"She's all right," Gemma said, and Mustardseed thought he sensed unease in her voice. "I'm taking her away next week. We're going back up north."

"She will enjoy that," said the woman. "Please give her my love."

"So that's all it is," Gemma said when they were alone again. "I'm taking my grandmother away for a week, and I can't lose my pitch here. Not with Christmas coming up."

"Do you live with your grandmother?" Mustardseed asked.

"Yes, me and her and my mother. We're going to Northumberland. Where she grew up. She can't drive any more, and she wants to go back again. The big house is being sold. Her brother died last year and his family don't want it. Sorry, am I boring you?"

"Not at all. So, you're driving up with your grandmother?"

"Yes." Gemma pulled a face. "It's quite a way, but I like driving."

"Your mother's not going then?"

"She's a head teacher. She can't take the time off. She'll even be busy over half term." Gemma fiddled with the Toblerone wrapper. "My grandmother…her name's Frances…she's not so well. I don't know…anyway we're going up next week, and that'll be lovely. She means the world to me."

"I'll be fine here," Mustardseed assured her. "You don't have to worry about the stall."

Now he opens the large street door and runs up the six flights to his flat. Gemma will be working tomorrow and Saturday. He's meeting her after the market to drive behind her to her house in South Stoke, so she can show him where the preserves are kept. When he's running the stall, he will have a key to her house; he'll have to drive over there at dawn to load up the van. He'd like to meet her mother first, so she can see who will be banging around downstairs each morning and evening for three days.

He takes out his mobile and glances at the screen. Two missed calls. He never heard it ring in the market. Both from RG. Shit, he was supposed to report back, assure RG everything was cool, but he stayed longer in the market talking to Gemma, hearing about her family, her life. She only has her mother and grandmother. Her parents were never married, and her father absconded years ago and lives in the States. Her grandfather died in a boating accident when she was very young; she hardly remembers him. The house she and her grandmother are going to is near a place called Fenwick. The heirs have said they can go and stay for a week before the house is sold. Gemma hasn't been to Northumberland for years. She has two guinea pigs called Guinness and Murphy, and he has memorised her registration plate. All good agent work, learning about the client, but giving little away of himself. But, as he dials RG's mobile and flicks open a beer, he knows that's not the only reason why he's deliberately found out so much about Gemma.

"He seems very nice," Gemma tells Frances.

She's rinsing vegetables at the sink for the guineas' meal. Cucumber, spinach, carrot, coriander, rocket.

"I thought he would be," Frances says.

"How did you hear of the agency?"

"Oh…I can't remember. I just saw the card somewhere and took it. I thought one day it might be useful."

Frances fills in another answer in her crossword. Gemma scoops a handful of vegetables onto a plate for Guinness and Murphy. She can hear the guineas squeaking in the living room. She takes the plate through and reaches in to nuzzle their furry black and white noses. Murphy is standing on his back legs with his paws on the hutch rails. Gemma scratches him on the head and slides the food onto the hay.

"He's coming over tomorrow night," Gemma says, returning to the kitchen. "So I can show him the stuff and how to get it. He's very professional. I'm sure he won't disturb Mummy too much."

She checks the time. On Thursday nights, her mother, Judy, has a late meeting after school. There's just time for a quick shower before she gets home. Gemma kicks off her shoes and pads up the narrow staircase. Their house is two cottages, knocked through, long and low on the hillside, overlooking the village of South Stoke.

Mustardseed known as Robert. She smiles as she turns her face to the warm water jet. She wonders what his name really is, runs through a selection in her head, but none of them fit. He's hard to name: Mustardseed, with his bright ponytail and faint golden stubble on his chin. How old is he? Early twenties, much the same as her, she imagines. She must have bored him stupid today, going on about Frances and Judy and Guinness and Murphy and Northumberland and the market. But he hadn't appeared bored. Once she'd started to talk, he'd asked her questions about her life, even about how to make jam and chutney and how to dry herbs. She'd almost told him her dream of one day opening a deli somewhere. She'd almost told him how afraid she was for her grandmother, eighty-two years old, with worsening health. But she didn't tell him those things because they are her most secret thoughts and not to be shared with a stranger.

On Saturday morning Mustardseed finds himself standing outside Green Park Brasserie. This is the other face of the station building, the old waiting room and ticket office, now a fashionable bistro. To the left of the Brasserie, a flight of steps leads into the lobby of the station. Mustardseed jogs up the steps. Through the open portal he can watch the

Farmers' Market. The square arena behind the bistro is packed with stalls; people are carrying woven tote bags of vegetables and paper bags of cakes. He can smell something with cinnamon – waffles maybe – cooking on a stove. It's impossible to see Gemma's stall from here. The walkway along the row of booths is crowded with more shoppers and a stray whippet, and all he can discern is the row of green-and-white striped awnings. The marching feet tap a hollow tattoo on the boards. He hesitates in the doorway and wonders whether or not to go in.

Last night, he followed Gemma home to her cottage in South Stoke. She showed him how the gate needs a hefty kick sometimes. Her house is made of two cottages, and she led him along an overgrown path in front of the building to the second front door.

"There's two of everything," she explained to him. "So I use this kitchen for the preserves."

He ducked his head as he followed her in, not that he's that tall, but the house made him feel he had to. There were plants on the front windowsill and, behind them, a stained-glass sunburst, vibrant even on a grey afternoon. The large metal fridge and hob looked out of place in the tiny kitchen. Gemma filled a scarlet kettle at the sink and took two patterned mugs from the wall cupboard.

A phone rang somewhere, muffled through the thick walls of the cottage, then stopped and he could just hear a woman's voice.

"I won't be disturbing your mother, will I?" he asked. "If I come straight to this kitchen?"

"She won't know you're here. She'll be asleep when you arrive on Saturday. The other days she'll have left for work. She gets in very early."

Now Mustardseed takes a step into the market. There's a bakery stall, just behind the CDs. Perhaps he could buy Gemma a piece of cake and take it up to her. No, just let it go. When Gemma returns from Northumberland, and she's no longer a client, then he can come and see her, talk to her. Not today. Reluctantly he turns his back on the colours and smells of the Farmers' Market and trots back down the steps.

The welcome blue sign: *Woodall Services, one mile*. Gemma flicks on her indicator and slides in behind a supermarket lorry in the left-hand lane. It's early afternoon, and they're travelling across the industrial heart of the country. The rough surface of the slow lane rumbles under the car's wheels. As she leaves the motorway, the sound of the traffic drops to a fuzzy grumble. She hears a squeak from the back seat. The guineas' hutch is strapped in securely, wedged with a sack of hay.

"We're here," she says to Frances. "We're at Sheffield." Her voice, loud over the engine, reminds her of childhood journeys: the smell of tomato sandwiches and coffee, stale from a flask, voices sudden and loud over the rumbling wheels.

Frances stirs in the passenger seat. She's been dozing on and off since Birmingham. Gemma doesn't mind. You can't talk on the motorway; you have to yell. Frances fumbles with knotted fingers in the handbag on her lap and pulls out her disabled parking badge.

Gemma finds a space by the entrance and parks. Her left shoulder aches. She sets the dial on the parking badge and props it up on the dashboard. In the back, the guineas are quiet now. She leans over, checks their water bottle is still attached and not dripping all over them. They will be all right on their own for ten minutes, with the window open a crack, while she and Frances go in to the Ladies.

Gemma gets Frances's stick out of the back, and holds open the passenger door. Frances stumbles, snatches at the door.

"Steady now." Gemma hands her the stick, waits for her to shuffle away before she locks the car.

They walk together up towards the complex. Frances climbs the steps, rather than using the ramp, one hand on the rail, the other on her stick. Gemma hovers on the step behind just in case. People shove past them, talking to each other or on mobiles, eating, smoking. Gemma realises how slowly Frances is walking. *Maybe it's just because we've been travelling,* she thinks. Anybody gets stiff after hours folded into a car. She's stiff too. But not really, not like this. A sign on the door to the disabled lavatory says it is out of order. Gemma takes Frances's arm to help her past the puddle of water that seeps out from under the door, and they move slowly towards the Ladies.

Frances hardly ever leaves the cottage now. She's never seen Gemma's stall at Green Park. At home, in a familiar environment, she manages all right. There's a cloakroom downstairs she can use in the day. Judy has been saying more and more lately that they should turn the downstairs study into a bedroom for Frances. Gemma agrees with her, but Frances refuses to leave her own room.

It's not just her walking though. A year ago, Frances was sent by her GP to see a renal consultant. She'd had high blood pressure for most of Gemma's life, but her tablets weren't controlling it. Her kidney function was impaired. Her sodium was low. Gemma took her to the appointment, fearful of dialysis machines and transplants. But neither of those came up. The physician took Frances's blood pressure. It was so high he took it again a few moments later. He prescribed different tablets and said he would see her again in six months. Gemma left the appointment confused. Surely if someone had kidney failure there was more that could be done than just changing blood pressure medication? At the six-month follow-up, they saw a different doctor – younger, probably a trainee – who found little change in Frances's blood pressure, and told her to stick with the new tablets. Frances's next appointment is in a few weeks; this time Gemma is going to ask Judy to take a couple of hours off to come too, see if she can be more forceful and find out exactly what can be done.

A fat woman buffets into Frances in the Ladies. Doors clang hollowly down the line. Water runs from a tap unchecked. Two Indian girls are applying kohl to their eyes in front of grimy mirrors. Gemma nudges open a cubicle, checks it's clean, and steers Frances inside. She takes the one next door, despite the clogged up paper down the pan, and squats painfully, reads the advert on the back of the door for incontinence pads.

When they get back to the car, they'll have a drink and a sandwich or some biscuits. She'll put a handful of greens into the guineas' hutch, and then they'll be on their way. She never told her mother how frightened she was taking Frances away on her own, how frightened she was shouldering that responsibility alone. She wishes suddenly for Mustardseed's strong and competent presence. She wouldn't be afraid if he were with them. He would know what to do whatever happened.

It's another bright blue autumn day. Mustardseed stumbles out of bed in the middle of the morning. The lozenge of sky through his cramped bedroom window hurts his eyes. He pulls on his running kit and trainers, and cuffs his hair back in an elastic band.

As he runs through St James Square and down the side of the Royal Crescent he wonders how Gemma is getting on in Northumberland. He hopes she is enjoying a crisp blue and gold day like he is. He hasn't heard from her. He does have her mobile number but he can't ring her before he's even done a day on the stall.

Running helps him sort through the grit in his head. If he's going to university in twelve months' time, he's got to get his application in. He only came to Bath as a stepping-stone. Camping, he called it. When he arrived here he still had his dream, but his dream was not to be. Whatever he's done in the past, whatever he has achieved, his future is not as a sportsman. Not any more, and it's time to decide what to do.

He has no roots in Bath. Much as he loves it, he wanted to move on. But now he isn't so sure. He has Googled lots of universities over the last few weeks: St Andrew's, Bangor, Durham. You can study chemistry all over the place. It's time for another adventure, another move. But in the last few days things have changed. Last night he spent hours on the University of Bath's website. And they have fantastic sports facilities. Why hadn't he ever considered studying there before? He doesn't have to run away. He could stay here, start to put down some roots, and see what grows and flowers from them.

The view is incredible. Gemma stands on the terrace at the back of Kyloe Mains. The fields, now shorn of summer grain, slope down from the hills to the A1 – the Great North Road – and the railway matching it stride for stride. Orange tiled roofs mark isolated farms and cottages, then the edge of the land crumbles into tidal flats, glassy with reflected sunlight and, further still, the ink-blue North Sea. The thin crescent of Holy Island lies to the north, its castle jutting from the sea and sand like a molar. To the south, the huge edifice of Bamburgh Castle, and the Farne Islands. Gemma can pick out the red and white stripes of the Longstone lighthouse. She would love to drive down to Aidan's Dunes and run on the sand as she did when she was younger, but she's afraid to leave Frances on her own. Perhaps Frances could come too and sit in the dunes car park, as Gemma strides through the marram grass, up and down the sandy hills, with the smell and the crash of the sea coming nearer and nearer. Through that hollowed-out bowl in the dunes – is there still a blackened washed-up log marking the way? – and onto the beach, where a salty wind smacks her face and silky steamers of weed caress her ankles as she paddles in the foaming shallows.

A tapping behind her makes her turn to the open French windows. Frances places her stick on the terrace and steps out beside Gemma. She's wearing a thick fleece, though it isn't even that cold, not for up here in October.

"I should have come here more often," Frances says. "I'm so pleased we're here now."

"It's a beautiful house." Gemma takes a step backwards towards the lawn, looks up at the windows above her. The back bedrooms have the same view, down the foothills to the coast and the islands. "D'you think they'll live here themselves? The people who're buying it? Or will it be another B & B?" She feels her throat go tight at the thought of this house in strangers' hands, at the thought of the generous bedrooms having corners shaved off to accommodate shower rooms.

"I don't know. I don't want to know."

"We could come up here again," Gemma starts. "The three of us. We could rent a cottage for a week or something. We wouldn't have to come near this house."

"No," Frances says. "Not for me. I shan't come here again. I just wanted to come and say my farewells. You can come back, Gemma. I hope you will come back." She turns unsteadily on the stones and steps back inside the living room.

Gemma shivers. It's colder than she first thought. Her forearms have risen in gooseflesh where she's rolled up her sleeves. She reaches down for the scissors and bowl on the battered wooden bench beside her. There's some longer grass by the stone walls. Guinness and Murphy will enjoy that.

She bends down and snips at the blades. She feels suddenly dizzy leaning over and straightens. Something has changed. She narrows her eyes, checks the panorama before her. It's the same. Sunlight on water, the flash of chrome and glass on the A1. An express train, heading southwards, snakes beneath the power cables, through level crossing after level crossing, where the track strides over the narrow lanes to the mud flats. The view is the same, but something is different. The sea sparkles, but the breeze is cold. Gemma feels, rather than sees, black pressing in on her from all sides, pressing in on the view. It's as though someone has taken a huge paintbrush and painted a broad, angry, black frame around the view.

Quickly she cuts a few more handfuls of grass then hurries across the lawn to the terrace. Inside the living room she pulls shut the heavy glass door and bolts it. Her arms and hands sting as they warm up.

Frances. Is she all right? It's Gemma's first thought on waking, it's the thought that pursues her through the days. She exhales in relief as she hears the flush from the downstairs cloakroom, then the tap tap tap of Frances's stick.

Gemma turns back to the French windows. It's still bright outside and sunny. No, not quite as bright or sunny. A film of cloud has streaked in, gauze across the sky. Rain may follow.

The guineas are wheeking in their hutch. They've smelt the grass.

"All right, guys. Let me wash it and you can have some now."

Gemma takes the bowl through to the kitchen to rinse the grass. She runs the tap at the sink, and rust-coloured water pops out with a spurt. There's a crack on the windowpane and she jumps. Droplets on the glass. The rain has come swiftly, almost unseen. Gemma leans in towards the window. She can just see the sea from this angle. The coast still lies in golden sunlight. If she were on the shore, she would look back to the Kyloe hills and see them veiled in thin mauve cloud.

She shakes the grass and scoops a handful onto a saucer. Stupid to get all twitchy because of a rainstorm. Weather comes in so quickly here, in this land of wide skies. '*The sun on your face, and the rain on your shoulder*,' Frances's brother, George, used to say. Yes, you can be looking ahead into a future seemingly bright with warm sunshine, and never know about the dark clouds swarming behind you. *But not me, not now,* Gemma thinks, as Murphy takes grass from her palm. *I've seen that darkness, and it's not behind me. It's all around, just waiting to swallow me.*

Green Park is something else on Saturdays. For the last two days Mustardseed has run the preserves stall and done more reading than selling. At a young age, he became used to travelling to tournaments, living out of a suitcase, and since then he has always taken books with him. He'd not realised how cold it would be in the market, with its vast open arch leading towards Sainsbury's. No wonder the other traders wore thick jumpers and scarves and mittens. On Thursday and Friday, there were the regular stalls: CDs, haberdashery, pewter jewellery, collectibles. The stall on his left was unoccupied, except for a crusty who leaned against it for fifteen minutes, smoking roll-ups and scowling at Mustardseed. On his other side, a woman selling sweets and handcrafted truffles watched his stall when he needed the Gents.

Today, Saturday, is the Farmers' Market. When he arrived at eight, all the undercover spaces were already taken with muddy vans and 4 x 4s. He had to park under the arch and carry the boxes of glass jars. Once his right shoulder seared with hot pain. He hadn't had trouble for ages, the boxes weren't that heavy – not for him – and he cursed his carelessness.

Somerset Tea is on his left today. Jim, the tea merchant, has already made him several cups of strange teas in a blackened mug. Mustardseed rinses his mouth out from his water bottle after a smoky red-black brew. Next time Jim offers, he'll just ask for an Earl Grey.

Mustardseed sells a jar of blackcurrant and a jar of strawberry, offers more assurances that Gemma is OK and will be back in the market next Thursday. He gazes up at the giant glass roof above him and the cool blue sky. It must have been a fabulous station. Now the panes are stained with bird shit and clogged with wet leaves; seagulls scuffle across the glass.

"Jim, would you watch the stall a moment?"

"Sure, Robert," Jim says, offering an open packet of green jasmine for a woman to smell.

Mustardseed strides down the wooden walkways, where once the platform would have stood, and into the main square of the market. His shoulder twinges, and he straightens his gait. There's a crowd at the CD stall; beyond that are the farmers' stalls. Mustardseed wanders into the square. There's a long vegetable stand, bright with autumn colours. At the front is a wooden crate of pumpkins – amber globes, tiny and huge – waiting for Hallowe'en. On the table behind are tied bunches of carrots, frilled cauliflowers, dusty purple beetroots, bony white parsnips. Cut them and smell the menthol.

He wanders on past wet cuts of fish in ice trays. There is venison, organic apple juice, a giant cauldron of soup, plucked fowl, trays of eggs, whole cheeses cut in half to reveal knobbly blue-black veins. The bakery. He reaches into the pocket of his jeans for some change (his money in the left pocket with his phone and keys; Gemma's float in the right pocket) and buys a Danish pastry, a triangle of chocolate fudge cake, and an interesting shaped loaf. Sometimes, above the noise of conversation and stamping feet, he can hear the mandolin player in the corner.

He walks down the ramp to the lower level in front of the Brasserie's back windows. Woven carpets unrolled onto the ground, wooden cabinets, a rack of bright clothes. Scented candles, pink and green handmade soap.

He should get back to the stall. He pulls the Danish out of his paper bag and takes a mouthful of currants and icing.

"Just in time," Jim says when he slides back into the booth. "I've put the kettle on."

Late afternoon and the market is quieter. The mandolin player has gone, the vegetable stall only has the straggly remains of its produce. The guy with the carpets outside the Brasserie is rolling them up, carrying them on his shoulder towards his van. Jim is talking at length to one of his regular customers. Mustardseed eases himself out from behind the stall. Through the giant roof arch, the sky is darkening. It's getting colder. The lamps have come on in the market. The bangs and thumps of tables being folded, boxes dumped on the floor. Van engines. Jim's customer walks on towards Sainsbury's with a carrier of bright blue tea packets.

"I'm going to call it a day, Robert," Jim says, unplugging his kettle from the mains under the floorboards. "Will I be seeing you again perhaps?"

"Sure," Mustardseed says. "I'll come to say hi to Gemma when she's back."

Jim starts gathering together his unsold tea. Pretty much everyone is leaving now. Nearly five thirty. Mustardseed retrieves his boxes, and places the remaining glass jars carefully inside them. He puts away Gemma's painted sign. He carries the produce to the van. When he comes back Jim has almost finished packing up. Cigarette butts drift on the ground. A stray Sainsbury's carrier bag, a Pepsi bottle, bits of paper. Some lads are skateboarding where the woven carpets lay earlier. The boys' voices echo under the giant roof. Mustardseed smiles wryly. The space, the thump of feet on wood, the echoes. It's like a huge squash court. Memories.

Leaving Kyloe Mains on Sunday is even harder than Gemma thought it would be. It's a misty morning and, when she stands on the back terrace, she can't even see the Farnes or Holy Island Castle. She feels tears. This country has betrayed her: this vast, ancient, uncompromising land. It won't even show its face, so she can say goodbye.

Turning south onto the A1, the litany of road signs – Fenham-le-Moor, Detchant, Elwick, Seahouses, Adderstone – fall behind Gemma's car, as the needle creeps up the speedometer, and the road slants inland from the sand flats. At Newcastle, the sun comes out from behind the flimsy cloud to glint on the Tyne. The border of the magical kingdom. Now just the solid, muscular upper body of England, and the soft south below that.

Gemma stops at Woodall again. Frances struggles with the walk to the complex and back, says she is out of breath. Gemma has loved this week away, more than she can say, just the two of them, talking about times gone by: Frances's childhood at Kyloe Mains with her brother, George; marrying Gemma's grandfather; having Judy and Anthony; Gemma's absent father in Maine, who she only hears from a couple of times a year. But now, with each mile under the car's wheels, Gemma feels a growing relief that soon she will be back with her mother who can share the responsibilities and worry – no, more than worry, the fear – of looking after a frail and special person.

"I would like to see you settled with a nice man before I go," Frances says suddenly.

"You'd better not be going anywhere then," Gemma says. "I don't think that'll happen any time soon." The cold terror she always feels when Frances speaks about a future without her.

Gemma's never found it easy to meet men. She had her first boyfriend during A-levels, but he went to university in Manchester and that was the end of that. After sixth form, she did various jobs in shops, and six months in telesales, but she never met anyone through work. An old schoolfriend introduced her to a cousin and that was good while it lasted but, after a few months, Gemma realised both she and the guy were bored and she ended their affair. They're still friends on Facebook, but now he's engaged. So many of her friends are getting hitched up, renting flats together. A couple of girls are married and several have had babies. Gemma sighs. She's only twenty-three, but it seems to get harder with every passing year.

Monday morning and the weather has changed. Mustardseed rejects his cap and puts on a hooded jacket. The rain is cold on his face and, for the first time, he can feel the breath of winter approaching. Vehicles spray up arcs of cloudy water from the gutters, and the traffic lights in George Street cast hazy red and green reflections on the tarmac. Rain lashes the Bath stone facades, staining them a dirty grey. Pedestrians jostle each other with umbrellas. Mustardseed notices the hems of people's trousers are soaked, and feels his own jeans flapping wetly at his ankles.

He walks down Milsom Street towards the agency. In his pocket is Gemma's key. He fingers the cold metal with his cold fingers. There is no letterbox on the door; he had said he would lock up on Saturday night and post it through the other front door, the one the family uses, but he hasn't done this. On Saturday night when he took the leftover preserves back to the cottage, there were lights on in the living room, and the curtains were not fully drawn. He could make out a woman – Gemma's mother, Judy – in an armchair, a phone to her ear, a glass of white wine in her hand. If she saw him through the gap in the curtains, she didn't wave or acknowledge him. He hesitated at the letterbox and pocketed the key. He would return it to Gemma in person.

RG has called Mustardseed in for payment and debriefing this morning. Mustardseed is just a little apprehensive. RG probably phoned Gemma first thing to check she was happy with everything. She may have said she hasn't had the key back. Well, it is quite reasonable to return a key to someone in person. The only problem is that without the agency van he'll have to get the bus to South Stoke, which kind of makes it a big deal. So be it. If Gemma is pleased to see him, she won't care. If she isn't – well, he isn't going to think about that just yet.

He rings the bell. Fairy answers the intercom curtly, and the door buzzes open. He shoves back his hood and frees up his ponytail. Up to the half landing and cloakroom, then up the second flight to the offices. RG's door is closed; Fairy's is open, and he can see her in the little kitchen, putting side plates away in the wall cupboard.

"Morning, Fairy," Mustardseed greets her.

"He's on the telephone," she says stiffly. "You'd better wait on the landing."

Mustardseed loiters outside the offices. Fairy bangs the cupboard door shut and goes back into her room. She doesn't invite him in or offer him tea and jam tarts. RG's door swings wide.

"Mustardseed, dear boy. Come on through. Fairy!" he calls. "Could we have some tea please?"

Mustardseed settles in the soft chair, and watches the rain sliding down the window behind RG's head.

"Did you enjoy your time at the market?"

"Yes. It was good, really good."

"I knew it. I knew it. When I gave you the assignment your face fell, but you enjoyed it after all."

Mustardseed smiles awkwardly. "It didn't sound as exciting as the others."

"In this line of work, one can never predict what will be exciting. It is that unpredictability that creates the excitement."

"Have you spoken to Gemma? Was she happy with what I did?" Mustardseed slides his finger through the key ring in his pocket.

Fairy comes in without knocking, carrying the tea tray.

"Ah, Earl Grey. Thank you." RG pours two cups. Fairy straightens some papers on the top of the filing cabinet and stalks out.

"What did she say?"

"Fairy?"

"No, no, Gemma. What did she say about me?"

"Gemma. Yes. She was very pleased with your work. She said she hoped you had enjoyed it."

"Good. Yes, I did enjoy it."

RG hands Mustardseed a hefty envelope. "Your money."

"Thank you." Mustardseed drinks Earl Grey. "Do you, er, have any more jobs coming up that might be suitable for me?"

"I had a call this morning, but unfortunately the client requires a female agent. I'm waiting for Peaseblossom to return my call. There is, however, a small job you can do for me. Are you free tomorrow?"

"Yes."

"The van's booked in for its MOT tomorrow. Would you be kind enough to pick it up at eight and then collect it whenever it's ready? No doubt there will be work to be done, but we'll sort that out later as I need it on Wednesday."

Mustardseed thinks. If he could collect the van tomorrow afternoon, he could drive over to South Stoke with Gemma's house key. That would be much better than going on a damp bus and arriving smelling like a wet dog.

"Mustardseed?"

"Oh, sorry, I was just thinking."

"Is this inconvenient?"

"It's fine. Sorry, what were you saying?"

"This is the garage." RG hands him a red and white business card. "I'll be on my mobile if you need me, but not between two and four. I'll meet you at the van at eight."

Mustardseed wanders back up Milsom Street. The sky is slaty and the rain still falls. Oncoming vehicles have their headlamps on. It feels more like late afternoon. He wonders if Gemma will ring him or RG before he can get the key to her. Surely, she wouldn't ring RG; surely, she would ring him instead. Should he just get the bus there this afternoon? No, Gemma only got home yesterday. She's probably busy doing stuff, making jam, washing clothes, catching up with her emails or whatever. He'll go tomorrow when he's picked up the van.

The alarm goes off at seven thirty. Mustardseed wakes to rain slapping on his attic window. He bundles under the quilt. Nothing to get up for. Not just yet. He's not going running in this weather. Something's nagging in his head. *Shit.* The van. He chucks the covers to the floor and shivers. He only closed his eyes for a second. He looks at the clock. Ten to eight. *Shit, shit, shit.* He grabs his running clothes, forces his feet into trainers. Looks like he is going running after all, or he'll never get to the van in time. He pulls on a hoodie and hurtles down the six flights. Outside, the street lamps give a queasy light to the grey morning. It's all downhill to the van. He lengthens his stride.

The RG van is kept on a strip of land at the end of a residential street by the Avon. Mustardseed isn't sure if it's parked legally but he's never seen a ticket on it. He suspects RG has an arrangement with someone somewhere.

Of course, RG is already there. He's twirling a large black umbrella, decorated with silver italics (*In thunder, lightning, or in rain?*) and glaring at his watch.

"I'm sorry," Mustardseed gasps, slithering on the wet flagstones. "I overslept."

RG holds out the keys, a glint of wet metal, then spins around and stalks away through the rain.

Mustardseed unlocks the door and gets in. Rain streams down the glass. He fires the engine, turns on lights and wipers. As he bumps off the uneven land and onto the road, he puts on the radio and twists up the heating. The garage is along London Road. He'll have to run home from there in his soaking clothes, and his muscles will be cold by then.

The rush-hour traffic grunts slowly through the city centre. He stalls the van at a pedestrian crossing and swears. He swerves onto the garage forecourt, only fifteen minutes late. Quickly, he hands over the keys and gives the guy on the desk his mobile number.

"Call me as soon as it's ready," he says.

Outside, he adjusts his hood, and starts for home and a hot bath.

From lunchtime Mustardseed checks his phone. No calls. Nothing. He's getting twitchy. Gemma must have realised he still has her key. He must get it back to her, and he wants to see her again and ask how her trip went. Now the job is finished, perhaps he could ask her if she'd like to meet up for a drink and a chat sometime. He smiles: if he asks her out he'll have to disclose his real name, but that won't matter now, will it?

It rains all day, and he stays in the flat. The small rooms and sloping ceilings are oppressive, especially with the insistent crack of rain on the windows. He's restless.

The garage doesn't phone until four. He can collect the van. There is work to be done for the MOT, of course, but that will be sorted out later. Mustardseed tells them Mr Goodfellow will be in touch to arrange a date.

When he slams the front door behind him the rain has stopped. The pavements are greasy with rainwater, but the sky is clearing. A cold wind rustles leaves from the trees in St James Square. The walk suddenly seems impossibly far. At last he sees the neon sign on the left.

They've fiddled with the seat. He adjusts it and turns into the traffic flow. Maybe he should have phoned Gemma but he's driving now, so he'll take his chances when he gets there. If she's not there, then OK, this time he will leave the key. That way he can ring her later to check she has got it, and he can ask her then on the phone if she would like to meet up.

He's surprised how nervous he is when he arrives in South Stoke. There's a patch of muddy grass by Gemma's garden gate for parking. Her Renault is not there. There are no cars there. Mustardseed is deflated. It looks like she's not around. He parks and turns off the engine. He should have called her. He'll just go up to the cottage and check in case she has parked somewhere else, or maybe her car is at a garage too.

He squelches through the puddles to the gate. It's stuck fast and he gives it a kick. Rainwater runs from the cottage gutter. There's a light on in the living room. Someone must be at home. He glances quickly in. An older woman is on the sofa. Gemma's grandmother, Frances.

He goes to the second door. The lights are off. Gemma's not in her kitchen. He bangs on the door, feeling stupid. No answer. He peers through the front window, through the hanging sunburst. The kitchen is empty. There are some glass jars on the tabletop, filled with something dark. He moves away from the door, turns, gazes out over the village below to the hills on the horizon. This hasn't worked out at all. It's all wrong. Now he just wants to get rid of the bloody key and take the van back to Bath.

He retraces his steps to the other door, the real front door, and lifts the heavy knocker. He waits for Frances to come to the door. It may take her a while, she's not in the best shape. Moments pass. Nothing happens. *Is she asleep?* he wonders. *Or deaf?* He bangs again. Still nothing. Perhaps she doesn't answer the door. But though she is old, from what Gemma's told him she's spunky. He can't imagine her not answering the door. Suddenly he is ill at ease.

He opens the letterbox and calls through.

"Hello. Mrs…Frances. It's Robert here, Gemma's…friend."

Jesus. Something is very very wrong. Everything's wrong. There's a way through from Gemma's kitchen to the main house. He checks the living room window on his way past. Frances is still on the sofa. She hasn't moved.

No, no, shit, fuck. His heart is soaring. He fumbles with the key, lets himself into the kitchen. It's dark in the cottage with no lights on. The room smells of garlic. He turns to the right. There's a lobby with a closed door on the other side. He tries the handle and he's in the living room, a long low-ceilinged room, probably two rooms knocked through. He runs over to the woman on the sofa.

"Frances?" he says loudly.

She's leaning to the side, propped on the sofa arm, but her neck has sagged down. Her eyes are staring. He's digging in his pocket for his phone with one hand; with the other he locates a fluttery carotid pulse. She's alive, she's alive. She must have had a stroke or something.

"Ambulance," he says.

The man on the phone wants details of the patient, of the events.

"Eighties," Mustardseed says. "She might have had a stroke. There's a pulse, but she's not responding. It's like she can't hear me."

Where the hell's Gemma?

He hangs up from the emergency services and finds her number in his mobile. When it clicks to voicemail he hangs up. He can't leave a message. Not about this. He doesn't even know which school her mother works at. There's nothing he can do except wait with Frances. He sits down beside her, takes her cold hand, and starts talking. In the corner the two guinea pigs rustle in their hay. Mustardseed waits for the howl of the ambulance and wonders if anyone will ask who he is and why he is in someone else's house, ringing 999 for a stranger.

Gemma hardly ever does anything. Anything except the market, that is. When Rebecca texted her last night, asking if she wanted to meet up in town on Tuesday, she felt like saying no, she had just driven back from Northumberland, she had chutneys to make, that she just didn't feel like it. Instead, though, she texted back and said yes, that would be lovely. She woke up early, chopped tomatoes and garlic till her hands throbbed, transferred the warm, sticky mixture into glass jars and left them to cool on the table.

The weather was so awful she felt even less inclined to go, but she didn't want to let Rebecca down. Before she went out she made tea for Frances, left her with a glass of water and the phone nearby on the table. She promised she wouldn't be too late back. As she drove into town, her wipers cutting a swathe through the raindrops, she told herself she had to have a life. Frances would be fine in the cottage alone. She was on other days. She would be today.

Gemma told Rebecca about her trip to Northumberland. Rebecca didn't ask who ran the stall in Green Park. She probably didn't realise being away would matter. They went into clothes shops and tried on dresses and tops and high-heeled shoes. Gemma bought some brown suede boots from New Look. They had coffee in Nero's. Rebecca asked Gemma if she'd like to stay on to eat in town, but Gemma said she really had to get back; she'd promised Frances.

Back at her car, she throws her new boots onto the back seat and puts the keys in the ignition. Before she drives off she checks her mobile. Missed calls from Mustardseed. Gemma smiles. She knows he still has her key, but that doesn't bother her. He's called her. As soon as she gets home she'll ring him back.

Mustardseed stands in the lane, waiting, watching for Gemma or her mother to come home. Frances has been taken away in the ambulance. Mustardseed simply said he was Robert, a friend of Gemma's. The paramedics didn't question this. Now he stands in the road, where a tractor has flattened mud into the tarmac, and waits. He's called Gemma two more times: still voicemail. She won't know it's him. She won't have stored his number. He'll just wait. He'll wait all evening if he has to. One of them must come home shortly.

He can hear a car approaching. Headlamps coming down the lane, slowing. It's Gemma's Clio. He stands aside. She stops when she sees him, slides down her window.

"Hello," she says. "Are you waiting for me? I'm sorry I missed your calls. Hang on, let me park."

She swings in behind the van, kills the engine and lights. She reaches for something on the back seat: a bulky carrier bag.

"Gemma," he begins, as she locks the car.

"You'd better move the van," she starts. "Mummy won't be too happy not to have her parking space. You can take it just down the road there. You do that and I'll put the kettle on."

"Gemma," he says again, more forcefully.

"What is it?" she asks.

"It's your grandmother. It's Frances. She's gone to hospital in an ambulance."

"What? How d'you know?" Gemma shoves past him and kicks the gate back.

"She's not there." Mustardseed jogs beside her. "Look, I came down to see you, to give you the key back. You weren't there. I tried the other door. I could see her in there, on the sofa. She wasn't moving. I used the key to get in and she didn't even know I was there. I called the ambulance."

"What happened? I must go to her."

"She improved a bit with the paramedics," he tells her, and it's not a lie.

Frances did stir when the ambulance arrived. She was barely coherent, but she was speaking. She didn't acknowledge him or ask what he was doing in her house. She didn't seem to notice him. He stood back, in the corner with the guineas. The paramedics told Frances they were taking her to hospital; she tried to refuse. Mustardseed watched them wheel her out to the ambulance, slide her in, bolt the doors, and then he was left alone in the cold grey afternoon, waiting for Gemma.

He follows her into the living room. She drops her shopping bag, slides her rucksack off her shoulder. The sofa is still dented from where Frances was sitting. A patchwork cushion has fallen to the floor.

"She was there, she was there when I left…there's her tea." Gemma picks up a mug from the coffee table. It's half-full of cold tea. "Does Mummy know?"

"I didn't know how to get hold of her," Mustardseed says helplessly. "I didn't know what to do. I thought I should follow Frances to the hospital because I found her, but then you'd come home and…"

"I'm frightened," Gemma cries. "She's always been here. I can't imagine…she's not been well…they say it's her kidneys…I must go to her."

Mustardseed wants to hug her, but she's standing away from him, with her arms crossed on her chest, and he doesn't like to step towards her.

"We need to tell your mother," he says gently. "Is she still at work?"

"She was going to Sainsbury's after work."

"Do you want me to call her for you?" he offers.

"I'll do it."

Gemma picks up the handset she left for Frances. Mustardseed doesn't know whether to walk out of the room and give her space, or to stay with her.

"Hospital…? No, I was with Rebecca. You know, Mustardseed…he came to bring back the key… I don't know…I haven't phoned them… I don't know…yes, he waited for me…yes, yes, OK." Gemma offers him the phone. "She says *can she talk to you*?"

Mustardseed takes the phone, imagines the woman he saw curled in the chair in this very room, with her drink in her hand.

"Hello?" he says.

"Can you tell me what's happened please?"
"I came over to return Gemma's key. There was no answer, but I could see your mother was in the chair. I knocked, thinking I could leave the key with her, but she didn't come to the door. She didn't move. I knew I had to get in to her, so I came in through Gemma's kitchen. She wasn't conscious. I felt a pulse. I rang the ambulance. I thought she'd had a stroke."
"What did the paramedics say?"
"Not a lot really. They just said she had to go in for investigations. I tried to call Gemma but I couldn't get her."
"Did they think it was serious?"
"I don't know."
"I'm in Sainsbury's at the moment," Judy says. "I'm just in the queue. I'll go straight to the hospital."
"Shall I drive Gemma up to meet you there?"
"Let me go on my own, see what they say. I'll call Gemma as soon as I hear anything."
"OK. I can stay with her if she'd me to. Until you get home."
"Thank you," says Judy. "And thank you for before. I'm sorry, we've not met…but thank you."
"I'll go to the hospital now," Gemma says.
"Please just stay there with Gemma for now," Judy says, overhearing. "I'll ring as soon as I can. Could I have a wine carrier please? I've got my own bags. Look, I have to go."
She hangs up the call.
"What's happening?" Gemma crumples down on the sofa where Frances had been. She reaches for the cushion. "She made this when I was little. This here," Gemma indicates pink flowered hexagons, "was one of my baby dresses."
"Your mum's going straight to the hospital when she's done the shopping. She asked me to stay with you until she has any news. If you'd like me to, that is."
"She doesn't want me to go there? What does she think it is?"
"She doesn't know any more than we do. She says she will call as soon as she can. You could phone the hospital but they probably won't tell you anything."
"I should be there."
"Your mum said you should wait here."
Gemma nods miserably. "You said you'd wait with me?"
"Yes, I can."
Gemma drops the cushion.
"Shall I make us a drink?" Mustardseed asks. He holds out his hand to help her up.
The family kitchen is busy, chaotic, with blue-washed wooden cupboards and bright Mexican tiles. There's a lime green table lamp on the worktop, numerous scraps of paper, a half-full bottle of red wine with a twisted metal stopper. Gemma yanks out the stopper, sloshes wine into two goblets.
"You only came to return the key," she says, pulling out a chair at the pine dining table.
"Well, and…"
She looks at him. He takes a mouthful of wine.
"What?"
"I was going to see if you'd like to meet up some time," he says at last. "Now the job's over, but now's not the time to talk about things like that."
"No." Gemma turns away and he can't read her profile.

"I'm so sorry, Gemma. I'm sorry about what's happened, and that it was me who found her, and that I had to be the one to tell you."

"I'm so glad you were here," she says, turning back to him. "If you hadn't..."

If he hadn't been there, Gemma would have returned home with her shopping bags to find her grandmother unconscious or dead even.

"Are you doing any other jobs for Mr Goodfellow?"

"Not at the moment."

"Is it your proper job?"

"For now," Mustardseed says. "I'm sort of in limbo. I do casual jobs. I'm making decisions about the future."

"What decisions?"

"About where I want to go to uni. I thought I'd go somewhere else, somewhere far away like Scotland, but now I'm not sure. I might apply for Bath."

"What do you want to study?"

"Chemistry."

"Oh," says Gemma, then, "Do you think she'll be all right? She will be all right, won't she?"

"Gemma, I don't know." He hesitates. "She was pretty poorly when I found her."

"But she was breathing. You said she had a pulse."

"She did, but it was faint, and it was like she was in a coma or something. She just wasn't aware of me."

Gemma scrapes back her chair. "I must feed Guinness and Murphy." She opens a tall fridge and takes out the salad box. It's full of plastic bags of greenery. She frantically shreds leaves into a sieve. "Could you bring me their bottle please?"

Mustardseed goes into the living room. The guineas are squeaking, rustling up and down in the hay. He reaches in and strokes each of the soft black and white noses. He unhooks their drinking bottle and takes it through to Gemma.

"One of the other agents, she had a job pet-sitting," he says.

Gemma breaks off from chopping cucumber to refill the bottle.

"Agents?" she repeats.

"That's what RG...Mr Goodfellow...calls us."

"Agent Mustardseed." She hands him back the bottle. "What are the others called?"

He opens his mouth, closes it. He doesn't know if he should tell her. "Cobweb, Moth, and Peaseblossom," he says at last. "Moth had to move into some guy's house when he was away, look after his cats."

"Why all the Shakespeare names?"

"It suits the agency."

"Do you like Shakespeare?"

"Yeah, I do. I found myself with time on my hands in my teens and I started reading a lot then. Shakespeare, all sorts."

He takes the bottle back to the guineas. He doesn't want to tell her he had all this time because he was often away at tournaments. He doesn't want to tell her how his dream ended, how he failed. Not today. One day, but not today.

As he attaches the bottle to the hutch he wonders what the next few days will bring. He wonders if Frances will live. He wonders how Gemma will cope if she doesn't. He turns at the sound of her footsteps.

"Here we are, boys." She scoops leaves, carrot and cucumber into the hutch. The guineas scuttle around, squeaking.

"Do you have pets?"

"No, I'm completely on my own. We had some rabbits when I was little."

They both start at the ring of the phone. Gemma hands Mustardseed the empty salad bowl and picks up the receiver. Mustardseed watches the guineas crunching on their vegetables. Which is Guinness and which is Murphy?

"How is she? What do they say? Well, they must know…what's happening…? Yes, he's here…We're just feeding the guineas… OK, I guess not… When can I see her?"

Mustardseed takes the bowl back to the kitchen. He drains his wineglass. Gemma comes back.

"What did she say?" he asks.

"Not much. They're still assessing her. They think there may be a urinary infection. Mummy says she can't do much more at the moment. She's coming home now, and we'll go up later this evening. She says would you like to stay to eat with us? I'll make a start on some pasta."

"No, I think you should have time with your mum tonight. I'll wait till she gets home. I should speak to her, say hello and that, and then I'll get off. I have to get the van back to RG."

"Could you move the van?" Gemma asks. "She'll have shopping to unload."

"Of course."

He goes out into the dark. It's still cold, and the wind is up. The gate is hanging open. He hopes RG hasn't gone looking for the van. Perhaps he's still in Bristol. At the gate, Mustardseed turns back to the long cottage. It looks cosy and homely with the lights on. Poor Gemma. He just wants to give her a hug, but still he doesn't like to. He rolls the van down the hill, parks on the verge and walks back to the house. Gemma is making a cheese sauce at the stove.

"Is it just you and your brother?" she asks.

"My brother?"

"Robert. Is it just you and him?"

"I've got two sisters. Lizzie and Jessie."

"Now you're not working for me, you could tell me your name."

Mustardseed sighs. He feels a right shit. He can't not tell her that, not tonight.

"Actually, it is Robert," he says. "I don't have a brother."

Rain speckles the windscreen, blurring the taillights ahead. Gemma is hunched low in the passenger seat of Judy's Audi. The heater is on high, and she is hot with the scarf around her neck.

Visiting hours are over by the time they arrive at the hospital. After dinner, which Gemma couldn't stomach, Judy showered and changed and phoned the hospital. She couldn't get any more information about a diagnosis but was told they could come in at any time. Frances is in Medical Admissions.

The car park is nearly empty at this time. The falling drizzle freckles the pools of rainwater in the tarmac. Judy parks. The two doors slamming sound hollow and loud. An ambulance comes nearer, shrieking; in the corner of the car park a hatchback's hazards are flashing as its alarm beeps. Gemma and Judy start for the main entrance. It's cold out of the car.

The main atrium is deserted, the shutters pulled down on the café, the shop closed and barred. The cleaners are on the corridors, with trailing Hoover cables. Judy hesitates at the signboard.

"This way," she says.

Gemma watches their two striding figures in the plate glass windows to the right. She can hear rumbling wheels from somewhere, but the trolley – or whatever it is – and the person pushing it never appear.

Frances is awake. A nurse is leaning over her, doing something with her hand. Gemma sees there's a needle in the back of it. Someone has removed Frances's clothes and dressed her in a hospital gown.

"Hello," Frances says as Gemma and Judy approach.

"How are you?" Judy asks.

Gemma can't speak. Frances is alert and smiling. It must all have been a mistake. Perhaps, Mustardseed overreacted. It was kind of him, but obviously Frances is fine.

"Can't you tell them to take this thing out?" Frances plucks at the needle in her hand.

"Now, come on, Frances," says the nurse. "We've had this conversation several times already." She turns to Judy. "Are you two all right with her now?"

"Thank you," Judy says shortly.

Gemma glances around the ward. She wonders if they should pull the curtains to, give Frances some privacy.

"Have you come to take me home?" Frances asks.

"What do the doctors say?" Gemma manages at last.

"I don't know. They don't tell me anything. When can I get out of here?"

"Gemma, you stay here," Judy says. "I'm going to find the doctor who's seen her. This is ridiculous. They must have some idea what the problem is."

"There's no problem," Frances says. "I'm fine. I want to go now. Gemma, love, can you find my clothes for me? I think they're in that green bag there."

"We can't just take you home," Gemma says. "We need to find out what's the matter with you."

Or could we? she wonders. *Could we not just bundle her in the car, and take her home, and the whole episode will become nothing more than a bad dream?* She's hot again, and unwinds her scarf.

Judy approaches with a tall, skinny man in a striped shirt. He has a stethoscope around his neck. He must be the doctor. He doesn't look old enough to be a consultant.

"Can I just check her medication with you?" he asks. "I understand neither of you were home at the time, and a friend called the ambulance?"

"I was at work," Judy says distantly, "and my daughter was out. We had no reason to think anything would happen today."

"Her medication?" the doctor repeats.

"Doxazosin, Atenolol, Furosemide, a statin of some kind–"

"Pravastain," Gemma interrupts.

"Domperidone, Gaviscon…"

"What's the Domperidone for?"

"She's had a hiatus hernia for some years."

"OK, thanks."

"So, what's the problem?" Judy asks. "Was it a stroke?"

"No, I don't think so. There's no indication for that. It looks like there's a urinary infection, which we will treat with antibiotics."

"That's not so bad," Gemma smiles at Frances.

"What?"

"Urinary infection. That can be treated, can't it?"

The doctor glances from Gemma to Judy.

"What?" Judy demands.

"Your mother's blood pressure is very low."

"But it's always high," Gemma says. "She's on medication to lower it."

"It's very low now. And her pulse rate is high. You know that she has severe kidney impairment."

"It's not serious," Judy says. "Not yet."

"She's seeing Dr Thomas soon," Gemma adds. "The renal consultant."

The doctor scribbles in the notes, pockets his pen.

"I'll leave you with her now," he says.

"Can someone take this thing out?" Frances fiddles again with the cannula in her hand.

"No, leave that," Gemma scolds, taking Frances's other hand.

Her hand feels tiny, cold yet sticky. Gemma suddenly realises that Frances has no idea about the conversation they've just had with the doctor. Her eyes are open and she is talking, but she's not there, she's not with them.

Guinness and Murphy are scratching in the hay. Gemma is alone with them in the living room. It's one in the morning. Judy went to bed at midnight after a quick call to her brother, Anthony. He's in Carlisle; there's nothing he can do. '*Go to bed, get some rest,*' she urged Gemma. Gemma went up to her little room under the eaves, and turned on the lamp, but she couldn't relax, and came down again to drink tea and sit with the guineas. One of them squeaks angrily. Gemma stirs from the sofa. Murphy is out, glaring at her with a cross black and white face. The clock ticks over the mantelpiece.

They gave the ward staff all their numbers, home and mobiles. The phones have been quiet. Gemma's mobile is on the coffee table. She even takes it to the bathroom with her.

She nudges Murphy back into his sleeping quarters. A scuffle breaks out again as he disturbs Guinness. She takes her empty mug into the kitchen and quietly climbs the stairs. The lamp is on in Judy's room. She pads in silently. Judy is sleeping. Gemma turns out the light and Judy stirs.

"What is it?" she says.

"Nothing," Gemma says.

"What time is it?"

"Just after one. Mummy, I'm going back."

"Back where?"

"To the hospital."

"Gemma, go to bed. You can't do anything."

"They said we could go back."

"I'm really tired. I can't go with you."

"I'm not asking you to. I'm going on my own. I'll have my phone."

Judy sighs. "Just be careful," she says.

As Gemma puts on her coat and collects her car keys she suddenly remembers Mustardseed. He asked her to text him and let him know what's happening. Quickly she takes out her phone.

'Urinary infection and low blood pressure. They are keeping her in. The Dr is concerned about her kidneys. I don't think he's told us everything. I'm going back there now. G.'

He's probably asleep, she thinks, as she hits send. She puts on the external light and closes the front door behind her. There's a damp film all over the car. The village is silent. She puts on full beam. She's tired. She was up early making tomato and garlic chutney. She really shouldn't be driving. Her mobile cheeps with a text. There's no one else on the road. She stops, grabs the phone from the passenger seat.

'Let me know how things go. Whatever time.'

In the city there is more traffic: a late-night bus, a police car with siren and strobes. There are still people wandering on the pavements, some shouting, two men shoving each other. Gemma turns into the hospital car park. She takes a ticket and the striped barrier rises to let her in. There are only a couple of other cars. She parks in the centre, where there are no shadows or dark corners. She runs across to the building, into the atrium and down the empty corridor. She passes no one on her way to Medical Admissions. The desk is deserted and the ward on low light. She recognises the voice of the nurse from behind closed curtains around another bed. The curtains bulge and the nurse comes out.

Frances is awake, her hands fluttering on the bed cover.

"Hey, I'm back," Gemma says.

"What time is it?"

"Nearly two o'clock."

"Have I been here a day?"

"No, just a few hours."

Frances looks unwell. Gemma looks for the doctor but he's not there. Frances has a drip of some kind – perhaps it's the antibiotics for her urinary infection.

"When can I go home?"

"I don't know. When you're better."

"I'm fine." Frances's fingers find the cannula in her hand. "Can you take this out for me?"

"No, you're on a drip. Leave it alone. It's not that bad."

"It hurts."

"It'll be out soon, when you come home."

"I might not come home."

"What d'you mean? You just said you wanted to come home."

"I won't be here for ever, Gemma."

"Stop that," Gemma cries.

The nurse glances up and comes over.

"Everything all right, Frances? Not trying to take out the drip again, are you?"

"It hurts," Frances says again.

Gemma feels hot tears in her eyes. Frances is falling further and further from her. She wishes she hadn't come back. This ward, this nurse with her frizzy hair, this half-light: it's all wrong, everything's wrong, and she suddenly feels so tired she can hardly stand, and she doesn't know how she'll be able to drive home.

There's a clock on the wall at the end of the ward. It's after two.

"I'm going to go and let you sleep now," she tells Frances, and leans down to kiss her on the forehead.

Walking back to the atrium she passes a man in theatre scrubs with a blue gown trailing behind him. A lift clanks loudly in its shaft; the doors creak open and a porter steps out, speaking into a hand-held radio.

In the atrium, the glass doors hiss apart. Gemma steps out and they hiss back behind her. A gust of wind whips the trees at the perimeter fence. She starts towards the car park. Her heart swoops. She turns behind her. Nothing. The wind again. She fumbles coins into the parking meter; she drops a fifty pence piece. A squall of rain hits her face. The night is hostile. She's running now, running towards her car, alone in the middle of the car park. She flings open the door and falls inside. The door slams and she exhales.

Suddenly she senses something; she jerks around, expecting to see – what? – in the back seat. Nothing but the splatter of rain on the rear window.

Her breathing calms a little. She holds her phone in her hand. He was awake not that long ago.

'She's really poorly. I don't know what to do. She's confused and doesn't know what's happening.'

She waits, holding the phone, as its screen fades. She must go home. She needs sleep. She's shivering. The ignition fires and she flicks on the headlamps. Her phone rings loudly. *Mustardseed* it says on the screen. Not the ward, not the ward.

"Gemma, where are you?"

"At the hospital. It's awful. I don't know what–"

"Are you staying there all night?" he asks.

"No, I'm in the car. I'm about to drive home. I'm so tired. I have to sleep."

She can feel her eyelids dropping.

"Come here. Come to mine. You can crash on the sofa. I don't want you driving home, when you're tired. Call your mum and tell her."

"I can't."

"Gemma, just come. I'll go and wait on the street for you. I'll help you find somewhere to park. You'll be safe with me, and you'll be nearer the hospital for the morning."

Mustardseed tugs jeans and a jumper over his shorts. He'd been in bed, not sleeping, wondering what was happening with Gemma and Frances, but not liking to call. He finds a visitors' parking permit pinned to his kitchen noticeboard, and writes in Gemma's registration number, memorised at Green Park. He runs down the six flights of stairs and opens the front door. It's cold, and the wind carries a cardboard Starbucks cup down the hill. Ragged clouds ride the sky. There is no one about. Yes, there is a parking space just a few doors up from his. He shivers in the chill, and waits for the sound of a car engine. At last headlamps. He gestures to the space. Gemma parks awkwardly, bumping the kerb.

"Here," he says, handing her the permit. "Put this on the dashboard."

She takes it from him, doesn't even glance at it, or the letters and numbers he's written on it.

"Did you call your mum?" he asks, as she locks the car.

"Yes."

"In here." He gestures for her to go first into the hall. He reaches past her for the light switch. "It's all the way to the top."

The lights expire as they reach the top landing, but he's left his flat door ajar and a warm lozenge of light spills out. He shows her into the living room, takes her coat and hangs it over the top of the door.

"Sit down," he says, gesturing to the sofa.

He's puffed up the cushions, got rid of the pile of rubbish on it: a newspaper, an unopened letter, a chocolate wrapper.

"Thanks," Gemma says and crumples down.

Gemma is so tired and her eyes are aching, but still she looks around the little room. The living room and kitchen are open-plan. A narrow breakfast bar separates the two. There are bookcases on either side of the hearth, packed with books, and there are more volumes on the floor. There's a framed Egon Schiele print, and a tall knobbly cactus at the window. The walls are a golden yellow, the sofa sienna. In the corner are two pairs of trainers and some racquets sheathed in dark cases.

Mustardseed slides behind the breakfast bar and turns on the kettle. His hair is loose tonight, tumbling down his back.

"I'm sure you could do with a cup of tea," he says.

"Tea, yes, thanks."

He holds up a bottle. "And some of this, perhaps?"

"I don't drink whisky."

"Just a little one then." He hands her a glass while he makes tea.

She gulps the whisky and it burns her mouth. Mustardseed places her mug on a low table, sits beside her on the sofa.

"Tell me what's happening," he says.

"Are you sure you don't mind me being here?"

"I'm sure. What do the doctors say?"

"They say it's a urinary infection, and her kidneys are bad. We knew she had bad kidneys, but no one told us this could happen. She was fine last week when we were away."

Was she fine? Gemma asks herself. Her walking was unsteady and she dozed a lot, but she was taking her tablets and was coherent to talk to, not like the frail shell she's become in a matter of hours.

"It's bad," she says, and drinks the last of the whisky. "It's bad. I'm frightened."

"What are they doing for her?"

"We saw the doctor earlier. He said they'd give her antibiotics for the infection. When I went in just now she had a drip… I suppose it was those. I couldn't see the doctor anywhere. She was fiddling with the needle, you know, the needle in her hand. She said it was hurting and she wanted it out. I know she can't have it out because of the drip, but no one was listening to her, the nurse, you know, it was like because she's old no one cares. They just talk over her."

"I'm so sorry, Gemma. If I'd only found her earlier…"

"You found her. She wasn't alone. You were there. I wanted her to meet you. I don't think she ever will now."

Now she's said it. She's never envisaged a life without Frances. Frances has always been there with her. It simply isn't possible to have a life without Frances, even though she's always known that one day that time would come. In her darkest moments she has wondered when, where, and how, but she's never imagined a narrative like this. When will the story end? Tonight? Tomorrow? It's already tomorrow. What is the date that will become one she'll never forget?

"Antibiotics are really good these days. If it was only today she became so ill, the chances are they can get the infection in the early stages."

"You play tennis?"

"What?"

"Tennis. The racquets."

"No, squash."

"Oh. Isn't that terribly energetic?"

"I guess so," he says.

"Are you very good?"

"I was."

"You don't play now?"

"I do a bit," he says. "With friends. I used to play properly. Yes, I was good. It's what I wanted to do, but I injured my shoulder and that was the end of it."

"You wanted to be a professional squash player? Did you win things then?"

"A few. England under 18s, England under 21s, I was in a European final, but I lost that."

"Jesus, you must be good."

Her head swims, from the whisky, or tiredness, or terror, or all three.

"I'm sorry," she says. "I'm keeping you awake."

"It's OK. Do you want to talk or do you want to sleep?"

"I don't know. I should go back to the hospital, shouldn't I?"

"No, she needs her rest and so do you." Mustardseed stands, gathers together glasses and mugs. "I think you should try to sleep now. I'll find you a blanket and a towel. The bathroom's…well, you can't get lost up here."

"I don't think I can sleep."

"Please try. Tomorrow may be a long day." He hands her a white towel and a stripy blanket. "Use the bathroom first, so I can make sure you're OK before I turn in."

She stands unsteadily and takes the towel into the bathroom. It's a tiny oblong off the hallway, jammed between the living room at the front and the bedroom at the back. The walls are a bright peppermint green. The shower curtain is red and white stripes. She closes the door, stares miserably at her reflection. She has nothing with her: no toothbrush, comb, deodorant, make-up. She squirts a caterpillar of toothpaste onto her fingers and scrubs it around her mouth. She splashes water on her face. That will have to do.

In the living room, Mustardseed has arranged the blanket on the sofa, organised cushions for pillows, placed a glass of water on the table. The lights in the galley kitchen are off. There's only the standard lamp casting a queasy circle of light. Gemma kicks off her shoes, and gets under the blanket.

"Try to sleep," he says again, clicking off the light.

He squeezes her shoulder gently as he walks by. For a moment Gemma wonders what would happen if she reached out, took his wrist, pulled him back to her, but now he has gone, and there's only the whirring of the bathroom fan and the muffled rush of tap water. She stares around the little room with its sloping walls and tiny square window. Her phone is on the coffee table. She'll hear it if it rings.

Mustardseed falls into bed. He's more tired than he realised. The fan whirrs on in the darkened bathroom, then stops. Gemma is quiet in the front room. He can't hear the snuffle of tears, or her restless movements on the sofa. Perhaps she is asleep.

For the first time in ages he's got a girl in the flat, a girl he really likes, and he can't do anything, say anything. Her grandmother is ill, possibly dying. It would be dreadful for him to –

A noise, a terrible noise. Gemma starts awake, confused. Neon light pulses from her phone on the table. She grabs it. It's her mother.

"Gemma, it's me."

"What's happened?"

"The hospital just called me. They say she's taken a turn for the worse. I spoke to one of the doctors. He said we should go in straightway."

"What's happened?"

"I don't know. He just said we really should go in as soon as possible."

Gemma swings her legs to the floor. Her jeans have been digging in and she can feel red pressure lines all over her flesh.

"I'll drive up now. Can you get there as well?"

"What's the time?" Gemma asks.

"Half six."

"Yes, yes, I'll come."

"They said she's been moved to Coronary Care."

"I thought it was kidneys?"

"Look, I don't know. That's what he told me. I'll see you soon, OK."

"OK."

Gemma turns. Mustardseed is in the doorway, wearing shorts and a printed T-shirt. She can't read the slogan in the half-light.

"Was that the hospital?" he asks.

"It was Mummy." Gemma stands up, tangles her feet in the trailing blanket, stumbles. He grabs her and steadies her.

"What's happened?"

"One of the doctors phoned her. I have to go to the hospital. She's worse. They said we should come now."

Still he's holding her arms. She feels if he let go, she would crumple.

"I'll come with you," he says.

"No, no, you don't have to."

"I want to. Give me five minutes."

He lets go of her, and she doesn't fall. She forces her feet into her shoes. She drinks the glass of water he left for her, refills it, drinks again. He comes out of the bathroom wearing the jeans and jumper he had on the night before. He runs a hand through his hair. Quickly Gemma goes into the bathroom; this time she avoids her face in the glass.

"Don't forget your phone." Mustardseed hands it to her when she comes out.

She pockets it and stumbles down the stairs while he locks the flat. Her feet are cold and clumsy. On the street outside she shivers in the grey dawn.

Mustardseed slams the passenger door. The windscreen is fogged with condensation. Gemma starts the engine. *It should be me driving her to the hospital,* he thinks angrily. He can't even give her a lift because he doesn't have a car, and he's returned the van keys to the agency.

Gemma jerks out of the parking space. A few early buses wheeze along, throwing up gutter water. Lights are coming on in flats and houses; sometimes a figure hurries along the pavement, hunched into a raincoat, carrying a brolly or a briefcase.

The sky has lightened to a gunmetal grey. *It's not raining yet, but it will,* Mustardseed thinks. When Gemma slides down her window to take a parking ticket the air that sucks in is cold and wintery. She drives under the barrier, the ticket in her mouth, the window still open. She parks, and flings open her door.

"I can't see her," she says, looking round the car park.

"Your mum?"

"I can't see her car."

"Do you want to wait for her?" he asks.

"No," Gemma says. "Let's go. Coronary Care. They've moved her to Coronary Care. I don't understand that. Her heart's fine."

Mustardseed doesn't know what to say. He just walks beside her, across the damp car park to the grim, grey edifice.

It seems to Gemma that she hasn't been away, that she hasn't been to Mustardseed's flat, that she hasn't slept. People are walking ahead of them through the glass doors to the atrium, staff on the early shifts. The shutters on the café are still down, the shop is still closed. Nothing has changed from the dark hours, except the people striding through, their heels clicking, to the artery corridors that branch off to wards and departments.

The door to Coronary Care is closed. There's an intercom. Gemma presses it urgently.

"Gemma Thompson," she says. "For my grandmother, Frances."

The door beeps. Mustardseed takes her arm. "I'll wait for you here."

Gemma hesitates. "No," she says. "Come in with me. I don't want to do this on my own."

Frances is in a bed straight ahead under a window. Her cubicle curtains are drawn on either side, open at the foot of the bed. The bright lights of the ward and the pewter square of sky make it appear like night time. A male nurse is fiddling with Frances's drip. On her upper arm is a blood pressure cuff.

"Hello again," Gemma says.

"Gemma," says Frances. "What are you doing back here?"

"I've come to see you."

"Who's that with you?"

"It's er…Robert," Gemma says. "A friend."

"Robert. You mean young Mustardseed?"

"Yes, Mustardseed," Gemma says, not caring what the nurse thinks.

"How long have I been here?" Frances demands. "What's the time?"

"Just gone seven."

"What are we having for dinner then?"

"It's seven in the morning," Gemma says gently. She turns to the nurse. "Why's she in here? I thought it was her kidneys. Can you tell me what you're doing?" She wishes Judy were here. She shouldn't be doing this on her own. But she's not on her own: Mustardseed is here.

"We're giving her an infusion of Dobutamine," the nurse says. "Her blood pressure is very low and her heart rate is too high. She has developed pulmonary oedema." He places an oxygen mask over Frances's face.

"Gemma, take this off for me." Frances tugs at the mask.

"No," Gemma whispers. "You need that. Leave it alone."

"She doesn't like it," the nurse says, adjusting the drip. "Her ECG was all right," he says over his shoulder as he leaves the bedside.

Gemma sits in the visitors' chair and takes Frances's hand. Frances says something but she can't hear her through the mask. From behind the side curtains a woman in the neighbouring bed is shouting '*turn off the lights, turn off the lights*' over and over.

Frances dislodges the oxygen mask.

"Is it night time?"

"No. It's not eight in the morning yet." Gemma slides the mask back on and gazes helplessly at Mustardseed.

Behind him the ward door opens and Judy comes in. She's wearing glasses today instead of her usual contact lenses.

"Gemma," she says. "Mum, I'm here now. How are you?"

"She keeps trying to take this off," Gemma says.

"Now don't do that," Judy says.

"Judy, get this thing off me," Frances says. "It's hurting my arm."

"It's for your blood pressure," Gemma says.

"I've got all these things in me. I've got a thing down here. A tube." Frances fiddles under the sheet.

"That's probably a catheter," Judy says.

"I'll wait for you outside," Mustardseed says, backing out of the cubicle.

'Turn off the lights, turn off the lights.'

"Is he looking after you?" Judy whispers to Gemma.

"He was lovely," she says. "I was so tired last night. I'm sorry I didn't come home."

"Mum," Judy starts. "Gemma's got herself a lovely boyfriend now. He's got beautiful hair."

Gemma opens her mouth, blushes, but Judy glares at her, and Gemma remembers Frances's words in the car, only days ago, about how she wanted Gemma to find a nice man before she died. *But he's not mine,* she thinks.

Judy takes her mother's wrist to stop her snatching at the mask, the cannula, the blood pressure cuff.

A man comes into the cubicle. He's holding a thick folder of notes. Gemma sees Frances's name written on it in black felt-tip.

"Ms Thompson?" he asks.

"Yes," Judy and Gemma say together.

"I'm Dr Tandy," he says. "I spoke to…?"

"Me," Judy says.

"Would you both come with me?"

Gemma glances at Judy.

"We're just going to speak to the doctor," Judy tells Frances. "We'll find out what they're going to do for you."

"Please come this way." Dr Tandy swishes out of the cubicle.

Gemma and Judy follow him. Gemma reaches for her mother's hand. The doctor leads them into a stuffy room with pink and brown chairs. Rain rattles on the window like a fistful of gravel. He indicates for them to sit. Gemma perches on the edge of a pink chair. The doctor slides the door sign to engaged, and closes the door.

"You are Mrs Thompson's daughter and granddaughter?" he starts, flicking out a biro.

"Yes," says Judy. "Can you please tell us what's the matter with her?"

"She's deteriorated since the early hours of the morning," he says. "Her blood pressure is dropping, and her heart rate is rising. We hope the inotropes – that's the Dobutamine infusion – will help with this, but she has pulmonary oedema as well."

"I thought this was a urinary infection," Gemma interrupts. "She wasn't that bad last night." She turns to Judy.

"She wasn't."

"During the night her condition worsened. Her kidneys are in a very bad way."

"You think she will die?" Judy asks.

Dr Tandy hesitates, fiddles with his pen. "Sometimes, despite our best efforts, the decision is made by the patient. Sometimes they simply decide when to leave us."

"She wouldn't," Gemma cries. "She doesn't want to leave us. She wouldn't just abandon us."

"This brings me onto something else," the doctor continues. "In the event of a cardiac arrest, resuscitation would, in all likelihood, prove to be futile. We need to consider the possibility of giving Mrs Thompson a dignified death, should that occur."

"What are you saying?" Judy asks tightly.

"If your mother were to suffer a cardiac arrest, it would not necessarily be in her best interests to resuscitate her. We have to balance quality of life and–"

"No," Gemma shouts. "I know what you're saying. You're saying you want her to die."

"It's not always kind to prolong life if that quality of life–"

"You are asking us if we will agree to your not attempting resuscitation?" Judy says. "The answer is no. We will not agree to that. My mother loves life. She would not want us to give up on her."

Judy stands. Gemma stumbles up beside her.

"Thank you for your time, Doctor," Judy continues. "We will go back to my mother now."

"Ms Thompson–"

"When you called me you were very calm, and very pleasant, and asked us to come in. I believed you wanted a positive discussion, but it seems you were asking us in just to have this conversation. The answer remains. No."

Judy opens the door and strides down the back corridor to the ward. Gemma follows. They don't think Frances is worth saving. She's old, she's getting confused. They don't care. For all the hi-tech equipment and drugs, if someone's old and infirm, they're worthless.

Mustardseed is sitting in the chair by Frances's bed. She seems to be sleeping, her head turned away from him. The mask is still on her face.

"Hi." He looks at them. "The door opened and I saw you going off with the doctor. I thought I should keep her company."

"Thank you," Gemma whispers.

Dr Tandy takes the folder of notes to the nurses' station. He says something to the male nurse, who glances towards Gemma. She doesn't look away. Dr Tandy walks over to Frances's cubicle.

"I'm going off shift now," he says. "One of the renal consultants will be coming to take a look at Frances shortly."

Gemma nods curtly, and the doctor leaves.

'Turn off the lights, turn off the lights.'

Judy takes a chair from a stack on the ward, sits down, reaches for Frances's hand.

"What's the news?" Mustardseed asks.

"Come with me," Gemma says. "I'll tell you outside."

She goes to the door; he's right behind her.

"What did he say?" he asks.

"He thinks there's no point," she says. "He says it's her kidneys. They're causing her blood pressure to be low or something. They're giving her something for it, which doesn't seem to be working. He says if she has an arrest, it's not worth trying to save her."

"What?"

"We said no," Gemma says. "We told them no, if anything like that happens, they must do whatever they can."

Something's ringing. Mustardseed takes his phone out of his pocket and glances at the screen. He hesitates a moment, then pockets the phone.

"Who's that?"

"It's not important."

"I should go back in," Gemma says.

Frances is awake, snatching at the oxygen mask. Judy secures it back on.

"I have to go into work just briefly," she says to Gemma. "I won't be long. Robert," she turns to Mustardseed. "I wonder, would you be kind enough to stay with Gemma? Just for an hour or so?"

"Of course."

"You don't have to," Gemma interrupts.

"Of course I will," he says again. "I don't have to do anything else. I'll stay, Gemma."

"Thank you." Judy stands up. "Mum, I'm just going away for a bit. I'll be back soon. Gemma and Robert are still here."

"How about a drink?" Gemma pours water unsteadily from the plastic jug at the bedside. She lifts the mask a moment and lets Frances drink a tiny sip.

Mustardseed hovers by the nurses' station. The renal consultant has arrived with his team; they have whipped the curtains shut at the foot of Frances's bed. Gemma's with them in there. Sometimes the curtains swell or sway as someone moves. He can't explain why, but he finds this sinister. His phone rings in his pocket. He takes it out. It's RG again. He can't keep not answering. The ringing dies, then the cheep of a voice message. Mustardseed shoves open the ward doors and goes outside. He will have to ring RG.

"Agent Mustardseed, you are still alive then?"

"I'm sorry I missed your call. I was–"

"Never mind all that now. I have a job for you. Rather late notice, I'm afraid. It's for tomorrow."

"It's not possible," Mustardseed interrupts. "I mean, I'm sorry, I can't do tomorrow."

"You can't do tomorrow? I haven't even given you the details."

"Whatever it is, I really can't do anything tomorrow."

"Mustardseed, you are supposed to give me dates in advance when you are not available for work."

"I know. I am sorry. It's…something's come up…"

The ward door flings open. It's Gemma. She not crying but her eyes are wild.

"Have you tried any of the others? I know Peaseblossom is always needing more money."

"It's not about the money, Mustardseed. It's about finding the right agent for the right job, and you would be perfect."

"I really am sorry," Mustardseed says. "But I can't. Let me ring you later and I'll explain."

"I thought you'd gone," Gemma cries.

"No, no. I had another call. I had to ring back."

"Was that Mr Goodfellow? Was he offering you a job?"

"Yes, and I said no."

"Why?"

"Because I want to be here. What did the renal guy say?"

"It wasn't Dr Thomas," Gemma says. "It was another one. He doesn't even know her. He's never met her before, and she was all vague, and I know he thinks she's lost her marbles, but she hasn't. She's never been like that. If it's her kidneys she must be dehydrated, right? And that makes people sound crazy, doesn't it?"

"Dehydration makes people very ill."

"He said something about her blood pressure not going up enough. It's always been too high before. It's so low today. He says they're going to give her lots of fluids to see if it'll rise. He says if it doesn't rise…"

"If it doesn't rise?"

"He says it may be too late."

"Did he say that in front of her?" Mustardseed asks.

"Not quite," Gemma says. "Outside on the ward. She could have heard though. He was loud. And I looked for you and you weren't there, and I thought you'd had enough and gone."

"I'm not going anywhere. I just told RG – Mr Goodfellow – I couldn't work tomorrow. I want to be here with you, whatever happens."

"Everyone keeps saying she's not going to make it. I told him, this renal one, I told him we wanted everything to be done."

"You've told two of them now," Mustardseed says. "Did they write it in the notes?"

"I don't know," Gemma says uneasily. "I should ring Mummy. Tell her what he said. I'm so tired."

"You'll need to get some rest at some point," he tells her. "When your mum comes back, if you and she want to go home for a bit I could stay with Frances if you like. So she's not alone."

"She's not crazy," Gemma cries. "They all think she's crazy, got Alzheimer's or something, but she hasn't. She's just ill, and they're not listening to me, and she's confused, and anyone would be confused in this place, wouldn't they, especially if they were dehydrated?"

"They would," he agrees. "And the drugs probably don't help either."

"Exactly. But they don't listen. They just think she's old and rambling, and she's blocking a bed, and that's all they care about."

"Ring your mum. See when she can get back."

Mustardseed stands back while Gemma calls Judy, watches the rain falling out of the cold sky. Tomorrow is Thursday. Gemma should be running her stall at Green Park. He wonders if she's thought about it at all. Probably not. If only he had a car, he could do it for her. There's no way RG will lend him the van. Without a car he can't get the preserves from South Stoke to the market.

Gemma's sitting beside Frances. Outside the window, the sky is lightening into a cold, cloudy autumn day. Frances still fiddles with the blood pressure cuff, the cannula, the mask. Sometimes Gemma offers her a sip of water. The male night nurse has gone now. Gemma's waiting for someone to come and start the fluid bolus to raise blood pressure. She watches the figures on the screen above the bed. She's not medical but she knows no one should have a blood pressure that low. She can't understand it: Frances's blood pressure has always been high. It's something to do with the renal failure. Renal failure: those two final words. Failure suggests something than cannot be turned around. The renal consultant, Dr – what was his name? She can't even remember – said dialysis would not be appropriate. Gemma was about to offer her own kidney to Frances, opened her mouth, closed it again. He would never agree to that. If Frances were twenty years younger, he might have talked about dialysis or transplant, but not at her age. No. Never.

Mustardseed has gone to get her a drink. She glances up, sensing movement in her peripheral vision, wanting him back, wanting Judy. It's neither of them. It's a nurse – a woman this time.

"I'm Amy," she says. "I've come to give your – grandmother? – some fluids."

'Turn off the lights, turn off the lights' through the flimsy side curtain.

Gemma sees Mustardseed coming back into the ward carrying bottles of Pepsi and chocolate. He hesitates when he sees the nurse.

"I'm just getting out of the way," Gemma says to Frances. "I'll be back when the nurse has finished with you."

She bites back the words too late. Like renal failure: they cannot be undone.

"What's happening?" Mustardseed hands her a cool bottle.

"She's having the fluids done now."

"Jesus, I thought they'd have done that. Why's everything so slow? It's not like they're over-run here."

There are only a few patients. Two nurses and a doctor are chatting at the nurses' station.

"Here's Mummy."

"Any news?" Judy asks.

"She's having the fluids," Gemma says again.

"But you said they were doing that when you phoned me. And they're only just doing it?"

"What I said," Mustardseed says.

"Gemma," Judy says. "You look absolutely wrecked. You must go home and have some rest."

"I'm so tired," Gemma says, and her voice wavers.

"Come here." Judy opens her arms, Gemma stumbles into them, and they hug each other, there in the middle of the ward, with Gemma's hand sticky from the chocolate.

"Judy," Mustardseed starts. "I said to Gemma while you were away that I could stay here for a while if you like, to let you both go home. You know, just to keep an eye on things."

Judy takes off her glasses and rubs her eyes. "That's very kind of you," she says. "But you look pretty done in yourself. I think we should all get some rest. We can't be here every minute. Honestly, Gemma."

The nurse is leaving Frances's cubicle. Gemma and Judy walk over. Gemma feels light-headed with fear, lack of sleep, lack of proper food. She wishes she hadn't asked Mustardseed to get chocolate because now she feels sick with its thick coating on her tongue.

Frances is on her side, facing the curtain.

"When am I going home?" She tugs off her mask again.

"Soon," Gemma says.

Judy frets with the bedding, strokes her mother's pale hair.

"Mum, we're going to go home for a bit. Just to get some rest. You should do the same, while you have these fluids."

"What fluids?"

"The renal doctor thought fluids would help your blood pressure," Gemma says.

"Is it very high? I've been taking my tablets."

"No, it's very low."

"It can't be low. It's never been low."

"Mum, stop worrying," Judy says. "Just please try to rest and we'll be back to see you in a couple of hours."

Gemma stoops to kiss Frances. She is hunched on her side. She looks so little, so frail.

"Just be here when I come back," Gemma whispers.

Mustardseed walks out of the hospital with Gemma and Judy. The wind tears at his hair and he stuffs it into his hood.

"Gemma," he begins. "What are you going to do about tomorrow?"

"What about tomorrow?" she asks.

"Green Park. I've been trying to think how I could–"

"Christ, I'd forgotten."

"I'd run the stall for you," he says. "Not as a job, as a friend. It's just I don't have a car and I don't know how I could get the stuff there."

"I can't ask you to run the stall."

"You haven't asked me. I'm offering. I'm not working tomorrow. You know that. I turned down the job RG was offering. I want to be with you and Frances, and do whatever I can, but if that means being at Green Park rather than here, I can do that. You know I know what to do."

"If you could, Robert, that would be so helpful," Judy says. "Even if it was just for a few hours, it would protect Gemma's interests."

"How can I get the stuff to the market?" he asks.

"I'll bring it in," Gemma says. "I'll come in first thing. I can do that. I just don't want to be stuck there all day. I can't. Then I'll come back at night."

"OK, that'll be fine."

"Are you sure you don't mind?"

"I don't mind," he tells her.

He doesn't mind. He's not known Gemma any time, but he wants to be part of her life, whatever that means. He feels oddly responsible for Frances too, as he was the one who found her. He'll do whatever he can do for Gemma at this time. He cannot imagine what's in her head.

"Are you sure you don't want me to stay with Frances for a while?"

"That's kind," Judy says, "but she's not herself. She won't know who you are, and I don't want her to get agitated or frightened."

"Sure," he agrees. "I understand."

"Are you up to driving?" Judy asks Gemma.

"I've just paid the parking. I have to take it now. I can't just leave it. It'd cost a fortune."

"Yes, they make a nice profit from the families of dying patients." Judy jabs her keys at the Audi.

"She's not dying," Gemma cries.

"Can you give Robert a lift home?"

"I'll walk," Mustardseed says. "Don't go out of your way, Gemma. Just go home and rest, and please call me and let me know what's happening."

He walks the few yards with Gemma to her car. The car park is full now. A sports car is idling, waiting for Judy to leave her space. Gemma opens the door, throws her half-empty Pepsi bottle on the passenger seat.

"Gemma."

"Yes?" She turns to him.

"Whatever they say to you, don't agree to anything. Tell your mum too when you get home."

"What do you mean?"

"They've said to you she might not…they said to you if the treatment fails…"

"There's nothing they can do."

"Have you heard of DNRs?" he asks.

"No, what's that?"

"It stands for Do Not Resuscitate. When they said to you Frances might have an arrest and there was nothing they could do it doesn't mean they would try to save her and fail. It means they wouldn't do anything."

"Yes, but we told them we didn't want that."

Mustardseed sighs. "My sister, Lizzie. She's a nurse in Birmingham. She's told me about these. They're standard practice. If a patient is very ill, and particularly if they're elderly or have dementia and so on. It's a form they fill in and keep in the notes. It means if the patient dies, they just don't do anything."

"But we told them!"

Mustardseed glances to Judy's car. She's pulled out of the space to let the sports car in, and she's waiting now between the rows of parked cars, waiting for Gemma. He wishes he'd mentioned this when Judy was around too.

"They will try to trick you into agreeing to this. They will pretend you have a say, and they'll ask you, but they will fill one in anyway unless you make a lot of noise. Whatever they say to you, you mustn't agree to anything. Keep saying she is still for resus. Have you got that? For resus."

"Yes, but they can't just let her die. They can't do that if we said no. We're the next of kin."

"Gemma. They do. They will pretend you agreed to it. That you felt it was giving her a dignified death. As if ignoring a dying patient is dignified."

"She's not dying yet."

"No," he says quickly. "But I'm sure this is going to come up. When you go in again, or when you ring up. They'll start putting pressure on you. Look, you must go if you're going to get some rest but get your mum to phone me when you get home. Then you must phone the ward and tell them Frances is still for resus. OK?"

"Yes, OK." Gemma looks close to tears.

"I'm so sorry. I'm so terribly sorry."

When he hugs her, he can feel the tension down her back. Her shoulders quake and she steps back, wiping her eyes with an angry fist.

"Drive carefully," he says.

She shudders out of the parking space, as though her feet are trembling. He watches the barrier lift for Judy to pass through, then fall again. Gemma's arm comes out of her open window; she forces the ticket in, the barrier rises again, and she is gone.

Mustardseed starts walking. Judy is right: he is tired. He needs sleep too. Recent events have been extraordinary. RG gave him the job running Gemma's stall. He really didn't want to do it but, not only did he find he enjoyed the market, with its eccentric traders, its enticing smells, its colours and noises, he met Gemma, and he knows, without any doubt, that he wants to be with her.

And Frances. Mustardseed does not believe now he will ever get the chance to know Frances. He would have liked to. She and Gemma were so close. No, are so close. His father's parents are both dead: they died when he was small. His mother's parents have lived in Spain for the past decade. He doesn't see them as much as he'd like to. He'll fly out very soon, he decides. Somehow he'll get the money and go and see them.

Gemma drives home behind Judy. Other cars cut in between them but once they're on the road to South Stoke they are together again. Judy brakes and parks on the churned up muddy ground where – only yesterday – Mustardseed left the van. Only yesterday Frances was sitting in the living room with Guinness and Murphy. Gemma parks behind Judy; together they walk up the path to the door. Guinness and Murphy squeak a welcome.

"Poor things," Judy says. "I had to chuck their breakfast at them this morning."

Gemma trails her hand in the hay and the guineas come bounding up.

"I have to talk to you," she says.

"What?"

"Something Mustardseed said in the car park. He says the hospital will try to get us to sign a form saying we don't want Frances to have resus. His sister is a nurse. She told him about it. He told us not to sign anything or agree to anything."

"We told the doctor that wasn't acceptable. I could see the way things were going. It's not like she's been in a coma for years. She's only just been admitted, for Christ's sake."

"I know. But he says they will try to trick us. They do it with elderly patients. He spoke to me but he wanted to speak to you. He said can you ring him?"

"He's a very nice boy," Judy says, taking out her phone. "I don't quite understand what's going on there with you two, but I like him. OK, what's his number?"

Gemma mumbles Mustardseed's number, embarrassed at Judy's comment. She's not sure what's going on either. When he came to the house only yesterday he said he'd come to see her, to see if she'd like to meet up now he wasn't working for her. Why would he do that if he didn't like her? She likes him, she likes him very much, but is her perception distorted in this dark time? Should she even be thinking these thoughts while Frances is dying in that awful place? But you can't stop your thoughts; they march on unchecked to destinations you don't even know exist.

Judy has taken her phone into the kitchen. Gemma hears those terrible letters – *DNR* – and other fragments: *Yes, yes…I did wonder… No I don't, we won't… Yes, thank you for looking after Gemma…I hope she can get a bit of rest now.*

She comes back into the living room. Gemma is still standing by the hutch. She feels so tired and heavy she's not sure she'll make it up the stairs.

"We have to get some rest," Judy says. "And then we'll go back in a couple of hours."

"What did he say?"

"Pretty much what you said. We're not agreeing to that. It's not what Mum would have wanted. She wanted to live for ages."

"Yes," Gemma whispers.

She starts up the stairs. She'll have a bath, change her clothes, lie down for a while.

Gemma's disorientated. Judy's standing over her bed. It's daylight. She feels wet and chilled. Something's wrong. Frances. Gemma struggles up. Of course: she is cold because her hair is still wet. How long has she been asleep? She fumbles for her alarm clock, knocks it to the floor without seeing the time.

"I've just rung the ward," Judy says, sitting on the edge of the bed. "I spoke to a nurse called Amy. She says she is looking after Mum."

"Yes, that's right. She did the fluids." Gemma's throat is cracked. She needs a drink. She needs fluids.

"This Amy said Mum's blood pressure was unrecordable it's got so low. She said Mum asked them to remove the cuff and refuses to have it taken manually now."

"What? Why?"

"You know how upset she was with the cuff and the cannula and all that stuff."

"But how can they check her blood pressure?"

"Apparently it did rise for a moment with the fluid and then dropped again. She said there was nothing they could do except make her comfortable, and she asked me to consider a DNR order. I said no."

"Good. No, not good. Nothing's good."

"We should go back."

"She is dying, isn't she?"
"I think so," Judy says.

They take Judy's car. Judy's mobile rings as they approach the hospital. Gemma grabs it.

"It's Anthony," she says.

"I called him just before I woke you." Judy turns into the hospital car park.

"Ant, it's Gemma."

Through the windscreen she gazes at the grim building. She's seen it in the stormy night with the trees twisting at the perimeter fence, and the wind roaring across the dark empty car park; she's seen it under the pewter dawn sky; and now in the cold white-blue of the afternoon. She answers Anthony's questions flatly, as Judy opens the window, tugs a parking ticket from the machine. The same rituals, the same patterns, done over and over now.

"He says he'll come down tomorrow," Gemma says, ending the call.

"He'll be too late," Judy says.

In Coronary Care, Frances's curtains are open. She's lying on her left side. She hasn't moved. Her eyes are closed. There is no oxygen mask.

"We're back," Gemma says.

Frances doesn't move or open her eyes.

"Mum, can you wake up?"

"Can you hear me? It's Gemma." Gemma meets Judy's eyes.

"She might be able to hear us," Judy says.

Gemma sits in the chair by Frances's head. The woman next door has quietened, asleep or dead, Gemma's not sure. She didn't even notice if the bed were occupied. Judy strides over to the nurses' station. Gemma strokes Frances's fingers. Her hand is tiny, thin, frail – all bone, like a guinea's hand – the vein mauve beneath the cannula. Gemma knows now that Frances will die in this ward, in this bed, maybe today, maybe tomorrow, maybe in a week's time. She will die in this blotchy hospital gown, with her hair all mussed up, and a catheter inside her, and a cannula spearing her vein. It will happen. Gemma's afraid. Afraid she won't be there when Frances dies, afraid she will be.

Judy comes back to the bed with Amy the nurse.

"We're not intervening any more," Amy says. "She's refused the blood pressure monitor and the oxygen. As I said on the phone, her blood pressure has become so low we couldn't record it. There really isn't any more we can do. She'll just slip away."

"Don't say that," Gemma cries. "She might hear you." She looks at Frances, still not moving, still not seeing, and thinks at that moment, how impossible these words seem.

"Would you come with me a moment?" the nurse asks.

Gemma struggles to her feet and follows Amy and Judy to the nurses' station. She turns back to the bed, but Frances hasn't moved.

"I believe Dr Tandy spoke to you this morning," the nurse begins, flicking open Frances's folder of notes. "He mentioned that if she were to suffer an arrest, it would not be appropriate to offer her resus."

Gemma balls her fists. She wishes Mustardseed were here.

"Also," the nurse continues, "I mentioned to–" she indicates towards Judy – "you on the phone that we need to discuss this with you in person."

"You aren't listening to us," Judy says. "The answer is no. I told the doctor that this morning, and I told you this afternoon."

Amy produces a red-edged form.

"We would like you to consider a Do Not Resuscitate form. It would allow your mother a quiet and dignified death, whereas CPR would be traumatic and, most likely, futile." She picks up a pen.

"No," Gemma says.

"How many times do I have to tell you?" Judy says. "We are not agreeing to this. If you're asking us you want our opinion, and we've given it."

The nurse slides the red form under the folder of notes. "I'm sure one of the doctors will speak to you," she says stiffly.

Judy's phone rings as they cross the ward.

"It's work," she says, walking swiftly to the exit to answer the call.

Gemma trails over to Frances's bed. She hasn't moved. She's breathing, and that's the only movement. Gemma thinks her breathing is louder, more strained. She traces her finger down Frances's jaw line, but still Frances does not wake.

"I have to go in again." Judy is back beside her.

"No."

"I'm sorry. I won't be long. I have to go in."

"But she might–"

"We can't be here every minute," Judy says. "I'll be an hour at most. Are you all right to stay or do you want to come with me?"

"I'll stay," Gemma says. "I don't trust them."

"Thanks. You could ring Robert and see if he could come up."

"I can't. I hardly know him."

"That doesn't seem to affect him. You should ring him and tell him what's happening. He's been very good to us."

"Yes. OK."

Gemma watches Judy leave the ward. The door sucks shut behind her.

'Turn off the lights, turn off the lights.'

Not dead then.

Gemma pulls the chair close to Frances, listens to her breathing. This is where she will die. This is where she will take – has taken – her last sight of the world. This cramped, stuffy cubicle, with swaying curtains on either side, stained in one place with dark-brown fluid. The water jug and beaker are still on the side table. Gemma's thirsty but she doesn't want to drink it. It looks warm and murky. She sits and waits. Don't let it happen when I'm on my own, she prays.

A young blond man steps into the cubicle with Frances's notes folder. He opens it clumsily in mid-air, settles it on his forearm. Gemma recognises him from the ward round. He must be one of renal consultant's juniors.

"I'm Dr Bainbridge," he says. "Renal registrar."

"She's not opening her eyes," Gemma says.

"She's developed pneumonia and sepsis," he tells her. "She really is very ill. I understand the staff nurse–"

"I'm not agreeing to it," Gemma says flatly. "Neither will my mother."

"Sometimes the medical team has to make a decision about what is in the patient's best interests," he says. "I understand you are resistant to a DNR, but I promise you there would be little benefit in performing resus on your grandmother. It would be much kinder and more appropriate to let her drift away, when the time's right."

"The time isn't right. And we should not be speaking about this beside her."

The registrar glances at Frances who is still, only breathing, the left side of her face pressed into the pillow.

"It may be necessary for us to make a decision on your behalf, weighing up the likelihood of success and quality of life for the patient. CPR is traumatic both for the patient and the family. Patients can become injured–"

"That doesn't matter if they're alive."

"The success rate of CPR is very low. Given your grandmother's condition–"

Gemma jumps as her phone rings. She tugs it from her pocket.

"Excuse me," she says, standing.

She would never normally be this rude but the registrar is frightening her. As she walks to the ward door she wonders: *Is it safe to leave Frances for just a moment? Will someone stifle her with a pillow?*

"How are things?"

He rang. Mustardseed rang. Perhaps he really does care. Gemma tells him how Frances doesn't respond, how she's already falling further and further away, what the nurse and the registrar are saying.

"I'm sorry," he says. "I was afraid of this. I've heard in some hospitals they put one straight into the notes in Intensive Care and such."

"They had one earlier. It wasn't filled in. Not yet. If they do that, there's nothing we can do to stop them, is there? And I know it's not what Frances would want. She'd want every chance of life, however small."

"Is your mum with you?"

"No, she's gone back to work for an hour. I'm on my own. I'm scared. I'm scared something will happen, that they'll do this form, that she'll die, that I won't be able to do anything."

"I'll come. I'll get a taxi."

"You can't do that."

"It'll take ages to walk. I'll call one now."

He hangs up before she can protest, but she wasn't going to protest any more. She wants him here with her.

Mustardseed runs down the stairs, opens the street door. Since he's got back home, he hasn't been able to concentrate on anything. He's managed to order a taxi for five minutes. He stamps up and down on the pavement until he sees the car approaching. He gets in the front seat. There's a stupid dangly thing hanging off the mirror that irritates him and a pungent smell from a so-called air-freshener.

When he gets to the ward Gemma is hunched in the bedside chair.

"She hasn't moved at all," she tells him.

He doesn't know what to say. Frances is going to die – he can see that – and forever he will be linked to that death in Gemma's mind. She may not want him because he is so tightly bound with this time: he and Frances woven together.

"She's never going to open her eyes," Gemma says. "The last thing I said to her was to be here when I got back, and when I got back, she'd gone. Where is she? She's not asleep…if she was asleep, she'd wake when I touch her, but she doesn't. I think even if I hurt her or hit her, she wouldn't wake."

"I think she's in a coma," he suggests quietly.

"People wake up from those. Years later sometimes."

"Yes. They do."

He looks at Frances, rather than at Gemma. He's told her what Lizzie said about the DNRs, but he hasn't yet told her the rest. *It will happen to Frances,* he thinks. He must tell Gemma, but he can't find the words. He should have it out with the nursing staff, but they'll just send for Security. He's not the next of kin. He's no one.

"If it hadn't been for her, I would never have met you," Gemma says suddenly.

"What?" He turns away from Frances, back to Gemma.

"She suggested Mr Goodfellow's agency. When I was saying I didn't see how I could go to Fenwick because other people were wanting to sell my sort of stuff at Green Park, she said I could get someone to run the stall and I said I couldn't ask anyone to do it and, anyway, people were too busy, and then she said she knew of the agency. She knew its name too. I Googled it and rang Mr Goodfellow."

Does Frances know we're here? Mustardseed wonders. *Can she hear us? Does she know where she is?* So many questions, and no one has those answers. Not even the medics. Frances is beyond all of them, on her way to that undiscovered country.

"Beautiful lady." Gemma strokes Frances's soft hair.

She's still curled on her left side, her cheek folded into the pillow. Her eyes are closed, but for a thin slit; through this Gemma can still see a dark blue iris. Her breathing is regular but ragged. Gemma wants to shout at her, tug her hair, slap her face, anything, anything at all, that will make her turn her head to Gemma, open her eyes, speak.

Gemma glances at the catheter bag strapped to the bed. There's only a tiny splash of dark urine. Everything is slowing down, becoming less. Frances, never a big woman, appears a fraction of her size, hunched under the thin covers. *Fading away,* Gemma thinks. Now she understands those words.

She should be remembering the good times, the happy times, even the times they argued. She should remember Frances playing with her as a little girl, teaching her the country lore of plants and hedgerows, showing her how to make jams and chutneys, consoling her when guinea pigs died, when her romances ended, when she didn't get a job she really wanted. She should be thinking about holidays in Northumberland, collecting shells on Aidan's Dunes, boat trips to the Farnes to see seals and puffins, the beautiful house and garden at Kyloe Mains. She should be thinking about anything other than this dreadful room, where her nerves jangle every time the phone rings on the nurses' station or someone raises their voice, but she doesn't think she'll ever be able to dig deeper in her memory. She will forever be able to recall the square of changing sky above the bed, the pattern of Frances's hospital gown, the stain on the cubicle curtain, the water level in the abandoned jug, and the rasp of laboured breathing.

She's trapped here, as trapped as Frances. She wants to run out into the cold afternoon, away from this place, with its shadow of death, but she cannot leave the ward. She checks the time on the wall clock. The hour is up and past. Judy should come back soon. She glances at her phone too. Yes, it reads the same time. The passage of time means little here in this room with no seasons, no day or night. She's aware of Mustardseed standing beside her, so close she could reach out to touch him but she does not dare.

"Here's your mum," he says.

Judy returns with a damp umbrella, not soaking, just enough to be greasy and clammy. Gemma scrapes back her chair, stands on spaghetti legs and stumbles out of the cubicle to meet her.

"No change," she says, turning to look at Frances.

From this further distance she looks even tinier, diminished; she's curling up, like a foetus once more, to be reborn into another world.

"What do they say now?" Judy asks. "Is she comfortable like that, do you think? Should we move her?"

"One of the renal doctors spoke to me," Gemma starts. "He says they're going to make the decision about resus. They asked us, like we had a choice, like we had an opinion that mattered, then they said they'll decide anyway, so why ask us?"

"Can they do that, Robert?"

"They have the final say," he says.

"I'll speak to them again," Judy says. "Jesus, I'm so tired. I had to go through some stuff with Doug. He's the deputy," she adds to Mustardseed. "He knows about Mum, you'd think he'd have tried to be co-operative just this once."

"Can I go outside?" Gemma asks. "Just for a few moments?"

"Of course."

"Gemma, wait!"

She turns.

"I need to tell you something," Mustardseed says. "Both of you." He glances at Frances. "Not here. Let's go outside."

Gemma glances at Judy, who nods. They go through the double doors, out onto the corridor.

"Something else Lizzie told me," Mustardseed starts. "When patients like Frances…when they say there's no hope…have you heard of the Liverpool Pathway?"

"I've heard the name," Judy says. "It's palliative care, right?"

"That's what they'd tell you if the subject came up. But it never does come up. When they say there's no hope for a patient, when they've done the DNR thing, then they start this Pathway, and it's nothing to do with care. They withdraw everything – water, food, medication. They give morphine, and something else, I can't remember. It knocks the patient out, in effect puts them in a coma until–"

"She was fine!" Gemma cries. "She was fine, and conscious, and then when we came back she was…a vegetable."

"They may have given her something then," Mustardseed says.

"I knew we shouldn't have left her, Mummy."

"Christ Almighty," Judy says. "You come to these places to be cured."

"I'm sorry," Mustardseed interrupts. "I didn't want to bring it up, but you had to know. You wouldn't have known otherwise. You need to know."

"I need some air," Gemma says.

"Let her go, Robert," she hears her mother say as she stumbles down the corridor. "She'll come back."

Outside Gemma gulps the air with its taste of recent rain. It's still only afternoon, but she can feel the encroaching night. It's more than just the setting of the sun she senses, and her arms tingle beneath her sleeves.

That room again. That awful pink and brown room. Gemma sits where she sat before; so does Judy. That ghastly nurse, Amy, is on Judy's other side. She jumps up as the consultant comes in, and closes the door with a satisfied click.

The consultant is the renal physician who came on the ward round with his registrar, Dr Bainbridge. He is holding Frances's notes. Gemma sees a thin red line amongst the paper, bright as a knife wound.

"I'm Dr Fleming," he says, sitting heavily. "Mrs Thompson has been under the care of my colleague, Dr Thomas, I see."

"Yes," says Judy.

"I hear that several people have spoken to you about a DNR order." He plucks the red-edged form from the folder. There's writing in the boxes.

"We never signed that!" Gemma shouts.

"We made it clear we would not agree to that."

"Mrs Thompson is really very unwell. To offer her resus should she arrest would only be traumatic for you and futile for her. We have explained this several times today. I am sure you would rather your mother, your grandmother, had a dignified death. A peaceful death. If she were to arrest, it would be impossible for us to get her back; if we did it would only be for moments. She is elderly and in poor health. She has pneumonia and sepsis."

"She wouldn't want this," Gemma cries. "She would want every chance."

"If she knew how ill she was–"

"She still would. She didn't give up. She never gave up. She won't give up now. Even though you're trying to kill her."

"Why has that form been filled in?" asks Judy. "The medical and nursing staff are well aware of our feelings."

Gemma glances at Judy, recalls Dr Bainbridge's words.

"In cases like this it becomes necessary for the medical team to make a decision on the patient's behalf if that patient is incapable of making a decision."

"It wouldn't matter if she were capable," Judy says. "If she chose something different to what you had in mind, it would be dismissed. As you have dismissed her because she is old and frail and is taking up a bed."

"It's nothing to do with beds," the nurse interrupts, leaning so close to Judy that Judy recoils. "We give the very best care to anyone – whatever their age."

"I assure you that is correct," says the consultant.

Gemma looks at Judy in despair. What she has been terrified of has happened. Someone has filled in the form. And what about the other, that Liverpool thing? Denying patients nutrition, drugging them unconscious? Her mother said she would bring it up, but when is she going to do that?

"We have made a very careful and considered decision based on the patient's health, co-morbidities, likelihood of survival, and quality of life. The decision was unanimous. It is not in Mrs Thompson's interests to list her for resus. I'm very sorry you feel as you do, but I am sure in time you will realise this was the right decision."

"No," Judy says. "We will not. You asked us if we would consider this and we said no. That should have been the end of it. If you are not interested in our opinion, why ask us? Just sign the form yourself and don't say a word to us."

"We hoped that you–"

"And what's with all this *we*?" Judy demands. "Someone must have taken ultimate responsibility for this. Is it you? I've never seen you before."

"He was here earlier," Gemma says quietly.

"It's a team decision," says Dr Fleming.

"So, no one has the guts to stand up and say *this is what I have chosen*. I've paid your salaries all my working life, and you don't even have the courtesy to do that." She stops, then, "My mother loved life. She will be afraid of death."

"We can give her some more morphine to keep her comfortable if necessary," he says, tapping the notes together.

"Some *more* morphine, did you say?"

The nurse glances at the consultant.

"We gave her some earlier," he says.

“I don’t recall anyone asking me or my daughter about that. Did anyone ask you, Gemma?”

Gemma shakes her head. She feels like she cannot speak.

“Why are you giving her morphine?”

“To keep her comfortable,” Amy butts in. “For any pain she has.”

“I don’t think she has any pain, except for an uncomfortable cannula. And how strange this morphine is given when neither of us were here, and stranger still that no one said anything about it until now. Until after that form was signed, sealed and delivered.” Judy jabs her finger towards the folder of notes. “Because once you’ve got that safely done, you can make another *team decision* to withdraw water and medication, get your Liverpool Pathway started.”

“The Liverpool Care Pathway–”

“Amy,” the doctor interrupts.

He flicks open the notes again, turns to the back. Gemma can see the word *Liverpool* on the top sheet. It blurs in her vision. Mustardseed was right: he was right, and it was already happening.

“The Liverpool Care Pathway has been devised to give the best possible care for terminally ill patients. It ensures their final hours are as free of stress as possible.”

“It denies them water and medicine.”

“Yes, unnecessary medicines are withdrawn, that is true. I mean, at a time like this, what would be the point of giving a patient a statin, for instance? Giving someone water could lead to a build-up of fluid in the lungs, which would be more distressing. “

“I want my mother taken off this death pathway immediately.”

“Ms Thompson, the team has spent a lot of time reviewing your mother, and we all agreed that, unfortunately, there is nothing more we can do for her. She did not respond to the fluids we gave her earlier and really that was the only thing that would have given her a chance, albeit a slim one. All we can do now is keep her comfortable.”

“By sedating her when we weren’t here, so we can’t even say goodbye to her.”

“Is keep her comfortable with the morphine, and let nature take its course.”

“It’s not nature taking its course; you’ve deliberately altered the course of nature.”

“Mrs Thompson will not survive this episode. I am sure you can see that. All we want is to ensure her last hours are dignified and pain-free. I have told you resuscitation would be inappropriate. There was no doubt amongst the team that a DNR was in the best possible interests of the patient, and the Liverpool…”

Frances will die. That’s all Gemma can think. She isn’t listening to her mother and the consultant any more. Frances will die, and she isn’t even being given a chance. If she stops breathing, no one will come rushing through the curtains with paddles and bags and adrenaline. They’ll just ignore her, if they’ve even noticed. She’ll die alone, unobserved, in this awful, awful place.

“When will she die?” she croaks.

Judy’s saying something about making a formal complaint; that ghoulish nurse is trying to put her hand on Judy’s arm.

“When will she die?” Gemma says again, and her voice sounds like the wavering voice of a pubescent boy.

The consultant turns to her, folds together the notes.

“I think she will die tonight.”

Gemma staggers out of the dreadful room, Judy's heels clicking behind her and, behind Judy, the heavy thump of the nurse. Somewhere behind the nurse is the consultant with his folder of notes and the red-edged death warrant.

Mustardseed is sitting on the chair beside Frances, his mouth moving. For a second Gemma thinks she has woken and they are talking to each other, but no, Frances is still hunched silently into the pillow. He's just talking quietly to her. She hasn't moved for hours.

"You were right," Gemma says. "They've done the form and this Liverpool thing. It's all done. They gave her morphine while we were away and now we'll never be able to speak to her, and tell her we love her."

"Shit, I am sorry." He stands and the chair scrapes on the floor. "You must tell her those things though. Maybe she can hear you."

"You don't believe that, do you?" Gemma asks him.

"I don't know," he says. Then, "She must be very dry. Have you got something you can moisten her mouth with?"

The jug of brackish water is still on the table, but Frances can't swallow. She needs intravenous fluids, but no one will give her any.

"I've got a tissue," Judy says, wrenches the lid off the water jug and dips the tissue into the liquid. Gemma watches her wipe Frances's lips. Frances doesn't respond. The window behind the bed shows a darker patch of sky. Evening, darkness, is approaching.

'Turn off the lights, turn off the lights.'

"What are we going to do?" Gemma asks.

Judy watches Frances, watches her uneven breathing.

"We can't stay here all night," she says. "I can't stand it. Let's go home and get something to eat, and then we'll come back."

Gemma doesn't want to stay there either. She's so afraid Frances will die when she is beside her, and no one will do anything to help. She'll have to live with that for the rest of her life.

"I can give you a lift," Judy says to Mustardseed.

She kisses her mother very gently on the forehead. There is no response.

"Beautiful lady," Gemma says again.

The three of them leave the ward together, without looking at the nurses' station where the ghastly Amy is doing something on the computer.

Now the window shows the murky city night. The ward is on low-lights. Gemma and Judy stand side-by-side at the foot of Frances's bed. She still has not moved. Her breathing is harsher.

"She looks so tiny," Gemma says.

She wonders if some time in the future she will recall the individual horrors of each visit to this ward or whether they will bleed into each other. No, she does know the answer. She will remember them all.

It's ten o'clock now. Gemma didn't want to come back after dinner because she was so frightened, but she couldn't tell Judy. Judy's frightened too. And angry.

"We should go," Judy says. "Let's say goodnight to her."

Gemma looks at Judy.

She will die tonight.

Gemma's on the sofa where Frances last sat. She's got Murphy on her knee. She strokes his soft black and white fur, his floppy ears. Sometimes he squeaks. In the hutch Guinness is banging around, tossing hay about, making tunnels. Now he's drinking; the ball bearing in the water bottle goes bang, bang, bang.

Judy's gone up for a bath. Gemma wonders if they will sleep tonight. She thinks she probably will, she's so tired and drained and unhappy. She's heard that many people die in the early hours – that cold, lonely time when the body runs slowest. She thinks this is what will happen. Judy told the night nurse – the male nurse who set up the Dobutamine – to call whatever the time. Gemma's frightened to fall asleep to be woken by the phone, knowing what has happened.

She stands and gently puts Murphy back in the hutch. Guinness growls softly from under the hay. Gemma rearranges the clumps, takes out a half-chewed carrot they've lost interest in. She looks at the time. Eleven twenty-five.

The phone rings, hard and loud. Gemma turns. The handset is flashing on its cradle. Judy's in the bath. She moves forward, takes it, hits green, and she can feel her own blood surging around her ears.

"Could I speak to Judy or Gemma Thompson?"

"It's Gemma," she says, folding down on the sofa.

She can hear noises from upstairs: the water gurgling, Judy's feet on the landing. Then Judy's standing there in a long T-shirt, with wet hair and a fluff of bubbles still on her leg.

"Was it peaceful?" Gemma asks the night nurse.

Is death ever peaceful? Is it peaceful when a stranger's signature on a form means everyone will walk away as you struggle for air? Did Frances regain consciousness at the end? Did she know she was dying? Did she think of Gemma or Judy, or her husband, lost so long ago? Did she cry out? Did she know where she was?

"I'm sorry," Gemma gasps. "Please speak to my mum."

She hands the phone to Judy, crumples down on the sofa, with the damp chewed carrot still in her hand.

It has happened. Frances has gone. Gone. Forever. Gemma knew it would have to happen one day, but she cannot envisage a life without Frances. She has always been there. The house is full of her things. She can't have gone. She simply can't. It isn't possible. Only yesterday morning she was well, cheerful. Or was she? She was a little subdued, but Gemma thought it was tiredness from the trip north. She will never sit on this sofa again. She will never sleep in her bed upstairs. In the kitchen her clothes are drying on the laundry rack. This can't be right. Never again. It's inconceivable. Frances wouldn't just go. She loved life too much.

Judy sits, puts her arm around Gemma, prises the carrot from her fingers.

"He said we can go and see her now," Judy says. "I would like to. They say we must go soon. I'll get dressed. Will you come?"

. Go soon. Or what? Frances will be taken away to the mortuary. Some cold place of dead people. Gemma's hazy about what happens to people after death. Will they demand a post-mortem? She feels she is twisting up inside. Not a post-mortem, not that. Isn't it enough that the hospital allowed her to die, wanted her to die? They can't want more than that.

She's crying but tears aren't enough. If she cries blood, it won't be enough. Nothing can express the desolation, the cold, the fear, that courses through her. She must live the rest of her life without Frances. She has go through everything without her – love, despair, having children, making a career, illness, her own death – all before she sees

Frances again, and she's not even comfortable with the idea of an afterlife, but that makes it even worse: Frances has ceased to exist in every way.

"Are you coming?" Judy stuffs wet hair into her coat. "You don't have to, but I would like to. You don't have to see her. You could wait on the corridor, but I'd really like you to come with me. Please."

"I'm coming. I do want to see her."

That terrible journey again. That car park, that building. The empty atrium, shutters pulled down at the café, the shop closed. The sound of a lift clanking somewhere. It's gone midnight and the corridors are deserted.

Gemma's heart rate bounds. She has never seen a dead person before. She's seen dead guineas: they lie limp, the light gone from their eyes. She knows their spirit, or soul, or essence – or whatever the hell it is that gives life – has departed.

The male nurse greets them quietly as they go onto the ward. The lights are on at the nurses' station. Frances's curtains are fully closed for the first time.

Gemma swallows. Her guts are pinched. She's not crying, not now, but she's afraid. Afraid that Frances's face will tell the narrative of her death, and that it was not peaceful.

Judy opens the curtains. Frances now lies on her back, her head facing upwards. She looks larger again, more like herself. Did she move to that position to die, Gemma wonders, or did the nurse lay her out flat? Her mouth is open a little, her profile sharp. Gemma tiptoes to her head. There's a tiny bloom of bruising behind her ear.

"She looks more like herself now," she says to Judy.

Judy nods.

"Distinguished," Gemma adds.

"Yes." Judy swipes the curtains closed again, and it's just the three of them, as it's been for so many years. For the last time.

"Beautiful lady." Gemma hovers her hand over Frances's fine hair; gently she brings it down. It's still soft, still fluffy.

I could lie down beside her, Gemma thinks. *I could lie down beside her and fall asleep with her.* She's not afraid any more, not of Frances. Afraid of the future without her, afraid of the next few days which she knows will be beyond terrible, but not afraid of the elegant lady on the bed.

"Did she know she was dying?" Gemma asks Judy.

"I don't know. No one can know."

"That form–" Gemma starts. "The Liverpool Pathway–"

"Not now," Judy interrupts. "Please. There's time for that later. We can decide what to do, but not now, not until…all this is over."

"We must do something."

"We will."

Mustardseed wakes. He's fallen asleep on the sofa with the lights on. His book has slipped to the floor. He stands, easing his muscles, and picks it up. It's just gone one. He wonders if Frances still lives. His phone is charging in the kitchen. He checks the screen. Nothing. He unplugs the phone and rings Gemma.

"Mustardseed," she says, and he knows. He knows in that instant that Frances has gone.

"I'm so sorry, Gemma," he says.

She tells him she and her mother have been to the hospital to see Frances. They are home now in South Stoke. She tells him she is relieved it is over.

“It was the waiting,” she says. “Wondering all the time when it would happen. I’m glad I wasn’t there but I sort of wish I had been. You know?”

“I can imagine,” he says. “Is there anything I can do for you?”

“You’ve done loads,” she tells him. “Shit, I have to get the stuff to the market in the morning.”

“Are you up to it?”

“I’ll do it. I’ll be there. I’m so tired but I don’t think I’ll be able to sleep now.”

“When I see you tomorrow,” he says, “can I give you a big hug?”

“Yes please,” says Gemma.

The house is as quiet as it gets. A few creaks. It’s an old house. Gemma thinks she might just stay up all night and take the preserves into Green Park for eight. It’s getting on for two now.

Where is Frances? She won’t be on the ward now. She’ll be in the mortuary. That terrible word. Gemma has only seen mortuaries on the TV: echoing tiled rooms, tall rows of fridges, metal tables, blood.

She gets out of bed, pads to Frances’s room. She holds her breath as she opens the door. Frances’s scent. *What am I doing?* she asks herself, but the pain is so raw, so intense, it seems she should just follow her feet into the bedroom. She turns on the bedside lamp.

The bed, neatly made. A fold of lavender nightdress under the pillow. Gemma lifts the quilt, gets into the bed, lays her head down. The alarm clock ticks. Gemma watches the second hand. The bedside table is cluttered: packets of tablets, half a tube of mints, a handbag mirror, two pens, a small torch. Gemma sits up slowly. They’ll have to go through Frances’s things. Her clothes, her papers, her personal possessions. Gently she opens the bedside drawer. More tablets, a packet of aspirin, a tube of hand cream. A black ring box. Gemma knows what’s in there. She lifts it out opens the box. Frances’s engagement ring, three tiny diamonds. Gemma slides it on her finger, lets the light catch the stones, slides it off, puts it back in the box. A few more pieces of special jewellery: a silver bracelet, an amethyst on a tangled chain. A photograph of Gemma’s grandfather in a Panama hat, a turquoise Grecian sea behind him. It was the last picture of him before he drowned. A few receipts. An envelope. Gemma lifts it out. It must be important to be in here. Should she look at it?

It has a local postmark. Gemma takes out the single sheet of white paper and gasps. The monogram at the top is the same RG that was on the van Mustardseed borrowed. The letter is dated May the previous year. Gemma can’t stop now.

‘Dear Mrs Thompson,

Many thanks for your cheque and for your kind comments about Agent Cobweb. I am delighted to hear you are so pleased with his work and will pass on your thanks and warmest wishes as you request.

Yours sincerely,

Robin Goodfellow’

Frances knew about the agency. She’d used the agency. What for? Gemma tries to remember anything she can from May last year. She can’t. She runs her hand through the drawer but there is nothing else. Now she will never know. She’ll never know what Agent Cobweb did for Frances. She wonders if Mustardseed could find out. No, he wouldn’t. It’s all confidential. And then: does it really matter? Whatever it was, it was the start of the thread that unravelled to lead her to Mustardseed. *Frances would have liked Mustardseed,* Gemma thinks. Even more than she liked Cobweb, whoever he is.

It's after two. In under six hours she'll see Mustardseed at Green Park, where it all began. Or did it, she asks, folding the letter, returning it to the drawer. Perhaps it began over a year ago.

Gemma sets the alarm for seven, turns off the lamp, and curls up under the cover, waiting for sleep.

Act IV

Lord, What Fools These Mortals Be!

It's only afternoon, but already the sky is darkening. Cobweb stops walking, gazes up at the giant golden edifice of Bath Abbey, floodlit from below. Behind the soaring towers and crenellations, the sky is dark turquoise with the sparkle of early stars. Cobweb's breath clouds in front of him, and he winds his scarf again around his throat.

The Christmas market comes to Bath for two weeks at the beginning of December. Abbey Courtyard is crowded with wooden booths, decorated with bright fairy lights and evergreen boughs. There are stalls selling jewellery, handmade soaps, patterned gloves, chocolates. There are candles, Christmas decorations, Russian dolls, and stained glass. Cobweb shoves his hands in his pockets as they are burning from the cold, and slides easily through the crowd. He stops at one of the booths and buys a paper cone of chestnuts. He recognises some of the shoppers, staggering about with carrier bags, but they do not recognise him, not even the woman who lives in his street. He's a master of disguise but, despite that, RG has voiced concern about his suitability as an agent. One day someone will recognise him from one of the TV parts he's had.

Cobweb loves Christmas, the drama and theatre of it all. He loves the coloured lights against the intense dark winter sky. He loves the strangeness of the tree outside the Abbey with its cold ambulance-blue bulbs. He loves the thin, stooped Father Christmas who wears a crimson hooded robe, and looks like a shaman from the Arctic tundra. He loves the flashing carousel and later, when true darkness has fallen, he'll ride one of the dipping painted horses.

He checks his watch. Time to go. RG called him that morning with a job offer. *Only you, dear Cobweb, can do this one*, he'd said. *Escort work, maybe,* Cobweb thinks. He gets a bit of that at this time of year, and he knows Mustardseed would never take that kind of assignment, especially now he's met that nice girl Gemma. Cobweb remembers an escort job last Christmas where the old queen client threatened him with a broken vodka bottle. This year, he's already got a New Year's Eve party job booked. *That one'll need a suit and a haircut,* he thinks ruefully. He's grown his hair out, it's thick and shaggy on his shoulders and currently an interesting pale silver. He leaves the market behind him, and the carousel, walks up towards the office and rings the bell. Fairy buzzes him in.

"How am I supposed to know who you are?" she grumbles. "Last time you were blond with spectacles. You could be anyone. You don't even sound the same."

"Chestnut, Fairy?" Cobweb holds out the cone.

Fairy sniffs, and helps herself to one of her extra strong menthol drops.

"Cobweb, Cobweb, come along in." RG has appeared in the doorway. "You're going to like this one," he chuckles. "Fairy, bring us some green tea, please, and those little macaroons."

Cobweb chucks his paper cone into the bin and follows RG into the back room. RG sits at his desk, does something on the laptop, while Cobweb settles on the other side.

"You're off to the south coast," RG says at last, as Fairy comes in with a tray. Green tea in a clear glass teapot. A plate of tiny coloured macaroons. RG pours tea. Cobweb warms his hands on the cup and they sting with the heat.

"What am I doing there?" Cobweb asks when RG doesn't elaborate further, but turns his head away, not quite hiding a mischievous grin.

"An acting role. Right up your street."

"OK, so what is it?"

"You have to impersonate someone at a hospital."

"A doctor?"

"Not a doctor." RG's twitching again with suppressed laughter.

"Not a doctor. A nurse then?"

"Not even close."

Cobweb drinks tea, thinks about it. "A manager? A porter?"

"Nowhere near. You'll never get it. You are going to be a decontamination operative."

"You mean a cleaner?" Cobweb imagines a ghastly striped tunic, hefty boots, and a lavatory brush.

"Don't look so down-hearted, Cobweb. You are going to the department Christmas party in place of this man."

Cobweb starts to wonder what a cleaner might wear to a party. "Why doesn't this cleaner want to go to the party?"

"Cleaner? I said decontamination operative. You're not a cleaner. You work in a department called Sterile Services. Your job is to sterilise the theatre equipment – scalpels, forceps, clamps and so on – then pack them up to go…wherever they go. Important work. Very…sterile."

"I'm going to the party pretending to be this sterile guy? Won't everyone else realise I'm not him?"

"It's a little more delicate than that. You are impersonating a man who doesn't exist. Three versions of him, in fact."

"Right," Cobweb grins. "You've got my attention."

RG hands over one of the agency cards. On the back is an email address and password.

"Gerry Pyles," Cobweb reads aloud.

"That's your name. You need to email that address, email yourself, so to speak. The clients will respond with the details. You can only communicate with them through this email. You'll all be using it."

"Who are the clients?"

"The clients are other decontamination operatives."

"And they've set up a fake email," Cobweb muses.

"They've set up a fake…sterile guy. Three versions of him." RG offers the macaroons to Cobweb again. "I know you're going to like this one. Do stay and enjoy the refreshments. I'm off home so all that remains is for me to say Oberon Out."

It started on a wet December Saturday a year ago, just a week before Christmas. At two o'clock Mark Swift, who was working overtime, left early. He tugged off his blues in the Gents changing room and threw them in the laundry skip. He didn't much relish the thought of getting home early though. Michelle would be in a foul mood as ever, the girls would be bored and miserable because she never had any time for them and, as soon as he was in the door, Eleanor would want his attention and he'd not get in the shower for an hour. Maybe he could drive into town and look in the bookshops for a while. But the sky through the small square window on the stairs was the colour of steel, and he knew the car parks would be packed solid on a Saturday afternoon with just a week's worth of shopping time left, and the idea of struggling through crowds of wet, despondent shoppers was as grim as the thought of Michelle.

He heard footsteps on the metal stairs behind him, and he turned to see who else was leaving. It was Donna. He held open the door at the bottom of the stairs for her. She had dark blonde hair in a tousled ponytail, which she was trying to stuff into the hood of her parka. Mark signed out in the book on reception and handed her the pen to do the same. It was cold in the lobby with only the glass front doors. Rain sliced down into dark puddles on the forecourt and the spindly trees bent and twisted in the wind.

"Are you parked nearby?" he asked Donna.

"I'm walking," she said.

Mark opened the heavy glass door, and the wind tore his face. Donna's parka ballooned and the hood blew off her head. The rain was icy and stinging.

"Would you like a lift?" he shouted above the wind.

He saw her hesitate a moment, fumbling with her hair, then, "That would be lovely. Thank you."

The metal gate to the car park was swinging to and fro, clanging against its post.

"I'm just here," he said, pointing to his battered Fiesta. He hoped it wasn't too disgusting inside. "Sorry," he said, shoving the key in the lock, "the zapper thing doesn't work." He got in, reached over to unlock the passenger door.

The ashtray was overflowing with Michelle's roll-ups, there was a plastic bottle in the passenger footwell and flakes of tobacco on the seat. He turned around. Most of the crap was in the back with the kids' car seats, but it was still squalid, and he was embarrassed.

"Where do you live?" he asked Donna.

She told him the road, and he shrugged apologetically. "You'll have to tell me where that is."

"Left at the McDonald's roundabout," she said, smoothing her fringe.

Mark opened the window to slide his permit into the slot. Rain splattered in onto his arm and into his eye. The barrier jerked up, and they left the hospital car park. The sky was ink-dark, and the traffic lights blurred into bright stars. It only took a few moments to reach Donna's house. He parked outside, beside a silver hatchback he took to be hers.

"I think that kept you a bit drier."

"Thanks, Mark," she said, and reached for the handle. As she opened the door, she said, "Do you have to get away or would you like a cup of tea?"

"Tea would be great," he said, and turned off the ignition.

He followed her up the steps into the hall. It was warm in the house. She took off her streaming parka and hooked it up with another couple of coats. On the floor was a pair of flowered wellies.

In the kitchen Donna filled the kettle, dropped tea bags into blue stripy mugs. Mark stood at the back door, watching the rain hammer into the churned-up lawn. The clouds were so dark and heavy he felt he could open the door, reach out and touch them, and they would burst. On the counter top was a bright pottery bowl containing three onions and a sweet potato. A child's drawing was taped to one of the wall cupboards.

"You have children?" he asked, gesturing to the picture. He didn't think she could have. There was no evidence of any in the house, no evidence of any other person.

"Oh no," she said, "that's Jack, my sister's boy." She unfastened her ponytail and shook out her wet hair. "Here, come and sit down."

Mark pulled out one of the chairs at the table and sat down. Donna handed him a mug of tea.

"Do you want an ashtray? I could get you a saucer."

"I don't smoke anymore," he said, confused for a second.

"Oh, I'm sorry. I saw the ashtray in the car."

"That's Michelle," he said. "It's not easy giving something up when you live with someone constantly doing it."

"That must be hard. Michelle's your partner?"

"My fiancée." He drank tea, looked away.

"Oh, congratulations. When are you getting married?"

"Not any time soon," he said. "Like they say on Facebook, *'it's complicated.'* We've got two girls. Eleanor and Susannah." Michelle might be a pain in the arse but he loved his children. "What about you? I mean, do you live here on your own? Sorry, I didn't..."

"It's fine. Yes, just me. The way I like it."

Mark's mobile rang in his pocket. "Excuse me." He glanced at the screen, cut off the call.

"Take it if you need to."

"It's only Michelle. I told her I'd be working till half three, don't know why she's ringing me."

Donna refilled the kettle. While it boiled she put away the plates and glasses on the drying rack. Mark fiddled with a pen, snapping the end so the nib shot out and retracted, shot out and retracted. Donna had been working in Sterile Services for some months now, but she'd hardly spoken to him before. During the week she worked eight till four, and Mark started at twelve and worked into the evening. The times when they were on a break together, he always seemed to be on his mobile. They had only been working together this Saturday because Norovirus had left the department short-staffed, and Donna had offered to help out.

"What are you doing at Christmas?" she asked, handing him a fresh tea.

"It'll just be us at home," he said. "I'll see my parents at some point as well."

She noted the use of *I*, not *we*. "Are you working next week?" she asked, suddenly hoping he would, that he might find time to come and talk to her.

"Only till Wednesday," he said.

"I'm there all week."

Mark's phone rang again. He swore and took it out.

"Just take it. It's fine."

"Sorry," he said and hit green.

Donna picked up an orange from the fruit bowl and played with it.

"I'll be back just after four," Mark said. "I'm working till half past...yes, I'm still at work."

It was the first lie.

It was the first lie.

As Mark drove out of Donna's close he grinned to himself. It was a small thing, to say he was still at work when he wasn't, but it felt monumental.

"If she knew I'd left work, she'd have been nagging me to go back sooner," he'd said to Donna at the time, and Donna just smiled and said he didn't have to explain himself to her. Mark knew it was more than that. Michelle would go crazy if she thought he was at another girl's house, drinking tea in her kitchen and talking to her. She'd already been so shitty to his female friends they'd withdrawn from him, and he knew she'd hacked into his emails.

The rain and wind had eased somewhat while he was at Donna's, and he no longer needed the wipers on. Fairy lights and Christmas trees twinkled brightly in house windows as he drove past. At last the heater kicked in and the car warmed up. He turned on the radio. *I must clean out that disgusting ashtray*, he thought. He'd do it on Sunday. Make the car look more presentable. He wished it didn't smell so much of stale tobacco.

On Monday morning Donna put on some make-up. She didn't usually bother. She didn't pretend to herself: she knew damn well why she was trying to look prettier. Not that there was any point. He had a partner, or fiancée, or whatever, who obviously never gave him five minutes' freedom. No one would stand a chance. *It's complicated*, he'd said. Whatever that meant. It meant no doubt that she drove him to despair, but he must love her really. He had two children with her. He wouldn't have done that if he didn't love her, would he? Or had she tricked him, deceived him, to keep him? If she had it was obviously working.

Donna checked her face and hair just before Mark was due to arrive, but he went straight to the autoclave, and she only saw him briefly in passing outside the tearoom. He said hi and smiled, but he looked tired and harassed.

The next day when Donna left at four, he was standing out on the forecourt, with his coat on over his blues talking into his phone. Donna felt cold just looking at him, as the flimsy material of his trousers flapped in the winter wind. She wondered what Michelle did for a job; probably she stayed at home with the kids which was why Mark did so much overtime on Saturdays. *That's an idea,* Donna thought, as she walked home. Perhaps she could do some more overtime. Mark implied he worked most Saturdays. Maybe she ought to look into that in the New Year. *What's the point?* she asked herself once more, as she waited for the crossing lights to change. *Because he isn't happy.*

This is the last chance I'll have to see him before he's off for Christmas, she thought on Wednesday morning. It was raining again: a cold driving rain that stung her eyes. The sky had hardly lightened by the time she arrived at the hospital roundabout. There was a blue sheen to the wet tarmac, and the smell of rain and exhaust fumes. As she walked up beside the main hospital car park, she saw the brave red and pink and yellow lights on the Christmas tree, luminously bright in the monochrome morning.

Mark arrived with one of the other technicians, an older guy called Brian, who worked the same shift. They nodded to Donna as they passed her by the changing rooms, but they were talking, something about money, and didn't stop.

In the afternoon, she found Mark at the dot matrix computer.

"Hi Donna," he said.

"You breaking up today?" she confirmed.

"Yup." He logged out of the system, and the hospital's blue screen came up.

"Just wanted to wish you a happy Christmas. You and…your family."

"Thanks," he said. "Sure it'll be the usual train wreck. You have a good one too. Hey," he added, as she turned away "Are you going to the department party on Friday?"

"No," she said.

"No, nor me," he said. "Wouldn't be allowed to. See you soon then."

Mark walked out to his Fiesta. There weren't that many cars in the car park at eight at night. Despite the amber lights round the perimeter of the car park, and the single red glow from the top of an aerial over the wall, he could still see the constellations: icy white sparks in an icy black sky. His breath clouded before him as he unlocked the car. It was as cold inside as out. His phone rang and he swore under his breath. Michelle again. He didn't answer, held the phone a moment in his hand. Then he texted: '*Staying on for an hour or so to cover.*' Then he turned the phone off and fired the ignition.

Donna heard the car outside, saw the flare of headlamps through the curtains. She stood up. The lights went off. It looked like the car was outside her house, but she wasn't expecting anyone. She flicked off the TV, then there was a rap at the door. She hoped it wasn't someone bringing a card or present that she had forgotten, but her lights were on: she couldn't pretend to be out. Her outside light was broken and she couldn't see anything though the muslin curtain at the front door.

"Hi," Mark said.

"Hi." She slid the chain off the door and he came into the hall.

"Are you busy? I would have called but I don't have your number."

"No," Donna said. "Not busy. Come in. Would you like tea? A glass of wine?"

"Tea please," he said. "I'm driving."

"Of course."

Donna filled the kettle. Mark sat at the table where he'd sat only a few days ago. The orange she had played with was still in the bowl with two dried-up lemons and some grapes.

"I wanted to see you before I go on holiday," he said suddenly. "I'm sorry I haven't been able to talk to you much at work… It's just I've been there a while now and some of them know a bit about my situation."

"Your situation?" She handed him a tea and sat at the table.

"Yes, Brian and some of the others. They know it's…"

"Complicated?"

"Kind of. Brian knows I'm not happy at home but I wouldn't want him to get the wrong idea or anything."

"The wrong idea?"

"Yes, I wouldn't want him to think that I, that you, you know what I mean."

"Of course," she said, embarrassed, then, "Are you looking forward to Christmas?"

"No," he said. "Michelle will drink too much, and pick fights all the time. The girls will be unhappy, and I'll probably find myself coming back to work early. That's what it's always like."

"I'm sorry," Donna said. "I'm sorry things are so bad."

"It's my fault. I should have got out before the girls came along. Now it makes it a whole load more difficult. I love my girls, I really do, but this can't go on. I don't know what to do. I'm sorry. You don't want to hear all this." He stood up, his mug still half-full. "I should go."

"No." Donna stood up too. "Don't go."

"I really should."

"No," she said again.

"Donna."

She didn't know if he moved towards her or if she moved towards him. When he kissed her, he tasted of Earl Grey.

Donna's sister Julie shook her head.

"What are you like? I suppose he said his wife doesn't understand him?"

"She doesn't."

Donna shoved another plate into the dishwasher. The kitchen surfaces were cluttered with the detritus of Christmas lunch: greasy plates, wine glasses, roasting trays. There was a wooden board with leftover beef slices on it, and a bin bag of torn wrapping paper. Donna knew she'd had too much Merlot; her head throbbed when she bent over.

"He just turned up at your house the other night?"

"Well yes, and he said how bad things were, and how unhappy he was and what a crappy Christmas he was going to have."

"And?"

"And then he kissed me," Donna said.

"Coming in a sec," Julie yelled in response to Jack's distant whine. She tipped the gravy down the sink. "Don't tell me you went to bed with him?"

Donna flushed, remembering. It had been quick, desperate. She lay there with her arms around his shoulders and thought that an hour ago he hadn't even knocked on the door. Abruptly, he peeled himself away from her.

"I'd better wash," he'd said.

"I'll get you a towel." Donna stumbled to her feet, pulled on her jumper and rummaged in the airing cupboard. She lay on her rumpled bed listening to the whoosh of the shower.

"Will you text me over Christmas?" he asked, as came back into the room, rubbing his arms with the towel. "That'll make me feel so much better. Give me your number." He took his phone from his pocket and turned it on. As the screen flashed alive the phone cheeped several times. "Oh, fuck off," he muttered to it.

"He's lovely," Donna said to Julie. "He makes me happy."

"He'll make you more unhappy than you could imagine," Julie said grimly, slamming the dishwasher shut.

New Year. January. Donna walked to work, in the grey half-light, gagging on the traffic fumes at the hospital roundabout. The Christmas tree was still there, still lit, but it looked sad now, obsolete, awaiting its destruction. And what of her? Was she too awaiting her destruction?

Just after eleven thirty she carried out some flattened cardboard boxes to the rubbish skip on the building's forecourt.

"Donna."

Mark ran cross the asphalt towards her. She tugged off her hat, let her ponytail fall down. He drew level with her.

"I'm working on Saturday," he said. "I could come over after."

"I'd like that," she said.

She didn't ask how he would manage it, what lies he would concoct. He wanted to come. That was enough.

"I've missed you," he said, and she smiled and blushed, and did not tell him how much, how very much, she'd missed him, and how the best things that happened to her over Christmas were getting his texts.

"We'd better go in," he said, and together they walked back to the door. "Here's Brian," he said, waving to the older man who was approaching from the car park gate.

Donna stuffed her hair back into her blue hat.

"Hi Mark, hi Donna," Brian said. "Good Christmas?"

"Yes," said Donna.

"No," said Mark, and laughed, and opened the glass door for Donna to go through.

Helen on reception glanced up as they crowded in. Mark and Brian signed in at the desk. Donna started up the stairs, remembering Mark's words about how Brian knew he was unhappy at home. She shouldered open the Ladies changing room. It was empty. *This is going to be so hard,* she thought. And Saturday was days away.

At four o'clock, Brian Webster bundled his coat on over his blues. He'd forgotten to post his letters before work. There was a postbox in the lobby of the main building. He'd walk down and post them on his break. He might even go into the coffee shop and buy a caramel slice. This New Year diet and exercise thing just wasn't working. He still hadn't got round to giving up smoking, and that was last year's resolution.

Once outside Sterile Services, he cupped his hands and lit a cigarette. Mark was pacing up and down with his mobile to his ear. Brian waved; Mark waved back, pulled an exasperated face. *He must be on to Michelle,* Brian thought, as he walked through the metal gates and onto the road. Mark had confided a few things to him, about Michelle's temper, her drinking, her uncontrollable rages and jealousy. Brian sighed. He wasn't happy at home either, but he couldn't say any of those things about his wife Joy. After twenty-five years of marriage they were still good friends, fond of each other. It was just that...Brian inhaled on his cigarette. He must not even think about it. Twenty-five years and three children couldn't have been a mistake, could they?

It was the middle of visiting time, and the patients' car park was busy. He walked beside a line of cars queuing at the barrier, over the zebra crossing, and into the warm fug of the hospital lobby. He stuffed the envelopes into the postbox, and walked on inside. He hardly ever came to the mother ship as Mark called it. Only a few times when he'd gone to theatres, or to use the cash machine, or to buy cakes or chocolate. He went into the coffee bar, straight to the cake counter. There was no one serving. He jiggled change in his hand, wishing he had the resolve to walk out before the assistant came back.

"I'm sorry, what can I get you?"

"Caramel slice, please," Brian said, and found himself staring into the darkest navy eyes he'd ever seen.

"I have to go. I'll see you later," Mark said.

"Call me later," Michelle demanded.

"I'll call when I leave."

"Call me on your next break."

"I can't. I'm nearly out of battery."

He ended the call. Suddenly he felt exhausted. As he walked back to the glass front door he scrolled through some of the texts Donna had sent him over Christmas. Gentle messages, saying she hoped he was having a relaxing break. *What a laugh,* he thought. No hassle, no demands. After about three messages he'd started to sign off with a couple of kisses; she mirrored him. He wanted to kiss her now. He swore and pocketed his phone. Saturday was too far away. It was lucky that Michelle wanted him to work overtime on Saturdays. He'd just leave an hour or so earlier and go to Donna's. Michelle would never know. She never saw his timesheets. She'd never notice an hour's discrepancy.

He reached out to open the door. Donna was on the other side. She smiled at him and stepped outside.

"I'm off home now," she said.

"Can I come?"

"Mark," she said, glancing over her shoulder.

"I know, I know."

"I'll see you tomorrow."

Georgia Shelley stared at her father's text in fury. How fucking dare he do that? Bloody shrink interfering in everyone else's business.

'Saw Bill McDonald today. He says they'll be recruiting for technicians in Sterile Services shortly. I said you'd be interested.'

She was quite capable of finding a job by herself, should the right one come up, and being some bottle-washer in the Sterile Services Department most certainly wasn't the right one. She was an artist, for fuck's sake. She hit delete, and trailed downstairs to the kitchen, poured a glass of red wine from the bottle standing on the worktop.

She'd left her art degree after only a year. It wasn't her fault things went wrong. It wasn't her fault she'd got pregnant by that idiot filmmaker, then had an abortion. It wasn't her fault she smoked too much weed. It wasn't her fault she never managed to get enough work together for the end of year show. Life conspired against her.

She'd been back at home with her father since the summer. There were no decent jobs here. The only reason he wanted her to work at the hospital was so he could keep an eye on her. Neil Shelley was a consultant psychiatrist who'd brought up Georgia single-handed after her mother died ten years ago. He hadn't really wanted her to go away to university because he couldn't watch her every move. He should be glad she was back at home, but he wasn't. She poured herself another glass and grimaced.

Bloody Bill McDonald in Recruitment. He used to live next door; that was how Neil had got to know him. Sometimes his wife had looked after Georgia when Neil was out on dates. Neil never remarried, never shared his home with anyone but Georgia, though a string of women, usually from the hospital – nurses, junior doctors, an audiologist – had appeared and disappeared through his life. There was no one at the moment, so he could fix all his attention on her.

Georgia trailed upstairs and into the spare room. This was supposed to be her studio. Her easel was in the corner; there was a canvas on it, stained with a blue-mauve acrylic wash. There were tubes of paint, brushes, and a palette, encrusted with rainbow colours. There was an old mug on the windowsill. Georgia sighed. She had no discipline to paint on her own. It must have been a week since she'd been in this room. She inspected the mug, found a furry growth at the bottom, and recoiled.

The problem was that she would have to find a job soon, she knew that. The Job Centre would start sending her for ghastly interviews at horrible places: bakeries, betting shops, supermarkets. The hospital might be better. There were all the junior doctors – surely some of them were single? Life was actually pretty boring at home on her own most of the day. Most of her old friends were away training in other cities. They'd come back at Christmas, some of them, and she'd met up with them, but it wasn't the same. They were all nearly half-way through their degrees, almost trained as teachers, marine biologists, engineers, lawyers. She met her old boyfriend from the sixth form at Christmas; he showed her a photo of the girl he'd just moved in with: a pudding-faced dismal specimen doing something in management. No, they had all moved away from Georgia, and she was the only one left standing, having achieved absolutely fuck all.

Maybe, just maybe, she might apply for the Sterile Services job after all. They probably wouldn't take her, but it would shut her father up, and if they did take her, well, it might offer a bit of amusement for a while. She might meet people she could go out with. It was almost impossible to get out at night the way things were.

She ran downstairs with the filthy mug. *OK,* she thought, *you win. I'll apply for the job, but not for the reasons you think.* She checked the kitchen clock. Just time to try out her new purple hair dye before her father came home.

Mark texted Donna at two on Saturday and said he was just leaving work and would be with her in a few moments. Donna exhaled, suddenly realising how afraid she had been. Afraid that he would say what happened before Christmas had been a mistake, that he could never do that again, that he loved Michelle and couldn't hurt her, or that Michelle had somehow found out, and he'd never be able to speak to her again.

She waited for the sound of his engine to come into the close. He slammed the car door, then there he was on the other side of the glass. He stepped into the hall and took her in his arms before she could shut the door behind him.

"It's been so long," he said.

"Yes," she said, breathlessly, fiddling with the key behind his back.

"I couldn't come any earlier. I have to have something to show for my Saturdays."

"Of course."

"Maybe one day I could bunk off," he mused, playing with her hair. "She wouldn't notice one day."

"How long have you got?" Donna took his hand, led him to the stairs.

"Till about three," he said.

"Oh."

She could not hide her disappointment. It was already nearly two fifteen. No, she should simply be glad he was here at all, that he had found a way to come to her.

Later, Donna lay with her head on Mark's shoulder, and his arm around her, but she could feel the tension in his body. She didn't want to move, didn't want to do anything that might provoke him to move, to reach for his clothes, his car keys, and walk out of the house. She lay there, hardly breathing, but silently aware that he was already thinking about leaving.

He shifted his arm, disentangled himself from her.

"I'm sorry," he said. "I have to wash and be off. Michelle thinks I'm working till three."

Donna glanced at the clock. It was quarter to three. He'd hardly been here. She flopped back on the pillow, watched him hurry out of the room. She'd put him a clean towel on the rack. The bathroom door closed, then the whistle of the shower. She sighed. It wasn't much, but it was all he could give. When he came back into the bedroom, with a towel around his waist, he smiled at her.

"I've just got time for a tea if you feel like making one."

She grabbed her dress and pulled it over her head. She didn't bother to untwist the knot of her tights on the floor. She padded downstairs to the kitchen, filled the kettle, set out mugs and tea bags. She heard his footsteps on the floorboards, then his voice.

"Coming," she called.

At the bottom of the stairs, she was just about to call up again, ask what he'd said, when she heard his voice again, the low metronome of someone on the phone. Someone on the phone who didn't want to be overheard. The kettle clicked off, and she went back to the kitchen, poured water onto the tea bags. Mark's feet running down the stairs.

"I'd better shove some cold water in it," he said, taking the mug off her and running it under the tap.

He gulped a few mouthfuls, gave her a hug.

"I have to go, sweetheart," he said, putting the half-full mug down on the table. "Text me later. Please."

"I will," Donna said.

She reached up and kissed him, but he was already moving away, towards the front door, towards his car, towards Michelle.

"See you on Monday," he said, kissed her again, and then he was gone.

She stood at the open door in her crumpled dress. The cold wind stung her bare legs. He reversed awkwardly out of the parking space and swung away down the close. Donna noticed her opposite neighbour at the front window looking out. She closed her door and went back inside. Her own tea was still too hot to drink.

It had been a week since Brian went to the coffee shop in the hospital, a week since that caramel slice and those midnight eyes. He tugged on his coat and started across the windswept tarmac.

Caramel slice or Danish? Brian mused, as he crossed into the car park. He imagined the golden sweetness of the caramel, the crumbly vanilla shortcake, and then he imagined the sticky white icing, the currants, the succulent cherry on top of a Danish.

He stopped on the corridor before the coffee shop. People barged past him. Someone clipped him with a wheelchair. Brian didn't notice. He simply stood there, watching the lithe figure bent over one of the tables, wiping the tea stains from the surface, straightening with a tray of dirty crocks, sliding gracefully behind the serving hatch.

Brian went into the coffee shop, suddenly aware of how unattractive he really would be to this beautiful youngster. A balding man in his fifties, overweight, smelling of tobacco, wearing trainers and a parka over blues.

There was a queue at the counter. Girls buying sandwiches. A couple wanting cappuccinos. He eyed the cakes. There were the Danish pastries, glistening with sugared icing; slices of chocolate cake, heavy with fondant; doughnuts that sparkled. A single caramel slice.

A hard-faced woman served the man in front of him, banging his teapot down so roughly it splashed on the tray and then there was the gorgeous creature once more, sliding behind the scraggy woman to Brian.

"Uh, I'll have a Danish pastry," Brian said, flustered of a sudden. "To take away."

"One Danish pastry coming up."

Brian watched the metal spatula slide under the cake, deftly scoop it up, slip it into a paper bag.

"Anything else I can do for you?"

"I'll have that caramel slice too," Brian said.

Anything to delay leaving. He wished he had time to eat his cakes at one of the tables. He handed over a note. As the change slid into his hand, he felt the sudden coolness of fingers against his skin. He looked up into those navy eyes.

"Enjoy your cakes," the young man said, and smiled at Brian. "See you again."

Before he turned to the next customer, Brian saw the ID card hanging from his belt. *Ashley Avery,* he said to himself, as he joined the chaos on the corridor. It didn't even sound like a real name. Ashley Avery. That was the young man's name. The name wasn't enough. Brian wanted to know more.

Sometimes it was difficult, Donna found. Sometimes she would want to reach out and touch Mark when she passed him on the corridor, or when he worked at the neighbouring sink. He would always smile, and sometimes she fancied there was a special message for her in his glance, but that was as far as it went. Once, she went into the staff room to make tea, and there he was, alone, filling the kettle. He turned at the sound of the door. Donna let it slam shut behind her. He kissed her and tweaked a strand of hair that had escaped from her hat. When the door opened again and some of the other girls came in, they were just standing side-by-side, dropping tea bags into the bin. Mark split his Kit Kat down the middle and handed her half, still wrapped in thin torn foil.

He came to see her every Saturday. He would text her as he was leaving, then five minutes later she would let him into her hall. He never had any extra time. At quarter to three exactly, he would go to the bathroom to shower, and Donna would go downstairs and make tea, and she knew that while he was dressing upstairs he was on the phone to Michelle. He was on the phone to Michelle in her bedroom. Donna didn't really think anything of this, except that each weekend it hurt more.

"I wish I'd–" he said once, as he was saying goodbye to her in the hall.

"Wish you'd what?"

"I wish I'd met you years ago."

Ashley Avery was standing over one of the tables. Brian hovered on the corridor watching him. Two young men were at the table drinking cappuccinos, eating eclairs. Ashley flicked a cloth over his shoulder, said something, the boys laughed. Brian moved closer.

"Have you a got a gig this Friday?" one of them asked.

"Absolutely. Nine o'clock. It's Lady Gaga this week," Ashley said. "I'd better say *ciao*. Here's one of my regulars." He smiled at Brian, with laughter in his eyes. "It's cake o'clock, is it?"

"I'll have a chicken salad roll," Brian blurted. He wondered whether to say he had overheard the boys' conversation about the gig and Lady Gaga. Was Ashley Avery a singer?

Ashley's dark blue eyes widened. "There's no such time as salad roll o'clock," he said.

Brian involuntarily helped himself to a banana from the fruit bowl.

"And this," he said.

"That bad, hey?" Ashley slid the bap and the banana into a paper bag, handed it across to Brian. "I'm sure you'd feel better having a nice caramel slice. Hmm?"

Brian trudged gloomily back to Sterile Services. He unzipped the banana and took a bite. Why the hell had he bought it? He hated bananas. Was he having a mid-life crisis? He thought about Ashley Avery and his blue eyes, his pale skin and chiselled cheekbones. His hair was dark, almost black, tousled to look like he'd just risen from bed. He wore an earring on one side, a dangling silver charm. Brian shoved the banana in a nearby bin and took his phone out of his coat pocket. As he walked he Googled Ashley Avery on his phone. He never expected to find anything, but there he was on the website for Clementines, the gay club in town. Brian spread his fingers across the screen and the image swelled. Ashley Avery with his hair slicked back, wearing something silver. He must be a regular at the club. Brian sighed, pocketed his phone. He knew where Clementines was, in one of the back streets behind the cathedral. Could he get there? Could he go there and watch Ashley Avery's gig? No. Joy expected him at the same time every night, and he'd have to invent a cover story.

He walked on towards Sterile Services. He'd supported his family for over twenty years. Surely now it was time for him to be himself, whatever that meant? Brian the cake o'clock man watching his young lover performing; clapping, shouting, laughing with their mutual friends in Clementines.

Ashley Avery wasn't the first man Brian had fancied. Of course not. But Brian was pretty sure all the others had been straight. When he'd first started work at the hospital a couple of years ago – after being made redundant from his managerial position in a waste disposal company – he'd fancied Mark Swift. Mark told Brian his home life was unhappy; Brian fantasised about easing Mark's pain. But that had all gone. Now there was no one but Ashley Avery.

On Friday there was a steely yellow stain in the sky. When Donna stepped outside at quarter to eight, there was a sparkling of ice on the parked cars, and the tarmac under her feet was black and treacherous. She went back in and replaced her hiking boots with her patterned wellies. She was late for work, treading carefully and deliberately, and several times she nearly skidded over on the ice.

In Sterile Services two people hadn't made it in because of the weather. Throughout the morning, as she glanced out of the windows, she saw the queasy light in the sky thicken and, when she took some rubbish out to the skip in only her thin blues, the cold almost took her breath away. She wondered if Mark would get in, whether the roads would have cleared or been gritted by the time he left home.

Just before twelve Brian locked his car and trudged towards Sterile Services. He clanged the metal gate behind him; it swung open again. The wind whistled coldly across the concrete forecourt. Brian glanced up to the staff room window on the upper floor and saw Donna standing there, hair loose from her hat, holding something – a mug? a sandwich? – and he waved. She waved back awkwardly and stepped away from the window, as though she'd been caught doing something she shouldn't. Who was she looking out for? Not him certainly. *Mark,* Brian thought suddenly. He had seen them talking furtively sometimes.

Not that he could cast any stones, he thought, as he stepped into reception, and the warmer air clogged in his throat. Tonight, Ashley Avery was doing his Lady Gaga gig in town. Brian wanted to go, but he hadn't the courage to make excuses to Joy and walk into a gay club, where he'd never been before, and he knew if he did, Ashley Avery's dark eyes would meet his, and Brian would see laughter, or worse, in them. He grabbed the pen and signed the entry book. He couldn't go. Not tonight. Forget it.

Donna came out of the Ladies, drying her hands on a paper towel. One of the other girls on her way in said, "It's snowing."

Donna looked out over the bleak forecourt. Soft flakes were spiralling downwards. She moved closer to the window, gazed up, straight into the underbelly of the clouds, until she felt dizzy with the falling specks. It was after twelve. Perhaps Mark wasn't coming in. She didn't know the roads around where he lived. Maybe the snow was already worse that way. As she turned away from the glass to go back to work she saw a figure running across the forecourt to the front door. His hood blew back, and she saw Mark's blond hair, then he disappeared under the awning below, and she heard the glass door bang, and his footsteps coming up the stairs. He almost cannoned into her.

"I'm late," he said.

"Don't fret. No one'll mind. Not today."

"Maybe not here," Mark said, taking his phone out. "I haven't called in."

Donna left him there, dialling on his phone. Michelle had only seen him an hour ago. Did he really have to call her as soon as he got to work? If it was just a one-off because of the snow, she could understand it, but Mark had to check in every day, on his breaks, and when he left. That wasn't normal.

The snow was starting to settle when Donna left at four. The outside lights had come on and shone weirdly in the dark, white light. She slithered across the forecourt in her wellies. On the main road, the traffic was creeping slowly, almost silently, all headlights and wipers. The snow on the pavement was impacted down into icy slush. Once she had to grab the fence post to stop herself falling.

At six thirty the supervisor told Mark to leave. She knew he had a long drive, some of it on narrow roads. He washed and changed quickly and ran down to reception to sign out. Snow covered the forecourt, trampled into icy footprints and tyre tracks. The flagstones leading to the metal gate were treacherous, and he walked on the grass instead. He was dreading the drive home. He was also pissed off because he didn't think he'd be able to do his overtime on Saturday. The roads would still be terrible. Only an idiot would drive out voluntarily in ice. But if he didn't work the next day, he wouldn't see Donna. He hadn't been able to catch her before she went, to tell her he probably wouldn't be able to make it. He would text her. No, he'd ring her. No, fuck it, he'd go and see her now.

Mark won't come tomorrow, Donna thought. She wished she'd been able to speak to him before she left, but he'd been talking to some of the others in the washroom, and she was afraid she would give herself away. She checked the time. Six thirty. She could text him instead. She was taken aback at how sad she felt that she wouldn't see him at the weekend. It only took a few times to create a pattern, and now Saturday afternoons between two and three were Mark time. She wouldn't know what to do with herself for that hour.

She hit send and peeled back the curtains. Snow drifted through the coronas of the street lamps: sickly pale orange flakes. Suddenly Donna was afraid for Mark, imagining his long drive home along icy roads, and in the dark. She closed the curtains as pale headlamps came into the close. It must be one of the neighbours coming home. No one would drive unless they had to.

In her hand her phone cheeped. '*I'm outside.*'

"What are you doing here?" she cried, opening the door.

Icy air blasted into the house, and Mark's mouth was cold when he kissed her.

"I got sent home early," he said. "Because of the weather."

Donna slammed the door, shivering at the chill.

"But, Mark, you should be going home then," she said. "The drive will be awful."

Mark shrugged, took off his damp coat. Donna hesitated. She should make him leave, make him set off as soon as he could. That would be the responsible thing to do, but Mark was sprawled on the sofa, patting the cushion next to him, so she said nothing, and sat beside him, with his arm around her, and his cold cheek against her warm one.

"Donna," he said at last.

"What?" She jerked around, suddenly terrified he had only come here this snowy night to tell her something she did not want to hear.

"I wondered…"

"What?" she said again.

"I wondered if I could stay here with you tonight?" he asked at last.

Donna stared at him, not speaking.

"Is that a problem?" Mark asked at last. "If it's not convenient, I'm sorry, I thought—"

"Of course, it's not a problem," Donna said. "It's the last thing I was expecting."

"If you'd rather I didn't, I really should get going. The snow and that."

Donna brought his hand to her mouth, kissed his palm.

"I'd love you to," she said. "But how are you going to do it? What are you going to say?"

"Don't worry about that," he said. "I'll phone her later."

"Would you like something to eat?"

"Later," he said, standing. "Come upstairs now."

He ran up ahead of her, and she followed more slowly, aware that tonight, because of the snow, everything would change, and the small lies would become a big lie. Through the landing window she saw the snow falling from the thick dark sky. Vehicles had left black tyre tracks on the road, and some kids were shouting somewhere. Snow was settling on roofs and lawns, and on parked cars.

"I'm glad you're not going home in this," she said, standing in the bedroom doorway, watching him tug off his jumper and shirt.

"So am I," he said.

Donna opened her eyes and glanced at the clock. Eight o'clock. Mark had wrapped himself around her, skin to skin. She needed to stretch but she didn't want to move. She couldn't tell from his silence if he slept or not but, as the clock ticked relentlessly on, she peeled away from him and he stirred.

"You should be making that call," she said reluctantly.

"Yes," he said, untangling himself from her, and immediately she felt cold.

She reached for her dressing gown. "I'll go and–"

"No, stay here, keep warm," he said, tapping on his phone. "Just be quiet."

Donna slid back under the covers as quietly as she could. She shouldn't be here for this conversation but she couldn't go now. His spare hand rested on the quilt over her tummy.

"Yes, terrible snow," Mark said. "I'm not even going to try to come back. No, not in that car. I'm staying in town with a friend from work… No, really, I can't… Don't be ridiculous, there probably aren't any trains… I'm not risking it, the roads are really dangerous. I'm going to stay here tonight…yes, someone from work. Gerry, you know, Gerry Pyles."

Donna glanced at Mark. Gerry Pyles. The name came so easily to him; it didn't sound like a name he'd made up on the spot.

"I must go. I haven't got my charger, and I'll need some battery for tomorrow… All right, I'll do that, I'll come as soon as I can."

He ended the call, checked the screen once more and turned off the phone. Only then did he turn to Donna.

"She doesn't want me to work tomorrow," he said. "She wants me to go back as soon as possible. I'm sorry."

"It's OK. You're here tonight," she said, then, "So who's Gerry Pyles?"

"Who indeed?" Mark laughed. "Gerry Pyles is you, sweetheart."

"But you made him sound real. Not like someone you'd just made up."

"I didn't just make him up. I've got your number in my phone under Gerry Pyles. I've mentioned him at home, you know, a guy at work I'm friends with. I said he worked Saturdays with me, so I had an alibi of sorts. Just being careful."

"Michelle wouldn't really go through your phone, would she?"

"I don't know," Mark said. "I kept your messages you sent me over Christmas, but then I deleted them. It was too big a risk. So now, all I have is your number under the name of Gerry Pyles."

"I see," Donna said, and smiled, wondering for a second if she should be concerned that Mark had made a false alibi so swiftly, as though he had done it before, as though he'd had affairs with other girls. That she wasn't special, just the last in a line.

"I'm going to have a shower," he said, then, "Did you say something about supper?"

Mark stood under the jet of warm water, and wondered why he was having a shower. He wasn't rushing off home to Michelle, so he didn't have to wash off the scent of Donna. It must be ritual; after he made love to Donna he washed. *Does it hurt her?* He didn't want to hurt her, not at all, but inevitably he would. He should have gone home in the ice and snow. Now he'd set a precedent, one which he could never follow, and it would hurt her. *Too late now,* he thought, wrapping himself in a fluffy green towel. He'd called Michelle. He was staying with Gerry. What he'd told Donna was true: she was in his phone under the name of Gerry Pyles.

One Saturday, when he'd got in, Michelle berated him for being late back. He'd been slow leaving Donna's, and then got caught up behind an accident. Instead of explaining he'd been stuck in traffic, he'd said that he had stayed to talk to someone at work after he'd phoned her.

"Who?" she demanded.

"Gerry," he said, picking up the TV guide, flicking through, trying to look casual, and wondering where the name Gerry had come from.

"You've never mentioned him before."

"Oh, he used to work nights," Mark invented, marvelling at how easily he lied. "He's just come onto days. He works weekends a lot."

"I've never heard of him," Michelle said, reaching for her tobacco tin. "What's his name? Gerry what?"

Mark glanced at that night's TV dramas to buy time. He'd been washing colo-rectal kits that day. He wondered if he might be getting haemorrhoids. "Piles," he said absently. "Er, that's with a Y. Pyles. Yes, Gerry Pyles. Good bloke."

Mark came out of Donna's bathroom and padded across the landing. He dressed quickly and turned on his phone just to check. Three missed calls from Michelle. He turned it off again. He would not look again. She couldn't find him. It was snowy outside; she had no car. She didn't know where Gerry Pyles lived. There was no way she could track him down, so why did he feel so apprehensive? Habit, he guessed, as he ran downstairs and into the kitchen, where Donna was heating a pan of water on the hob and measuring out spaghetti. She smiled at him and he thought how lovely she looked with her hair tangled, and a flush on her cheekbones. She handed him cheese and the grater, and he whistled quietly to himself as he worked, and outside the snow still fell, white flakes from a dark sky.

Donna woke first. It was just light. She was very cold. She moved slowly, not wanting to wake Mark, knowing that once he woke he would leave. She slid her arms into her dressing gown and padded to the window. It was no longer snowing. Their two cars wore sparkling white crowns. There were tyre tracks running down the road and, despite the hour, jumbled footprints on the opposite pavement. She went to the bathroom, cleaned her teeth and rubbed water on her cheeks. She'd lost her Saturday hour with Mark, but what had she gained? They'd cooked together, eaten together in front of the TV, shared a bottle of wine, and come to bed early to make love and talk into the early hours. It had been the most wonderful night – the most wonderful surprise – of her life and now, with the coming of daylight, it had gone, would melt into nothing, as the snow would melt into water.

Monday morning, and Donna was in the washroom, the dirty room. It was a vast cavernous place, high ceilinged like a warehouse. There were sinks along both sides for soaking the instruments when they arrived from theatre. Congealed blood could be stubborn, especially in the hinges of forceps and haemostats, and needed to be soaked off manually.

Donna had been assigned a trolley of packs from the delivery suite. She scanned the first into the computer and emptied the instruments with a discordant clang onto the workbench. She was cold in her blues. The snow had gone and, with it, the enchantment. Mark hadn't texted her on Sunday, and she found herself almost dreading his arrival at lunchtime.

Once her instruments were soaked, she loaded them onto a carriage for the tunnel washer. She glanced at the clock. Eleven. Only an hour until Mark arrived. It was harder and harder to be with him at work, and not let something slip. Sometimes he was at the neighbouring sink; sometimes they were in the packing room together, and he would look over at her, only his eyes visible between his hat and mask, and she felt that her desire and her love – yes, her love – must be obvious for everyone to see.

As Donna sent her carriage into the tunnel washer, Brian came into the washroom, calling out cheery greetings over the bass beat on the radio. It was so noisy with the constant music, the raised voices, the metallic clanging of steel on steel. Donna shivered again.

There were two tunnel washers, with a viewing chamber between them. Donna walked in, exhaling at the sudden warmth on her bare arms. Her instruments were in the first chamber, being washed before disinfection. She watched the water sloshing against the pane. On the opposite side another load was rattling through from the disinfection chamber to the drying area, to be blasted with hot air for fifteen minutes, before being unloaded in the packing room. Donna stood there a moment, simply breathing the heat, and the hypnotic gurgling of the washer, as her load hovered between the states of dirty and clean.

Dirty and clean. That was everything in Sterile Services. The washroom was the dirty room, where bloodstained instruments came in from theatres and outpatient clinics. Through the washers they went and emerged into the packing room or clean room. The boundaries were rigidly drawn. But the boundaries that now governed her life were not so simple. After Mark left her bed he washed. It was like he was purging her from him, as though she were the dirty room, and Michelle the clean room. No, that wasn't fair. Anyone would wash in those circumstances, wouldn't they? And yet, watching her instruments move on into the ultrasonic chamber of imploding bubbles, she could not reject the image from her mind. Dirty, clean, dirty, clean.

"You OK, Donna?"

She turned, startled.

Brian stood in the entrance to the washer, an LMA in his hand, like a deformed flower.

"Yes, fine, thanks," she said. "Just warming up in here."

"You sure? You looked, I don't know, sad."

"I'm not sad," she lied, and followed him out into the cold and the noise of the washroom.

It was cold in the car park. Donna stuffed her hands into her pockets and wished she'd brought gloves. The metal gate between the car park and the forecourt of Sterile Services clanged noisily against its post. Donna took a few steps down the gravel path to try to keep warm. She checked her watch. Nearly six-thirty. She had come too early. Overhead the sky was dark and cloudless. The stars looked cold. There was a group of people chatting further down a row of cars; Donna adjusted her hood and turned away. She couldn't see Mark's car amongst the parked vehicles.

The gate clanged loudly again and she turned. It was Mark. He waved and ran down to where she stood.

"It's at the far end," he said, gesturing to the darkest corner of the car park. His breath formed a cold white cloud as though he were smoking.

Their feet crunched on the gravel. Mark unlocked the car and Donna slid inside. It was as cold, or colder, inside the car, and smelt of Michelle's cigarettes.

"You must have gone home and come straight back again," he said, sliding a cold hand inside her coat, inside her jumper.

"I don't care," she said, and she didn't.

That afternoon Mark had stopped by her sink in the washroom.

"Can you come up this evening?" he asked quietly. "Meet me in the car park at half six."

"Is something wrong?" she asked.

"Nothing," he said. "I just want to see you."

Then he'd moved away, and said something to Brian at the next sink. Donna glanced at Brian under her lashes, saw him watching Mark walk away. Brian shook his head imperceptibly and turned back to his work. Donna wheeled her load to the nearest washer carriage, suddenly glad not to be beside Brian. Mark was talking to the supervisor in the corner, didn't acknowledge her as she stacked her haemostats into the carriage.

It was so cold in the car, and Mark's hands on her skin were colder still. Through the blurry windscreen she could see the drooping black leaves of the hedge, then a slice of navy sky, and the single red eye of the communications mast behind the wall.

"I can't work this Saturday. I'm sorry," Mark said.

"Oh," Donna said. "What's happening?"

"It's Michelle's birthday," he said at last. "I can't work."

"OK," Donna said, and she knew her voice sounded small and probably sulky.

She never asked anything about Michelle. She had never seen a photo of her. She only knew what Mark volunteered, which was very little. She knew Michelle was the stepsister of his friend's ex-girlfriend, and that was how they'd met. She knew Michelle was older than him.

"How old is she?" she asked.

He hesitated. "Thirty-nine."

Donna caught her breath, surprised. Mark was thirty to her twenty-five, but she hadn't realised there was such an age difference between Mark and Michelle. Michelle was nearly fifteen years older than she was. Donna wavered. Surely, she should feel young and desirable, but she didn't, she felt threatened, threatened by a woman with more experience of life than she'd had, the mother of two girls.

Mark lifted aside her hair to kiss her again.

"I am sorry," he said again.

"It doesn't matter," Donna lied.

What should she expect? Of course, there would be weekends when he couldn't work, when Michelle or the children demanded his time. She knew all this, she knew all this from the start. She remembered Julie's words, and felt a prickle of unease.

"I would much rather be with you," Mark said. "I've been trying to think of a way round it, but I can't. It's only one weekend."

"Only one weekend."

"I have to get back," Mark said. "Give me a cuddle."

Donna let herself slide into the brief warmth of his arms. She could get through one weekend without him. Mark opened his door and Donna squinted as the car light came on.

"I'll see you tomorrow," Mark said, putting his arm around her, as they walked back through the car park, "then it'll be the weekend, and you know how fast they go, then it'll be Monday again, and not too long until the next Saturday."

They stopped at the gate. It was closed against its post, quiet for once. They stood, facing each other, breath clouding between their mouths.

"You're lovely, Donna," Mark said quietly. "I'll miss you so much this weekend."

He pulled her to him and kissed her quickly, then he swung open the gate and she was alone under the stars. She turned to leave the car park and froze. She was not alone under the stars. A chunky figure was hunched up against the wall. Under a dark coat, she saw the pale trousers of hospital blues. A vapour cloud that was not cold breath; the glowing red dot of a cigarette. Brian. Donna's face burnt in the cold. Brian was looking away, turned towards the countryside behind the car park, but Donna knew he'd seen, heard. She reached up; her hood had fallen down. She tugged it up roughly and crunched out of the car park, only feet away from Brian. She kept her head down and he did not speak to her.

Mark watched Michelle across the table. The candle flame turned her red hair to gold, accentuated her cheekbones. He knew the man on the next table was admiring her. He sighed. It was so difficult. She really was a looker, and there must be something good there or they wouldn't have stuck it out so long. Nearly ten years since they first got together. They'd been through so much, and now, on her thirty-second birthday, he was sitting opposite her, knowing he had been unfaithful. Not once, but many times. He justified this to himself, saying that it was Michelle's temperament, her jealousy, her drinking, that had driven him to Donna. Michelle hadn't drunk like that when they'd first met. He couldn't recall when it started; it was something that crept up on all sides, like the rising tide on mudflats. Michelle didn't go back to work after Eleanor was born, then Susannah came along soon after, and still she didn't go back. When he got home he found her drunk and weeping, or shouting, the babies abandoned. She'd yell at him, accuse him of being late because he was with a woman. Once he had been, but Michelle threatened to take the girls away, and he couldn't risk anything again. Then he started working at the hospital, and there was no one till Donna. Donna was different – unsure of herself, anxious to make him happy – but needy. She needed reassurances, which was why he had lied about Michelle's age. Michelle had given him his two beautiful girls, but she had isolated him from his friends and, to an extent, his family too. He needed more. He needed Donna.

The waiter came and cleared their dessert plates, asked if they'd like coffee. Mark nodded his assent; Michelle ordered a whisky. He didn't rise to it; it was her birthday dinner. It was the first time they'd eaten out in ages. He had dropped the girls off at his parents' earlier that afternoon, his early ease with his family awkward now with Michelle's ghost between them.

The meal had been wonderful. The food was lovely, and Michelle was laughing and happy. He had seen the glances she gave him under her lashes, promises of things to come later. He reached out for her hand and brought it to his lips.

His phoned cheeped in his pocket and he automatically dug it out. Was it his parents? Were the girls all right? He glanced at the screen under the tablecloth.

"Who is it?" Michelle asked, as the waiter placed whisky and coffee on the table.

"Thanks," Mark said to the waiter to buy time.

"Who is it?" Michelle demanded again, her voice harder, flint-edged.

"Only Gerry," he said, putting the phone away, and tearing open a sachet of sugar.

"What does he want?"

"Oh, nothing. Just a funny story from work today."

"Didn't you tell him we were going out tonight?"

"Yes," Mark said. "Of course."

In truth he was angry with Donna. He wondered if it was a challenge she'd thrown down, whether she was testing what he was doing this Saturday night, Michelle's birthday. He didn't write back to her; he couldn't there and then in the restaurant and, for a moment, he played with ignoring her altogether. What she'd done had broken the boundary, texting him when he was out with Michelle. He drank coffee, gazed at the other diners, at a tray of meals being brought out, at the blackboard where a waitress was scrubbing out one of the starters with a damp cloth.

Michelle lit up a cigarette as soon as they got into the car. Mark opened the window a crack and cold air sucked in.

"Thank you for tonight," Michelle said suddenly. "It was great to go out again."

Mark turned to her briefly, squeezed her leg. "I'm glad you enjoyed it."

"I did." Michelle smoked, gazed out of the window. "Maybe we can make things happy again," she said. "I do love you."

"I love you too."

Mark hadn't replied. Donna wished she hadn't texted him. She knew it was Michelle's birthday. She knew it was a mistake. If she hadn't had that last glass of wine, she probably wouldn't have done it.

Her Saturday afternoon had been bleak without Mark. She was almost afraid at how dependent on him she had become in such a short time. She had gone into town, looked in a few shops, bought some earrings and a new skirt, picked up many books in Waterstone's and read the blurbs, and replaced them on the three-for-two tables.

As the afternoon slipped into the evening, she imagined Mark and Michelle leaving for an evening out, a meal, or a club. She didn't know what Michelle looked like but, at thirty-nine, with drinking and smoking habits, she must be lined around the eyes, with dull skin, and grey hairs.

Donna had waited until after nine to text Mark and, at midnight, when he still hadn't replied, she went to bed. She was tired and fell asleep with the light on. Something woke her; she reached out to turn off the lamp, scooped up her phone. That was what had woken her. Mark had texted. '*Sorry, didn't check my phone till now. Sleep well.*' Donna stared at the message until the screen died to black. It was after one thirty. *He must have waited for Michelle to go to sleep,* she decided. But, if that were the case, surely, he could have said something more? And where were his usual kisses? She should not have texted him today. It was stupid. He was pissed off, and now she was upset. She flicked off the lamp but she didn't sleep for hours.

On Sunday morning, she made a half-hearted attempt at housework. She cleaned the bathroom, trailed the Hoover round, straightened a few ornaments and dusted around them. She kept her phone in her pocket; when it rang, she almost dropped the vase she was holding. *Mark*, the screen said.

"Hi," he said. "I'm sorry about last night. It was a bit awkward."

"That's OK," Donna exhaled, realising suddenly how many times she used those words to Mark. "I'm sorry too. Can you talk now?"

"Kind of," he said, and the line crackled, and she imagined him walking away somewhere. She wondered if he were in the house. No, he must be out somewhere: in a shop, on a walk.

"I'm really looking forward to Monday," he said.

"Me too," Donna said, even though their shifts only crossed for a few hours, and often they were working in different areas.

"Yeah, OK," Mark said and his voice was harder, more distant. "Look, Gerry, I've got to go. I'll see you next week. Cheers."

He hung up before Donna could speak. Gerry Pyles, her alter ego.

Brian gulped the sudden warm air as he entered the hospital. He felt more relaxed coming to the coffee bar these days; Ashley always smiled at him, and asked how he was, as though they were old friends. Sometimes, Brian dared to imagine Ashley was even flirting with him, as he handed over a sticky bun or a caramel slice. Brian didn't order salad rolls any more. He was what he was: an overweight man in his fifties who smoked too much and exercised too little, and might possibly be falling in love with a beautiful nightclub singer. And that was OK. More than ever before, Brian felt at home in his body and in his mind. He had a secret and it sustained him. It fuelled him.

He wasn't the only one with a secret. He'd known there was something with Donna, since the day of the snow, when he saw her looking so anxiously out of the window. After that he had watched them at work, and sensed something – an awkwardness and an intimacy – that could mean only one thing. Then, the other week, he'd been outside at six-thirty having a cigarette, and Donna and Mark had walked together towards the gate, arms around each other, and Mark had kissed her and said she was lovely, and how much he'd miss her at the weekend. Brian knew Mark worked overtime most Saturdays but, as far as he was aware, Donna didn't. So, what did that mean? Was Mark meeting Donna after work somewhere?

The following day Brian had felt embarrassed with both of them. Donna looked away when he approached, muttered her replies to his questions. He thought they'd not noticed him, but he realised then that she had and, as well as that, she was miserable because Mark wasn't working that weekend. Brian even felt a faint simmer of jealousy, recalling how, once upon a time, he'd gazed at Mark's floppy blond hair and wanted to reach out and touch it, how he'd imagined Mark's mouth on his own. Donna knew the feel of Mark's hair, the taste of his kiss, and ridiculously, he resented her, but then, remembering Ashley, his jealousy dissolved like breath on a winter's night.

Now Brian strode into the coffee bar. Ashley was sorting crisps in wicker baskets. Brian recognised the two boys sitting at a table by the counter. They were the two who'd asked Ashley about his Lady Gaga gig. Today they were in uniform, one in theatre blues and one in a healthcare's tunic. The one in blues called Ashley over.

"Hello Brian," Ashley purred, as Brian walked in. "And how is the steamy world of Sterile Services this afternoon?"

The other boys chorused hellos to Brian, smiled up at him, this friend of Ashley's. Ashley introduced them as Paul, an ODP in trauma theatres, and Carl, a healthcare on the Gastro ward. Paul was fiddling on his phone, and thrust it at Ashley.

"In a moment, darling," Ashley said, sliding back behind the counter. "Let me look after Brian first, then we'll both come and take a look."

Brian flushed with pleasure at the word *both*, opened his mouth to order a caramel slice, already anticipating the heavy sweetness of toffee and shortbread, but there were none left in the glass cabinet.

"Do not despair," Ashley laughed. "When we got down to the last caramel slice, I took the liberty of hiding it under the counter in case you came along. And if you hadn't, I would have had it myself for you." He handed Brian the cake on a plate. "Come on, sit down with the boys and look at my gig."

"Your gig?"

"Yes, last week's," Ashley said, taking money off a woman for a bottle of Pepsi. "It was Rihanna night. You should have come. You must come. You know where Clementines is?

"Yes, yes," Brian said, allowed himself to be steered by Ashley to the boys' table.

Paul tapped his screen. Brian quickly bit a chunk of cake. His mouth was dry and it was hard to chew. There was Ashley on the screen, wearing the tiniest metallic costume Brian had seen, arching his back, looking like he was sucking off the mike. Brian swallowed the cake with difficulty. He couldn't even concentrate on Ashley's singing. He felt hot under his jacket. He needed a drink.

"Hang on," Ashley said. "Got to go."

Paul thrust the phone towards Brian, but he couldn't take it with his sticky fingers.

"He's…incredible," he managed at last.

"You must come down," Carl said. "We're always there, unless we're working. I missed the Madonna night. I was on a late shift."

"I will," Brian said hoarsely. He dumped his plate on the table amongst the boys' cups and plates. "I must get back now."

"We'll look out for you, Brian," Paul called.

Brian waved at them, and looked for Ashley, but he was at the cappuccino machine and had his back to the room. Brian was almost grateful. Outside in the cooler air, he realised he felt sick from gobbling the caramel slice too quickly. Or was it something else? Was it that, seeing Ashley's video, seeing him in his world, had discomforted Brian, even embarrassed him? Because Brian was embarrassed. He was obviously accepted, even liked, by Ashley and his friends, but they belonged to one world and he belonged to another. Theirs was a world without boundaries, a world of overt sexuality and glitzy costumes, whereas he was a staid married man with children, and to cross that line would be a betrayal of everything he had strived for all these years. He hunched his shoulders into the wind, and walked back to Sterile Services.

A couple of weeks passed before Brian saw Ashley again. He had a week off, and he and Joy went to stay with their daughter Ruth in Cardiff. While he was away, he tried not to think about Ashley. Sometimes he failed, and Googled images of his performances at Clementines. He looked him up on Facebook, while he sat in the car waiting for Joy and Ruth to come back from a shopping trip. Ashley's Facebook photo was from one of his performances. He had many friends. Brian recognised Paul and Carl from the hospital. There were photos too: Ashley in Clementines, Ashley in drag, Ashley almost naked – except for a pair of shades – lying on a beach somewhere blue and gold, Ashley laughing over drinks with friends, Ashley with his arm around a bony-faced man with a ponytail. Brian's finger hovered over *Add Friend* box. No, he couldn't.

He returned to work but he avoided the coffee bar. He wanted to see Ashley but he was afraid, embarrassed. When the boys showed him the video of Ashley's gig, everything had changed. Brian felt the gulf widen between him and this beautiful young man. He craved Ashley as he craved the thick sweetness of a caramel slice, and in the same instant was repelled by his gluttony.

"You walking down?" Mark asked one afternoon at four.

"What?" Brian asked. He was in the lobby shoving his arms into his coat, going out for a smoke.

"I thought you went down to get a cake about now?"

"Oh, er, no, not today," Brain said, patting his pockets for cigarettes and lighter.

He watched Mark jog across the asphalt to where Donna was dawdling. Mark caught up with Donna; she turned to him, then they moved behind the spindly trees and Brian could see no more. He cupped his hands and lit a cigarette, moving in the opposite direction, towards the clanging gate and the car park where he first saw Donna and Mark together that night.

If he could just get through another week without Ashley, he thought, he would have broken it, whatever it was. He wouldn't go to the coffee bar again.

A couple of days later, he was working alone in the autoclave room. The packaged sets of instruments came through from the sterile packing room on a conveyor belt. They were packed in material with pores which opened in the heat to let the steam in, and then closed to form a seal, and were bound with autoclave tape that changed colour to certify the correct temperature had been reached. At the far end of the room, the previous load of instruments cooled under the whirring fan.

"Hey, Brian."

Brian jumped at the voice, loud over the fan. It was Mark.

"Delivery for you just arrived."

"Delivery?"

"Yeah, I was just taking some rubbish out and this guy – a porter I think – came up to me with a big envelope for you. I've left it by the dot matrix. It's a bit… squishy."

"Squishy?"

Mark shrugged. "See for yourself."

Brian followed him into the cavernous dispatch area where the surgical kits were piled on trolleys, waiting to be sent back to theatres, the delivery suite, or to GP surgeries.

"There you are." Mark gestured to a brown envelope beside the dot matrix computer, the device that logged each and every instrument by the pattern of dots engraved into the steel.

Brian picked up the envelope. '*Brian, Sterile Services*' in a flamboyant, loopy script. Mark was right: the parcel was squishy, almost greasy. Brian ripped it open, and a familiar sweet waft of vanilla and caramel rushed out. Brian felt his face burn.

"What is it? Smells like cake."

"It's nothing…just a joke." Brian clutched the parcel to his chest.

Mark chuckled, shook his head and walked off.

Brian opened the envelope again. The caramel slice was flattened on one side. There was a white paper napkin folded inside. He pulled it out. The same loopy script: '*I can't eat them all myself. A.*'

Brian didn't go to the coffee bar for a few days. He didn't acknowledge the caramel slice. He shouldn't. He should just forget the whole crazy interlude, delete the internet history on his phone, and get on with his life, his job, and family.

One afternoon, he was out the front, smoking on his own, just before four. Some of the eight-till-four shift came out of the building, calling their goodbyes, heading for the car park. Brian raised his hand and waved to them. Donna peeled away from the group, started across the asphalt to walk home. Brian watched her turn right at the gate and disappear behind the scrubby trees. He knew she knew he was watching her, that he knew her secret. He tossed his cigarette down, ground his heel into its smoking tip and strode out of the car park. Donna was ahead of him, her hands in her coat pockets. He crossed the road on the zebra and went into the main car park.

The coffee bar was surprisingly quiet for the middle of the afternoon. Ashley and the scraggy woman were behind the counter, Ashley with his back to the room, preparing cappuccino at the machine. The woman squeezed behind him to clear some tables. Brian hesitated. Ashley turned and handed two frothy bowls of cappuccino to the man at the till. As he took the money, he looked up and saw Brian. Brian walked over to him, words clamming up in his mouth.

"Hello stranger," said Ashley. "I can't keep doing a mail order service."

"Oh, uh, yes, thank you for that. It was…most welcome."

"I wondered if we'd ever see you again down here."

"I was away for a while. I went to stay…went to Cardiff, and then I was just busy."

"Come with me." Ashley slid out from behind the hatch. "Back in five," he shouted to the scraggy woman.

"What is it?" Brian asked.

"I could do with some fresh air."

Outside the main doors Ashley turned to Brian.

"The boys put you off, didn't they?"

"What boys?"

"Paul and Carl. They showed you the video of me, and you didn't like it."

"Oh, I…"

"I don't think you liked what you saw. It's only an act, you know. A performance. That's what I do."

"Yes, you're…you're very good. It's just…"

"So, when are you coming to see me? Or aren't you?"

"I will sometime," Brian said miserably. "It's that…I can't…it's not easy."

"I know it's not easy."

"No, no you don't. You see, it's a gay club and…"

"You're married," Ashley finished for him.

"How did you know?"

Ashley laughed. "Your wedding ring might be a giveaway."

"Oh."

"It's not only that. I knew you were from the start. You're not the only one. Believe me. There are quite a few guys down there who are married. No one'll mind."

"Someone might see me."

"That works both ways."

Brian shivered. The wind was cold. Under his coat his blues were thin, and the trousers flapped around his legs with a crack.

"I'll try. I do want to come. Yes, you're right. When I saw the video, I thought I don't belong in that world."

"Anyone can belong down there," Ashley said. "Not everyone's gay. We have students, gangs of girls." He grinned. "We'll make you really welcome. Even if I'm not performing, I go down a couple of times a week."

"I'll find a way," Brian said. "Somehow."

He couldn't think how, not right now, but there had to be a way. If Mark and Donna found ways to meet in secret, surely, he could find a way to spend an hour or so in a bar.

"I've got a Whitney Houston night in a couple of weeks," Ashley said. "Come as my guest. Look, I'll have to get back or I'll never hear the end of it. See you soon, yes?"

"Yes," Brian said.

The vast glass doors hissed open and swallowed Ashley inside. Brian checked his watch. He'd gone over his break. He started walking fast, and suddenly realised he hadn't even bought a cake.

Georgia quickly read through her application one final time and hit send. A box flashed up on the screen, thanking her for her application to the NHS. It was done. She'd applied for the Sterile Services job as soon as her father told her it was on the internet. She'd surprised herself, because she'd actually tried to beef herself up, make herself sound as though she might be employable. She didn't know much about the department, only that they cleaned the instruments from theatre. It didn't sound much fun, swilling up to your elbows in bloody, shitty water, but she guessed they had protective clothing, so they couldn't catch HIV or whatever. And she wouldn't have to stay there long. Once she was in the NHS, she could apply for another job with greater ease, a PA perhaps to one of the managers.

She glanced at herself in the mirror. She was delighted with her black and purple striped hair, and the silver crescent of hoops in each ear, but they weren't quite what a PA would look like, and there was no way she was going to cut and perm her hair and wear a pin-striped trouser suit like some drone. Never mind, there were other jobs: maybe in one of the labs. That could be interesting. But once she'd hooked herself a junior doctor, she might not have to worry about work that much, might even get back to a bit of painting.

Things had been so much better at home since Michelle's birthday. Michelle was kinder to the girls, had even cut back on her drinking. Mark didn't believe it would last forever but, right now, he was almost happy.

It was Sunday afternoon and Michelle was lying on the sofa with Susannah cuddled up to her. Eleanor was playing with her dolls on the rug. Michelle's red-gold hair was falling loose from its tortoiseshell comb, and she reached up with one hand to let it down. As she dropped the comb on the coffee table, she looked over at him and smiled, a memory of the night before, and a promise of the night to come. And Mark smiled back and wondered, not for the first time recently, how he had got so caught up with Donna, and why.

Just before Christmas things had been as bad as they'd ever been. Michelle was drinking and smoking all the time, and yelling at the girls for no reason because of the drink. Once she'd hit Mark in a drunken rage, and it was only the sight of Eleanor, crying and confused in the bedroom doorway, that stopped him hitting her back.

Making a fuss of Michelle for her birthday had definitely been worthwhile. She'd seemed so surprised when he told her he had booked a restaurant table, and asked his parents to baby-sit. He realised that it had been months since he'd done anything for her. Maybe he wasn't the only one feeling neglected. Since that night she'd welcomed him into bed at night; once she had persuaded him to bunk off work for the day and, as soon as the girls were at school, she'd taken his hand and led him back upstairs. He'd told Donna he'd had an upset stomach.

Donna. Mark sighed. What the hell was he doing? Compared to Michelle, Donna seemed pale and very young, with her yearning eyes, and yet he could not bring himself to tell her it was over because he knew he would miss those secret Saturday afternoons, and her obvious devotion, and he was also very aware that soon, any day now, Michelle would start drinking more and more, would scream at him over nothing and turn her back on him in bed. No, he had to keep Donna as well. He just had to ensure Michelle never found out. With the watertight alibi of Gerry Pyles, he was confident he could handle the situation.

Brian glanced behind him to make sure no one was following him. He dangled his car keys in his hand to make it look as though he'd forgotten something. He hurried through the metal gate, leaving it to bang on its post. The wind picked up a few dry leaves in the car park. Brian shivered under his coat and wondered if he could be bothered to walk all the way to his car to make the phone call. Standing still would be very cold though. He dialled Joy at home, and started walking through the rows of parked cars, checking over his shoulder to make sure no one from Sterile Services was nearby to hear his lie.

"Hello, love," he said.

"Is everything all right?" she asked, and it occurred to him suddenly that he never phoned her from work – unlike Mark with Michelle – and now he was only doing it to tell a lie, the cover-up for the worst thing he had ever done in all their years together. He felt sick, nearly bailed out.

"Everything's fine," he said instead. "It's just, well, we're really short of people today. They've asked if I could stay on for a bit tonight."

"But it's Friday night. What do you mean *for a bit*?"

"Oh, uh, couple of hours, I think. Till the night people arrive."

"I suppose dinner will keep," Joy said. "I was going to do that casserole. I'll eat mine though."

"I'm sorry to be a nuisance. It's just they are really stuck today. I'll call you when I'm leaving."

Brian hung up and pocketed his phone. He felt a right shit. Part of him wanted to call Joy again and say he'd scrub it, the department would have to manage without him, and he would drive home and eat casserole with her in front of the telly. But he didn't. He started back across the car park. Overhead he heard the distant buzzing of the Air Ambulance coming closer every second. Someone reversed out of a parking space and roared off in a cloud of dust and grit. Brian stopped a moment and lit a cigarette, reassuring movements of lighting and inhaling, but they did nothing to steady him inside.

When Brian arrived at Clementines he hovered outside the door for a moment, almost too terrified to enter. Through the windows he could see coloured lights flickering pink, green, blue. He could hear people talking and shouting, and music. Ashley was in there; Ashley was expecting him. He only had to push open the door, but still he dithered. Two young men ran across the road and went inside. Brian sighed miserably. He'd lied to Joy to do this. He couldn't bail out now. He checked his phone one more time – no messages – and turned it off. Then, at last, he climbed the two steps and opened the door.

The bar was full. He had no idea a gay bar would be so busy. The coloured lights flashed; someone turned up the volume of the music. It was a song he recognised but he didn't know the singer. There were groups of men on the settles, some in jeans and jumpers, others in frilled shirts and leathers. There were girls too, in groups and couples. He'd never felt so out of place in his life. Suddenly he saw Paul from work. Paul was sitting at a table near the stage. And yes, the man with his back to Brian, that was Carl. Carl was talking to a third person with a lot of complicated make-up. Brian wasn't sure if it was a man in drag or a girl. As he stared, Paul looked up and waved. He jabbed Carl on the shoulder. Carl turned, waved too, beckoned Brian over. Brian hesitated, mimed drinking, and turned to the bar, where a devastatingly handsome blond man in a tight vest asked him what he would like. Brian glanced along the bar. People were drinking cocktails, pink and green like the fairy lights, with striped straws and umbrellas. He ordered a scotch and soda, half expecting the beautiful man to laugh at him, but of course he did not, simply held a glass under the amber bottle, and Brian watched the ripple of his muscles under the vest.

"You made it then." Paul squeezed along his bench to make room for Brian.

The man in drag, or whoever it was, had gone. Carl leaned over the table to Brian.

"We thought you weren't coming. Ashley would have been distraught. He was so hoping you would come."

Brian felt his face burn, but before he could speak the crowd shrieked and whistled, and there was Ashley, sparkling in silver and turquoise, stopping to kiss a girl with rainbow-striped hair. As he stepped up onto the stage he saw Brian and flashed him a smile that hit Brian's bloodstream faster than a caramel slice.

Donna was uneasy. It was Friday night, and usually she would be looking forward to Saturday and Mark's visit, but this time she was apprehensive. She couldn't really explain it, just that the last few weeks he'd arrived just a fraction later after doing his overtime and he'd stopped phoning Michelle from her house. Instead, he would kiss her goodbye in the hall and sit in the car on the parking strip outside and call home. Sometimes Donna crept upstairs and gently moved the bedroom curtain aside and watched him behind the wheel, the phone to his ear. It saddened her: there he was, outside her house for a further ten minutes, but not with her. Not that she wanted to hear him on the phone to Michelle. Of course she didn't, but it was almost worse just seeing a slice of his face through the windscreen, not knowing what he was saying. The sound of his car ignition firing was bleak, and then he would be away.

This Friday at work Donna kept thinking Mark was going to take her to one side and say he wasn't going to be working at the weekend or, worse, that he was, but that he could not come and see her afterwards. By the time she got home she had a headache with anxiety. She wanted to text him, say something about the next day just to get the reassurance that all was well, but she was afraid to.

Ashley finished with *I Will Always Love You*. Brian wondered what the words meant to Ashley, whether there was someone – a man – somewhere who he loved. The crowd roared and shrieked. Ashley grinned, suddenly the Ashley from the coffee bar once again, and replaced the mike. He jumped off the stage.

"Shove over," he said to Paul. "Brian's here as my guest tonight."

Paul grumbled good-naturedly and moved onto a stool that Ashley had hooked out from under the table. Ashley slid onto the settle beside Brian. The beautiful man in the vest appeared with a tumbler of dark liquid.

"One rum and Coke," he said, dropping two pink straws in and placing the glass in front of Ashley.

"And drinks for these three, please. Brian, what are you on?"

"Oh, uh, I'll just have a diet Coke," Brian said. "Driving, you see."

The barman gathered up the empties with a glassy crackle.

"Did you enjoy that, then?" Ashley asked Brian.

"You're amazing," Brian said.

"We want him to go on *X Factor*," said Carl.

"No, no, I like what I do. I'd rather be here with you lovely boys."

"He's right, you should apply," Brian said. "Think of the money, the opportunities." He visualised Ashley, glittering and gorgeous on the television, being interviewed, signing a record contract, living the celebrity lifestyle, and suddenly realised, too late, that if Ashley did all that, he would be even further removed from him. "Well, not if you don't want to," he finished lamely, grateful to see the barman arriving with a scarlet tray of drinks.

Brian gulped his Coke. He wasn't wearing a watch and his phone was turned off in his pocket. He didn't know what the time was. He tried to glance at the watch on Paul's wrist, but his sleeve hid the face.

"Tell me about yourself, Brian."

"Me? Oh well, not much to say."

A young man with a shaved head leaned over the table.

"Don't you dare disappear without coming to see me," he said to Ashley.

"I won't, darling. I'll be doing the rounds later, but Brian can only be here for a short while and I want to talk to him first."

Brian blushed as the man joined the group on the neighbouring table. They were a mixture: boys and girls. Brian didn't even know if they were all gay or not, or whether they were the students Ashley had told him about. That had always been his problem, never knowing who was and who wasn't. Mark, for instance. Brian had really fancied Mark once, and other men too, going back years, but they never ever gave him a hint that they might be interested. For the first time in his life, with Ashley, he had found a man who might, just maybe –

"Brian, talk to me."

So, he did. He told Ashley about Joy and the children, about his job in Sterile Services, how before that he'd been the regional manager of a wheelie bin company until he'd been made redundant. He expected Ashley to laugh, but he didn't, just sucked the viscous black liquid through the two straws, and watched Brian with steady eyes outlined in dark kohl.

"Sorry, I'm pretty boring really."

"I don't think you're boring at all," Ashley said, and squeezed his hand.

Across the table Paul wriggled out of his jumper and suddenly Brian saw the face of his watch. It was long after ten. He'd have to go. He felt like Cinderella leaving the ball.

"I have to go," he said to Ashley. "I'm sorry. It's just…"

"I know, I understand. Thank you for coming. It meant a lot to me. I hope you'll come again."

"I will," Brian said. "I promise." *Somehow.* "Goodnight everyone."

"Night, Brian," said Paul and Carl.

Brian paused at the doorway and looked back into the vibrancy and colour of the bar. Already the bald man and the rainbow-haired girl were bearing down on Ashley. He was laughing and hugging the girl, then waving to someone else across the room. Brian wrenched open the door and stepped out into the night. The cathedral was floodlit from beneath, and the soaring pinnacles shone with a pale gold light against the dark blue of the night sky. There were stars and a stray streak of cloud. He could still hear the noise from inside Clementines. He dug out his phone and, with rising panic, turned it on. Two missed calls and a text from Joy. He dialled home, walking quickly through town towards the car park.

"I was getting worried," Joy said when she answered. "I tried to get you a few times. I was going to phone the department at half ten."

Shit.

"I'm sorry, love," Brian said, jogging across a pedestrian crossing. "I'm leaving now."

Shit, shit, shit, he thought. Imagine if Joy had called the department and someone had told her that he'd left at eight as usual. Brian felt cold sweat under his arms. He'd promised Ashley he would go to Clementines again, and he must. He hadn't enjoyed a night out so much for ages. It was part of his life now, the gay bar, but he would have to keep his phone out all evening on the table in front him, like Mark would, and run out into the street to speak to Joy should she ring.

He unlocked the car and shoved the key in the ignition. That was all he could do, unless he could come up with some other alibi.

Donna almost sobbed with relief when she saw Mark's car pull up outside her house on Saturday. A moment later, he was in the hall, kissing her, twisting his fist in her hair.

"Is everything all right?" she asked, pulling back, watching his eyes for evasion.

"Of course, everything's all right," he said, taking her hand to lead her upstairs.

She hesitated. "It's just…I'm probably being silly…I wasn't sure if I'd upset you or something."

"You? Upset me? Silly girl." He kissed her again, started up the stairs. "You keep me sane, give me something to look forward to."

At the top of the stairs he turned back to her.

"I'm sorry if I've been a bit weird or something. I've had a few worries. I didn't want to burden you with them."

"You can talk to me. You know that. About anything."

"I know, but I don't think you'd want to hear about these."

"Oh," Donna said. "I see."

"Things aren't very happy at home. You know that. But lately…ah, forget it, I'm here now. Come to bed."

Half an hour later, Mark lay on his back, gazing at the lampshade over Donna's bed. He'd have to get up and shower in a moment. He turned his head. Donna smiled at him. He reached out to her long hair. He couldn't give her up if he wanted to. Neither could he leave Michelle and the girls. He wanted everything, all of them. He hadn't liked lying to Donna earlier; neither did he like lying to Michelle at the moment because she was being lovely. But he knew that would change. He knew her patterns by now. Just the night before he'd noticed she'd started on the vodka again. It wouldn't be long before she turned vile again; during those times he needed Donna more than ever.

"It's my birthday on Thursday," he said, reluctantly throwing off the quilt. "Can you get the day off?"

"Day off?" Donna sat up and the covers fell away from her.

Mark glanced down appreciatively.

"I could go off sick," he said. "I mean I'd tell Michelle I was working, but I could phone work on my way over. What do you say?"

"You mean we could have a whole day together?"

"Well, from lunchtime."

"I'd love that," Donna said.

"I must get a shower." Mark dropped a kiss on her rumpled hair and went into the bathroom.

Nine o'clock on Monday morning. Georgia stifled a yawn as her father drew up on a dusty asphalt forecourt. There was a grim-looking building ahead, two storeys, with glass double doors. *Sterile Services* it said over the portal.

"You've got money for the bus home?" Neil asked.

"Sure." Georgia flicked down the visor mirror and checked her face. She used her nail to scrape off a stray flake of eyeliner.

"OK. I'll see you at home tonight then. Good luck."

Georgia got out and slammed the door. Neil waved once and roared off towards the hospital and the consultants' car park. Georgia tugged her black mini down on her hips and stared at the building. It wasn't anywhere near the hospital itself. It didn't look as though there would be any junior doctors in sight. There were a couple of white NHS courier vans parked outside, and a giant skip overflowing with cardboard and debris. At the far side of the building there appeared to be some muddy grass, edged with skinny trees. Georgia glanced down the access road to a red and white striped barrier. It only led to another car park.

Her interview wasn't till nine thirty but there was nowhere else to go.

"It's a bit fucking bleak," she muttered out loud, and started towards the double doors.

The problem with Sterile Services was that it was a twenty-four hours a day department. Donna couldn't leave an answer machine message saying she was ill; whatever time she phoned someone would be there to answer the call. In the end she rang at midnight, as Wednesday tumbled into Thursday, Mark's birthday. One of the night crew eventually picked up the phone. She said that she had been sick and would not be coming in the following day. The guy on the phone grunted and hung up, and she hoped he'd write it down, let the day supervisor know.

She woke at seven and snuggled back under the quilt, listening to the grinding of the bin lorry outside, and the shouts of the bin men. An hour later she got out of bed and bathed, and sent Mark a happy birthday text. He didn't reply. Donna chucked her phone down once more in frustration. Just after eleven thirty he called her.

"I'll be with you in about half an hour," he said.

Donna re-adjusted the ribbons on his birthday present. She'd raced into town after he left her house on Saturday and chosen him a fountain pen, black, engraved with silver knotwork. As she'd slipped the slim parcel into her rucksack, she realised she hardly knew what his writing looked like.

Mark dumped his phone on the passenger seat and pulled out once more into the traffic flow. He'd called work and told them he was ill. Then he had called Donna to say he'd be with her shortly. But there was one more call to make: he would have to speak to Michelle at twelve to tell her he had arrived at work. The last few days had not been good. Michelle was drinking again. Only last night she made Eleanor cry. She told him she'd bought his birthday presents off the internet, but they hadn't arrived yet, and Mark knew they never would. He drove slowly, not wanting to get to Donna's too early. He parked at the kerbside in the road behind her house and rang Michelle. From here he could see Donna's kitchen window and the jumble of vases on her sill. Once he thought he saw her wander into the kitchen.

"I have to go," Mark said to Michelle. "It's nearly twelve."

"Call me later," she said.

"I'll try," he said, and turned off the phone.

"Will I see you tomorrow night?" Ashley asked Brian.

Brian took the caramel slice that Ashley had wrapped up for him. He didn't know how to tell Ashley that he was getting sick of caramel slices, that their sweetness now hit the back of his throat like a wasp and made him nauseous for hours afterwards.

"Are you performing?" he asked, taking a tentative bite, ready for the sugar rush.

"Not tomorrow," Ashley said. "But I'll be there anyway. I'd love to see you."

"I don't think I can," Brian said sadly. "I need some time to think how I can do this. I can't keep saying I'm working late."

"No," Ashley agreed. He grabbed a paper napkin off the counter and took a biro out of his pocket, "Here's my number. Give me a call if you can come. Or if you want to talk or whatever."

"Thank you," Brian stuttered.

His hand brushed Ashley's as he took the folded napkin. The paper was vaguely sticky to the touch. He slid it into his pocket. On his way back to Sterile Services he dumped the rest of the caramel slice in the bin. There was no way he could tell Joy he was working late again, even though the department was short-staffed. Both Mark and Donna were away, apparently ill, as well as one girl on maternity leave, and two others off on long-term sick leave. The managers were recruiting new staff. There had been interviews on Monday.

Brian sniffed. He didn't believe Mark and Donna were both ill. They were off somewhere or in bed, living their secret lives. They had to say they couldn't work whereas he had to say he was doing overtime. What a mess.

Quarter to twelve on Friday lunchtime. Donna threw her jacket around her shoulders, grabbed an apple from her rucksack and ran down the steps to the glass doors. Only twenty-four hours ago, she'd been waiting for Mark at her house. They'd driven out to a pub a few miles into the country and sat outside in the cold spring air drinking wine under an umbrella. Mark had asked if she wanted to eat, but she shook her head, aware, as always, of the clock ticking, counting down her time with him.

"I'm not hungry either," he said, and swept up his car keys from the wooden table, took her hand and led her back to the car.

Driving home in the sunlight, Donna's eyes caught a frail glitter on the dashboard. A long hair, bright red copper. She'd never imagined Michelle with red hair. Fascinated, she moved her legs searching the seat for more.

"Are you OK?" Mark asked, and she flushed, and sat still the rest of the way home, with her eye on the bright flash of hair in front of her.

As she trailed through the metal gate to the car park crunching her apple she thought again of that bright hair. It made her uneasy, uncomfortable. It was something intimate, the kind of thing people used for witchcraft. It disturbed her.

A figure was walking towards her. Brian. She tossed her apple core into the undergrowth and shoved her hands in her pockets.

"Hi Donna. You better today?" Brian chucked down a cigarette and ground his heel into the glowing stub.

"Yes, thanks." Donna looked away.

Mark was driving into the car park. He didn't wave or even look at Donna and Brian.

"Oh well, I'd better sign in and get on with it," Brian said, and walked off.

Donna trotted down to the further end of the car park. She could see Mark's blond head as he got out of the car. She heard the door slam. He started walking towards her. She smiled, thinking of the day before. Mark wasn't smiling as he greeted her. She felt sick.

"Is everything all right?" she asked.

Mark touched her briefly on the shoulder.

"Nothing you need to worry about," he said.

"You can always tell me. I've told you that."

Mark sighed, looked away across the car roofs to the hazy fields and hedges.

"Things aren't so great at home," he said.

Donna opened her mouth to say *I'm sorry*, then stopped. She wasn't sorry. The last thing in the world she wanted was for Mark to have a happy home life. No, she didn't wish unhappiness on him. It was so difficult and confusing.

"Michelle's drinking again," he said, as they walked up to the gate.

"Oh," Donna said.

"The girls are unhappy. She was foul to me last night."

"On your birthday?"

"On my birthday. Actually, I don't think she even said *happy birthday* to me."

"Oh Mark."

He kissed her quickly and kicked open the gate. Brian was talking to a couple of the girls on the forecourt. The girls wandered off towards the car park. Brian opened the metal door and gestured for Donna and Mark to go through. Mark picked up the pen on the desk to sign in. Donna ran on upstairs, leaving him and Brian talking to the receptionist. She scrubbed in again and went back to the dirty room, back to the clatter of instruments, the roar of the washers, and the constant thump of the radio. She was surprised to see Mark come in to join her; she thought he was rota-ed into the packing room. She watched him unpack a trolley of steel tools onto the draining board and glance at the checklist. He looked tense and taut. More so than usual.

Mark gazed into the bowl of rusty water in front of him. It was stained with the blood of strangers. The radio was pounding into his head. He wished someone would turn it off or tug out the plug. He was aware of Donna at her own sink on the other side of the room, behind him. He was getting out of his depth. He didn't know what to do. He didn't know anyone he could talk to. *If only Eleanor and Susannah hadn't happened,* he thought, as he had so often thought and, like every other time, he almost gagged on his thoughts. He wouldn't be without them. Not for anything or anyone. They tied him to Michelle, but would he really want to be free of her?

He emptied the sink and wheeled his instruments over to the tunnel washer. A fat woman in too-tight blues was loading her own haul into the other washer, with a lot of clattering. Behind her, Mark could see Donna at her sink, reaching over for instruments, then lowering them into water. Her ponytail was slipping out from under her hat. He stood there a moment, looking at the strip of pale skin between her hat and the top of her tunic, and he wanted to tiptoe over to her, put his arms around her, and kiss that soft warm skin, as he had the previous day, when she stood at the kitchen worktop waiting for the kettle to boil, and he'd lifted aside her loose hair. The fat woman slammed her load into the washer and straightened.

Donna checked the wall clock. Three-thirty. Half an hour to go. She turned to see what Mark was doing. He was back at his sink again. One of the supervisors came hurrying into the washroom with a scrap of paper in his hand. Donna watched idly. Suddenly, he was heading for Mark. Mark turned as the other man tapped him on the shoulder, showed him the piece of paper. Mark snapped off his gloves, snatched the paper and ran though the room.

"Mark," Donna started, as he brushed past her, but he didn't stop.

The supervisor was talking to a couple of other technicians. No one was looking. Donna slipped out of the room and ran upstairs. She opened the door of the tearoom. It was empty. She hesitated outside the Gents' changing room. She thought she could hear a voice. It sounded like Mark. The clang of a locker. She shrank back against the wall as the door opened. Mark had changed into his own clothes.

"What's happened?" Donna cried.

"Stupid bitch," Mark said.

"What?"

"Not you. Just had a message to call the school. Michelle never picked up the girls. They're still at the school now. I have to go."

"Will you–" Donna started, as he crashed down the stairs. "Will you come and see me tomorrow?" she whispered.

She went into the tearoom and stood at the window, watching him striding across the forecourt. He wrenched open the gate and disappeared around the corner. Donna trudged back downstairs. She still had to clear up her own work area.

Somehow Donna managed not to text Mark that evening. She didn't text him on Saturday morning either. She wondered whether to walk up to the hospital, see if his car was in the car park. At twelve, he texted her saying he wasn't working. There were kisses at the bottom, but there was a typo in the message, and Donna imagined him sending it secretly, in a hurry, unable to check it. She wrote back: '*OK. Hope everything is all right. XXX.*' He didn't text again.

On Monday, twelve o'clock came and went. Brian arrived; so did the rest of the afternoon shift, but no Mark. Donna ran up to her locker to check her phone. Nothing. The screen remained cruelly dark. At the end of her shift, she was in the changing rooms tearing off her blues, trying to crush the rising flutter of butterflies in her stomach, when two of the other women came in. Donna couldn't see them as she was changing behind a row of lockers, but she recognised their voices.

"I think he's got trouble at home," said one. "With his wife or girlfriend or whatever she is."

Donna froze, her dirty blues scrunched in her hand.

"What d'you mean?" asked the other.

"I think she's an alky. Just a few things Brian said. You know she left the kids at school the other day? That's why he rushed off on Friday."

"I was away Friday. What happened?"

"Not sure really. He had a call from the school and went tearing off. Brian said he was taking the week off to sort things out or something."

A locker door slammed shut, the click of a key, the rustle of a carrier bag.

"Such a shame. Mark's a sweetheart, isn't he? He loves those kids so much."

Donna swallowed bile as the two women banged out of the changing room. She chucked her blues in the skip and thrust open the door, desperate to be out of the stench of shoes and old deodorant.

Michelle was in bed again. Mark stood in the doorway, gazing helplessly at her. There was an overflowing ashtray on the bedside table. The room smelt of tobacco. Michelle's hair was dull and lank, and her face blotchy. He stared at her, wondering in those moments, how he could ever have desired her. He scooped up the ashtray and swept the stray curls of tobacco into his palm. Michelle stirred and mumbled, threw the quilt off her shoulders. She was still wearing the same T-shirt she'd been wearing the previous day when he'd arrived home, having dropped the girls at his parents' house.

He ran downstairs with the ashtray and chucked the contents into the bin on top of the empty glass bottles. He swilled it under the tap. The smell would be on his hands for ages. He didn't want to take it back up to her, but if he didn't she'd probably set fire to the quilt or something. He trudged back up and, as he came onto the landing, he heard the chime of his phone. A new message. *Shit.* He'd forgotten it was charging on his side of the bed. Michelle was sitting up, reaching across the pillows for it.

"I'll get it," Mark said, snatching for the phone, but Michelle had it first, and tugged it out of its charging cable.

"A text," she said. "From Gerry Pyles."

"Give that to me." Mark surprised himself with his strength as he knocked it from her grasp.

"Gerry Pyles. Always Gerry fucking Pyles," she said. "Who the fuck is Gerry Pyles?"

"Someone I work with." Mark glanced at Donna's text: '*Are you taking time off? Please text me when you can. Miss you xxx.*' He hit delete swiftly.

"Yeah right. So why can't I see the text?"

"Because it's not your phone. I don't look at your texts."

"Yes, you do."

"No, I don't."

Mark pocketed his phone and ran downstairs, leaving Michelle swearing in the bedroom. A few moments later, he heard her stomping across the landing to the bathroom. His parents were delighted to have the girls, but he knew they'd read the despair in his eyes, and seen through the lies about Michelle being ill. He sighed. He wanted the girls home, but it was no place for them right now. It was no place for him either. He wished he was with Donna. In the kitchen he quickly wrote back to her, reassuring her that he was OK, and asking her not to text again until he contacted her.

Brian watched Donna at her sink. She looked utterly wretched. He knew why. Mark was off, and with Michelle. People were gossiping about his situation, his problems. Brian had overheard one of the girls saying Mark should look for someone else, that she was available. He hoped Donna hadn't heard that. He sent his load into the washer and walked over to her.

"I'm going down for a cake at four. Would you like to come with me?"

Donna jumped, sloshing water. "I go home at four," she said.

"I know, but I thought a cake and a chat might cheer you up."

Donna turned away, back to her stained water.

"If it's any consolation, I don't think he's having a very good time," Brian said quietly. "I'll meet you out the front if you'd like to come. My shout."

He walked away back to his own sink. He suddenly had the urge to take Donna down to the coffee bar, to introduce her to Ashley, to show her that he too had his own troubles, his own secrets.

Brian was outside on the asphalt when Donna came out. He was smoking, and walking slowly towards the road.

"Brian," Donna called.

He turned and chucked down his cigarette. Donna jogged over to him.

"Changed your mind?" Brian smiled at her.

"Yes, thanks. I'm not in a hurry to get home."

"Have you heard from Mark?"

Donna hesitated. "He texted me and asked me not to text at the moment. Things must be very difficult." She was fishing; she knew it.

"I don't know," Brian said. "I know he has some troubles, but I don't know the details."

"She's a bitch and a drunk. She's horrible to him and to the girls. He's so unhappy." She waited for Brian to agree, but he took her arm and led her across the road to the main entrance. "What do you know, Brian?"

"Like I said, not much."

Inside the hospital it was hot. Donna unzipped her jacket. Brian dodged past a dithering wheelchair.

"You often come here for cake," Donna said. "Mark said you had a special delivery."

"My friend works here," Brian mumbled.

They queued at the counter. Brian was looking all around the café.

"Your friend not here?"

"Doesn't look like it."

Donna chose a piece of iced lemon cake; Brian a Florentine. He handed over a note to the grumpy woman behind the till.

"No Ashley today?" he asked.

"He's off sick." The woman handed him his change roughly, and dropped a coin onto his tray.

Brian gestured to a table near the window. Donna hung her jacket on the back of the chair, and busied herself with milk and teapot.

"I don't understand why Mark won't let me text him," she said abruptly. "We have a code, a false name."

"What d'you mean?"

Donna forked up cake. "Mark invented this guy called Gerry Pyles who works in our department. He's got my number stored under Gerry Pyles, so she won't suspect anything."

"An invented alibi." Brian chewed his Florentine,

"You don't approve?"

"Not that. I think it would be most useful."

"Hey Brian!" A young man in blues slapped Brian on the shoulder. "How're you doing?"

"Paul, yes, not so bad. Ashley's not well, I hear?"

The young man pulled a face. "He's got laryngitis. He can't sing. Can't talk either. He must be going spare."

"What? Oh no. Is he OK?"

"On voice rest. He said he might come down on Friday just to see everyone. Will you be–?" He broke off suddenly.

Donna gazed out of the window at the seagulls pecking in the consultants' carpark.

"I don't think I can," Brian said sadly. "It's difficult."

"Sure, I know. Hope to see you."

"Your friend's a singer then?" Donna asked when Paul had gone.

"Yes." Brian picked up his paper napkin and fiddled with it.

"Where does he sing?"

"Clementines. In town."

"The gay bar?"

"That's the one."

"Is he good?"

"Very."

"I would never have imagined you going to a gay bar, Brian. What does Joy think about that?" Donna grinned and drank tea. Brian looked wretched, and Donna suddenly understood. "She doesn't know, does she?"

"No," Brian said quietly.

Donna put down her cup. The cake had hit her blood stream. She felt a bit queasy.

Brian tore the napkin into pieces. "I've never done anything like this before. And I haven't been unfaithful to Joy."

"Is it this Ashley? The singer?"

"Yes and no." Brian met her eyes at last. "I got to know him down here and he was the most beautiful man I'd ever met. He kept asking me to go to the club, but that meant lying to Joy. I did go though. Once. I told her I was working late to cover people who were away."

"Paul's gay, too, isn't he?"

"Yes, he's a friend of Ashley's. And another fellow called Carl. I met them both here too. They're so friendly and kind. They welcomed me down at the bar. They know I'm married and it's really hard for me, but it's the whole thing, you know, the whole world. It just feels right. Are you shocked?"

"Not shocked," Donna said. "Surprised maybe. I would never have guessed. You're leading a double life too."

"I am."

Donna said nothing.

Brian finished his drink, checked his watch, and scraped his chair back with a clatter. "I have to go. Please don't say anything about this to anyone. Not even Mark."

Brian hurried back to Sterile Services. *I'm really bloody unfit,* he thought grimly. His heart was racing – though that might partly be anxiety at what he'd said to Donna – and his breathing was ragged. He must cut down on the cigarettes and try to lose some weight. He should join a gym. There was one near the hospital. He could go after work once or twice a week. Brian stopped, his heart hammering. If he went to a gym after work, he would be late home. That could be his alibi. He started walking again. He could go to the gym some nights, and on Fridays he could go to Clementines, but he could tell Joy he was at the gym again. He jogged over the road to the open forecourt of Sterile Services. The gym was very expensive. He had seen the prices when he'd half-heartedly Googled it before. He couldn't really afford it. A gym wasn't necessary to cut down on smoking, and to eat more sensibly. But he could tell Joy he needed to go. He could tell Joy he was going on a Friday night, and then he'd be free to go to Clementines. He hesitated outside the glass door to the department. Donna's words caught in his mind: '*Mark invented this guy called Gerry Pyles who works in our department.*' He could use Gerry Pyles too. After all, he didn't exist, so no one would get into trouble. He could tell Joy he was joining a gym with a colleague, Gerry Pyles, and that they'd be going on Fridays after work. Brian almost choked on his own audacity then, as quickly, he felt a rush of relief, like when a painkiller eased a headache. He ran up the stairs, not noticing his breathlessness and aching muscles. *Yes, Gerry Pyles,* he chuckled to himself.

Donna held out the sheet of paper to the girl in front of her. Georgia Shelley was young, nineteen, twenty, Donna guessed. Under her sterile hat, her hair was long and black, streaked with purple. She had huge black lines of kohl around her eyes, and rings in her ears.

"What is it?" Georgia took the paper from her.

"It's a list of what goes into a basic orthopaedic set," Donna explained. "New people always start here in the packing room. Watch what I do to pack a kit, and you'll soon learn the various instruments, and what they look like."

Georgia gazed at the rows of cramped type on the list in her hand. *Jesus*. What the fuck was she doing here? This was going to be hell. She might actually die of boredom or, at the very least, end up one of her father's patients. The list said there were seventy items in a basic orthopaedic kit. *If you didn't have OCD before you started here, you sure as hell would get it,* she thought, watching the man on the next bench counting some kind of forceps.

"OK, let's start." Donna, the rather wet girl she'd been assigned to, gestured to Georgia's head. "You've got a bit of hair hanging out."

Donna was finding it hard to teach Georgia. The girl wasn't interested. Her eyes were always wandering around the packing room. Donna thought back to her first day, and the woman, who had since retired, who showed her what to do, in exactly the way Donna was trying to teach Georgia. Donna too felt she would never remember the names and appearances of the different types of forceps, clips, retractors, and scissors. She also remembered how trapped she felt in the packing room, with its sealed doors and one-way air pressure. As the hand on the clock eased on towards twelve, she felt queasy. Surely Mark would be back today. She hadn't seen him for two weekends. She'd only had a few texts from him, sometimes sent in the middle of the night.

At ten to twelve she told Georgia she had to go out to make a phone call. She met Mark on the forecourt.

"Donna, Donna, I'm so sorry," he said.

"Are you all right?" Donna asked, aching for him to kiss her.

"I'm fine," Mark said. "Everything's OK."

"What does that mean?" Donna asked warily.

"It means I'll be working Saturdays again." Mark waved to Brian who was coming across towards them.

"Mark," Donna said quickly. "Brian knows."

"Brian knows what?"

"Brian knows about us. About you and me."

Mark glanced over to Brian again. "How the fuck did that happen?"

"He guessed," Donna said.

"Hi Donna," Brian said. "How are things, Mark?"

"OK," Mark said tersely. "Look, I have to go and report in and all that after last week." He shoved through the glass doors.

"You're pleased to see him back," Brian said to Donna.

"Oh yes," she said, watching Mark signing the register through the blurry glass. He straightened, chucked the pen down, and ran up the stairs.

"Have the new people started?" Brian asked.

"I'm mentoring one of them." Donna rolled her eyes.

"Any good?"

"Difficult. She's a consultant's daughter. Full of herself. There's another one, a guy, but I haven't seen much of him. I think the others are on a later shift."

Brian let himself into the Gents changing room. Mark, already changed, was just ending a phone call on his mobile. Brian helped himself to a clean set of blues. There was another man in the changing room, digging in a rucksack. He must be the new bloke Donna had mentioned. Brian changed quickly, hid a couple of sticks of chewing gum in his pocket, and followed Mark out.

He wheeled a trolley of dirties to a sink. *Yes, the new people started today. One of them, Gerry, he's just joined a gym. I'm going down with him after work on Friday to have a look. You know I need to get fit, Joy. If it looks good, I might join as well. I could go once a week or so.*

"Brian, you made it." Ashley was sitting at the bar when Brian walked into Clementines on Friday night.

He knew Ashley wasn't performing; he'd seen him at the coffee bar in the week. His voice was better, though a little hoarse, but he'd said he would be at the club on Friday night.

"Just a diet Coke," Brian said to the beautiful barman.

He flushed as he groped in his pocket for change. Joy thought he was at the gym with Gerry Pyles. Soon he would have to go home and tell her all about it, and how he was going to join and go down once a week after work. On a Friday. He'd have to tell her about Gerry Pyles too. How old he was, what he looked like, was he married. Women wanted to know these things. He had to keep a cool head. Whatever he said tonight he was stuck with. He couldn't turn back. If he'd created a monster he had to live with it. But not now. He would worry about all that on the drive home.

"Sorry, what did you say?" Brian bent his head to Ashley.

On the stage, framed with winking fairy lights, someone was doing karaoke, bellowing *Mamma Mia*.

"Paul and Carl aren't here tonight. I have you to myself. Come and sit down."

Brian picked up his glass and cold liquid sloshed onto his wrist as he followed Ashley into the back room of the pub. Hands reached out to pluck Ashley's sleeve as he moved through the crowds. All the tables were taken, but some girls shoved up along a horseshoe-shaped leather sofa, and Ashley and Brian squeezed in on the end. The girls were drinking rainbow cocktails, their voices already loud. Brian could feel the hard length of Ashley's leg beside his own thigh. He gulped Coke quickly.

"Are they working?" he asked, for something to say. "Paul and Carl?"

"Paul's gone to stay with his folks; Carl's doing something, I can't remember what." Brian had to lean close to Ashley to hear him over the girls' drunken laughter. "How did you manage to get here tonight?" Ashley asked.

Brian hesitated. Ashley had asked him the question straight. He wasn't hungry for a sordid tale of deceit and lies; he simply wanted to know how Brian had managed it.

"I had to tell a few lies," he said at last. "Lies to Joy."

"I didn't think you'd have told her the truth." Ashley sucked rum and Coke through the straw, his indigo eyes on Brian. "You don't have to tell me," he said, and suddenly put his hand over Brian's. "I don't have to know."

"You do," Brian cried, flustered at the cool feel of Ashley's fingers on his, on his wedding ring. "I told Joy I was at the gym."

"I didn't know you went to the gym. Is that the one Paul goes to?"

"I don't go to the gym," Brian said sadly. "Do I look like I go to the gym?

"Ah." Ashley flicked his drink with the straw.

"I told her I was going with a guy from work. I said I was going to look around and if I liked it I was going to join. I'm not really joining."

"Who's the guy from work? Will he keep your secret?"

"Oh yes," Brian laughed ruefully. "He'll keep it."

Friday night and Georgia was at home on her own. Neil was out on a blind date with some woman he'd met on Plenty of Fish. Georgia wondered if she'd have to risk internet dating too. After a whole week in Sterile Services she hadn't seen a junior doctor once. She hadn't seen anyone really, except the drones in the department, moving like blue robots amongst the washers and autoclaves. She'd spent the first week in the packing room with Donna, who was supposed to be teaching her how to assemble kits. But Donna was too busy looking everywhere for that Mark Swift guy, who started at midday. Twice he'd been in the packing room too, and Georgia had seen the dark stain on Donna's cheeks, and registered her distracted air. Once, out of boredom, she'd even asked Donna a few questions about the job, but Donna had been gazing at Mark's shoulders as he leaned over his own bench in front of them, and she'd had to repeat her question two more times.

Another time she'd gone into the staff room, and found Donna and Mark standing close together by the kettle, apparently making tea. Yeah, right. She had asked around discreetly when Donna was out of the room and found out that not only did Mark have a girlfriend or partner or whatever, but he had two kids as well. *What the hell does he see in Donna?* Georgia wondered. Donna was wet. For a moment Georgia considered Mark Swift: tall, blond, blue eyes, good muscles from what she'd seen under his scrubs. Had he looked at her with interest? Was he getting sick of the simpering Donna and her soulful glances over her mask? No, Mark Swift was a waste of time. She could see that even if Donna couldn't. He'd do on a dark night, and she wouldn't refuse him if he offered, but she couldn't be bothered to put herself out to take him from Donna. He was a losing wicket, as her father would say.

The most interesting person she'd met so far was Brian Webster. She'd met him outside the first afternoon when she'd gone for a smoke, and he'd given her a light. He was old and was losing his hair, and he needed to shed a few stone, but Georgia liked him. She could sense frustration, and almost helplessness, roiling beneath his surface which matched her own. He was pissed off with his lot, seeking something more. A mid-life crisis of some kind.

She laughed. Her father would have enough to keep him going for weeks in that department.

"I'm going away shortly," Ashley said.

"Holiday?" Brian asked.

"Working."

"Where are you working? How long will you be away?"

Brian swallowed the painful desolation in his voice. Just when he'd got his alibi worked out, and Ashley was leaving. Leaving! He could not imagine it: no Ashley at the coffee bar, no Ashley at the club. The Coke tasted too sweet, the girls were too drunk, the fairy lights too abrasive.

"I work on the cruise ships in the Med." Ashley finished his drink. "I've done it for the last couple of years."

"As a singer?"

"As a singer. It's great. I love it. I'll be off at the end of May. Hey, Brian, don't look like that. I'll be back in September."

"That's a long time."

"I'll send you postcards from Venice and Athens."

Ashley met his eyes and Brian smiled. He would. Brian knew that.

"You must still come down here," Ashley said. "Come with Paul and Carl. They'll still be here. Top up?"

Brian stumbled to his feet to let Ashley out to the bar. When he sat down again, next to a fat girl with spiky crimson hair, he turned around, watching Ashley's dark, lithe figure snaking to the bar. Ashley was talking to a young man in tinted glasses. Ashley rested his hand on the man's arm, laughed and moved on. Brian sighed. The very day he'd started the Gerry Pyles fiasco, Ashley told him he was going away. He should be pleased for Ashley, but he felt only the cold, hollow ache of loneliness. The fat girl shrieked at something her companion said, and Brian flinched. What was he thinking? Ashley liked him – he knew that – but no more. He didn't know who Ashley loved, if he loved anyone, but Brian knew it was not him. Somehow, he would live with it. Somehow, he would continue the lie he had started and come to Clementines on Friday nights. He liked the bar, he liked the atmosphere; it felt right to him. He would come to Clementines and wait for Ashley to return from the Med.

Ashley clicked two glasses down on the table, both with coloured straws and ice cubes.

"I hope I've got them the right way round," Ashley grinned, and squeezed onto the bench beside Brian.

"Tell me about the cruise ships, then," Brian said. "Where will you be going?"

Brian left Ashley in the bar, talking to the man in glasses and his boyfriend. The evenings were warmer now, but he was cold after the heat of the bar on his skin. He hesitated with the keys in the ignition. Should he call Joy and say he was coming now? No, it would set a precedent like Mark had. Instead he glanced at the screen on his phone. Nothing. Joy believed him. He twisted the key, angry at the surge of disloyalty he felt. He could go home and say he didn't like the gym and wasn't going to join. He thought of Ashley and his friends at the club, the sparkly lights, the laughter, the acceptance. *No.*

As he drove home he tried to create an image of Gerry Pyles in his mind. He had to get this right. It took his mind off the sting of his betrayal. Gerry Pyles was new to the department. He was younger than Brian, thirties probably. Rugged, muscular, short hair, possibly a tattoo. He liked sport obviously. His home life? It couldn't be too complicated. He had a girlfriend. No children. He lived out of town on the other side. That was enough for now. He could add details, flesh him out, over the coming weeks.

"It'll end in tears," Julie said.

Donna had taken some time off. She was in town with Julie, sitting at a grimy table in Starbucks.

"We're very careful," Donna said.

"I can't believe you've kept it going so long." Julie stirred sugar into her coffee.

"Like I said, we're careful. She'll never know. She's not interested enough in him to find out, and we have an alibi anyway. Mark's invented him. He's invented someone at work, so if I text she'll think it's from him."

"Not if she reads your texts she won't."

Donna faltered. "She wouldn't do that. She'd see on the screen it was from Gerry. Mark's told her all about him."

"Told her all about someone who doesn't exist? This is insane, Donna. The more lies there are, the more likely it is to go tits up."

"It won't," Donna said. "It won't," she repeated more firmly.

"What does Michelle know about Gerry Pyles?" Donna asked Mark on Saturday.

She was aware of him watching the clock, his body already sprung to jump out of bed and shower before driving away from her.

He turned to face her. "What do you mean?"

"I mean, what does she think he's like?"

"I dunno." Mark sat up in the bed, rubbed his eyes.

"Mark, it's important. She might ask you. You need to know, have your story straight."

"I just said he used to work nights and now works days. It doesn't matter, does it? It's only to make things a bit easier for me. I must have a shower."

Donna lay back, listening to the familiar whoosh of the shower behind the bathroom door. Not for the first time, she wondered what was going to happen. How long was this situation going to last? Would Mark want to keep her as his mistress indefinitely? She wavered in her thoughts: sometimes she was content for that, glad to have her precious hour on a Saturday with him, glad to see him at work, and to sometimes take a kiss from him in the tearoom; most times she longed for more, longed for a man she could ring up whenever she wanted, a man who did not demand deceit. The problem was that such a man was never going to be Mark. He said sometimes how he wished he could leave Michelle, but Donna knew this was a fantasy. He would never leave his children. Whatever path Mark chose, Michelle would always be there beside him.

On Monday afternoon, Donna watched Georgia assemble a kit.

"Doesn't anything ever happen in this place?" Georgia asked.

"What sort of thing?"

"Anything. We don't ever see anyone from the hospital. There's no life here, just the same old people all the time."

"I like it like that," Donna said.

"I suppose you would," Georgia said. "Where is Mark today?"

"I don't know. In the washroom or the autoclave, I suppose. What's Mark got to do with anything?" Donna wished she could bite back the last question.

"Oh, come on, Donna," Georgia said, ticking off the final item on her list. "I'm not blind, you know, or stupid. Brian knows too."

"Yes, I know Brian knows. Did he tell you?"

"He didn't have to. He just confirmed it."

"Well, bloody Brian should concentrate on his own fucked-up life."

"Why's his life fucked-up? I like Brian."

"I like Brian too," Donna said. "But he shouldn't have said anything. He might have told someone else."

"No, he hasn't. We were just having a fag and I said something about you shagging Mark, and he said yes, it had been going on quite a while, and Mark had a shitty home life. So, come on, spill the beans, what's Brian's problem?"

Donna hesitated. She did like Brian, but she was angry with him for talking about her and Mark to the precocious Georgia.

"Oh, nothing," she said. "Just pissed off with his life, I think."

"Jesus, aren't we all? Look, I'm getting a lift with my dad after work tonight. He doesn't finish till half four. Will you walk over to the hospital with me? See if we can find some junior doctors."

"I don't want a junior doctor."

"Well, I do. Come on, it's only half an hour."

Donna sighed. She just wanted to go home. "All right, then."

They left the department at four and walked down to the main hospital. The road was solid with traffic as it always was at rush hour, and the air was thickened with exhaust fumes.

"Where do the junior docs hang out, then?" Georgia asked.

"I don't know. You'd know better than me. Your dad's a consultant."

"He's only a shrink. I don't want another shrink, thanks. I want a surgeon or a cardiologist."

Donna glanced at Georgia. She wore cut-off jeans over lacy tights. Her hair was long, black and purple striped, with a new flash of neon pink over one temple. The amount of eye make-up she wore made Donna's eyes feel gritty. She wondered if Georgia would really appeal to a young doctor.

“Why don’t we go and have some cake in the café?” Donna suggested. “We’ll see who goes by.”

“Excellent. Cake and people-watching. Doctors always look after their stomachs.”

A very attractive young man served them. He had dark-blue eyes and a wide smile.

“Queer as a coot,” Georgia said under her breath as they carried their drinks and cakes to a spare table near the entrance, so they could watch the passers-by on the main corridor.

“Of course,” Donna said, as realisation hit her.

“Of course what?” Georgia angled her chair, so she had a better view of the doddering patients and erratic wheelchairs going by.

Donna glanced back to the counter, where the man was handing over change to another customer.

“Of course what?” Georgia demanded again.

“That guy,” Donna said at last. “He’s gay.”

“Well, yes, obviously.” Georgia rolled her eyes.

“Hang on.” Donna jumped up and ran back to the counter to grab some spare napkins. This time she glanced at the young man’s name badge. Ashley Avery. That was him. Brian’s friend, Ashley. The singer at the gay club.

“I’m right,” she said, returning to the table. “It’s him. Ashley Avery.”

“Who’s Ashley Avery?” Georgia forked up cake, and glanced at her mobile. “Oh Christ, he’s going to be late. Stupid wanker. I should have just got the bus again.” She jabbed a quick text, and dropped the phone into her bag.

“Brian’s friend,” Donna said. “He’s a nightclub singer at Clementines. That’s the gay bar.”

“I know what Clementines is.” Georgia’s phone cheeped again and she took it out. “Oh, shut up,” she muttered to the screen, and banged out another text. “I’ve told him to come here when he’s done.” She twisted around to look at Ashley. “Brian’s friend? Do you mean friend or *friend*?”

“I’m not sure.” Donna felt guilty now for spilling Brian’s beans, but she was still pissed off with him talking about her affair with Mark, especially to Georgia. She was pretty sure Georgia had no discretion.

“So that’s it, then?” Georgia murmured. “Brian goes both ways.”

“For Christ’s sake, don’t say anything. I’m the only one who knows.”

“Keep your wig on. Who would I tell? Look, I don’t give a fuck what other people do. You, Mark, Brian, whatever. Maybe that department’s a bit more interesting than I thought. Hey, what d’you reckon to him?” Georgia nodded to a man in theatre blues with a stethoscope around his neck, who was grabbing a pack of crisps from the basket.

“I don’t know,” Donna said. “Not my type.”

“Why, cos he’s single?” Georgia jabbed Donna in the ribs.

Neil Shelley arrived at five. He was a tall, slim man with neat hair and a sports jacket. Donna couldn’t see any resemblance to Georgia in his face.

“This is Donna from work,” Georgia said.

“How do you do? I’m Neil. How’s she getting on in Sterile Services?”

“She’s doing fine,” Donna said.

“Donna’s been mentoring me.” Georgia said. “And we’re going out on the town one night soon, isn’t that right?” She turned to Donna and pulled a desperate face.

“Much better for you to go together,” Neil said, before Donna could speak. “Girls shouldn’t go out alone.”

“Oh, don’t start.” Georgia shouldered her bag. “See you tomorrow, Donna.”

"I don't go out," Donna protested the next day.

"What d'you mean, you don't go out? What do you do?"

"Do?" Donna echoed. What did she do? Not a lot was the truth. "I like my own company," she improvised. "I read. I watch films. Sometimes I cook."

"And sit around waiting for Blondie to show up?"

"He only comes on Saturdays," Donna said. "Saturday afternoons."

"Not much in it for you, is there? Is he going to ditch her or what?"

Donna shrugged. "I don't know. Don't think so."

"Well, come out with me. You might find a better offer."

"I don't want a better offer."

"You set your standards too low," Georgia said, then, "Look. Please come out with me. The old fool won't let me go on my own. He's just as likely to stalk me or something."

"He's only concerned about you," Donna said. She'd liked the look of Neil; he seemed quiet and gentlemanly. "You're only twenty."

"Yeah, and I've lived away and done all kinds of shit. Since I've been back he's been so overbearing it's terrible. Come out with me, come and pick me up or whatever so he can see you're really coming, and then maybe he'll shut the fuck up, and leave me alone. There's no life in this place. I've got to get out and pull someone, or I'll end up like him trawling around sleazy internet dating sites."

Donna sighed. She felt mean, but she hated pubs and nightlife. She didn't like crowds or noise, loud music and clubbing.

"How about Friday?" Georgia demanded.

"All right, Friday," Donna said weakly.

On Friday, Brian turned into the gravel car park and chugged slowly along the lines of cars looking for a space. He felt queasy. On the back seat was an old hold-all with his gym kit in. Joy was delighted he'd enjoyed his visit to the gym with Gerry Pyles, and had gone out and bought him new shorts, and sports socks, and a special water bottle. He'd just stopped her wasting money on expensive new Nikes, by saying he had a pair, almost unworn, at the back of the cupboard; he could wear those, as he obviously couldn't use his work ones for the gym.

Brian swerved into a parking space. He was on a one-way ride now. He couldn't un-invent the gym or Gerry Pyles; he just had to go with it. He turned off the ignition and opened the door. At least he would see Ashley tonight.

Donna agreed to meet Georgia outside Starbucks at half eight. Neil was bringing Georgia into town in the car. A black BMW drew up at the kerb. The passenger door flung open, and Georgia stumbled out in huge heels and a very short skirt.

"Thanks. See you later." She slammed the door shut.

On the other side Neil got out and leaned on the roof.

"Hello Donna," he said. "Have you girls got enough money for taxis?"

"Yes, we're fine," Georgia said.

"Donna can come back to ours after if you like," Neil said. "If you need me, just ring me. I'll be at home."

"See what I mean?" Georgia glowered as Neil drove off down the main street.

"He's only looking after you," Donna said. "Come on, then, where are we going?"

"Let's try over there." Georgia nodded to a wine bar on the opposite side of the road.

A couple of young men eyed her long legs as she wobbled over the cobbles. Donna felt plain and frumpy in her jeans and shirt as she followed Georgia into the darkened interior.

They found a corner booth and carried their drinks over. There were empties on the table, and wet glass marks on the beer mats. Georgia tipped tonic into her vodka. Donna swallowed a small mouthful of wine.

The music was too loud, and the bar was already crowded. Donna had to lean forward to speak to Georgia across the damp table.

"Your mum?" she asked. "Does she live somewhere else?"

"She's dead," Georgia said, as a barman with tattooed biceps swept up the dirty glasses onto his tray.

"Oh," Donna said. "I'm so sorry."

"It was ten years ago." Georgia drank, watching the barman sliding behind the bar with his loaded tray. "It's why he's like he is."

"Who, your dad?"

"Yeah, why he's such a dinosaur about me going out and that."

"Why?" Donna asked.

"It's not the same here anyway. We were living in London at the time. She was attacked in the street and mugged. She died of head injuries."

"No wonder he's so protective of you," Donna said. "That's terrible."

Georgia played with her glass. "I'm not such a hard bitch, you know," she said. "I'm just desperate for some independence, to be my own person and all that, but he won't let me do anything." She drank and grinned at Donna. "He likes you. He'll be OK if you hang out with me."

They stayed for two drinks, then Georgia suggested they try somewhere else.

"There's no life for a Friday night," she grumbled, flicking her jacket around her shoulders and straightening her skirt.

It was easier this time. While he was in Clementines, Brian refused to think about Joy or Gerry Pyles or the gym. He had the drive home to practise what he would say. He'd Googled the gym often enough, so he could describe it to Joy; he'd read up on the rowing machines and the bench press.

Ashley wasn't singing. He was sitting beside Brian on a settle. Paul and Carl were opposite. Behind the bar the fairy lights flashed and flickered. Brian relaxed against the back of the settle. He wished he didn't have to keep checking the time.

"Let's go in here," said Georgia outside Clementines.

"That's the gay bar."

Georgia rolled her blackened eyes. "I know that. It'll be great. Hey, Brian might be here."

"I thought you wanted a man. You won't find one in there."

"I want to find some life. I want to find interesting people." Georgia had already opened the door.

Donna glanced quickly around and reluctantly followed Georgia inside. The bar was like a grotto, hung with pulsing coloured lights. *This isn't right,* Donna thought. *What am I doing in a gay bar? What's Georgia doing in a gay bar?*

"So many gorgeous men," Georgia shouted. "Do you think we can convert them? Look!" She pointed across the room. "There he is. Brian. With that guy from the café. You know, what's his name?"

Donna followed Georgia's gaze. There was Brian, raising a drink to his mouth. He was laughing at something, his face was relaxed. *He looks years younger,* Donna thought.

"I'll get the drinks. You go over and tell him we're here. Find some chairs for us." Georgia marched up to the bar.

"I'll have an orange juice," Donna called.

She hesitated. Suddenly Brian looked over towards her. He put down his drink. Next to him Ashley also turned. Donna felt heat in her face, as though she were the one caught out. Slowly she started across the bar towards them.

"Donna?" Brian asked uncertainly.

"I'm with Georgia."

"In here?"

Donna shrugged. "She wanted to come here. I thought she was trying to pull, but she insisted we came here."

"It's more fun in here," Ashley said. "Hey, Brian, shove along and we can squeeze one of the ladies in. Carl, grab that stool."

Carl hooked a spare stool with his foot and dragged it up to the table. Georgia arrived with two glasses.

"I asked for a juice," Donna said, wishing she had driven into town, had a genuine reason not to drink.

"Well, you've got wine. Evening, boys. Mind if we join you?" Georgia put her glass down next to Ashley's and slid in beside him.

Donna sighed and sat down on the stool. She felt completely out of things, stuck on the end of the table, out of the group. Brian quickly introduced Paul and Carl; Donna remembered one of them from the coffee bar. She sipped her wine. It was very cold. The others were all laughing at something. Ashley was fingering Georgia's long coloured hair.

Brian glanced at his watch again. He'd have to go. If he were late home, he could blow everything. He wasn't sure how this could happen: Joy wouldn't ring the gym to see if he'd been there, but he just knew that, even in deception – or, maybe more so in deception – there were rules and they must be obeyed. He slid on his jacket and tapped the pockets for his cigarettes and phone.

"Oh, Brian," Georgia cried. "You can't leave us now."

"I have to. The gym'll be closing shortly."

"The gym?" Georgia asked.

"It's where I say I am," he mumbled. "I must go."

"Night, Brian," the others chorused.

"See you next week," Ashley added. "After all this time at the gym I'm sure you can squeeze in a caramel slice."

Donna watched Brian walk to the door. She wished she could go too. Ashley and Georgia had spread out on the settle. There was no room for her there too; she was still stuck on the end. She wondered if anyone would notice if she just disappeared.

Up on the stage a couple of men in drag were dancing. Someone turned up the music volume and dimmed the overhead lights.

Georgia slammed down her empty glass. "Who's going to dance with me, then?" She stood up, adjusting her skirt again. "No point dancing with a straight man. They're crap. Ashley?"

Donna saw Ashley glance at her swiftly. "Not this time," he smiled at Georgia. "Paul's a great dancer though."

"I'll dance," Paul said.

"Donna? You going to dance with Carl?"

"Oh, er, no," Donna said. "I'm no good."

"Suit yourself." Georgia squeezed behind her and took Paul by the hand.

"Hey, wait up." Carl downed his drink and followed them to the stage.

The coloured lights tuned their bodies red and green. Georgia's skirt rode higher up her legs. Under her tights Donna thought she saw a flash of neon pink knickers.

"Donna?"

She turned. Ashley had moved down the settle and was next to her. She saw he had a beautiful face: all cheekbones and smoky midnight eyes.

"What's up, Donna? You don't seem to be having fun."

She shrugged. Stupidly, she felt tears in her eyes. She couldn't tell him. She couldn't tell him that she was crying because she was out with a girl she hardly knew, and now she'd ended up in a gay bar, when all she wanted was to be out with the man she loved, like anyone else, but that, because of Mark's impossible situation, it would never happen. She shrugged and gestured towards Georgia.

"I'm not like her," she said, and she knew she sounded petulant, but she couldn't help it.

"She's only enjoying herself," Ashley said. "I wish you were too. You can have fun here. You won't get men hitting on you. You can just relax, have fun."

"I don't like going out really," she said. "I'm not a drinker or a dancer."

"I'm not staying late tonight," Ashley said. "I'm tired. Would you like me to walk you home?"

"Oh no," Donna said hastily. "You don't have to do that."

Paul was heading for the bar, taking out his wallet. Georgia was dancing with Carl. As Paul passed the table he mimed drinking. Ashley shook his head.

When Paul came back, holding an unsteady tray of glasses, Ashley said, "Donna and I are going to head off now."

Donna tried protesting as Ashley helped her into her coat. Georgia saw and came stumbling off the dance floor.

"You're going as well?" She asked Ashley, Donna noticed, not her.

"Yeah, I'm not up for a late one tonight. Here, give me your number."

He pulled out his phone and handed it to Georgia, who punched in her number.

"Ready, Donna?" Ashley asked, and offered her his arm.

Georgia kicked off her shoes and scrambled back to the dance floor, and the queasy, undulating lights.

Outside, the night was cool. The sky was milky overhead, stained with street lamps.

"You can't walk me home," Donna said. "I live by the hospital."

"At least let me walk you to the taxis then."

Donna felt the prick of tears in her eyes again, as she walked through the city night with this beautiful young man, who was so wrong, but so kind.

"Will you be OK?" he asked her. "Do you want me to come back with you for a bit? You seem so unhappy."

"It's nothing," Donna said. "Just that I miss someone who can't be with me."

"I see," Ashley said. "There's not much I can say that will help. Just know you're always welcome at the bar. Now, are you going to give me your number too?"

"You want my number?"

"Only if that's all right with you."

"Yes, yes, of course it's all right. I'm sorry."

"You can always text me," Ashley said. "If you're feeling down. We have fun at Clementines, but there are quite a few people there who have pain in their lives too."

"Brian, you mean?"

"He's one, yes." Ashley gestured to the taxi rank, where a car had just pulled into the kerb. "There's a cab. Don't be a stranger, Donna."

"Did you have a good night with Donna and the boys?" Brian asked.

He and Georgia were sitting smoking on a bench at the side of the Sterile Services building.

"Wonderful night," she said. "Carl had to almost carry me out."

"Did Donna have fun?"

Georgia shrugged. "She left pretty soon after you. She went off with Ashley. He said he was going anyway, but I think he went because of her. She was a right wet weekend in there. Dunno what her problem is. Well, yeah, I do, I suppose. It's Blondie."

"He doesn't make her very happy," Brian said. "I wish she could find someone else."

"She's not interested."

"She was happier before him. She's so strained and drawn these days."

Georgia turned to Brian. "You notice things, don't you? Thing is, I need Donna." She flicked out another cigarette and offered the packet to Brian. "I don't know anyone here much these days. My dad won't let me do anything. I need someone to go out with." She inhaled thoughtfully. "I guess he has his reasons, but I want a bit of a life. I need a cover, you know?"

"An alibi?" Brian said slowly. "That's what I needed too."

"So you could go to Clementines?"

"I had to make up something. Someone. I made up someone at work. Someone who went the gym."

"You mean you said you were going with Blondie or someone?"

"No, I really made him up. Well, not exactly. He already existed. It was Mark, actually, who made him up first. Donna told me. Hasn't she told you?"

"Told me what?"

"About Gerry Pyles?"

Donna followed Mark into the tearoom. It was empty, but there was a lingering curry smell emanating from the microwave. Mark held out his hand for Donna's mug.

Donna stood at the window, looking down into the car park. Sometimes when she was alone with Mark at work she found she didn't know what to say to him. He handed her a tea and threw himself down in one of the soft chairs.

"Georgia and Brian seem to have hit it off," Donna said.

Below, she watched the two of them meandering back towards the building. Georgia pulled a blue hat out of her pocket and started to fold up her hair inside it.

"I thought it was his gay friends she liked." Mark yawned and swung his legs up onto the coffee table.

"That was Friday," Donna said.

On Saturday, when Mark had come over, she'd told him a little about the night before in Clementines with Georgia and Brian and Ashley and the others. She didn't tell him how upset she'd got, and she didn't tell him how Ashley walked her to the cab. She didn't tell him how she'd rather have been out with him.

She left the window and sat beside him. He squeezed her hand, but he didn't kiss her. Outside footsteps came closer. The door opened, and Mark snatched his hand away.

"Hey," Georgia drawled. "This is where you're hiding."

"I'm not hiding," Donna mumbled.

"Good work, Blondie," she said to Mark. "Very sneaky. I like it."

"Georgia," Donna started. She had a bad feeling.

"Well, Brian knows. You must have told him."

Mark stood up and slammed down his mug. "Look, I don't know what the hell you're–"

"Georgia knows," Donna said.

"Knows what?"

"About us."

"There's nothing to know. I'm going back to work."

"For God's sake, I've known about that for ages," Georgia said. "I'm talking about Gerry Pyles. Though what the hell kind of name is Pyles?"

The tea tasted foul in Donna's mouth. At the door Mark stopped and turned.

"I don't know what you're on about," he said.

"I didn't know it was a state secret. Brian told me you'd made up a guy to use as an alibi. He knows because Donna told him." Georgia glared at Donna. "And now he's using him too."

Donna felt her face flood. She couldn't look up at Mark.

"Fantastic idea," Georgia went on. "I want to borrow him."

"Well, why not, it seems everyone else has."

"Mark," Donna wailed.

"Chill out," Georgia snapped. "What the fuck does it matter? No one's going to know."

"It seems half the department knows. If this gets out–"

"It won't. Sit down, Blondie, and listen."

"And stop calling me that."

"Whatever. Listen. I don't know what your Gerry Pyles is like. Brian's is a fitness fanatic at the gym."

"What gym?" asked Mark. "Brian at a gym?"

"Brian tells his wife he's at the gym with Gerry Pyles when he's really at the gay bar. I don't want a bodybuilder for an alibi, I want a gay best friend to go clubbing with. So when I use Gerry Pyles he won't even be the same guy. You can do what you like with him. It's just a name, isn't it? *What's in a name* and all that?"

"*What's in a name*?" Mark repeated.

At last Donna met his eyes. He looked defeated.

"Why did you tell Brian?" he asked her.

"I'm sorry. I don't know. It was when you were, when things… I was miserable."

"You're always miserable," Georgia said.

They all froze as the door opened.

"Ah, there you all are," said Brian.

"Great." Georgia grabbed his arm. "We're just talking about Gerry."

"Shit, Mark, I'm sorry. It's just it's such a good idea, and we all seem to need a cover story."

"We should get this sorted out properly," Georgia said. "We need an email and so on. Then we can write to ourselves or each other or whatever, make it more realistic."

"Yes, an email," Brian agreed.

"We'll get together and talk it over." Georgia accepted a stick of gum from Brian.

"We need to get back to work," Mark said stiffly, and grabbed the door handle.

"And don't take it out on Donna," Georgia called after him. "It's much better now there's a team of us."

"Thanks, you two," Donna said bitterly.

"Chill. Blondie'll come round. He's an egomaniac; he'll love the idea we're all using his creation. And, speaking of getting together, Ashley's texted us all, says we should go to the coffee bar tomorrow afternoon. Paul and Carl will be there."

"He hasn't texted me."

"He did," Brian said. "It was a round robin just now. You'll come, yes, Donna?"

"I don't know," she said, and brushed past them and out of the door, after Mark.

Mark clanged two trolleys together in the autoclave room, and the noise jarred through his ears. He was furious that first Brian, and now the ghastly Georgia, knew about Gerry Pyles. Gerry Pyles was his secret, his and Donna's, and now Donna had destroyed it by blabbing. He was disappointed with her: he thought she would never say anything to anybody. At the same time, he felt guilty that she should be in this position. Of course his situation made her unhappy. That was inevitable, but he couldn't do anything about it, could he?

He wandered down the long room to where the completed, sterilised sets were cooling under the whirring wall fan. What had Georgia said? That Gerry Pyles was her gay best friend. She didn't need to invent a gay best friend; didn't she know enough of them? And Brian? He said Gerry Pyles was some gym freak. Outrageous. Gerry was neither of those things. Mark should know. He invented him.

"Are you coming to meet the boys then?" Georgia asked.

It was Tuesday afternoon at four. Georgia had changed out of her scrubs into another improbable skirt and a top with a zig-zag hem. Brian had tugged a hoodie over his blues, even though it was a warm and sunny afternoon.

Donna shouldered her rucksack. "No, I want to speak to Mark."

"He's on the phone." Georgia indicated to Mark, who was standing near the metal gate, with his mobile to his ear.

"I know, but I'll speak to him after, and then I'll just head off home."

"Suit yourself. Come on, Brian, or your break'll be over before it's started."

Donna stood on the asphalt watching Brian and Georgia stride away from Sterile Services. Once Georgia wobbled on her heels and Brian grabbed her arm to steady her. They disappeared behind the new growth on the spindly trees.

Mark still hadn't turned around. He was scuffing the ground with the toe of his trainer. Donna hitched her rucksack on her back. Really, she just wanted to go home and have a bath, but she hadn't had a chance to talk to Mark since the terrible scene the previous day. He had said hi to her and smiled, but she could feel her heart rate rushing with anxiety all the time. She knew Mark was angry about Gerry Pyles. She had to talk to him, make sure everything was OK. The worst thing she could have done would have been to rush off with Georgia and Brian.

"Are you going out with that nice Donna again?" Neil asked Georgia after dinner that night.

"Probably."

Neil reached for a pen and folded the *Times 2* to do the polygon.

"I'm going out on Friday night," Georgia ventured, watching Neil write a word at the top of the paper.

"With Donna?" He looked up.

"She might come." Georgia picked up the wine bottle and checked the level. She knew it was empty, but it gave her a prop. "It might just be me and Gerry." She pretended to read the label on the back of the bottle. The delicate ink drawing of Chile was blurred with a dark trickle of wine.

"Who?" Neil put down his pen.

"Gerry. Gerry Pyles," Georgia said. Why the fuck had Blondie called him Pyles? "He's new in my department."

"In Sterile Services?"

"Yes, that is my department." She banged down the bottle. She'd started it. She had to finish it now.

"So who is he? How old is he? What's he like?"

"He's gay, so don't go getting ideas."

"You're going out with a gay man?"

"Not going out like that," Georgia sighed. "Just going out for a drink and a bit of a dance."

"How old is he?" Neil repeated.

"How old?" *Shit.* She hadn't really thought this through. "Twenties, I think. He's very intelligent, cultured. He's…" She hesitated. Not a painter, like the idiots from uni. Not a singer like Ashley. "A poet."

"A poet? Is he published? Is he any good?"

"He's very secretive about his poetry. Doesn't want the people at work knowing about it, you know."

Neil picked up his pen again. "A gay poet," he said. "Well, as long as he looks after you and sees you home, or into a taxi."

"He'll do that for sure," Georgia said.

Donna never expected Mark to ring her when he left at eight that night. She hadn't been able to talk to him at the end of her shift. When, at last, he'd ended the call, he'd sprinted back towards the glass doors.

"Mark."

"I'm late," he'd said. "I'll call you when I finish."

She stood there, watching the glass door swing shut, then trudged across the car park towards home.

"I'm sorry," Donna said to Mark when she picked up the phone that evening. "I'm so sorry I said anything to Brian. I didn't know he'd tell anyone else."

"It doesn't matter," Mark said. "Well, it does, but we can't do anything about it now."

"Have you got time to call round?"

"I can't, Donna. I'm in the car. I'm just about to go home. I'll see you tomorrow."

Friday night in Clementines. Brian gazed around the table at his friends: Georgia, Carl and Paul, and beautiful Ashley. Ashley caught his eye and smiled at him. Brian sighed. Ashley was leaving in just over a week's time. He'd be gone for three months. Brian drank and traced the narrative in his head from his first encounter with those smoky blue eyes to this night in the bar, surrounded by friends, accepted and liked for what he was, or for what he wasn't, or for what he wished he could be. Over the weeks, his fantasies about Ashley had dissolved. Ashley was beautiful, talented, vibrant, but not for Brian. And yet, Brian knew Ashley liked him, and would remember him when he was hundreds of miles away on his cruise ships. He hadn't won Ashley for himself, but he had gained a whole new world, and new friends, and they would always be there, and then, one day, at the end of summer, Ashley would return.

"Did you ask Donna to come tonight?" Ashley asked Georgia.

"I did, and I texted her this evening as well, but she wouldn't. She's getting ready for Blondie turning up tomorrow. She's still pissed off with me and Brian for using Gerry Pyles."

"Did you tell your dad about him?" Paul asked.

"I said he was a poet," Georgia said.

"You could have just said you were out with us," Carl suggested. "We work at the hospital. He could have checked us out."

"It's easier to have someone in the department, and someone who isn't real. What do you mean, checked you out?"

"You know, checked we were who you said we were…" Carl trailed off.

"Oh fuck," Georgia said.

"Agency worker," Paul said. "Gerry Pyles is an agency worker. That's why he won't be able to find anything on him."

"Good thinking. Let's hope I don't get so drunk I forget that."

"Are we going to do anything for your farewell, Ashley?" Paul asked.

"Oh, let's," Georgia said. "Let's go out or something. When are you off?"

"A week on Monday."

"So, we could do something next weekend?"

"Not Sunday," said Carl. "I'm working."

"I'll be with my mum on Sunday," Ashley said. "We could do something on Saturday."

"What would you like to do?" Georgia asked. "Theatre, meal?"

Ashley laughed. "I'd love to go to the zoo."

"The zoo?" Paul echoed.

"I love the zoo. I haven't been for ages." Georgia stood up. "Who's for a top-up? The zoo it is."

Brian put his hand over his glass. "I'll have to be off soon," he said.

"Or Gerry Pyles turns into a pumpkin," Georgia called as she stalked to the bar.

"Can you come on Saturday?" Ashley asked Brian.

"I don't know. I don't expect so."

"Oh, Brian."

"You must go anyway. Have a wonderful day. Maybe I can meet you there."

Brian finished his drink. He didn't see how he could get away on a Saturday. There would be the Tesco shopping in the morning, then DIY or a visit to the garden centre. Joy would never believe he was going to the gym again. He stood up and reached for his jacket.

Ashley leaned forward and put his hand on Brian's wrist. "We'll ask Donna to come with us," he said. "A day out would do her so much good."

Mark parked outside Donna's on Saturday. He was a few minutes earlier than usual but, even so, he was surprised that she hadn't been looking out for him, wasn't already opening the door. Her car was there. She was in. Of course she was in.

As he locked the car he heard the house door opening. She looked wretched.

"What's up?" he asked.

She closed the door, fiddled with the key and chain.

"You're angry with me."

"No, I'm not." He ruffled her hair and kissed her.

Yes, he had been. Very angry. But he couldn't do anything about it now. He'd created a monster with Gerry Pyles. Maybe Georgia was right in some way: maybe if they were all in on the secret they could help each other out. He sure as hell wasn't going to hand Gerry Pyles over to them, and lose all control of him. A fitness freak? A gay best friend? The problem was when he tried to imagine his Gerry Pyles he drew a blank.

"It doesn't matter," he said to Donna. "It'll be OK."

For now he was stuck in this syndicate of liars.

Mark left at the usual time. Donna stood in the little hall, listening to the sound of his car until it blurred into the background whine of traffic. She checked the door was locked and trailed upstairs. She still felt it: that acute loss when he left her house. The bed was still rumpled from where they had lain; in the bathroom the shower dripped cold water into the bath. His damp towel was thrown across the rail.

Her phone cheeped in the bedroom. She dropped the towel on the floor and ran to read the message. It must be from Mark. Perhaps he was coming back? Of course not. Stupid girl. He had left her radar now until next weekend. She opened the message. It was from Ashley, asking her to go to the zoo with him, Georgia, Paul and Carl – and possibly Brian – next Saturday afternoon. It was his final outing with his friends before leaving for the cruise liners. Saturday afternoon. Donna stared at the tiny type until the screen went black. She couldn't go. Not on a Saturday afternoon. That was her time with Mark. She couldn't lose that. Anyway, they didn't really want her there. She'd be alone, out of it, as she had been stuck on the end of the table in Clementines. Could Mark come too? Donna hesitated with the phone in her hand. If he came too she wouldn't be alone. It was a Saturday; he could pretend he was working late. Of course not. Stupid girl. He would never do that. He would never break his pattern. Every week he arrived and left at the same time. She knew that, even when he fucked her, he was watching the clock.

"The zoo?" Neil asked. "With that Perry bloke?"

For a second Georgia couldn't think who he was talking about. "Oh, Gerry," she said at last. "Yes, he might come. And some others from work."

"Who are the others?"

"They're not from my department. They're…Gerry's friends."

"How are you getting there?"

"One of them will drive. Not sure who yet," she said.

It was probably going to be Ashley but, whoever it was, they were going to meet her in town.

"D'you remember that time with Mick's boys?" Neil asked.

Georgia scowled. The last time she'd been to the zoo, at fourteen or thereabouts, she'd wanted to watch the penguins being fed, the meerkats, the toucans with their giant colourful beaks. Her two younger male cousins had rushed off to the adventure playground, where one of them had come hurtling down the slide onto the other one's head, amid screams and recriminations, spoiling the day. Georgia remembered Neil holding a tarantula, which she wasn't too sure of. She hadn't been to the zoo since then.

Ashley, Paul, and Carl were definitely coming. Brian was still dithering, saying he might be able to meet them there for fifteen minutes, but she didn't think he would be able to. Brian would say goodbye to Ashley on Friday night when he left Clementines and, on Saturday, he'd be stuck at home with his wife, wishing he were at the zoo. Donna, of course, had refused to come, because Blondie would be coming over for a shag. Georgia sighed with irritation. Donna was so wet. If Blondie made her happy, then she should cheer up, take what she could from him, when it was convenient for her. If he made her upset – and she seemed to be upset all the bloody time now – she should tell him where to get off. Still, he had been useful with the Gerry Pyles thing. As Georgia had predicted, Blondie had grudgingly said the others could use the alibi, as long as there were no fuck ups. Georgia was going to set up an email soon. Somewhere upstairs she had an old pay-as-you-go phone. It might be handy if Gerry had a phone too, but who would look after it? It would have to be a communal phone. Complicated. She shrugged. She would worry about that some other time.

Brian was desolate. Ashley had just come down from the stage, wiping his face with a handkerchief. He'd been doing old favourites and requests. For the last time. No, the last time for three months, Brian corrected. He swilled his Coke around the ice cubes and drank. Cruise ships were dangerous places. Sometimes they sank. There was norovirus. Ashley might meet someone, another gorgeous young man, and run off to Greece with him. He might never return.

"Cheer up, Brian." Ashley put his hand over Brian's. "It's not for ever."

"Are you sure you can't come tomorrow?" Paul asked.

"I can't. It's just too difficult."

Not only was he sad that he could not enjoy an afternoon out with Ashley, he was jealous of the others for being there when he couldn't. It was ridiculous, he knew that. They had no more claim on Ashley than he did.

"Is Donna going?" he asked.

Georgia rolled her eyes. "She won't give up a precious hour with Blondie."

"Ah, don't be like that," Ashley said. "If she needs to be at home that's fine."

Brian stood up. "I have to go."

"Now, don't stop going to the gym, just because Ashley's not here," Carl grinned. "Ashley will want to see your hot gym bod when he gets back."

Brian waved goodnight to Georgia, Paul and Carl, and walked out into the twilight with Ashley.

Donna opened the front door and looked down the close. It was Saturday afternoon, and Mark was fifteen minutes late. He was exact, obsessed, with his timings. Something was wrong. She checked her phone once more. Nothing. No text, no missed call, no voicemail. She jumped off the step and stood in the empty parking space where, so many times before, his scruffy car had waited. It was a hot day, at the end of May. Summer was coming. She could hear an ice-cream van further up the estate and the sounds of kids shouting somewhere. Music thudded from an open window opposite. Her neighbours were getting on with their weekends. Maybe some of them were wondering why the Fiesta that turned up every Saturday was not there. She ran back up the steps out of the sun's heat, and into the hall. Still nothing on her phone, and he was over twenty minutes late. He wasn't coming. He could have told her. She could have gone to the zoo with the others. She hesitated, about to text him. No, bugger it, she could call him. It would only come up as Gerry Pyles, after all. The phone went straight to voicemail. She didn't leave a message.

Georgia shoved her Magnum wrapper into a nearby bin and crunched into the chocolate. Her hair whipped around and stuck to her sticky lips.

"Shame Brian and Donna couldn't come," Paul said, as they wandered up a narrow track towards the tropical house.

"Shame Gerry couldn't come," sniggered Carl. "He could have done some performance poetry by the lion pen."

"Or press-ups," Paul offered.

Georgia shoved at Carl. "What the hell have we started?"

"I think it's great," Ashley said, licking a trail of vanilla ice cream from the side of his cone. "Really funny. There you are, all different people needing a completely different cover story. Genius. I'm almost sorry I'm going away. Things are getting interesting."

"Will your dad want to meet Gerry?" Carl asked Georgia.

They stood outside the tropical house eating the last of their ice creams.

"I sincerely hope not," she said. "Or one of you guys will have to pretend to be him."

"He'll have seen us around the place. Ashley'll have to do it when he comes back."

"No way. He's seen me in the coffee bar."

"Oh shit." Georgia dropped her wooden stick into Carl's outstretched hand. Carl jogged down the track to a bin.

"I'm sure it won't go that far," Ashley said to Georgia.

"He'll just have to leave the department quickly," Paul suggested. "That's the trouble with agency staff."

There really wasn't any point staring out of the bedroom window. Mark wasn't coming. It was now the time he would normally be leaving. Had he overheard Georgia saying something about the trip to the zoo and thought she was going too? Donna wondered. Surely he would have asked her. Was he all right? There was no way she could find out. Miserably, she went into the bathroom, and wiped off her make-up. Had he stood her up because of Gerry Pyles? With her face still blobby with cream, she dialled the Sterile Services department. She didn't know the weekend staff well, vaguely recognised the Scottish accent of the supervisor.

"Is Mark Swift there?" she asked, without introducing herself.

"Mark's not working today. He should be in next week."

Donna hung up. So he knew he wasn't coming in and he couldn't even send her a text. With the phone still in her hand, she texted Georgia: *'Are you having fun?'*

"It's Donna." Georgia squinted at the screen in the sunlight and read out the text.

"Is she coming to join us?" Ashley asked.

"No, Blondie's just left. This is the time he goes." Georgia pocketed her phone. "Come on, let's go and find these capybaras."

"I love capybaras. They're so gloomy." Ashley grabbed Georgia and waltzed her down the path, bumping into a party of teenagers coming the other way.

"Donna could drive up now, couldn't she?" Carl asked. "If she's on her own. She could be here in twenty minutes."

"She won't though," Georgia said. "She's as OCD as Blondie in her own way. Saturdays are sacred."

Donna handed back Georgia's phone to her.

"Looks fun," she said.

"You should have come," Georgia said, and dumped half her sandwich in its screwed-up foil.

They were sitting with Brian at the picnic bench at the side of Sterile Services. Georgia flicked open a pair of sunglasses and slid them over her black-lined eyes.

Donna shrugged. "I would have, but I thought Mark was coming, and he didn't, and I still haven't heard from him. Where is he? When I rang they said he'd be in this week."

Mark wasn't at work. No one seemed to know why he was away. Donna couldn't ask anyone directly; all she could do was to eavesdrop on the supervisors' conversations, but no one had mentioned anything. She hated the way whenever Mark broke his rigid patterns she felt sick, terrified, almost too frozen to move, afraid that something had happened and Michelle had found out, and that he was going to tell her he could no longer come to her on Saturdays.

"Maybe one of the kids was ill," Brian suggested.

"You going to the coffee bar at four?" Georgia asked Brian.

"Ashley won't be there."

"I don't think Paul or Carl are working today either," she said.

Donna took her own phone out. "I'm going to call him. Anything could have happened. He could be ill, hurt, whatever."

"Is that sensible?" Brian asked.

"I can't stand this. I have to know. Suppose he's waiting to hear from me? He must think I don't care."

"He won't think that," Georgia snorted, and shredded her abandoned crust into crumbs.

"It'll only come up as Gerry Pyles," Donna said, sounding more confident than she felt. Inside, her heart was thumping, and she felt light-headed with nausea, but she had to know.

The phone rang out. Georgia threw crumbs to a jackdaw who was strutting on the scuffed-up grass nearby.

"Mark's phone," said a woman's voice.

Donna jumped, gasped, didn't speak.

"Mark's phone," the woman said again. "Who is this?"

Donna hit red and the screen died.

"What happened?" Brian asked.

"It was her. She answered his phone."

Georgia shoved her glasses onto her head. "What did she sound like?"

"I don't know. Why was she doing that? Why didn't he answer? He must be ill or something."

On the wooden table Donna's phone rang. The screen pulsed into neon life. *Mark*, it said.

"That'll be her again," Donna gulped. "I can't answer it." She rejected the call, and the phone died.

"What does your voicemail say?" Georgia lit a cigarette and shoved the pack to Brian.

"What d'you mean?"

"I mean, does it say *this is Donna here*?"

"Oh, no, no, it's just the pre-recorded one."

"Phew," Brian said, as the phone rang again.

"She ain't going to let this go." Georgia threw the rest of the crust to the jackdaw, who hopped nearer the table. "Has she left a message?"

"No. What can I do? I won't know if it's her or Mark. I can't just not answer. It's supposed to be Gerry's phone."

"Then get Gerry to call her back."

"How?" Donna wailed. She was almost in tears now. This was how it was all going to end, with her own stupidity.

"You just need a man to pretend to be Gerry. There's a man." Georgia pointed at Brian.

"Yes, yes." Donna pushed her phone at him. "Ring back and say you're Gerry. Quick, before she calls again."

"What the fuck do I say?"

"Say you were ringing to see if Mark was going to meet you," Georgia suggested.

"Meet me where? He's not here."

"Next Saturday. He told her Gerry works Saturdays, didn't he?"

"I don't know. Yes, yes, of course," Donna stumbled.

"OK, say you were seeing if he was going to meet you."

The phone rang again. Brian jumped.

"Answer it," Georgia yelled.

Brian hit green. He felt sick.

"Hello," he said. "Gerry Pyles speaking."

Georgia choked on her cigarette. Donna's eyes were watery, like she was about to cry. Brian fiddled with the cigarette pack on the table in front of him.

"I was hoping to speak to Mark," he said.

"Mark's ill," Michelle said. "Why do you need to speak to him? Who are you?"

"I work with Mark," Brian said. "I wondered how he was…I…er…wondered if he was going to be around this weekend."

"This weekend? What do you mean?"

Brian gazed helplessly at Georgia. She had her sunglasses on again, and he couldn't read her eyes.

"If he was working…sometimes we do stuff after work on Saturday."

"What stuff? I don't know what you're on about. Mark only works till three on Saturday. He doesn't do stuff."

"Oh, well, sometimes we finish early and do stuff." Brian gestured at Georgia for inspiration. Georgia was watching the jackdaw. "Birdwatching," Brian exhaled.

There was silence for a moment. Then, "Birdwatching? Mark doesn't know anything about birdwatching."

"We're learning," Brian said, and his confidence swelled. "We knock off a bit early on Saturdays and go and see what we can find. Saw a…woodpecker last Saturday."

"Mark was here last Saturday," Michelle said.

"The Saturday before, I mean. Yes, a woodpecker, just here, in the grounds. Pecking wood."

Georgia had her head in her arms on the table, and her shoulders were shaking. Donna was waving her hands desperately.

"Just tell Mark I called, please," Brian said. "The name's Pyles. Gerry Pyles."

When he hung up he was sweating.

Georgia howled. "*The name's Pyles. Gerry Pyles*. Birdwatching. Fucking hell, Brian, that was fantastic."

"I didn't know what to say," Brian gabbled, handing Donna back her sweaty phone. "Oh, Donna, don't cry. She thinks he's real now."

"What will Mark say? He'll know it was us."

"He should have fucking called you at the weekend, then, shouldn't he?" Georgia stood up, still chuckling. "Now, he's gonna have to start twitching. If he's not already. Come on, guys, we're desperately late."

"He'll be furious," Donna whispered.

"He'll get over it," Georgia said. "A few afternoons stuck in a hide full of guano and he'll be begging you to ask him round."

Brian swallowed a laugh. The jackdaw flew off. *Jesus,* Brian thought. *It was lucky the bloody jackdaw was there.* He put his arm around Donna as they followed Georgia back to the building.

"I'm sorry, Donna," he said. "I didn't know what to say. All I've done is set up an alibi for you anyway. Mark goes birdwatching on a Saturday afternoon, but he would have preferred she didn't know because it's a bit sad. Nothing really wrong with that. Not a strip club or anything. Harmless."

Pyles. Gerry Pyles. The three-headed beast: gym fanatic, gay poet, twitcher.

"Birdwatching?" Mark scowled at Donna. "What the fuck have you been doing? Who was that on the phone anyway? Was it Brian?"

"Yes, it was Brian," she said. "I had to get him to do it. She…Michelle…kept calling back. She wouldn't have stopped. Why was she answering your phone anyway?"

"I was in bed," he said. "I haven't been well. I still don't feel well. I only came back today to sort out what the hell you three witches have been concocting."

That wasn't quite true. He'd felt queasy and dizzy on Saturday and hadn't wanted to come to work, or even go to Donna's, and he hadn't had a chance to call her or text her. Susannah was ill too, and Michelle resentful at having to wipe up the little girl's vomit.

Mark knew, as soon as he came back to work, Donna would be nagging him about why he hadn't called her on Saturday, and he was still worn out from the bug, and couldn't face trying to explain to her that sometimes, just sometimes, he had other things on his mind, including his family, and that he wasn't on-call to her, but he knew that also sounded cruel, and that if she really irritated him that much he'd call the whole thing off, and he couldn't – and wouldn't – do that. But by Tuesday morning he'd had enough of Michelle's whining, and the smell of her cigarettes made him nauseous again; once he was sure Susannah was over the worst of it, he got into the car to drive to work with a mixture of relief and uneasiness.

"He had to say something," Donna said. "I didn't tell him to say birdwatching. He made it up."

"Michelle thinks I go birdwatching with Gerry Pyles on Saturday afternoons instead of being here. She wants to go through my pay slips."

“Well, you’re not working till three, are you?” Donna challenged him. “So she’ll only find that it all matches up.”

She slammed out of the staff room. Mark gazed at the door quivering it its frame. *Robin, sparrow, blue tit, seagull, thrush, starling*. He ran through the birds he knew in his head. *Puffin, magpie, cuckoo, pigeon*. He knew more than he thought. *Golden eagle, bullfinch, wagtail, barn owl, heron*. He’d seen a heron only a year or so back. A beautiful elegant silhouette in the river shallows. Actually, he wouldn’t mind knowing a bit more about birds. Maybe he and Eleanor could go birdwatching in the summer holidays. Quickly, he opened up Amazon on his phone and started scrolling through bird books.

On Friday night, Brian left Clementines at the usual time. It was the first time without Ashley. Paul hadn’t been there either, so it was just him, Georgia and Carl. Georgia had tried to get Donna to come down, but Donna hadn’t answered the text. No one had heard from Ashley yet. Brian didn’t even know where he was.

He parked outside his house and grabbed his gym bag from the back seat. It was ridiculous. Every Friday, as soon as he got in, he bundled his freshly laundered, unworn gym clothes straight into the washing machine before Joy could see that there were no creases, no sweat stains, on them.

As he unlocked the door, he heard Joy’s voice, saying, “Ah, Dad’s back from the gym now. Have a word with him.” She came out of the kitchen with the phone in her hand. “It’s Ruth.”

Without thinking Brian dropped the hold-all on the hall floor and took the phone.

“Ruth, sweetheart, how are you?”

Joy bent to pick up the hold-all.

“No, don’t,” Brian yelped.

“What?” Ruth cried.

“Don’t what?” Joy asked.

He snatched the gym bag off her.

“Got some other stuff in there,” he said, and strode upstairs with the phone to his ear. He half expected Joy to follow him, but she didn’t. He padded into the bathroom and, as quietly as possible, turned on the tap, and splashed his gym shirt with water under the arms and across the back.

“What are you doing?” Ruth asked.

“Just in the bathroom.”

“Sounds like it. Are you taking a slash?”

“No. No, of course not. Just washing.” He turned his gym socks inside out, and crumpled them with his wet hand.

“I suppose you want to have a shower after the gym,” Ruth said.

“Well, yes, I do, really. Can’t stand being sweaty and I don’t like showering there.”

At the weekend Georgia sent a round robin to Brian, Donna, and Mark at their work emails from Gerry Pyles’ new email address. In it she included the password. She’d struggled to come up with something suitable for all the Gerries. In the end she’d chosen ‘*decontaminated*’. Perfect. Now, they could email themselves, or each other, from Gerry, and could even show the emails to the relevant people. Marvellous. She hadn’t found her old pay-as-you-go phone and, in any case, she realised that wouldn’t be much use because Michelle already thought Donna’s number was Gerry’s. The email would be sufficient.

“Am I going to meet Perry Gyles?” Neil asked her later.

“It’s Gerry Pyles,” Georgia said. “Why can’t you get that right?”

“I once knew a registrar called Perry Gyles,” Neil mused. “Why don’t you invite him up for dinner?”

“The registrar?”

“Your friend.” Neil glared. “I don’t have a problem with gay people. You know that. Invite him to dinner.”

“Urrgh…he’s vegetarian.”

“I love cooking. We could have a pasta dish or a risotto.”

Oh Christ, Georgia thought. Gerry might have to go on holiday for a week or two. With luck, if she encouraged him, Neil might go back onto Plenty of Fish with renewed enthusiasm and find another distraction.

Friday night, and Brian was alone in the Gents changing room at eight o’clock. He opened the door a couple of inches. Quiet on the corridor and on the stairs. Mark was working, but it was mostly girls tonight. The coast looked clear. He unzipped his gym hold-all and took out his shirt. Holding the fabric taut with two hands, he nudged the tap with his elbow. A huge spurt of cold water splashed the shirt and his face. Brian swore and jumped back, as the door opened and Mark came in.

“You OK?” Mark tugged off his blue tunic and chucked it in the laundry skip.

Brian averted his eyes uneasily from Mark’s muscles. He turned off the icy jet of water and wrung out the shirt in the bowl. No one could sweat that much. *Shit.*

“*British Birds*?” Donna held up the large shiny paperback.

Mark stood in the bedroom door wrapped in a towel. As ever, his hair was dry. He had perfected the art of showering without wetting his head.

“That was in my rucksack,” he said.

“It had fallen out.” Donna sat cross-legged on the bed and leafed through the book. “Are you really going birdwatching?”

Mark let the towel drop and reached for his shirt. “I want a hobby to do with Eleanor. She should know more about nature. Birds are interesting. We’ll get a nesting box for next spring. See if we can get some blue tits.”

He buttoned his shirt and held out a hand for the book. Donna handed it to him silently. He stowed it away in his rucksack and flapped out his jeans.

“Are you doing it because of what Brian said?”

“No, I’m doing it for me and Eleanor.”

When he’d gone, Donna thought over the conversation. Mark had turned the whole thing round: what had started out as an alibi to spend time with her was now a family interest. He’d still cuddled her in the hall, and stroked her hair, and kissed her goodbye, but she knew now that everything would always begin and end with Michelle and his girls. It didn’t matter how horrible Michelle was to him, how much she drank and smoked, how badly she treated the kids, however old she was, nothing was ever going to shatter that unit: certainly not Donna.

Without Ashley, Brian stopped going to the coffee shop. He sat with Georgia on the picnic bench, and sometimes Donna joined them and, once or twice, Mark. Brian refused cigarettes from Georgia. Not going to the coffee shop meant no more caramel slices either. He was determined that Ashley would see a real change in him when he returned. He might not be going to the gym, but he was damn well going to try to lose weight and increase his fitness.

Georgia snapped her lighter at a cigarette. Brian closed his eyes. He hadn't actually stopped; he'd just cut down. He was so tempted just to have one; instead he unwrapped a fresh stick of gum and watched Mark stalking a chaffinch along the fence.

"That was genius, Brian, birdwatching," Georgia said. "You've opened up a whole new world for him."

Mark came back, his eyes on his phone. "He moved just when I was about to take the picture," he grumbled. "Got some good goldfinches the other day. Look, Donna."

"Sure, you don't want one?" Georgia waved the cigarettes at Brian.

He shook his head. He didn't really need cigarettes. Ashley had emailed him from Malta.

Brian and Joy went away for two weeks' caravanning in South Wales. They saw Ruth and met her new boyfriend. Their other daughter, Sarah, drove down from Chester and spent a couple of nights in the tiny spare bedroom in the caravan.

Georgia had free texts and kept Brian up to date with what was happening at work. Paul had introduced her to his straight neighbour and she'd gone out with him a couple of times (with Gerry Pyles, of course) until she decided she preferred his friend, Andy, who had long blond hair, and an earring. He'd dropped out of a marine biology degree and was now working in a bar, and doing a bit of busking with his guitar. She couldn't introduce him to her father because of the hair and the failed degree and the busking, so she was still using Gerry Pyles. '*He's a bit like my Gerry might be*,' she texted Brian, '*but he is definitely straight. Pecs to die for. I'm keeping him away from you.*'

Mark had changed his ringtone to some kind of birdsong, Georgia told Brian. She had suggested to Mark he could use a duck to identify Michelle calling. He had forgotten Donna's birthday and only remembered when he saw Georgia giving her some Thornton's. Donna had fled home in tears, and Georgia had told Mark, on pain of death, not to go to the hospital shop and buy her wilting carnations.

Brian had to turn his phone onto silent, so Joy would not hear the relentless cheerful beeps of Georgia's messages in the intimacy of the caravan. If she knew he was talking to a young girl like Georgia, she'd be disturbed, but Georgia was no threat.

He looked at Facebook on his phone. Georgia, Donna, Paul and Carl were friends with Ashley, but Brian didn't dare add him. Ashley hadn't added any new pictures. Brian looked again at the one of him with the bony-faced young man. *Not Ashley's boyfriend,* Brian thought. They just didn't look like that. There was almost something familiar about the other guy. He looked a bit like someone off the TV, but Brian couldn't think who that might be.

'Postcard for you from Naples,' Georgia texted. *'I put it in your pigeon-hole. What sort of hole has Blondie got? Duck? Ostrich? Dodo?'*

Donna took some holiday in August when Mark was away as well. Sometimes he texted her from his camping trip with Michelle and the girls; sometimes he sent her a photo of a bird he'd seen. Donna deleted these pictures.

Georgia dumped Andy, the failed marine biologist, after he nicked thirty quid from her wallet.

"Today's the day then," Georgia said to Brian. "Are you coming, Donna?"

"I'm coming," Donna said.

Georgia glanced at Brian. He grinned back. Since the birthday fiasco, Donna had grown some balls. Georgia had told Brian that Mark had left work early that day, and Donna later said he had gone to hers with flowers – from a proper florist and wrapped in pink marbled paper – and chocolates and a book token.

"The time went really quickly, didn't it?" Donna asked Brian.

Brian shrugged. Every day he'd wondered where Ashley was, who he was with, whether he'd met a young man, and whether he would ever come back to England. He'd received emails and cards – as had Georgia and Donna – but he still didn't dare believe Ashley would return. And now today, tonight, Ashley was meeting them all in Clementines.

Brian felt sick walking towards the bar. The evening was cool, as evenings at the end of August could be, and he shivered, remembering for a moment, that first time he had shuffled through the door and into the world of light and colour inside.

Ashley was at the bar with Georgia and Donna. Brian simply stood in the doorway and gazed at him. His skin was golden from the southern sun, his hair had grown, thick and dark over the collar of his shirt. He moved his hand to make a point, and Brian saw again the long, slim, mobile fingers.

Georgia looked up. "Brian!"

Ashley turned, slid off his stool and came over to Brian.

"Brian," he said, kissing him on the cheek. "So, so, good to see you. You look great. Must be all that time at the gym. We have so much catching up to do."

He steered Brian towards the bar.

"I'm going with Ashley next summer," Georgia said. "See if I can find a rich widower."

Mark felt a fool writing to himself from a fake email.

'Are you working this Saturday? Thought we could head down to the estuary for an hour.

Let me know.

Gerry'

He opened up his own emails and left the message open on his laptop when Michelle was around.

"What the fuck is the point of birdwatching?" she demanded. "I still can't forgive you. You lied to me. You said you worked till three, and really you were off twitching."

"It's a wholesome hobby," Mark said. "And look how interested Eleanor is."

"Perhaps you should let her go with you on Saturdays then?"

Thank God Michelle doesn't have a car, Mark thought. He closed down the internet. She couldn't have seen through the alibi, could she?

Georgia left Sterile Services at four o'clock. Donna had a week off, and she had no one to walk with. Autumn had come quickly, and the wind was cool. She stopped and zipped up her jacket. There was a slow-moving line of cars heading for the exit. She veered off the path and took a short-cut under the trees. There were toadstools growing here: some yellow and waxy like boiled potatoes, some pale with brown sprinkles on top like cappuccino, and two – no, three – pink-white golf balls of new Fly Agaric. In the coming days the balls would darken to red, and swell into bright domes. Georgia tentatively touched one with the sole of her shoe.

They were all living in stasis. Mark and Donna had been carrying on for almost a year, and nothing had changed. Mark pretended to go birdwatching when in reality he was fucking Donna for an hour. Donna, though she had hardened imperceptibly, still would not risk losing that hour a week.

Brian trotted off to Clementines every Friday night and gazed at Ashley on the stage, or across the table, but would never truly belong, would never truly be gay, because he was a married father of three, and he would never walk away from that, and would never tell Joy how confused he was.

And what about her? Gerry Pyles had been a useful ally for her nights out in Clementines, and then later with Andy, and she had used him once or twice to go clubbing with Paul and Carl on a Saturday night, where she had met a few men, but none she really wanted. If she was honest, she preferred the gay club and her strange cronies from the hospital.

Brian threw his dirty blues into the skip and tugged on his own shirt. It was looser than it had been six months ago. Cutting down his carbohydrates and junk had worked, and he hadn't even been near a gym. He was sure his breathing was better now he smoked fewer cigarettes. Joy had commented on his slimmer body, and he had turned away, feigning embarrassment, when she said how good the gym was for him. He could never tell Joy how he really spent his Friday evenings. He could not even imagine how betrayed she would feel, or how cruel that would be. It would have to remain his secret forever. He sighed. Sometimes that thought made him feel very tired.

Mark shouldered open the door to the changing room as Brian was leaving.

"Night, Brian," he said.

Brian looks a bit grim, a bit depressed, he thought. Well, it would be a strain deceiving his wife like that week in, week out. Mark stiffened. Wasn't that exactly what he was doing too? He should stop it. Nothing could ever come of it. He could never be with Donna in the way she wanted, and he wouldn't want that anyway.

He changed quickly, turning his back as a couple of the other guys came in. It was Thursday. Only Friday, and a short day on Saturday, and he would be in Donna's bed again. He smiled as he zipped up his hoodie, and wished he had time to call on her before he went home. Birdsong trilled from his pocket. Michelle on the phone again.

Georgia was the first to see the posters. One of the supervisors was sticking one on the wall as she came out of the Ladies.

"Are you going to the Christmas party, Donna?" she asked later.

They were sitting outside on the bench. It was freezing cold, and they were both shivery in blues under winter coats, but it was the only place where Georgia could smoke discreetly.

"I don't think so," Donna said.

"Fuck it, I knew you'd say that. You didn't even think about it, you didn't even consider it, you just said no. Blondie might be there."

"He won't be. He didn't go last year. He said he couldn't because of her. It was one of our first conversations."

"Wow, your affair got off to an exciting start, didn't it? Talking about a night out neither of you was going to have."

"You know he can't do stuff like that. And I don't go out much."

"Let's ask him when he arrives," Georgia said. "And Brian. I bet Brian and Joy always go. I'll ask them later. I think we should all go."

"Mark's off today and tomorrow," Donna said. "And she wouldn't let him go without her."

"So she might come. Wouldn't you like to see what she looks like? He's never shown you a photo, has he? She's old, she drinks and smokes. Surely you want to see her?"

"You drink and smoke," Donna says.

"Yeah well, we're different generations."

Donna hesitated. Georgia was right. There were twenty years between her and Michelle.

Mark walked back into the living room with a mug of tea in his hand. He hadn't heard Michelle come downstairs. She was leaning over his laptop, her bright hair falling over her cheek. He could see from the angle of her arm that she was using the mouse pad. He stopped and the tea sloshed over the top of the mug. He knew instantly she'd seen something she didn't like. He'd had several windows open: Amazon, a bird watching site, Google, his emails.

She looked up.

"What's with this Gerry Pyles guy?" she said.

Oh fuck, Mark thought. Someone must have emailed him as Gerry Pyles. It wouldn't be Donna. It'd be Georgia. She was a loose cannon. Oh fuck.

"What about him? I was just Googling some stuff about puffins to send him." That, at least, was almost true. He had been Googling puffins.

"He's emailed you," Michelle said. "Asking if you are going to the Christmas party at work. Is he asking you on a date?"

"Ah, don't be daft." Mark wished she would stand aside and let him look at the screen, and see what Georgia, Donna, Brian, whoever-the-fuck-it-was, had written.

"He wants to know if you're going. I notice he doesn't ask if I'm going. Why doesn't he want me to go? Why does he want you to himself?"

"Let me look." Mark put down his drink and shoved her aside. He should be bollocking her for going into his emails, opening a message, but he knew if he did it would make things worse.

'Hey Mark,

Hope you are enjoying your time off. Wanted to ask you if were coming to the Christmas do. It's on the 21st December at the White Rose. The rest of the gang will be there.

Cheers,

Gerry'

Mark stared at the message. Georgia. Why the fuck had she done that? Couldn't she have waited until he was back at work?

"So, who's the rest of the gang? What gang? More bloody twitchers?"

"No, no," Mark stumbled over his words. "Just people at work. Um, Brian, you know about Brian."

"Brian and who else?"

"Oh, uh, Georgia, Donna." He drank tea to avoid her eyes. He should never have said Donna.

"I think we should go to this party. Your parents can have the girls. Write back and tell him we'll both come."

"But you never want me to go to things."

"Not on your own, no," Michelle said. "But I'd like to meet this Gerry Pyles. There's something about him I'm not sure of."

"I'll tell him at work." Mark moved to close the internet.

"No, write back now," Michelle said, and her voice was suddenly hard. "Or shall I?"

"Would you like to come to the Christmas do?" Brian asked Joy. "It's at the White Rose this year, you know, the big hotel."

"Of course," Joy said.

Brian knew she would want to go. They had always gone together. Joy enjoyed an occasion to dress up, and the White Rose was pretty swanky, or so he'd heard. Perhaps he could buy her a new dress to wear.

"Will your friend be there?" Joy asked.

"What friend?" Brian asked. Ashley? How could she know about Ashley?

"Your friend Gerry, silly."

Oh Jesus. Gerry Pyles.

"What's the White Rose like?" Georgia asked Neil.

She knew he'd taken a few Plenty of Fish women there on dates. She'd never been there, thought it was fusty and old fart-ish.

"Not your scene, I don't think," Neil said. "Why?"

"The Sterile Services party's going to be there," she said. "Grim choice, I reckon."

"I like it," Neil said. "It's discreet, quiet. Good whisky selection. Are you going to this party, then?"

"Damn right I will."

"You're going with Donna?"

"Donna probably won't go." Georgia stopped. She shouldn't have said that; it was telling him too much.

"So, who will you go with? Perry?"

Phew. Of course.

"I've told you God knows how many times. It's Gerry."

"Gerry then. You going with him?"

"I'm sure he'll be my date."

"It'd be nice to meet him," Neil sniffed. "I hope he'll come and pick you up from the house, introduce himself to me properly. About time he did."

Georgia gulped.

"What the hell were you thinking of?" Mark hissed to Georgia in the tearoom.

"Chill, Blondie. I was trying to do you a favour." Georgia tossed her apple core into the pedal bin and wiped her hands on her blues.

"You should change your tunic. That's dirty. And what do you mean, a favour?"

"Donna was being a drip as usual. Saying she wasn't going to come. I thought if she knew you were coming she would."

"Michelle saw it. Now she wants to come too. That's not going to make Donna come, is it? She stood over me, telling me what to write back."

"Yes, I gathered that." Georgia hesitated in the doorway. "I'm sorry, Blondie. I wrote it to you. I didn't think you'd be letting her read your messages."

"I couldn't stop her. Does Donna know about this?"

"She's not here today. Her sister's ill, and she has to look after the kid or something."

Mark sighed, helped himself to a biscuit from the open packet.

"Christ, these are stale. Can't anyone wrap things up round here?"

The door swung back. Brian came in, still in his outdoor clothes. He opened the fridge and put his food on one of the crowded shelves.

"Everything OK?" he asked.

"No." Mark bit into another stale biscuit. "Georgia here wrote me an email from Gerry Pyles about the fucking Christmas party, and Michelle saw it, and now I've got to go with her, and Donna will be upset."

"Gerry Pyles has jinxed that party," Brian said, checking the kettle for water. "Like a fool I asked Joy if she wanted to come. Well, I say like a fool, but we always go. Anyway, she said yes, then asked if Gerry Pyles was going to be there, because she wanted to meet the man who'd helped me get my six pack."

"Six pack's a bit of a fantasy," Georgia said. "Actually, I did the same. I told Dad I'd be going with Gerry Pyles, and he said I'd got to get him to come to the house and be respectable and honourable and all that shit. Looks like we've all fucked up."

"Oh marvellous." Mark swept up some stray crumbs in his hand, and chucked them into the bin on top of Georgia's apple. "Now Michelle, Joy, and your old man are all expecting to meet this guy. And guess what? He doesn't exist."

"Well, you made him up." Georgia shouted. "You started it."

"You all stole him."

"We adapted him. My dad thinks he's gay. Joy thinks he's a muscle man."

"Michelle thinks he's a twitcher," Mark finished.

"So, we're not just one man short," Brian said. "We're three men short."

"It's easy. He can't go," Georgia said.

"Yes, he has to work," Brian agreed. "He works the evening shift before the gym."

"He works the early shift with me," Georgia corrected him. She felt laughter in her throat. It was so absurd.

"In your email to me, you implied he was definitely going."

"Shit, Blondie, you're right."

There was just the two of them in the bar. Brian thought back wistfully to those early heady days when he thought he and Ashley might – just might – but no, of course not.

"You OK, Brian?" Ashley asked.

Georgia was at home with an ear infection. She'd been off work and was taking antibiotics. Donna was at home doing whatever she did on her own at home on Friday evenings when she didn't come to Clementines. Paul was off with other friends elsewhere. Carl was – Brian didn't know where Carl was. It was just him and Ashley at a corner table, under a string of neon pink fairy lights, with the beat of Lady Gaga throbbing in his ears.

"I'm in a bit of a mess, actually," he confessed. "We all are."

"What kind of mess?" Ashley asked. "Who's *we*?"

"Me, Georgia, that idiot Mark."

"What about Donna?"

Brian drank to avoid Ashley's eyes. He knew that, for all her stubbornness, or shyness or whatever it was, Ashley was very fond of Donna, and protective of her.

"Donna too, in a roundabout way."

"You'd better tell me. Perhaps I can help."

"I doubt it." Brian hesitated. "Oh, it's stupid. It was Georgia's fault really." He drained his glass, told Ashley about the department Christmas party, about how he and Joy always went together, how she was now expecting to meet Gerry Pyles and, as if that weren't enough, Georgia's father and Mark's girlfriend were also expecting to meet him.

"And Georgia told Mark that Gerry was definitely going to be there. And they won't believe us if he's not. Georgia's father's getting really heavy wanting to meet him. I wonder if he doesn't approve of gay men."

"He's a shrink, right?" Ashley laughed.

Brian smiled. "If Donna comes, she'll see Mark with his girlfriend. She thinks Mark's only still with her for the kids, and she is a bit of a nutter, always ringing him at work, and making him ring her and that, but I don't think he has any intention of leaving her or making more time for Donna or anything. He's just stringing her along. Donna, I mean. I used to like Mark, and I used to feel sorry for him, being unhappy at home, but now I think he's a bit of a shit." Brian stopped.

Was he not also a bit of a shit? A monstrous shit, in fact. He picked up his glass but it was empty. He swallowed the crushed remains of the ice to soothe the heat of his guilt.

"Donna shouldn't go," Ashley said. "She shouldn't see this Michelle woman."

"Georgia's making her go. She thinks Donna should check out the enemy."

"The enemy may not be quite what Georgia imagines."

"Exactly."

"Unless perhaps Donna could go with me," Ashley suggested. "Could I be her plus one? Do you think she'd like that?"

"You?" Brian gasped. "You at our party?"

Ashley at the Christmas party. Brian could look at him all evening, and he wouldn't be jealous of him being with Donna. It was unimaginable; it was wonderful.

"You could ask her," he managed at last.

"I will. If she wants to go. She mustn't go alone."

"No," Brian agreed. "But what about bloody Gerry Pyles? If he's not there, Joy or Michelle might start asking people and then they'll find out he doesn't exist. Shit, shit, shit. What have we done?"

"You need someone to be Gerry Pyles."

"You?" Brian gasped again. "You'd come with Donna and pretend to be Gerry Pyles?"

"Of course not. How can I go with Donna if Gerry Pyles has to pick up Georgia and get the third degree from the shrink?"

"We could sort out something," Brain said. "I'm sure we could. You'd also have to talk about the gym."

"I don't know anything about the gym."

"And birdwatching."

"Brian. No," Ashley said firmly. "I'll come with Donna to support her, but I can't be Gerry Pyles."

Brian gazed sadly at Ashley. Wonderful, perfect Ashley, who perhaps wasn't so wonderful or perfect after all: he wouldn't help out in a crisis.

"You're a singer, a performer. You could pull it off."

"Don't be ridiculous. Georgia's father's seen me at the coffee bar."

There was a smile nudging the corners of Ashley's mouth. Brian felt a cold flood of disappointment. Ashley was laughing at them, at him.

"However," Ashley reached into his jacket for a pen. "I do know a man who could do it."

"Who could be Gerry Pyles?"

Ashley pulled out an old Sainsbury's receipt. He glanced at it, turned it over and began writing on the back. Brian watched those loopy letters forming under the Biro, the writing he'd first seen when Ashley sent a caramel slice to Sterile Services for him.

"I can't remember the website exactly, but Google that." He handed Brian the scrap of crumpled paper.

"Robin Goodfellow Agency, Bath," Brian read. "Bath? That's miles away. What is this place? Who's Robin Goodfellow? I don't understand."

"I knew someone once in Bath. He worked for this agency. He did other things too, a bit of acting, a bit of escorting, a bit of I-don't-know-what really. He'd do it."

"He's Robin Goodfellow?" Brian asked doubtfully.

"No, that's the guy who owns the agency."

"Your friend works for him?"

"Yes. He could do it. He's done weirder things, or so he told me."

"But Bath?"

"He'd travel. He could be Gerry Pyles, in all his forms."

"So, what's his name?"

"That's not important," Ashley said. "He's a man of many aliases, of many lives. He used to work for the agency under the name of Cobweb."

"What sort of a name's that?"

"A code name."

"This all sounds a bit MI5, James Bond. Is it legal, this agency? What do they do?"

"It's as legal as the jobs they're given. There's nothing illegal about someone pretending to be someone else for a few hours to keep the peace in three families, is there?"

"I suppose not."

Ashley tapped the screen on his phone, handed it to Brian. It was Facebook. It was the photograph he'd seen before when he was looking at Ashley's profile. Ashley with that bony-faced, longhaired man.

"That's him. But I doubt he looks like that now. He changes like a chameleon."

"How did you meet him?" Brian asked, wavering at the thought of his wonderful, perfect Ashley being mixed up with secret agents, illegal practices, an undercover world.

"I lived in Bath briefly. I met him in a gay bar."

"Was he your boyfriend?"

"I don't think he has boyfriends. Not like that. Or girlfriends either. You'll see what I mean when you meet him."

That doesn't answer my question, Brian wanted to say, but he did not speak. It did not matter who Ashley had known, who he had been with, even who he loved, many years ago in another city.

"Were you singing in the gay bar?" he asked instead.

"Yes, just starting out. It was called Riff Raff's. My old friend Martin ran it. Amazing place."

"Is it still going?"

"Absolutely."

"I'll Google it too," Brian said.

"Don't even think of going there, Brian. They'd eat you alive in Riff Raff's." Ashley smiled, remembering other days, another life.

Cobweb swings his long legs off the Travelodge bed and crosses to the door. He's stayed in so many of these places for work. They're all the same. White duvet with only two pillows, hairy sofa bed, upturned smeary glass and sliver of soap in the bathroom where the light makes his skin look green and waxy.

He checks through the spyhole. Yes, it's Ashley. It's been a couple of years since they last met. Like the Travelodge room, he's the same, but in a good way, an attractive and familiar way: dark blue-violet eyes, slender hips, wide smile.

"Ashley," Cobweb says at last. "Long, long time, no see."

"Not so for me," Ashley says. "I've seen you on TV quite a few times. You may look different, but I'd always know you."

"Come in. We must check all this stuff. You've got photos?"

"Of course."

As the door swings shut, Ashley takes out his phone, swipes the screen a few times.

"Here you are. Here's Brian. He's a darling, poor thing. This is Georgia, your date for this evening, and here's Mark. Oh, and this is the lovely Donna, who's coming with me. She's Mark's mistress."

Cobweb slides his finger back and forth on the screen. Of course, he had asked Brian, Georgia, and Mark for photos when he contacted them, but he'd asked Ashley to take some for him as well. Nothing can go wrong.

"So, let's see what you've got, then," Ashley says, taking the phone back.

Cobweb gestures to the hairy sofa: a flowing tunic, a medallion, rubber wristbands, John Lennon bottle ends, a Blackberry, a patterned scarf, a geeky watch.

"We'll check them all off," he says, unzipping a large black hold-all. Inside are three smaller bags: one blue, one red, one green. "Then we colour co-ordinate them. I need my own clothes too, of course, to escape in."

"You'll only have to be the gay poet at Georgia's house," Ashley says. "Once you get to the hotel you can ditch him. Unless you take her home at the end."

"Anything could happen," Cobweb says. "We have to have everything prepared." He bends down to a cardboard box on the bedroom floor. "This is the best bit. This is for Brian's Gerry Pyles."

"Oh Jesus," Ashley guffaws. "How the hell are you going to manage that?"

"That's why I have you as a PA," Cobweb says.

Can I get away with it? Georgia asks herself. *Can we get away with it?* Employing a man known only as Cobweb, for fuck's sake, to impersonate three fake people? It's insane.

She's ditched the pink stripe in her hair, gone back to the black and purple. She's wearing a tiny, clinging black dress over cobweb-patterned tights. Cobwebs. She's only just seen the humour in that.

Neil's going out tonight with that Annette again. He met her on Plenty of Fish. *It's a good job there are plenty of fish in the sea,* Georgia muses, as Neil gets through them at a cracking pace. She met Annette a few days ago. Older than Neil, with long hair, going silver, and amber earrings. She's an antiques dealer or restorer or something, and she does reflexology on the side. *She seems OK,* Georgia thinks, but she'd better not assume she'll still be around in a few months' time because they rarely are these days. Georgia doesn't know where Neil's taking Annette for dinner. She wishes they'd leave before her, but oh no, Neil wants to meet Perry – sorry, Gerry – after all this time. What the hell is this Cobweb guy going to be like?

"Wow, you look amazing," Mark says to Michelle as she spins in front of the mirror.

Her dress is a simple shift, turquoise with purple Celtic patterns on. She's scooped her hair up with that tortoiseshell clasp thing. Mark, who is on leave today, knows she has had a bottle of wine during the afternoon, but she seems OK at the moment. She's applied her make-up without any wobbly lines but, more to the point, she's calm and pleasant. He's really proud to be seen beside her, as long as she doesn't get all mouthy. He wonders how he can stop her drinking at the party, realises he cannot.

And then there's Donna. He wishes and wishes she weren't coming. He wants to text her and tell her not to come. He knows how upset she will be, seeing him with Michelle. He knows damn well the picture he has painted of Michelle has not been entirely true. Yes, she drinks and smokes. Yes, she did forget to pick up the girls once. Yes, she is a real bitch at times. But. He looks at her again, at how the bedroom light catches the copper of her hair, and her gold earrings, and he wishes for a moment he could just tumble her to the bed, shove up that shift, unravel her hair, and fuck her; then, later, to open a bottle of wine and spend the night in a hazy, boozy dream with her, rather than face the double horrors of a tearful, wounded Donna, and a stranger pretending to be a man he, Mark, invented, in order to be unfaithful for an hour every Saturday.

Brian's worked a shorter shift today and gone home early. This close to Christmas, many of the operating lists are cancelled, blanked out in red on the rotas pinned to the noticeboards, as the surgeons and anaesthetists and theatre staff are on holiday. Sterile Services is quieter, and the supervisor didn't bat an eyelid when Brian asked a few days ago if he could leave early on Friday.

He's bought Joy a new dress for the party. It's a mauve floral print. He bought her new shoes as well, but she says they pinch at the toes, so she'll be wearing an older pair. She went to the hairdresser yesterday to get her roots done, and a new cut.

She's so excited about the party; more than she has been any other time. She can't wait to meet Gerry Pyles. If it weren't for him, Brian would still be fat and wheezy, still smoking. Joy can't wait to thank Gerry for helping Brian before it was too late.

Donna feels sick. Really sick and terrified. Tonight, she will see Michelle, the woman Mark shares his life with, the mother of his children, who sleeps beside him every night. Every night, but that one time, the night of the snow.

Today there is nothing funny about hiring this agent from Bath. Donna knows the evening will not be one of laughter for her, but one of tears. If Michelle is beautiful, she will be destroyed; if she is ugly, she will cry *why, why, why* into her pillow tonight. *Why does he stay with her?* He cares enough about Michelle to go along with this insane idea of hiring this friend of Ashley's. That's how much he wants to appease and please her.

Donna drags a brush through her hair again. It's loose down her back. She wears a ponytail at work, so she can shove it into her hat easily. She doesn't know any fancy ways to put up her hair. She only has scrunchies, no fancy clips or clasps. This dress is a bad idea. It's a midnight blue maxi her mother bought her. She's too dumpy to wear it. She runs her hand along the wardrobe rail to see what else she has. Ashley will be here any moment in the taxi. She has to leave with him, if she's going, because he is helping Cobweb with his masquerade. She tugs out a short black dress. Too boring. A red one with a cut-away back. Too slutty. And she probably wouldn't get into it these days. She hears a car draw up outside, a horn. She runs to the bedroom window and looks out. There's the taxi, with its neon roof sign, headlights on, engine growling. From her bag her phone rings. Ashley.

Leaving the two dresses in pools on her bed she clicks off the light and goes downstairs.

Annette and Neil are in the living room, sitting on the sofa, talking quietly. Neil's wearing a cravat – one Georgia gave him several years ago – and Annette is wearing a drapy pashmina thing that looks like a carpet. The last time they went out, Neil insisted on bringing Annette back to the house to meet Georgia. He's always done that, brought them home to meet her very early. *Perhaps that's why he gets through so many fish,* Georgia often thinks. Tonight, she suspects Annette will be back at the house after their date and, most likely, will be there in the morning too.

Georgia is in the hall, hovering, waiting for Cobweb. Supposing he doesn't turn up?

"Your date is late," Neil calls out to her.

"Oh, well, don't worry, you two go on out." Georgia comes to stand in the living room doorway.

"No, we'll wait. I want to meet him at last."

"Have you and Perry been going out long, Georgia?" Annette asks.

"We're not going out," Georgia mumbles. "He's gay. And it's Gerry, not Perry."

"My fault," Neil says benevolently. "I keep calling him Perry. Is he coming in a cab or in his own car?"

"Oh, uh, I'm not sure."

The knock on the door startles Georgia. *Oh shit, this is it.* Neil and Annette both stand. Annette's got her carpet thing twisted, and she tugs it ineffectually.

Georgia clicks the chain off the door and opens it.

"Georgie, darling. You look divine."

"Uh, Pe – Gerry, great to…see you."

Cobweb is wearing dark trousers with a voluminous smock under a black velvet jacket. There's a pink lily pinned through his button hole, and at his throat he has a patterned scarf. His dark hair is long on his shoulders. Attached to his lapel is the red twist of a Terence Higgins ribbon and a rainbow Gay Pride badge.

You'll do, she is about to say; just in time remembers she cannot.

"Perry, how do you do?" Neil's offering his hand to Cobweb. "About time you came here. I kept asking Georgia to bring you back for dinner. Anyone would think she didn't want me to meet you. I told her I was quite capable of rustling up a little vegetarian something. Georgia, you did check there were vegetarian options tonight, didn't you?"

"Yes, yes, of course," Georgia says, shoving her arms into her jacket.

"Georgia tells me you're a poet."

"Ah, Georgie, that's so sweet and flattering. Mr Shelley, sorry *Doctor* Shelley, I scribble a few lines here and there, and hope they sometimes make people think a little on life, and love, and the world. I always have my little book with me just in case." He taps his breast pocket and Georgia sees a small hard-backed notebook.

"We should really be going." Georgia picks up her bag and reaches once again for the door handle.

"Well, young man, I hope to see you again. You look after my little girl tonight."

"For Christ's sake, I've been going out with Gerry for ages." Georgia rolls her eyes and takes Cobweb firmly by the arm.

"Georgia very much enjoyed going to Gay Pride with you and your friends," Neil says, as they step out into the cold.

Georgia tries to remember when the hell she said she was going to Gay Pride. *An alibi for a day out with Andy,* she thinks.

"What's in the bag?" Donna asks Ashley, as the taxi drives away.

They are standing outside the White Rose. The hotel is in the middle of town, but down a dark private drive off one of the streets. Floodlights bleach the Georgian façade of the building to a white-gold. In the centre of the car park is a bare, spindly tree, hung with red and blue fairy lights. The lights are cold; Donna shivers suddenly with chill and dread.

"Come on, old girl, let's get you inside."

"The bag?" she asks again, and gestures at the large hold-all in Ashley's hand.

"Just a few props for Cobweb," he says.

A car door slams. "Donna, Donna!"

Donna turns, her head heavy on her neck. It's one of the girls from work, wobbling on high heels. Donna waves, but doesn't wait, lets Ashley steer her towards the porch and the lights inside.

"Now, don't approach Mark," Ashley hisses at her. "I guarantee he will come to find you."

"Perhaps they won't come," Donna suggests. She doesn't even know if that's what she wants. Imagine all this tension, all this adrenaline, for nothing, just seeping out of her body, through the soles of her shoes and into the opulent crimson carpet of the White Rose.

They show their tickets to a flunky in reception who gestures them through to the back bar. Ashley's been here before and knows the way. He guides Donna through the public bar, up a short flight of stairs, and through a further, private seating area. The walls are heavy with burgundy, gold and green, hung with gilt mirrors and boughs of holly. Donna checks her reflection in one of the ornate mirrors, and recoils. The dress makes her look fat; her cheeks are pink from the cold outside, and her mascara has smudged under one eye.

In the back bar, the lights are low, with strobes swooping across the dance floor. Donna hesitates in the doorway Yes, she recognises the features of the people standing at the bar, and hovering over the long tables of snacks, as those of her colleagues, but they look all wrong. She hardly ever sees these people in their own casual clothes, let alone suits and party dresses. Oh God, one of the supervisors is wearing a Santa hat. Someone always has to.

"Where's your car?" Georgia asks Cobweb.

"At the Travelodge," he says quietly.

"Bloody hell, we've got to walk then?"

"It's only ten minutes. I checked earlier."

Under an orange streetlamp Cobweb takes her hand and twirls her around. As she spins, she glances back up the road. Neil is standing at the garden gate, watching them. The lumpy shape of Annette is in the open doorway, a silhouette against the lamplight spilling out.

"They're watching us," Georgia hisses.

"I thought they would," says Cobweb.

Ashley's put a glass of white wine in front of Donna. They're sitting together at one of the tables. Donna is hunched into the corner, watching the double doors. The supervisor in the Santa hat and his wife come over to say hello, but Donna doesn't invite them to sit at the table. Ashley's drinking Coke, allegedly without his usual rum, to keep a clear head, and his foot is hooked through the handle of the hold-all under the table. Donna wishes she hadn't come, wishes she'd turned all the lights off before Ashley's taxi came, and he would have had to go without her.

"Here they are," Ashley says.

Donna snaps her head towards the doors; she was momentarily distracted watching a couple of the other girls helping themselves to tapas and crisps from the food table. Her heart rate drops. It's Georgia and a tall, bony, camp-looking man in a smock with a trailing scarf and a flower in his buttonhole.

"Donna, Ashley, meet my poet friend, Gerry Pyles," Georgia says loudly.

Brian and Joy are late leaving. It's Brian's fault. He's had diarrhoea several times in the last half hour. How the hell has he come to this: a man who lies to his wife about secretly visiting a gay club, and who has now chipped in his share to hire a man to pretend to be someone who doesn't exist. And what happens next? After this party?

Donna stands as Cobweb kisses her cheeks: left, right, then left again. She doesn't know what to say, what to call him. Gerry seems stupid; Cobweb worse. It's all right for Georgia. She's got into all this, arm-in-arm with Cobweb, tweaking the flower on his jacket. She hasn't really got anything to lose now. She's safely got to the hotel without too much hassle from her father – and Donna's sure Georgia exaggerates how he goes on – and Cobweb can ditch the velvet jacket and the red ribbon for the rest of the evening, as that Gerry Pyles has done his bit.

"Cobweb," Ashley says, nods his head towards the double doors.

"Go for it, boys," Georgia downs her vodka. "I'll look after Donna."

Ashley shoulders the hold-all. Donna doesn't notice him walking away, or Cobweb following discreetly towards the Gents at the far end. She is vaguely aware of scraping her chair back, the noise it makes on the floor, audible above *Walking in the Air*, and she realises she is standing.

"Fuck her, what a slag," Georgia says. "She shouldn't be wearing that at her age."

The flashing lights turn Mark's face green. Donna knows he has seen her; then he moves away towards the bar tugging Michelle's arm. Michelle is as tall as he is. Her hair looks pale in the lights, but Donna knows it is red from the strand she found in the car. It's piled on top of her head exposing a slim, white throat. She's wearing a short shift, one that Donna would never have dared to wear. Donna slumps down on her chair once more, reaches for her wine.

"I told you, don't worry about her," Georgia shouts. "Come on, let's get something to eat while the boys get ready."

"Where are they?" Donna asks.

"Getting ready for Twitcher Gerry. Come on, let's see the old cow in close up."

"I don't want–"

"You can't sit here on your own all night like a lemon. The other guys will wonder what's the matter with you. And surely you want to see Blondie squirm?"

Not really, Donna thinks. *I don't want to be here at all. I should have listened to my heart, stayed at home, never known.* She lets Georgia haul her up, march her towards the bar and the food. People speak to her, bending to her ear to be heard over the music, and she responds, she must do, but she has little idea of what she's saying. She's watching Michelle tip a glass of ruby-black wine to her mouth, watching her scanning the room, looking for someone.

"So, where is he then?" Michelle shouts over the music.

"Who?" Mark plays dumb.

He'd seen Ashley and another man – he must be Cobweb – moving swiftly, stealthily, through the bar with a hold-all. He couldn't see Cobweb closely; all he noticed was a flowing scarf over something black. But he did see Donna's face, saw Georgia's mouth opening harshly, and he knew they had seen him and Michelle. Why the fuck had Donna come here tonight, knowing he would be bringing Michelle? Was it to hurt herself or make him feel guilty? He was feeling guilty already and he knew from her expression she was hurting. In her shoes he wouldn't have come. Would he?

"Gerry fucking Pyles." Michelle cracks down her glass on the bar. "He was the one who asked you on this date, wasn't he?"

"He'll be here soon, I guess," Mark says lamely.

He wishes he could have something stronger than half a lager, but he's driving.

Michelle fiddles with her hair clasp, glares around the room. She doesn't know any of the people from Sterile Services. She's never been to a department party or function. Neither has he.

"Come on, I'll introduce you to a few people," Mark says.

A tap on his shoulder.

"Mark, old chum. Good to see you."

He stares a moment at the man in front of him, uses the loud music to delay speaking.

"Gerry," he says at last.

Cobweb's eyes, behind John Lennon glasses, are impassive. He gives nothing away. He's lost that flowing scarf; now he's wearing a shirt with a patterned tie. One sleeve is rolled up to reveal a huge geeky watch on his wrist. His hair looks like it has been tamed with gel or water.

"You must be the lovely Michelle," Cobweb says.

"Oh, uh, yes, this is Michelle. Michelle, this is Gerry Pyles, who I–"

"Spend a lot of time with when you're supposed to be working."

"Ah. Michelle, don't be hard on him. He was embarrassed at telling you what we were doing."

"And what were you doing?"

"Birdwatching. That's all. Nothing sinister in a bit of birdwatching, but Mark here thought you'd laugh. By the way, Mark, I've got those photos you wanted to see."

He takes a mobile phone out of his pocket, scrolls through.

"Oh yes," Mark says. "Great, the photos."

What fucking photos?

"The raptors," Cobweb swipes his finger across the screen.

How the fuck had the man got photos of buzzards and kestrels plugged into this phone?

"Look at that one, the female. Isn't she a beauty?"

"Let me see," says Michelle.

"I didn't think you were interested in birds."

"She's not," Mark interjects.

"No, I'm not, but I want to see. Mark, get me another." Michelle gestures to her glass. "What else have you got on there, Gerry?"

Mark freezes. What else has Cobweb got on the phone? He knows Michelle, knows how she'll snatch that phone and go through it.

"Gerry." He feels really weird saying this name, the name he made up. Christ, he only made it up so he could see Donna. Now look where that fling has landed him. "Can I get you a drink?"

"Thanks, Mark. I'll have a Glenmorangie." Cobweb turns back to Michelle. "You need a wee dram when you're birdwatching in the Highlands."

We're not birdwatching in the Highlands, Mark thinks. Why couldn't Cobweb have something sensible like wine or beer? Mark nods to the barman, orders the drinks, and another half lager for himself. He hopes Cobweb can hold his drink OK.

Donna's watching the three of them at the bar. Cobweb is showing Michelle something on a phone.

"What are they doing?" she asks Ashley.

"He's got a phone full of birds," Ashley says.

"Text BIRDS to 1234 for sexy chat," Georgia snorts. "Oh, bloody hell, here's Brian. Ashley, you'd better stand by with your magic bag."

Donna stares sadly at the plate in front of her chosen by Georgia: chicken leg, mini pasty, crisps, a triangle of cheese.

"I'll get you a refill," Ashley says.

"Ah, cheers, vodka and tonic," says Georgia. "Shall I get us some more food?"

"Donna?" Ashley asks.

"Orange juice."

She doesn't want orange juice – it'll be too acidic – but, if she drinks any more wine, she'll cry. Mark won't leave Michelle. She's stunning, and she doesn't look almost forty. Donna wonders if she misheard Mark? Maybe close to she looks her age, with the lines and blotches of alcohol and tobacco. Somehow Donna knows she won't.

"Look after the bag." Ashley springs to his feet, heads to the bar.

Donna watches him tap Cobweb slightly. Cobweb doesn't flinch, is still hunched over the phone with Mark and Michelle. Michelle looks bored and irritated. She's fiddling with her empty glass. Ashley picks up a whisky glass and downs the contents. The barman hands him a juice and Georgia's vodka.

"You nicking other people's drinks?" Georgia asks him when he returns.

"It was Cobweb's," Ashley explains. "He's got to keep his wits about him. They never even noticed."

Cobweb turns, inclines his head.

"I need a cigarette," Michelle says.

"You'll have to go out then," Mark tells her.

He's sweating like hell. Cobweb seems unruffled. He's shown Michelle so many photos of birds she's bored rigid.

"Are you coming?" she asks Mark.

"No, I'm going to say hello to a few people, get some food."

"I'll see you shortly then." She scowls at him and Cobweb. "Don't go disappearing into a hide or something."

As she stalks out of the bar, Cobweb peels away from Mark's side before he can say a word to him. The whisky glass is empty, but Mark can't recall seeing Cobweb drink it.

"Oh Christ, here's Blondie."

Donna watches Mark sidling towards her through the crowd. He doesn't stop to talk, even when one of the girls catches his arm.

"I suppose you want me to make myself scarce," Georgia says. "OK, I'm off to the Ladies."

"Georgia," Mark says.

"Blondie. Did you get away with it?"

"I think so. He had birds and everything on his phone. Where is he now?"

"Getting changed." Georgia nods towards Brian and Joy, who are talking with several other people. "Just don't fuck this up, Blondie."

"Donna, Donna, at last I can come and see you," Mark says, as Georgia struts away.

Donna tries to smile. If she looks wretched, she will appear even more unattractive than Michelle.

Georgia weaves across the dance floor, stopping to take a handful of crisps from the food table. On the corridor, the two doors of the Ladies and the Gents are facing her; to her left the passage opens out into the public bar. She hears the noise of voices and the occasional clink of glasses. Cobweb and Ashley are still in the Gents with the hold-all, she guesses. She opens the door to the Ladies.

Immediately, she inhales the heady scent of lilies. There's a vase of cut blooms next to the row of basins. A long mirror reflects the three cubicles; two are ajar and one is locked. Behind each basin is a glass bottle of liquid soap: green, white, pink. A lavatory flushes, then the closed door opens. A woman with long greying hair comes out, walks to the basins, squirts green soap onto her hands, runs the taps. Georgia's about to turn and flee, but Annette has seen her in the mirror.

"Georgia, hello," she says, shaking her hands three times over the bowl.

"What are you doing here?" Georgia stumbles.

Annette reaches for paper towels, dries her hands slowly, deliberately. She's no longer wearing that carpet thing.

"It was Neil's idea."

"Well, of course. Spying on me, no doubt. I thought you were going out for dinner."

"So did I," Annette says, carefully dropping her damp paper into the chrome pedal bin. "Neil wanted to come here and just check you were OK."

"Of course I'm OK. I'm an adult. I've been to university, you know. I don't need him spying on me all the time. It's outrageous. It's embarrassing."

"It is," Annette says calmly. "Believe me, I don't want to spend my evening in this depressing place with its gloomy furniture, watching my date for the evening peering around for any sight of you, and wondering how he can gatecrash a private party."

"Why's he here?"
"It's your friend, Gerry. He's not sure about him."
"What d'you mean, not sure?"
"I don't know. His words, not mine."
"You sound pretty pissed off too."
"Look, Georgia, your dad's a nice man, but I don't think I'll be seeing him again. If he can't let his daughter go out with friends from work, then I really don't think he's the man for me. I hope you enjoy your night."
Georgia watches the heavy door bang to behind Annette as she leaves. She stands, breathing the scent of lilies and the elusive citrus of Annette's perfume.

Cobweb and Ashley are squashed into a cubicle in the Gents. The hold-all is on the floor. There's no room to move.
"Do people really want to shag in these places?"
"The stories I could tell you from my past," Cobweb says.
The water he used to smooth his hair has dried, leaving it sticky. He cuffs it back into a ponytail, swaps the geeky watch for a selection of brightly coloured rubber wristbands. Ashley drops a medallion around his neck.
"OK, get blowing," Cobweb says.
Ashley bends down, with his head nearly going down the pan, and tugs out the pair of inflatable arms.
"Here, you do one."
"You've got singers' lungs."
"Jeez."
Ashley starts blowing, and the rubber biceps inflate. He chokes with laughter, tries to fasten the bung.
"Fuck it, that's too tight," Cobweb says. "I can hardly move. Let it out a bit."
Air farts out of the rubber arm. Cobweb freezes. There's someone outside in the Gents.

Brian's got guts ache again. He's got to find the Gents. Looking around he can see Mark at a side table with Donna, close but not touching. Georgia is nowhere to be seen; nor is Ashley. There's no one who might be Cobweb, the agent from Bath. What the hell's going on?
Joy is talking happily to a couple of the women and their husbands. Brian is terrified she will ask one of them about Gerry Pyles, but if he doesn't get to the Gents soon, he's going to shit himself. They are all taking about holidays and foreign travel at the moment; surely that can't lead into the gym, Brian's health kick, and Gerry Pyles?
Brian dodges colleagues to get out of the bar. The door to the Gents opens and a man comes out.
"I wouldn't go in there if I were you," he says to Brian.
"Oh, but…" Brian trails off. This man must also have diarrhoea, must have made a God-awful stink.
"I wouldn't like to think what's going on in there. There seem to be two men in the cubicle, doing…well, I don't know. Something to do with blowing and something being too tight."
Brian's bowel is about to let rip inside his best trousers. The door to the Ladies opens and Georgia comes out.

"What the fuck are you doing?" she yells.

"What?" Brian asks, confused.

"Not you, him," she shrieks, pointing at the man. "You're spying on me. Even Annette thinks you're a nutter, and she's going to dump you tonight. She told me."

"She already has. She's calling a taxi. We only came here to check everything was all right. There was something about Gerry that I just didn't like. Something not right."

"Oh, because he's gay?"

The man – Georgia's father – is still barring the door to the Gents.

"I'm sorry," Brian says weakly, and pushes past Georgia into the Ladies.

"Is that a friend of yours?" Neil demands, pointing to the closed door of the Ladies.

"Yes, that's Brian. He works with me."

"Is he a man or a woman? He just went into the Ladies."

"Because you wouldn't get out of the way. When you gotta go…"

Shit, Georgia thinks. Cobweb and Ashley are trapped in the Gents. *Shit* again: did her father see them? No, they must be in a cubicle, but they'll be coming out any minute. She grabs Neil's arm and tugs him away to the public bar.

"Come on, I'll have a drink with you," she says.

"But don't you want to be with your friends? Where's Gerry?"

"He had to make a phone call," Georgia improvises and leads Neil away from the lavatories.

Luckily no one comes into the Ladies. Brian washes his hands quickly with pink liquid soap and scoots out. He opens the door to the Gents. There's no one in there. Cobweb and Ashley, if that's who they were, must be back at the party.

At first Brian can't see Joy anywhere. In the low light, fractured by strobes across the dance floor, he sees Mark at the bar, with a glamorous-looking bird – bad choice of word in the circumstances – who surely can't be Michelle, from what Mark's said about her. Suddenly Brian sees Joy. She's sitting at the table with Donna. She probably saw Donna looking sad and went to talk to her. Joy's kind. Brian feels such a shit sometimes.

"Hello, Donna," Brian says, pulling out a spare chair.

"Donna here was looking a bit lonely," Joy says.

"Have you seen Georgia?" Donna asks Brian.

"Uh, no." It seems the safest answer.

"Ah, here's Ashley." Donna looks relieved.

Brian drops his gaze to the plate of food Donna has pushed away. He can't look at Ashley, not with Joy only across the table. He stares at the half-nibbled mini pasty on the plate. Ashley's introducing himself to Joy, saying he has come with Donna. At last, Brian looks up, and there's Ashley, sitting in the next chair, one ankle resting on the opposite knee. Between Brian and Ashley is a large dark bag. Ashley's wearing a neon pink frilled shirt Brian has seen him wear before, and he has a long silver earring. If they were in Clementines now, Ashley might place his hand over Brian's in that way that he does, that doesn't mean they're lovers – Brian knows they will never be – but means that Ashley likes him, and cares about him, and understands him, probably more than he understands himself.

It's so much quieter in the main bar. Georgia throws herself down in the huge burgundy leather chair that Annette must have been sitting in. There's half a glass of red wine on the low table. It has a lipstick mark on its rim. Georgia picks up the glass and sniffs. Cab Sav probably. She twirls it, so the lipstick mark is away from her, and takes a mouthful.

Shit. Holy fucking shit. She's got to text Ashley. He's the emergency contact. And Brian and Donna just in case. Even Blondie. No, he's a liability.

She fumbles in her bag for her phone, drops her cigarettes on the floor – she could use one now – and snatches at her phone.

'SOS – Dad's here. I need Gay Gerry,' she texts to Ashley, Donna, and Brian.

As she hits send Neil appears with a vodka and tonic for her, and some sort of whisky.

"Excuse me a moment." Ashley jumps up, the screen of his phone still glowing.

He dodges past a few people. Brian's phone vibrates in his pocket. Something is happening; something is going wrong. Donna too is watching Ashley. Joy alone is unconcerned. Brian sees Ashley speaking to someone leaning against the wall. He takes his phone out and cups it in his hand. Phew. Georgia needing her gay poet back because of her old man. That could have gone badly wrong. Brian should have thought of that and told Ashley himself. But how could he with Joy there?

Ashley returns to the table. The other man walks just behind him. He's wearing a tight satin-look shirt over insanely big biceps. There's a medallion around his neck. He has a ponytail. In one hand is a pint of beer, in the other a plate of food, but his arms are bent in a peculiar way because of the size of his muscles.

"Brian, mate." Cobweb puts his beer down on the table, and slaps Brian on the shoulder.

Brian's face goes purple in embarrassment; he's so grateful for the half-dark.

"Gerry," he says, standing up awkwardly, knocking the table, and Cobweb's pint, so beer froth slops over the glass. "Gerry, meet my wife, Joy."

"Pleased to meet you," Cobweb says to Joy. "Hey, Donna, how's it going?"

"Hi Gerry," Donna says.

"Brian, you'll have to work twice as hard at the gym next time, seeing as you're missing a session tonight," Cobweb says, through a mouthful of cold sausage.

"You've done a fantastic job with Brian." Joy smiles indulgently. "He's a changed man since you took him in hand."

Ashley sniggers and mimes wanking under the table.

"Brian's got a bit of work to do, haven't you, mate?" Cobweb pinches Brian's reduced midriff. "But we'll get him there. Protein. That's the key." He gestures to his plate of sausages, chicken legs and cheese slices. "Kill that carb. Hey, had any more thoughts about that half marathon, have you?"

"Half marathon? You never told me about that," Joy says.

Ashley takes a large gulp of Cobweb's beer while Joy gazes at Brian.

"Is that safe?" she asks Cobweb. "I mean, a half marathon's a long way. And Brian's not as young as you. Or as fit. Shouldn't he get his heart checked out first?"

"It's only 13.1 miles, Joy. Or 21 k. We'll start off with a few 5 k runs, see how you get on."

"Great," Brian says faintly, not meeting Ashley's midnight eyes. "But I might just get a MOT first. Make sure I'm fit for duty."

"I think that's a good idea," Joy agrees. "I'm sure everything's fine, but better to be safe than sorry."

"Very sensible, Joy. Brian, you've got a diamond there. I'll see you all later." Cobweb dumps his plate, bearing two chicken bones, on the table.

"Don't forget your drink," Joy cries, and hands the wet glass of beer to him.

Cobweb swings his giant arms and stomps off.

"Brian, are Mark and his girlfriend here?" Joy asks.

Ashley kicks Brian sharply.

"They're over there," he says, points to where Mark and Michelle – she must be the glamorous bird – seem to be having an argument.

"Let's go and say hello then. Donna, Ashley, we'll leave you in peace."

As Brian follows Joy, he sees Ashley pick up the bag and run after Cobweb. He just sees Cobweb hand Ashley the pint of bitter, then Joy tugs at his arm, and he has to look away, back to Mark and the tall redhead who's gesticulating wildly at him.

"I thought you were supposed to be keeping a clear head," Cobweb hisses.

Ashley has taken the pint of bitter into the Gents and has balanced it on the cistern.

"I'm just being a good PA," Ashley says, unzipping the hold-all, and whipping out the smock and velvet jacket. "Here, undo your hair."

"What the hell is Georgia's old man doing here?" Cobweb asks, letting out the bung from the first of his artificial biceps. "Jesus, they hurt."

"He's checking up on her or something. I don't know." Ashley gulps beer, and smoothes down Cobweb's velvet lapels.

"How much have you had tonight?"

"Just a couple of rum and Cokes, a whisky and this beer. Hey, what does Gay Gerry drink?"

"Campari and soda, please, Georgie darling."

Georgia is starting to feel a bit woozy herself now. Neil has followed her back to the party and, just in time, Cobweb emerged from the Gents as Gay Gerry. She carries the Campari and her own vodka back to the food table, where Neil has buttonholed Cobweb.

"One of my colleagues is doing some research about young homosexuals," Neil says. "She's writing about the sociosexual orientation of gay males."

"Gerry, here's your drink," Georgia interrupts.

"Would anyone notice if I had a nibble? I thought Annette and I were going for dinner in town." Neil takes a plate and heaps on a slice of flan, a chicken leg, a couple of sandwiches and some crisps. "So, I was wondering, Perry, if you'd be interested in talking to her? I could give you her number, and tell her you're a friend of Georgia's."

"Don't be stupid, Dad. Of course, he doesn't want to be in a research project." Georgia hands Cobweb a plate of food.

"Georgia, what are you doing?"

"What?"

"You've given him chicken. You know he's a vegetarian."

"Oh, fuck, sorry, Gerry. Look, I'll have it. Here's some quiche."

"Thank you, sweetie," Cobweb says. "In the New Year, I'll be giving up gluten, dairy products, caffeine, and alcohol, but quiche is perfect tonight."

As Cobweb waves quiche in Neil's face, Georgia watches Ashley down the Campari with a grimace.

"Gerry, I really want to say thank you," Joy says. "You've done so much for Brian. I'm ever so grateful."

"Brian, what did I say about the carbs?" Cobweb flexes his blow-up biceps and glances quickly around the bar for Georgia and Neil.

He'd said he needed the Gents again – to become Gym Gerry – and could only hope that Neil didn't follow him and Ashley in there to check out their sociosexual orientation. Neil, now on another whisky, seems to be going the same way as Georgia and Ashley.

"Oh, uh, well, it's Christmas, isn't it? It's a party." Brian gulps and swallows the last of his sausage roll.

"Is your partner here with you tonight?" Joy asks Cobweb.

"No, Tracey's working tonight."

"She works at Sainsbury's," Brian interrupts.

"Of course, I think Brian told me she worked there. Is she working over the weekend?"

"She's off on Sunday. Working tomorrow. But that's OK. I'll be working out most of the day. In the pool by 6 am. Do you fancy a swim, Brian?"

"You can go if you like," Joy smiles.

"I haven't been swimming for years," Brian falters.

"You did in Spain last year."

"That's not Gerry's kind of swimming."

"It's been an absolute pleasure, Joy," Cobweb says. "But I'm going to head off now. Busy day tomorrow."

He leans down awkwardly with his rubber biceps to kiss Joy and his medallion bangs her on the boobs. As he straightens, he feels something moving. Something like a bung. Oh fuck, his left arm is deflating with a fart which he hopes is obliterated by the music.

"You know, Georgia, I think you might have been given the heave-ho too tonight," Neil says.

"What?"

"Perry. He seems very taken with that nice-looking friend of Donna's. Where is Donna, anyway? I'd like to say hello to her. What's the world coming to, two lovely girls having to take gay men to the works do?"

"Shit, this is harder than I thought it'd be," Cobweb says to Ashley, as he struggles out of Gym Gerry's tight shirt. One of the inflatable arms falls to the floor like a used Durex.

Ashley shrieks and unpops the other bung with a giant fart.

"Shut the fuck up. We'll have Dr Shelley in here in a moment. Best case scenario: Gay Gerry has a weak bladder."

Ashley shrieks again, twisted up.

"Christ, you're pissed," Cobweb grumbles and rummages for the clip-on tie and glasses.

Ashley is leaning drunkenly against the cubicle door. "Even I've never had Campari before."

"I don't recommend you have it again."

The external door opens. Footsteps then a knock on the cubicle door.

"It's Dr Shelley," Ashley giggles.

"It's Mark. Get on with it. Donna and Georgia are keeping Shelley out of the way."

"I'm coming," says Cobweb, inching open the door. "Ashley, you bloody sober up or I'll flush your head down the pan."

He runs his hand under the taps and smarms his hair down.

"Come on," Mark hisses.

"Oh look, it's Bill Oddie again. I thought he'd left."

"I bumped into him in the Gents," Mark says. "We were just having a chat about birding over Christmas."

"Are you ACDC, Mark?" Michelle yells. "What the fuck is going on here?"

"I was just in the Gents and–"

"Just in the Gents? You spend your spare time with this weirdo behind my back, then you disappear into the Gents for a *chat* with him, and look – he's wearing a Gay Pride badge." Michelle reaches out and tugs the rainbow motif off Cobweb's tie. It must only be a clip-on tie, because the whole thing comes away in her hand. "I knew you were lying, Mark. I knew you were up to something, but a man. A man! What the fuck am I going to tell the girls?"

She picks up a pint of beer off the bar beside her and chucks it in Mark's face.

"Urrgh," Mark splutters, as cold froth hits his eyes.

"Hey, what's going on? That was my drink."

Mark wipes beer from his eyes. Oh Christ, it's the deputy manager scowling at him.

"What were you thinking of?"

"I'm sorry, I'm sorry." Ashley has sobered up quickly. "I must have got it muddled up or something."

"I have to go. Now."

Cobweb flaps out a pair of black jeans and a cashmere sweater. His own clothes. He rakes his hand through his hair, twists the giant watch off his wrist.

"You're just going?"

"Just going." Cobweb smiles wryly.

"I thought I'd take Donna clubbing," Ashley says. "Georgia too if she can get away from her dad."

"Take him too," Cobweb grins.

"Stay in touch?" Ashley asks.

Donna sees Michelle throw the beer at Mark, sees Cobweb sidle away, minus his tie, sees Mark grovelling to the deputy manager. She watches Mark drag a screaming Michelle through the double doors, without looking back, without looking for her.

Georgia and Neil come wobbling over to the table. They're both drunk. Brian and Joy are there too. Then Ashley.

"Do you want to go on somewhere, Donna?" Ashley asks her, following her gaze to where the double doors are closing after Mark and Michelle.

Donna doesn't want to, but she doesn't want to go home alone, sober, lying awake, wondering why Michelle threw beer at Mark, and what that means for her. She knows Mark isn't working the next day; she suddenly realises she won't see him again before Christmas.

"OK," she says.

"Georgia?" Ashley asks.

"Oh, fuck it, what the hell. Dad, I'll see you later."
"Where's Perry?" Neil asks.
"Gerry?" Joy says. "He's gone. He said he was going swimming first thing."
"Swimming? He didn't look like the swimming type. I thought you and he…" He trails off, looking at Ashley.
"Me and Gerry?" Ashley asks. "Oh, no, no, nothing going on there."
"Gerry's got a partner," Joy butts in, looking confused. "Her name's Tracey."
"No, you're wrong there." Neil drains his whisky glass. "He's as gay as a… Hey," he turns to Ashley. "One of my friends is making a study of gay men. I don't suppose you'd be interested in being interviewed for it?"
"Will you stop asking people that?" Georgia bellows.
"I don't think Gerry's gay," Joy mutters to Brian. "He didn't look a bit gay to me. You don't think he is, do you?"
"I wouldn't know," Brian says. "How can you tell what some people are?"
"D'you know, I wouldn't mind being interviewed at all," Ashley says. "Come on girls, let's get into town." He stands, with a girl on each arm. "Dr Shelley, are you walking with us?"
"Yeah, all right then."
"Don't worry about Annette," Georgia says. "Plenty more fish in the sea."

Cobweb stands in the car park. The rear lights of Mark's car disappear erratically around a bend in the drive. The red and blue fairy lights sway in the tree overhead. It's very cold. Loud voices behind him. He turns. It's Ashley with Donna and Georgia and Georgia's father. They don't see him. He quickens his pace and jogs up the drive. There are no lights under the winter trees, and he disappears into the darkness.

Act V
Almost Fairytime

It's two days before Christmas. There's a sparkle of snow on the pavements of Bath, falling like shards of amber through the coronas of the streetlights. RG has opened the sash window in the office and is leaning out into the cold. The Christmas lights hang across the street in spirals of red and gold. It's a Sunday, so the shops have shut by now, but there are still people straggling by with carrier bags, sometimes slithering on a treacherous paving slab.

"Shut that window," Fairy grumbles.

She's laying out another feast on the table: gingerbread hearts, chocolate truffles, mince pies, crystallised fruits. There is mulled wine and schnapps. She has strung up winking coloured lights around the room and lit three fat white church candles. There's a wreath of holly on the office door, and RG has hung a spray of mistletoe from the lintel.

"Christmas," Fairy sniffs. "So much effort for one day."

RG looks up and down the street, sees the first two guests coming.

"Come on up," he calls down, and they turn to wave at him above. He reaches for the intercom on the wall by Fairy's desk.

"Who is it?" Fairy asks.

"Surprise," he says.

Mustardseed and Gemma come into the office. They're flushed from the cold. Mustardseed's wearing a brightly-patterned woolly hat over his ponytail.

"Mustardseed, dear boy." Robin clasps his hand. "An excellent first six months with us."

"Thanks, RG," Mustardseed grins. "This is Gemma."

"Delighted to meet you at last, Gemma." RG stands back and looks at her. *Yes, the resemblance is definitely there.* "I met your grandmother," he says. "You look very much like her. A lovely lady."

"She was," Gemma says.

"Is," RG corrects her. "She hasn't left you."

The intercom rings, and Fairy grabs it. "Peaseblossom, good evening."

There's a rush of cold air up the stairs as the street door opens. RG hears Peaseblossom and a man talking as they come up. He's never asked the agents to bring a plus one before, but this year has been a time of finding new loves and old.

"Robin, Fairy, Mustardseed, happy early Christmas," Peaseblossom says. "Gemma, I did so hope Mustardseed would bring you. I've heard lovely things about you from him."

Gemma blushes and nudges Mustardseed, who puts an arm around her and squeezes her close.

"This is Luke," Peaseblossom says, introducing the shaggy-haired man beside her.

Fairy arches an eyebrow, as the intercom rings again.

Moth and Cobweb arrive together with Moth's little boy, Cosmo, who's wearing a long stripy scarf that almost trails on the floor. Cobweb shrugs off his black velvet cloak and hooks it on the hat stand.

"Excuse me," Luke says. "I think we've met before."

Cobweb studies him a second and grins. "We have," he said.

"I knew it, I knew it," cries Peaseblossom. "I knew you two would have met."

"We've had an interesting year," RG says, handing a glass of mulled wine to Moth. "Some intriguing cases, yes?"

Cobweb pulls a dice out of Cosmo's ear, holds it in his palm, closes and opens his fist and it's disappeared.

"Do it again," Cosmo urges.

"You haven't brought anyone with you, Cobweb," Peaseblossom says.

"I never do," he smiles. "And after the job I did on Friday, I don't think I would ever take a date to a Christmas party."

"Do tell us more." Peaseblossom takes another gingerbread heart.

"You know the rules, Peaseblossom."

"Yes, but, Robin, I always seem to break them and things end up happily ever after."

"Let's just say I don't know that they will for the clients I was working for," Cobweb says.

"Why are you fidgeting?" Moth ruffles Cosmo's shiny brown hair.

"Something in my shoe, Mummy." He tugs off his trainer with flashing LED lights and finds Cobweb's dice inside.

"What are everyone's plans for the new year?" RG asks.

"Get the PhD finished," Moth starts. "When it's warmer I'm taking Cozzie to Wales for a few days."

"Aberystwyth, by any chance?"

"Might be," Moth smiles at him. "I'd like to introduce him to a friend there."

"I've applied for uni." Mustardseed scoops up a handful of nuts.

"You're not leaving us?" RG is shocked. He never saw that coming, and he sees most things.

"No chance," Mustardseed grins. "I'm staying in Bath. Gemma wants to expand her business, so I'll be helping her with that as well. Not that I'm much of a cook, though I made her birthday cake the other week."

"It was lovely," Gemma says.

"I'll be needing a cake soon," Peaseblossom says.

"I thought your birthday was in July?" Moth asks her.

Peaseblossom looks at Luke and takes his hand. "It's a wedding cake we'll be needing. Luke and I are getting married."

"Again," Luke adds.

"That's wonderful news." Moth gives her a hug.

"Congratulations," Mustardseed and Gemma cry together.

"That's lovely." Cobweb kisses Peaseblossom. "So pleased for you."

"This calls for another drink. Glasses please."

"Just remember what happened at the last wedding," Fairy says, and Peaseblossom smiles and laughs.

RG hands out the drinks. He's secretly delighted that Fairy and Peaseblossom are friends now, and all because of his helping hand with the two sonnets.

"A toast," he cries. "To Peaseblossom and Luke."

"Can we go to the wedding, Mummy?" Cosmo asks.

"Of course you can," Peaseblossom smiles. "You'd make a wonderful wedding elf. We have one elf already who'll be coming, but I'd love to have two elves."

A strange year indeed, RG muses. Peaseblossom, Mustardseed, and Moth have all found love or friendship through their assignments. And Cobweb?

"What about you, Cobweb?" he asks. "What will you be doing this year?"

"I never know what's in store."

“If only we could find someone for you.”

“Peaseblossom, don’t even try,” he laughs. “Actually, it was really weird. That job I did on Friday. I got that through an old friend. He knew the clients needed some help and suggested the agency, and that I would be the right person to do it. He used to live in Bath. I met him in Riff Raff’s a few times.”

“You never told me,” Moth says. “Was he an old boyfriend?”

“No, nothing like that,” Cobweb says and grins. “But we’ll keep in touch.”

“Might be another wedding cake for you, Mustardseed.” Peaseblossom jabs Mustardseed in the arm.

“Where will you two be living?” Moth asks.

“I still have a place in London,” Luke says. “I have to because of my work. We’ll live between Bath and London, see how it goes.”

“I might keep him longer this time if I’m not under his feet.”

Luke smiles and strokes Peaseblossom’s hair. RG looks at the circle of faces. Mustardseed and Gemma. Peaseblossom and Luke. He knows Cobweb and Moth are friends away from work, and that Cobweb adores Cosmo. Still, he can’t imagine Cobweb settling down with anyone. No one really knows Cobweb; no one ever could. No one even knows what he’ll look like from day to day, which is a source of endless amusement for Cosmo.

They drink, they eat, they laugh. Somehow Cobweb corners Fairy under the mistletoe.

Peaseblossom and Luke are the first to leave. Luke’s staying with her in Bath over Christmas. RG leans on the windowsill again and watches them walk away, holding hands. At the bottom of Milson Street Luke stops Peaseblossom and kisses her under the snowflakes.

Mustardseed and Gemma leave next. RG smiles at Gemma. He remembers her grandmother Frances well, and the job Cobweb did for her. He remembers Frances telling him about Gemma. *She would be happy if she knew,* he thinks. Mustardseed is a decent young man.

“Why don’t you ever show me how to do it?” Cosmo asks

“Because it’s magic.” Cobweb flutters a red silk scarf.

“Come on, Cozzie.” Moth feeds his arms into his coat.

“I’ll walk you home,” Cobweb offers, and flaps out his giant cloak.

“You go, Fairy,” RG says, when the street door bangs shut after Cobweb, Moth, and Cosmo. “I’ll sort out this lot.”

“You mean you want to eat it all yourself.”

“You can have a doggy-bag.”

“No, thank you. I have had quite enough sweet food for today. You can gorge yourself stupid.”

“Have a very happy Christmas, Fairy,” he says, as she drops her handbag over her head and puts one arm through the strap.

He hands her a tiny, glittering parcel.

“And you, whatever you may be up to.” She takes her umbrella from the corner of the room and hooks it over her wrist. “Thank you for this. I’ll open it on Twelfth Night.”

He’s alone at last. He nibbles a piece of gingerbread and pours another glass of schnapps. How many of these agents will still be working for him by next Christmas? Peaseblossom may have gone to London; Mustardseed may find the work no longer suits his lifestyle; Cobweb’s face may have become too well known, even with the wigs and make-up. RG smiles. He would have loved to see Cobweb at that hospital Christmas party. *Moth will still be here,* RG thinks, unless she suddenly decides that west Wales would be a better place for Cosmo to grow up. Only time will tell.

He puts the remaining delicacies into the freezer, throws away the dregs of the mulled wine. He snuffs out the candles and clicks off the fairy lights. There's a scattering of crumbs by the door, where Cosmo dropped a piece of cake, and Mustardseed trod on it. RG goes into the tiny kitchen, comes back with a broom to sweep behind the door.

CPSIA information can be obtained
at www.ICGtesting.com
Printed in the USA
BVHW041131310519
549793BV00008B/259/P